He slid his hands to her elbows, stopping her. "I'm not treating our first time together like we're teenagers looking for a fast thrill in a game room. We're not only too old for that, we deserve better."

Dusting her hands as if she was done, she hurried away. "Fine. This is all I have, Bryce. All I can do."

He touched her shoulder and she stopped. Did she want him to change her mind? Show her how much he cared about her? "If it were me. . .If our positions were reversed, and I was the one with scars, what would you do right now, Kylie? Would you let me run away? Continue to be afraid?" She covered her face. "I am afraid."

He could barely hear her. He asked just as quietly, "Of me?"

"Strangely enough, no. But yes, maybe of you most of all."

D1578628

GUNSLINGER

BY
ANGI MORGAN

MILLS
BOON

First Published in Great Britain 2016
By Mills & Boon, an imprint of HarperCollins*Publishers*
1 London Bridge Street, London, SE1 9GF

© 2016 Angela Platt

ISBN: 978-0-263-91910-3

46-0716

Our policy is to use papers that are natural, renewable and recyclable products and made from wood grown in sustainable forests. The logging and manufacturing processes conform to the legal environmental regulations of the country of origin.

Printed and bound in Spain
by CPI, Barcelona

Angi Morgan writes Mills & Boon Intrigue novels "where honor and danger collide with love." She combines actual Texas settings with characters who are in realistic and dangerous situations. Angi's work has been a finalist for numerous awards, including the Booksellers' Best Award and the Daphne du Maurier Award. Angi and her husband live in north Texas.

Visit her website, www.angimorgan.com, or follow her on Facebook at Angi Morgan Books. She loves to hang out with fans in her closed group: bit.ly/angifriends.

There is never a book completed without
my pals Jan and Robin.

This one also goes to my wonderful agent, Jill, and to
the patience of my amazing editor, Allison! Thanks,
ladies, for hanging in there with me.

Prologue

Austin, Texas, five years ago

Sissy Jorgenson-Tenoreno attempted a smile at her friends to make the empty parking lot less spooky. It didn't work. "This is an odd place to meet, even for Xander."

The food truck's inside lights were glowing. So were the Christmas lights strung around the single picnic table out front. Daddy Cade's Po'Boys didn't seem to be one of the more popular gourmet trucks in town. Good thing she'd brought her entourage of Darren, Janna and Linda with her.

Xander should think twice if he thought she'd meet him anywhere alone.

"Your soon-to-be ex-husband probably chose this place because he knew you'd never eat here," Darren said. "You make every calorie count twice. Especially now that you need your figure back."

She was still the same size as when they'd eloped eight months ago. In fact, the outfit she was wearing had been bought on their unofficial honeymoon trip to Paris.

"Sissy Jorgenson shouldn't be forced to come to a place like this," Janna complained. "You should send the police for your things. Even the cat."

Xander's father owns the police.

Did it really bother her that they talked as if they understood the life she'd led before getting married? Teen model, then married to the mob? They had no clue. Not really. A different location every week was glamorous to them. A different hotel each week was appealing. A life of travel and what appeared to be one party after another.

Even the parties got old. The same faces night after night. There weren't any sleepy movie days in front of the television. No study binges, no spontaneous orders of pizza and beer. No darting to the store for milk and bread, which were never on the menu anyway.

One day someone might ask what had been going through her mind when she got married. Her friends shrugged the divorce off as if it was no big deal. What had she expected? Happily ever after? Looking back, she hadn't really expected anything. She might not have known what marriage would be like, but she knew what she wanted.

The answer was so simple. She'd wanted a home. A place to belong, a family and a pet. She'd never had one and always wanted to save the strays she saw while travel-ing. Instead, being married was equivalent to being locked inside a mansion surrounded by people who had no love in their hearts.

"I need a bottle of water or maybe this place sells Gel Shots. Five or six of those and we'll be ready to party again." Linda staggered across the gravel parking lot to the food truck and banged on the window. When no one answered, she swayed back to the group. "I'm so envious. In three days you'll be jet-setting halfway across the world for a fabulous Roman adventure. I, on the other hand, will be starting another boring semester of school."

While starving herself to drop down to her agent's ideal weight, she'd be wishing every minute for her friend's boring life.

"Anybody want a fried oyster po'boy? Of course Sissy's

answer is no. She can't waste calories on stinky food. The bun alone would be—"

Sissy tuned them out and let them make fun of the way she'd eaten while staying with them over the past two months. They didn't understand that drastic measures were needed if she wanted her career back.

Even at the same weight there was the perception of what her body should be. She had to be thinner, taller, sleeker—more everything—to get back on top of the heap of girls who came along every day.

Fortunately, she hadn't been out of the paparazzi's eye very long. Her husband had made certain she'd been on his arm for special events. The press asked if she planned to return to her career after the honeymoon was over. Xander had assured them several times that their life would be a never-ending honeymoon.

But Xander Tenoreno was a liar and horrible person. If there was a villain in her life, it would be him. She was walking away from the divorce almost destitute. She'd been a dumb kid and rushed into marriage without a prenup. He'd taken everything. They'd been playing whose divorce attorney was the toughest until she'd realized that she could start over if she walked away.

It didn't matter. All she wanted was Miss Kitty, mainly to save her from the wrath of the household. None of the family was happy about the divorce. They didn't believe in it and took 'till death do you part' very literally.

No matter what Xander said or did, he couldn't keep her down. He could keep all of the money. According to her agent, she was still in high demand because of the public life she'd led, but she was almost *old* in model years. Old and only just celebrating her twenty-first birthday next week.

She looked around at the isolated parking lot and wondered if Xander was trying to frighten her. He didn't have to try hard. Would Xander or his family stoop to something that would hurt her friends? She shook her head, answering herself. Even they wouldn't be that public.

"What happened between you two, Sissy? Why did your Mr. Hunky-poo start sleeping around? He was so much fun to party with." Linda asked, hands on her hips, expecting an answer.

Okay, everyone in the parking lot expected an answer. After all, her life was continually up for discussion. Her every move was up for debate.

The threats and demands had been plentiful after their wedding vows but she hadn't told anyone. Not a soul. Not even her attorney. "I was supposed to stay at the mansion and be traipsed out whenever he needed someone to hang on his arm. It wasn't my scene."

"Barefoot, pregnant and cooking over a hot stove? You?" Janna laughed and everyone joined in.

That scenario would never have happened, but it was close. Of course she didn't get pregnant. Then a dozen doctors all agreed that there was no reason they couldn't have children. The consensus was that they shouldn't be in such a hurry. Give it time. But Xander had just quit. He tended to want immediate gratification for everything he did. People seemed to show up injured if he didn't.

"I don't have to think about that anymore." She laced her fingers, then pulled them apart, sitting on them to keep still. *He can't hurt me if I'm not there.*

The Tenoreno family wanted her out of the way.

Gone. Forever.

As long as he'd finally agreed to give her Miss Kitty, she could leave Texas and never look back. She looked around at the isolated food trailer. No other cars. No parking lot lights. It was just such an odd place for a man who liked everything shiny and new.

Including his women.

"It's eight forty-five. How long do we have to wait? That new band is opening at the Bat House. Is he always this late?" Darren paced.

"Yes. Time means nothing to him." She'd never thought he'd be here on the dot. But if roles were reversed and she was the one late, he would euthanize Miss Kitty as he'd threatened more than once to keep Sissy in line.

A super big SUV drove by. Smoke curled from the dark windows as it slowed. The bass of the music inside echoed through her chest it was so loud. Her friends danced to the hip-hop rhythm.

"We need music," Janna said, dancing to the fading beat over to the food truck window. "Come on. Can't you open up for a second? Even for water?"

Sissy swatted at her neck and shivered. It felt like something was crawling on her. Or maybe someone had walked on her grave. Wasn't that the saying? She discovered a tendril of her long hair had blown free from its intricate braid and tickled her skin. Her imagination had gone super wild.

As if she wasn't already scared enough. Now the thought of spiders in her hair had her all itchy. Another vehicle approached the three-way intersection with the same low bass thump. Another SUV?

Was it her imagination or an odd premonition that made her stand and move to the side of the trailer? She didn't know. But as the SUV drew even with the lot, she saw the gun barrel in the open window. She screamed. She dialed the number she'd had ready on her cell since they'd arrived.

The gunfire was maddeningly loud. She tried to get to the car. The gravel popped up in front of her hitting her legs first one direction and then the other. They shot all around her, missing. She was their target. She didn't doubt that for a second.

"Nine-one-one, what's your emergency?"

The voice was drowned out by more rapid fire of another weapon. Laughter from the men as they opened the car doors. She wanted to recognize one of the men who followed the Tenoreno family everywhere. She couldn't be certain. But the family wanted her out of the way.

Gone. Forever.

There was nowhere to run. No one to call out to for help. She was about to die and wanted to scream louder. Scream hysterically.

The phone was still in her palm. She couldn't be certain the police would respond. Her husband might have paid them to avoid the area. She prayed someone decent was on the other end of the call, trying to discover what was happening in this remote parking lot.

The gunfire stopped.

Sissy looked up, blinking hard to see her attackers. Maybe they were just trying to scare—another burst. Linda's screams were cut off. Janna's followed. Her eyes never shut as she fell to the ground.

The stinging fire in her side whipped her around. Another stabbed through her arm like a hot knife through butter…quick, silently tearing her flesh. A third and fourth pierced under her arm that had flown above her head.

Darren wrapped his arms around her but they fell. She landed hard under him. His body protected her from the full force of the bullets. The white gravel that had been hard to walk through minutes earlier turned dark. It registered but there was no pain. She couldn't catch her breath, couldn't speak.

The phone wasn't in her hand. It had bounced away. The case had popped open, but the light was still on. Someone still listened.

It was interesting what registered in her mind during those few life-ending seconds. Trivial information like the spots of blood now on the metal legs of the table. Or the burned-out bulb on the twinkle lights at the rear of the lot.

The noise of the bass hip-hop and guns faded away to be replaced by sirens.

What did any detail around her matter? She'd been shot…more than once. She was about to die. There was no one left to truly grieve for her. She'd said goodbye to a greedy family long ago. Her only friends were dead because she hadn't wanted to be alone to face her ex-husband.

After all their sacrifice, she would still die alone.

What good had she accomplished in her life? She knew how to walk in high heels and how to throw her hair over her shoulder before placing her hand on her hip.

Somehow she dragged her hand to her side and cried out from the pain. She wanted to tell someone the truth. Leave some sort of message about who had killed her. There wasn't a way to reach her phone. She couldn't move Darren.

Her last thought should have been about kittens or something good. Instead the only thing that repeated over and over again was a never-to-be-seen headline…

Xander Tenoreno Had Killed His Wife, Sissy Jorgenson, and No One Would Ever Know.

Chapter One

Hico, Texas, present day

"Shirtless? Of course I'm shirtless." Bryce Johnson yanked the muscle shirt over his head, catching it on his ear. "What legitimate undercover Texas Ranger mows a lawn trying to get a woman's attention wearing a shirt?"

"I bet you have your glasses on, too." There was a familiar sound from his partner, Jesse Ryder, as he held the phone to his chest and laughed. "And…um…don't forget your Sig is showing."

Bryce scrambled behind his back. He gave up and went inside to drop his weapon, shirt and glasses. He didn't need to see up close to mow the lawn anyway. The briskness of the AC helped cool his frustration. A little.

"You know…" Jesse continued laughing. "If just taking your shirt off doesn't work, you could try a speedo and a giant sombrero."

"Har har har."

Jesse should be giving him legitimate advice for his first undercover assignment. Not poking him with a big stick through the phone. It didn't matter. His partner was three for three this morning and it seemed like Bryce was about to strike out.

This weekend was his final at bat.

"Seriously, man, is there a problem? If you don't get

her attention today, you might as well hang it up. They're going to pull the plug and move on."

"We don't know for a fact this is Tenoreno's ex-wife."

"Now, look, Bryce. You sold Major Parker on this assignment because you were certain this woman was the ex. What's changed your mind?"

"Nothing. But there's been no evidence or action that solidifies my hunch either."

"Hunch? Hunch?" Jesse's voice rose in decibels and octaves. "You know how important this is to me, pal. The state's attorney needs a slam dunk in the courtroom this fall. If this isn't the ex, you need to move on and find her. We don't have time for you to play a hunch."

The picture he'd burned into his memory could be a match. *Was* a match as far as he was concerned. He was certain. But short of walking up to her and asking if she had a bullet-wound scar on her abdomen and two others under her arm, there was no proof.

He needed proof or her admission since he didn't want to ask her outright. He couldn't ask the time of day or to borrow a cup of sugar. Her house was secure and locked up tighter than the local bank.

"When I'm not fixing something on this rental—which was a part of the deal you hatched up—I'm spending my spare time running more searches. You can't guilt-trip me into working harder. I haven't had a day off in weeks."

"I know, man. We just don't have time to waste."

There was a lot more to this case than just finding a potential witness. The Tenoreno family had already tried to kill law officers to make the case fall apart. As far as they knew, the crime family was still searching for the primary witness under Company F protection.

"Then let me get back outside and come up with a way to introduce myself." He disconnected before his partner could try to give him more advice. His head was swimming with all the suggestions from the Rangers in his company.

He left his service weapon in the lockbox he'd brought with him last week. Short trips back to Waco down Texas 6 had yielded more than a couple of suitcases of his stuff. The house was furnished, but he'd brought items to make it livable. Including his television and game station.

Livable? More like bachelorized.

The July heat pounded on his shoulders as he finished the outside chores. Not a bright idea for skin that hadn't seen the light of day in years. He'd listened to advice from another Texas Ranger about how to get a woman's attention, and today he was desperate.

Bryce was finally on an assignment that didn't include a computer. For the most part anyway. He was undercover. On his own and getting sunburned.

It had been a while since his back had seen the sun and done yardwork. Too long apparently. He'd just finished the lawn—the burning-dried-up-grass-with-no-trees-in-the-yard lawn. Patches of it were more dirt than the combo of overgrown weeds that he'd just plowed through.

If he didn't get closer to his target this weekend, his undercover time was done. Nothing he did and nowhere he'd been seemed to catch Kylie Scott's eye. Twice he'd been thrown next to her by town matchmakers. Twice they'd had polite conversation. Twice he'd been certain he'd broken through her protective shell. And twice he'd been wrong.

Holding his straw hat away from him, he turned the water hose on himself with the other. Spitting-hot water hit his skin but quickly soothed the burn. Probably wasn't good against sun protection, but he was just dang hot and wanted to cool down fast.

He also needed a minute to watch the house across the street and two doors down. She had been taking care of lawn maintenance on a Saturday morning, too. Conservatively dressed in shorts and a long-sleeved shirt, Kylie Scott wasn't flashy. No bikini tops to work on her tan.

Pecan Street was empty now and Kylie's garage door was shut. He should put the yard tools away and return to the half-assed air-conditioning. He'd missed when she'd finished up and moved inside.

"Some undercover cop you turned out to be." He'd talked more to himself in the past week than he'd ever admit. The red shoulders were just going to get worse. He might as well head to the store and grab some ointment. Or maybe he could ask to borrow some from Kylie.

Taking a drink from the hose, he contemplated that until there was a puddle of mud next to him. How could he meet her?

Former teen supermodel Sissy Jorgenson, the ex-wife of a short-lived marriage to Xander Tenoreno was hiding and doing a damn good job of it. Her ex was the state's real target. It would help their case if they had more evidence against the Texas crime family and Company F had been assigned to obtain it.

Bottom line, Xander was also looking for his ex-bride. The rumor circulating was that she had evidence against him that had kept her alive. True or false, Bryce didn't know. His goal was to find Sissy/Kylie and convince her to hand over her evidence against the Tenorenos.

Head of the family, Paul Tenoreno, was behind bars without bail facing trial in September. The final blow would be to add his son Xander as a cellmate. Bryce soaked his head, then shook his hair from side to side. Water sprayed like his brother's dog shaking after swimming in their pool.

"As good as that feels, you might not want to greet your neighbors that way."

He recognized Kylie's voice, spun around. She screamed

a little and hopped backward. He'd soaked her shirt with the water hose.

"Dammit, that was careless of me. Sorry." Bryce wiped his eyes free of droplets still clinging to his skin.

"Wow, that was a bit of a shock." She fanned her shirt front, but didn't run home.

"I, uh…didn't hear you come up."

"I hope so, because if you wanted to have a wet T-shirt contest… Well, you'd need a shirt." She nodded toward him, wringing the edge of her shirt onto her multicolored toenails.

Wait. What? Was she flirting with him?

Without his glasses and with water dripping into his eyes, he could barely see her facial expression, just her bright smile. True wheat-blond hair was pulled into a ponytail and stuck through the back of a ball cap. She was the right height of about five feet eleven. She wasn't rail-thin, but slender enough to be a teenage model who had left the business.

"Come to think about it, we probably do have some guys on this street who wouldn't mind serving as the judges. You'd win of course."

"Huh? Oh. Right." He couldn't think of anything to say.

"You're making a bigger puddle." She pointed to his feet.

Bryce jumped toward the faucet and turned off the water, cursing under his breath at his ineptness. He slowly stood, ready to see where this strange encounter would lead.

"Bryce? I don't mean to impose, but I need your help. That is, if you could spare a few minutes."

"I don't have any plans."

She relaxed and let out a long sigh. "Oh good. It shouldn't take long. I noticed that you have an extension ladder and wondered if you could get my pole saw out of the tree in my backyard."

"Sure." *Flirting?* Wishful thinking was more like it.

He retrieved the ladder from the garage and headed down the middle of the small town street.

"Need help?"

"Not at all, I got this."

She was already walking next to him as if she'd known how he would answer. The ladder was more awkward than heavy. Sort of like their conversation. He had an opportunity now and couldn't think of anything he might ask that wouldn't sound suspicious.

Last thing he needed was for her to take off and disappear. He'd never hear the end of that at the office.

"I've noticed that you don't talk much."

"Not really. If I'm honest, I haven't gotten much practice lately." He rested the ladder on the inside of her fence as she worked the combination lock on the gate. If she wasn't the former Sissy Tenoreno, something had happened to Kylie Scott to make her overcautious.

"Are we being honest?" She smiled shyly, focusing on removing the lock.

The temperature should have dropped when they walked under the oak shade tree. But he could swear it rose several degrees when she stole a look before she pushed up her sunglasses.

In the past couple of weeks, he'd never seen her eyes up close. Even without his glasses, her long eyelashes, tinted a rich dark brown, hadn't hidden the quick peek she'd taken of his chest.

Instead of the bright blue eyes from her modeling days, they were a deep dark brown—almost black—when she didn't hide behind mirrored shades. Definitely not the color of Sissy's, but the shape...

No doubt remained.

Kylie Scott was the woman he'd been searching for.

KYLIE OPENED THE gate and Bryce grabbed the ladder on the other side. She dropped the lock back through the slots, then removed it before he noticed—hopefully. It was silly to be so paranoid.

But paranoia had taught her to be hypervigilant with her safety. She wasn't used to leaving the locks out of place.

Even when no one appeared to be on the street. Even when she had a very capable-looking man standing next to her, it went against her habits to leave the gate unlocked. But she managed it by sticking the padlock inside her pocket.

"I was trimming a dead limb and the saw got stuck."

"Lucky I was around."

"I have some iced tea. Can I get you some?"

"That would be great."

"Okay." She rubbed her palms together and stepped to the porch. She tried to turn her back on Bryce and walk like a normal person through her kitchen door.

It didn't happen. She hesitated, waiting for him to lean the ladder on the tree. He just watched her act like an unsteady idiot. Bryce was practically a stranger. She'd only met him a couple of times in town.

"I hope you like it sweetened. That's all I have."

"Sure. I'll get this down."

"Thanks so much. It's stuck up there pretty good." Oh my gosh. She was babbling, trying to wait him out. If he'd just look away, she could dart into the kitchen.

Kylie had never been a normal teenage girl, but she was certain this was how they acted. Flushed, embarrassed, unsure of themselves—everything that she was experiencing for the first time. She'd been a full-time employee by the time she'd reached puberty. The boys she'd known back then had never been mature enough for her tastes.

Needless to say, the men who accepted her as an adult at that age hadn't been good for her. Well, spilled milk and all that…whatever the saying was. She'd moved past it. She was in a good place and didn't have to think about that any longer.

Throwing her shoulders back, she turned, leaving herself vulnerable to a nonexistent attack. She slid the glass door open and marched to the refrigerator for the pitcher. Two glasses sat on a pretty little tray she'd picked up at the antique shop this week. She added a freshly sliced lemon to a matching bowl and poured the tea.

Five years. She'd survived five years. Her life was changing and it was time to keep her promise to herself. If she could survive this long without being discovered, it was time to start living again.

Taking a second, she watched Bryce tug on the pole trying to free the tiny saw. He arranged the ladder soundly in place, shook it a little to see if it was steady, then climbed.

It had been a very long time since she'd allowed herself friends. Then again, being Bryce's friend wasn't too high on her agenda. She'd watched him out in the yard fixing up Mrs. Mackey's rental. He'd stopped by the pie shop while she'd been at lunch.

It might be a coincidence, but Hico was a very small town. If there was a visitor here for a couple of hours, a resident was likely to encounter them a couple of times. So running into a neighbor at the store and pie shop was almost predictable.

She hadn't been the only woman catching a second or third glimpse of his straight nose and dimpled chin. A constant five o'clock shadow had never done anything for her before getting a look at Bryce. She was full-blown giddily attracted to every muscle his tight T-shirts exploited.

The view as he climbed the ladder wasn't helping to cool her heat.

Mrs. Mackey had praised Bryce's ability as a handyman and suggested his skills not be wasted while he was living on their street. At face value her statement had been so innocent. Then the other ladies who had conveniently stopped by the museum had all giggled.

"If they could see you right now, they'd probably faint or have heart attacks. They definitely would if they knew what my plans for him are." She took the dish towel and fanned her flaming cheeks. Dipping her head, she closed her eyes, embarrassed by her desires. "What are you thinking, Kylie? Yes, it's been a while. But you can't just ask him to bed. You deserve more than that."

With her mind made up to slow her racing thoughts, she met her helpful neighbor at the bottom of the ladder. He stepped onto the grass, tree trimmer in hand, following her to two chairs and a small patio table—her fourth anniversary present to herself.

No matter what she kept telling her mind to do, she couldn't avoid the manly chest turning a feminine shade of pink. He took a sip of tea, then gulped it down.

"That's really good. Just hit the spot."

"Thanks again for the help, Bryce. If you hadn't been home, I'd be watching that pole saw rust."

"I doubt that, but anytime." He tipped his straw hat in her direction.

"That's interesting."

"What?"

"The hat-tipping thing. No one under the age of sixty has ever tipped their hat to me before. In fact, I'd never seen it until I moved to Hico. People wave when they pass in their cars. They acknowledge me on the sidewalk. They even open the museum door, wave and go on their way."

"I'd say they're just being friendly." He finished off his tea and set the glass down.

"It's the reason I stayed here. I hadn't planned on it, but I'm glad I did."

"That's right. You work in the Billy the Kid Museum."

He took another long gulp of his tea. "I used to make my brother pretend he was Billy the Kid when we were practicing quick draw."

That's what she wanted…to be so relaxed and easy going. She sipped. It had been five years. Maybe it was possible? "And who would you pretend to be?"

"The sheriff."

"Why not the outlaw? I thought kids wanted to be the cool gunslinger who shot things up?" She noticed he actually looked a little embarrassed. "Did you play cops and robbers, too?"

"I think I got in trouble one too many times for shooting birds with my BB gun. Too many lectures on how I should be a better example. Besides, the good guys always win."

"I've heard that."

Before she could think again if she was the good or the bad, she heard his cell vibrate.

He jumped to his feet and reached into his back pocket. "Excuse me a second, I have to take this."

Kylie tried not to listen. Maybe it was a habit mixed with genuine curiosity, but she felt uncomfortable and moved out of earshot to the tree. It wasn't difficult to discern the phone call was upsetting to Bryce. His side of the conversation was a lot of one-word responses. His body language became very stiff and formal. She sipped her tea, looking at the dead limb that still needed to be trimmed back to the trunk.

When he returned, Bryce dropped his hands to his knees, bending at the waist to lean forward.

Kylie set her glass down, approaching cautiously. No matter how much she wanted to know this man, she didn't. That was a fact that she couldn't push aside. "Is something wrong?"

"Everything, I'm afraid. Someone couldn't do their

job correctly and my timetable's been advanced." He straightened.

The sadness and concern didn't belong on his handsome features. The urge to wipe them aside was too strong to ignore. She recognized it and held it in a secret place where she kept most of her emotions.

"I'm sorry, Bryce. I hope things work out for the best."

"I hope so, too. There's something you should know, Kylie." Bryce rested his hands on his hips. "If I can find you...so can Xander Tenoreno."

Chapter Two

Kylie could feel the blood drain from her face as fast as it had in her knees. Barely able to stand, she sort of rocked before catching herself on the tree trunk. Her ex-husband's name hadn't been said in front of her for almost four years. She wanted to run. Hide.

Bryce watched her reaction. He saw it all. She knew what the fright looked like and she hadn't hidden it. The look on his face confirmed for her that he knew he'd found the right person. She couldn't deny it. Well, she could, but it wouldn't do her any good. He wouldn't believe her.

"Are you a cop?"

He shook his head, squinted, then rubbed the back of his neck as if he was mad for being right. An odd reaction from someone who had completely wrecked her life.

She looked at the serving tray and the ceramic outdoor table it sat on. Neither would cross over to her new life. Whatever that ended up being. Just the things that fit inside two suitcases. Nothing more. Not even the laptop. She couldn't borrow a car. He'd just follow.

Everything stayed here.

The escape plan was in place. The cash was in a box under the bathroom sink along with a passible ID. All she had to do was fake whatever Mr. Unbelievable standing in front of her wanted.

"If you worked for Xander, I'd already be dead. So who

are you?" All the excitement of finally having the courage to face Bryce sort of evaporated along with any moisture in the heated air.

"Bryce Johnson. I'm a Texas Ranger here to help you."

"Help me right out of my comfortable home and life you mean." She picked up the tea glasses, along with the tray. Another wave of sadness crashed into her heart at the thought of leaving. "It was that silly picture for the online article, wasn't it?"

He nodded. "And your eyes. You changed the color but not the vitality that's there."

"Strange words from a man who probably just got me killed." She walked across the porch, the lock heavy in her pocket. The urge to run to the fence and secure the gate made her stop before opening the door. Bryce was following and paused on the steps.

"We can help you, if you allow us to."

"I told the police, and anyone else who would listen, everything that happened that night." The nightmare images forced her to stare at a pure drop of water sliding down the empty glass. If she shut her eyes or even blinked, she'd be transported back to the white gravel stained with blood.

"Kylie."

Startled by the shock of his touch, she dropped the tray. One glass shattered and one rolled across the wooden porch. "Isn't that weird? Ever wonder why sometimes they break and sometimes they don't?"

"All the time." He knelt beside her to pick up the broken pieces. "I didn't mean to scare you."

"What did you expect when you announced that my ex could find me? Is he really looking again?"

Their eyes met and held as he asked, "Again?"

Nice eyes. Such a shame.

Kylie mentally shook it off. None of the attraction was real. He was a flippin' Texas Ranger and not the good-looking handyman across the street. He was here with sneaky ulterior motives. She stood, confused by all the emotions making her want to cry.

Not in front of him, though. She would not cry until she was on a bus heading to the airport. No one cared if she cried on the bus.

She carefully balanced the tray on the wooden porch rail and took a step toward the door. "Who was on the call you took and what did they say?"

"Austin PD."

Her fingers wrapped around the screen door's handle. "My case never made it to court. They assured me there was a lack of evidence. I have no idea what you're referring to or why you're here. So why don't you just cut to the part where you've put my life in danger."

"Are you aware your father-in-law—"

"Ex-father-in-law."

"Right. Look, Miss Jorgenson."

"Wrong again. My name is Kylie Scott. Sissy Jorgenson died with the first bullet. She doesn't exist anymore." She took advantage of Bryce's awkward silence. He politely backed up to allow her to get inside and wedge the screen between them.

A good hostess would open the screen farther and invite him into the kitchen. The hot July air was thick and getting hotter. A bead of sweat rolled across her skin and wedged between her breasts, squeezed together by her sports bra.

Her voice and body might appear to be calm, but she was hyperaware of every second of panic she stopped from bubbling to the surface. Knees about to buckle, she wanted to run inside and leave the handsome Texas Ranger locked out on her stoop.

Bryce took off his hat, getting closer to the screen. He raised his hand toward the handle, but changed his mind at the last minute.

"I'm not sure what I can say. It was never my intention to use scare tactics to get you to listen to me. I wanted you to trust me before I had to tell you."

"That was never going to happen. I can't—won't—trust anyone like that again. You're wasting your time. Not to mention the taxpayers' dollars." She let the screen shut but didn't make a move to close the inner door. Why was she was putting off the inevitable?

Maybe she didn't want to leave. Or shoot, it really was because his concerned look crinkled the corner of his eyes. And he looked different without his glasses. Maybe that wasn't concern and he just couldn't focus.

Whatever the reason, he'd taken his hat off and his hair had a cute little flip where his hat had rested. He was seriously adorable-looking—whether guys liked to be thought of that way or not. And yes, she didn't want to shut the door in his face.

"The gentlemanly thing for you to do is leave now." She edged the door closed a little more.

"You're right. Leaving would be polite. But right now, I'm a Texas Ranger...not a gentleman."

The screen popped open and her reflexes moved her backward into the kitchen. He was through the door quickly, shutting it and turning the dead bolt. Once that was done he turned to her, hat in hand, bare-chested and terribly sunburned.

"You'll forgive me, Kylie. I've got my orders and I need to make sure you're clear on a few facts." He gestured to the small table in the corner. She joined him. "You see, someone—we assume Tenoreno—is actively looking for you. His father is in jail awaiting trial for murdering his mother."

"I heard. Don't you think I keep up with them?"

"What you might not know is that we think Xander doesn't want his father cleared. He's taking over the family business. He also knows that we're building a case against him. You can help strengthen the state's case." He leaned forward on his knees, slowly spinning that silly straw hat brim through his fingers.

"No. No. No. A thousand times no. I don't have any evidence to help you. Don't you think I tried that before the divorce? If I could have blackmailed him for my freedom, I would have."

"The rumors aren't true, then." He totally looked the part of a workingman. Somebody who fixed things for a living. He's not, she reminded herself, staying angry. He deceived her and all the residents of Hico.

"Does Mrs. Mackey know you're a cop?" She placed both her feet flat on the ground and sat straight in her chair. She knew all about body language and she was being as inhospitable as possible.

"Not a cop."

"Is there a difference?"

"Technicalities mostly. Honor. A code that's hard to understand." He set the hat on one knee and leaned back against the vinyl chair.

She understood all too well why he winced. It was the reason she wore a special UV-protected shirt with long sleeves. "I have some aloe that will help that burn."

"I'll be okay. If you wouldn't mind answering a few questions about the Tenorenos—" He pulled free of the chair, gritting his teeth so hard the muscles jumped in his jaw.

"I'll be right back."

Summing up her options had become second nature. She hadn't been spontaneous in five lonely years. It had taken over an hour to decide to ask Bryce to retrieve her pole saw.

Should she grab the handgun she'd hidden in the bathroom in case of a bad situation like this?

It should have already been decided. She'd weighed all the variables when she'd bought the gun and learned how to use it. If Bryce hadn't been in the house, she'd be talking to herself, debating. But he was in the house and he'd most likely leave if she just asked.

That was the rub. She hadn't asked.

Why? She was ready to move past living this way and had made the decision after she'd met him last week. That's why. He was already part of an idea that would rescue her from her routine.

She looked at herself in the bathroom mirror. The gun was in a hidden compartment behind a picture. It had taken her weeks to build it herself. The result was amateurish, but it was covered by a frame and no one knew about it.

Pulling the aloe from the cupboard, she longed to be brave or a little fearless. It had been quite a while since she'd felt like life was to be lived with reckless abandon.

"Get lost?" Bryce's deep voice penetrated her body like a shock. He stood at the edge of the kitchen. He hadn't followed.

Her breath caught in her throat like an air bubble or hiccup. Maybe it was more like trying not to cry. Whatever it was, she was uncertain and confused. There was no reason to automatically trust this man.

No reason to help him with answers about the Tenorenos or his sunburn.

Bottle of lotion in hand, she turned to his smiling pink face confident that she'd thought out her plan a thousand times and it was the right thing to do. She shoved the lotion into his chest. He caught it with one hand while the other held on to his hat.

"As much as I want to celebrate five years of freedom, I know that I'll never be free from the Tenoreno family. I had hopes but nothing will change that. So I'd like you to leave, Bryce. Just go away."

BRYCE HAD BEEN asked to leave. As a Texas Ranger, he should. As a man who had delivered news that clearly upset this woman...he couldn't.

"You have no reason to trust me, Kylie." He watched her chest rise, inhaling air to state her defense and pushed on before she could. "I do see why trusting anyone would be almost impossible. You asked me what the difference was between a cop and a Texas Ranger. We don't have an agenda."

"I'd still like you to leave and I think you have to now."

"I'm not leaving until I explain."

"I wish you wouldn't." She flattened against the wall.

Was she afraid? She should be. Her ex-husband was turning out to be as bad and deceptive as his father. "Xander Tenoreno lost the police detail this morning. There's a chance he could be headed here."

He wondered how Kylie had ever managed to fool anyone about her fake history. With every mention of her ex's name she paled and practically became a different person. Her entire demeanor changed. Now was no different, her eyes darted to the bath, her hand rubbed her side—probably one of the bullet-wound scars.

"You told Xander so you could get me to do your bidding. You're all the same. Out only for your own selfish interests—"

"Kylie!" He raised his voice and reached for her wrist.

A couple of seconds later, the bottle of lotion she'd given him went flying against the wall and he was lying on his back wondering how he'd been outmaneuvered.

"Oh my God, I'm so sorry. I've done that in practice, but never...I didn't mean to—oh, no." Kylie knelt next to him alternating between a pat on his shoulder and his head.

"You've been taking...martial arts." He needed a second to get his lungs working correctly.

"Aikido. It just sort of kicked in. I knew I was nervous.

I guess I should have tried to calm down." She covered her mouth. "Can you get up?"

"I think I'll just wait here for a second."

She smiled. It was worth being knocked to his back to see her relax enough to smile like that.

"You know, I never thought it would work. The moves are so practiced and mechanical. This is really sort of cool."

"Tell that to my back."

"I'm so sorry. Are you going to be okay?" Her touch was cooling to his burning skin.

"All but my pride. If that's an auto response, I'd hate to see what you can do when you're deliberately provoked."

"I'd probably freeze in my tracks." She looked comfortable. His knees would be screaming sitting bent like that.

"Is that why you have a gun stashed back there?"

"What? How did you know?"

"Your reaction." He rose to one elbow. "The way you keep looking in that direction. You almost twitched."

Her blond hair framed her face as she leaned forward. "I can see that I need to practice my self-control."

"Well you sure as hell don't need to practice throwing a man to the ground. That was more than a little embarrassing."

"Part of aikido is to react without thinking. Defending yourself without giving away what you're about to do. I've practiced during class, but there hasn't been any reason to actually use it here in Hico."

"Until now." He stretched his back, confident everything was still in one piece. "I didn't mean to make you feel threatened."

"The only thing you did was reemphasize my reality. I was fooling myself thinking things would change."

She was retreating again. Talking behind her hand, wrapping the other around her waist. He wasn't going to let her demonstrate more aikido to make her feel better. He pulled himself to a sitting position and leaned against the wall.

"Can you hand me that lotion? Maybe rub some on my back and shoulders before I go?"

"Okay, guy from down the street, you're definitely ready to leave." She tossed the bottle to his gut.

He trapped it, squeezed some of the green goo on his palm and slapped his shoulder. "I really could use some help."

"You managed to get burned all by yourself."

"You're joking, but the reason I'm burned is because I was trying to impress you."

She scooted on her knees to be next to him, extending her hand. He swiped the lotion onto her fingers. She squirted a lot more across his shoulders, the sudden chill made him wince.

What a change a couple of minutes made. She'd been so frightened that she'd flipped him to his back with a defensive move and now she was rubbing aloe on his shoulders. She'd also gone from petrified to smiling.

"My research might have given an indication of who we were searching for, triggering someone else's search. I trust everyone who I'm directly involved with in this case. But some parts of it are out of my control. I didn't mean to lead your ex-husband to you."

The light rubbing across his shoulders slowed for a second. Kylie spread the aloe, remaining silent behind him with her face and expressions hidden. He didn't want her to be nervous again. He preferred her smiling. So did his back.

"Your aikido. That was a great move. What's it called?"

"Aiki otoshi. It's a blending drop. I like it because you don't have to lift or flip your opponent."

"I noticed that. You hit my knees together and there

wasn't anything I could do to stop the fall. You're good. That wasn't a beginner's move."

She moved away, replacing the cap to the lotion. "Keep it."

"Even though I didn't mean to put you in danger, I think you need to come with me, Kylie. We can keep you safe."

They were sitting on the floor. She'd created a corner where she could see both doors, but was protected from anyone looking inside by the couch and walls. He noticed the mirrors strategically hung on the wall and one on a bookshelf.

Kylie Scott had a lot of precautions in place. She'd studied self-defense and probably was a crack shot with whatever weapon she had hidden in her bathroom. But it still wasn't a match for a man with endless resources and contacts like her ex-husband.

"You didn't see anything while you lived in the house? Is there any place he might keep important files?" he asked.

"I don't mean to be insensitive, but didn't the murders earlier this year get you inside that bleak mansion?"

"Only relating to the murders. The Tenorenos' lawyers made certain of that."

"Look, Bryce. I know you think you can protect me. You may really want to. But we both know it's just not true. At some point you'll have to walk away and I'll be alone. I can't worry about other people. I have to think about staying alive."

"Come to Waco. Let the attorneys run some questions past you. We'll keep it confidential. No one will know, but you might be able to help us shut down their operation."

"Stop it. I wasn't around their daily deals with lowlifes. When I stayed there I was kept from everything. No one helped me. Isabella was such a nice woman, but never on my side. It was her son one hundred percent." Kylie stood and pointed toward the door.

"You don't have to face this alone." He got to his feet, making one last plea. "We can help you put him away for the murders of your friends."

She covered her face with both hands. She looked up with determination, shaking her head.

"You said Xander wanted to take over the business. He doesn't need to find me to do that. He never believed in divorce and couldn't stand the idea that I would leave him. Plain and simple, as soon as I left him, he wanted me dead."

Chapter Three

"I know she's going to run. What do you want me to do about it?" Bryce had taken only enough time to change his clothes. The aloe on his shoulders helped the initial sting, but he should have worn a T-shirt. Now was not the time to be concerned about sunburn pain.

"Follow her," Major Parker said firmly. "You're certain she understands the consequences of rejecting our offer of protection?"

"Yes, sir." He rubbed his lower back. "She thinks she can take care of herself."

"It was good work finding her, Johnson. Real good work."

"Thank you, sir."

I just hope she doesn't get killed.

Hico, Texas wasn't large. It wasn't even a medium-sized town. If Kylie Scott was headed out of town, she really was at a crossroads to head in any direction. She'd given him no indication where that might be.

Maybe he could rule out east to Waco. Northeast toward Fort Worth and an international airport? Northwest to Stephenville and too many small towns to name? Or southwest to Mexico? There wasn't a warrant. No reason to detain her. No legal reason to keep her from running.

Whichever direction she decided, it would be today. He'd seen that look in her eyes. Panicked with a plan. She was leaving, all right. And it looked like her ride had just pulled up.

The old Chevy pickup stopped by Kylie's house most afternoons. She worked two part-time jobs and the older man gave her rides. Bryce had met her at the Billy the Kid Museum downtown where she walked a mile to work three days a week.

The other job he'd heard about from Mrs. Mackey. Fred Snell drove her to ranches right outside town where she worked cleaning barns with teens who needed community service. Mrs. Mackey had elaborated that Kylie was a good listener.

This afternoon she looked like every afternoon she hitched a ride. Nothing more than a small backpack in her hand and a pair of work gloves. But he'd seen that look.

Fred backed up out of the driveway. Without a plan of what he was going to do, Bryce stepped off his porch and jogged to the street. He waved Fred over. Kylie glared at him, but rolled down the window.

"Hey, Kylie. Mr. Snell, I think Mrs. Mackey introduced us at the café last Wednesday. Nice to see you again." The older gent bobbed his head. "I was wondering if you could use another hand."

"What's that? I'm a little hard of hearing."

"He asked if he could come with us today." Kylie shook her head.

Fred looked around her and squinted at the window. "Yeah, you're Mackey's handyman. We can always use another pair of young hands and a strong back. We're clearing some brush out at the Childerses's. Scoot over to the middle, Kylie."

"I don't think this is a good idea, Fred." She looked from one man to the other. Bryce could tell she was scrambling for an excuse to not open the door. "He needs gloves and has a horrible sunburn. He might get sick from it."

"Nonsense, Kylie. I have lots of extra gloves. You hand 'em out to the kids. Plenty of men work when their shoulders are red. Besides, you make us use sunscreen." He nodded and the debate was over.

Kylie scooted while he opened the door. Her eyes shot daggers—no other way to describe it—into Bryce's heart. He should be a dead man after those sharp points had stabbed him multiple times.

Fred stepped on the gas and the old truck chugged as loud as a train down Pecan Street. "Might as well leave that window down, son. AC went out in this thing back in '79."

There wasn't much small talk between the roar of the engine and the wind blowing through the cab. He dropped his arm behind Kylie to make a little more room and ended up with an elbow in his ribs.

"Ouch. What was that for?"

"The least you could have done is left your gun at home. I'm surprised you're not wearing a white hat since you're trying to come to my rescue." She wiggled on the old vinyl seat, trying to gain space between their hips.

"Now, Kylie, darlin', I'm going to downshift in a few. Scoot back over to our new volunteer." Fred kept his eyes straight ahead, one elbow out the window and one hand on the wheel.

One look at his upturned lips and anyone could tell he thought he was helping two lovebirds take flight. Fred hadn't been exaggerating about shifting soon. They turned taking a road that was more dust than dirt.

Their driver rolled up his window and Bryce took the hint. It was better to sweat and be able to breathe.

"Want to take off your extra shirt?" he asked close to Kylie's ear.

She shook her head and pulled the long-sleeve shirt closed at the neck. In the past two weeks he hadn't seen her in short sleeves. *Battle scars*. She'd been shot four times in that drive-by.

They reached their destination and Bryce would have a hard time if he had to drive back by himself. His shirt was sticking to his skin. He winced when Kylie lightly patted him between his shoulders.

"Thanks for coming to help," she said loudly.

Fred acknowledged and gave a wave to follow. Other cars and trucks were close by. A few young people milled around the corner of the house, coming to attention when Fred approached.

"I thought you worked with a couple of kids cleaning barns."

"Today is special. A tornado came through the property in the spring and we need to clear it out. The Childers family has donated the wood to the teen group. They plan to sell it for firewood."

"Know how to use a chain saw, son?" Fred asked from where three were being gassed up.

"Yes, sir. Grew up around them."

"Grab a pair of gloves from behind the seat and come get a refresher. We don't allow anyone who hasn't graduated to use one." He pointedly turned to the kid at his elbow and shook his head.

"You don't have to do this, you know." Kylie threw her bag over her shoulder and pulled her gloves on.

She acted like running away was the furthest thing from her mind. No one would have guessed that she wasn't moving through her life like normal. Her biggest worry at the moment seemed to be how they'd get all the wood back to town.

Xander Tenoreno was out there. No one was watching him. He could be meeting with a hired gun, sending one of his men or planning—yeah, he could be planning to take care of his ex-wife himself. Bryce had seen some of the gruesome results the Texas Mafia families had left in their wake. How could he convince her to come with him?

"Kylie, why don't you take Bryce, Calvert and Martin on your team. Everybody clear on the rules?" Fred asked.

"What rules?" He nudged Kylie before she could walk too far away.

"The team that stacks the most wood wins a bunch of donations from the town. Daydreaming isn't allowed…we want to win. Right, guys?"

"Whatever," they both answered, clearly not excited.

"Martin, do you mind lugging this thing and taking Bryce to the worksite? I need to say hi to Mrs. Childers."

"No prob."

Bryce was torn. He needed to keep Kylie in sight. Whatever her plan, she wasn't leaving without her shoulder bag. "Why don't I carry this for you?"

"That's all right. No need."

"I insist." He took it off her arm, playing a little tug-of-war until she let go.

"Fine." She ran up the hill to the house joining a woman on the porch.

As much as he wanted to hear that conversation, he felt it was necessary to maintain his cover story with Kylie's friends. If she announced he was a Texas Ranger…who would show up on her doorstep?

Then again, what if that was what the conversation was right at this moment?

"YOU'RE CERTAIN IT will be okay?" Kylie asked.

"Of course I am. I'll explain everything to Richard later. He'll take the grandkids in the four wheeler and catch Little Bit tomorrow. No big deal. They'll have a blast."

"I can't tell you how much I appreciate this, Lisa."

"On the other hand, maybe you should tell me what's

wrong. You aren't afraid of the tall and good-looking one over there. Are you? Is that what this is all about?"

"No. I don't want to involve him." She watched the last of the teams disappear into the trees.

"Well, maybe you should. He looks like someone who could fix a couple of problems."

"Remember, we just talked about ordering pizza for the kids and getting water down the hill."

"I'll have Little Bit saddled and ready to go at four, but I don't understand why you're all set to visit the Turners. I could run you over in the car a lot faster."

"I've been looking forward to my ride on Little Bit all week and I don't want Fred to miss out on his pizza. So I'll hop the fence and walk. I love to walk. Jan said she didn't mind bringing me home."

Kylie took a couple of steps away and realized this might be the last time she'd see Lisa. She ran back to the bottom step and threw her arms around the older woman's neck. She never hugged, but the people in Hico had helped her in so many ways.

"I'm a better person for knowing you and all my friends here. You guys have been so good to me. Thanks."

Lisa didn't let go. "You've got me a little scared now, Kylie. What have you gotten yourself into?"

She'd practiced this laugh in the mirror a thousand times when she'd been modeling. Her carefree, nothing-in-the-world-matters laugh that she'd perfected came off beautifully. Five years and she could fake it with the best of them.

"Seriously, nothing's wrong. I'm watching movies with Jan."

"If something happens to you... Well, I'll just never forgive myself."

"Nothing will. Promise." She skipped down the hill, horrified at the lies she'd told.

One of the things she hadn't missed from her old life was liars and users. People who had hung around her, claiming to be her friends, but who just wanted a free ride. They told her whatever lies were convenient. She'd let them and didn't care.

Not until four of them had died. One saving her life. Everything changed then.

Sissy really had died that night. She'd been a character invented out of necessity. Kylie was her real name. During those long days in the hospital, she had talked to herself in the mirror. Forcing her mind to reconnect to that real person.

Unable to attend the funerals of her friends... Scared that Xander would send someone to finish the job... Speaking only to her lawyer... She planned and prepared to run and hide. Leaving everything had been because of Xander. But leaving...that was all her idea.

She'd done it once when she'd signed on to become a model at the age of thirteen. Leaving the disaster of a life back then had been easy. Emancipation had been easy. Turning twenty-one and wheeling away from the hospital wasn't hard. It had saved her life. She was sure of it.

But today would be the hardest thing she'd ever done.

It didn't take long to catch up with the kids. "Hey slowpokes. I thought you'd be racing to get started. Once we finish this project, Bryce promised us all pizza."

"I what?"

"Pizza. Remember?" She caught up with him, looped her arm through his and the bag hanging over his shoulder. "You don't mind springing for pizza after all this hard work, do you? Or should I tell them that Rangers don't make enough money to buy three or four pies?"

"Pizza it is."

She broke apart from him, snagging her bag in the process. But she laughed and faked her way to the twisted trees. She plunged into the work, refusing to think of what was in store over the next few days.

Her map, compass, money and change of socks were with her. She'd had a moment of brilliance after Bryce had left. They'd be watching for her on every form of transportation. Xander might not know exactly how she looked now, but the people prosecuting his father did. They would trump up charges and arrest her. And he'd find her.

That was one thing she was certain about. There had already been one scandal this year about crooked state attorneys and politicians on the payroll of Paul Tenoreno.

"I don't know what you're planning, but you aren't going to shake me." Bryce walked up with a heavy-duty limb trimmer thingy.

"I have no idea what you're talking about." Her tree was ready to be cut. She signaled Martin who could handle the chain saw. She dug her earplugs out of her pocket. "Do you have ear protection? No? You might want to work on the next tree, then."

Bryce was angry. It showed in the way he chopped small limbs off and threw them into a pile. The kids then moved the brush to a larger pile that would be a bonfire later in the fall for their school. They worked. Hard.

Load after load of fireplace-size logs were added into a trailer that the ATV pulled up the hill. Richard was keeping track of how many were loaded by what team. Bryce was obviously in pain. Not from the physical labor—it was clear his muscles could handle that—it was the sunburn. His tight-fitting jeans didn't help much either. He'd switched from little limb lopping to splitting wood with an ax.

"If you guys moved about six feet, I think you'd be in the shade." She handed Bryce a bottle of water and lowered her voice, saying, "I think you could take off your shirt and stop rubbing your sunburn, too."

"You were right about my holster not being empty," he whispered back.

"I can stash it in my drawstring bag. It won't be out of your sight."

Did she have an ulterior motive? Not at first. She didn't want to steal his gun. But… No. She wouldn't steal his gun. Before she left, she'd hide it in the barn. It would be out of sight and out of reach of the two granddaughters.

"You might as well put your phone in here, too." She blocked the view of him removing his weapon and placing it inside. "You can hear it if it rings."

That would be hidden, too. Hopefully it would slow him down not to have his phone.

"Wait." He shrugged out of his shirt. The light pink of that morning had turned a deep red. Small white spots—blisters—had formed from getting hot again. "The bag stays with me. You're moving around. I'm staying put."

Swinging the ax, he lodged it in a log and moved everything to the shade, taking her travel items and dropping them in his line of sight. Darn him. And it was almost time to go.

The last thing she wanted was to bring all these people into her problems. She couldn't create a diversion without a lot of repercussions. How was she going to get out of this? She shook her head as it came to her. It was the perfect excuse to head back to the house.

She finished up the last tree. The kids and parent volunteers had been great. The heat wasn't too bad since most of the area was still shaded. And in this little gully there was even a hint of a breeze.

I'm going to miss this so much.

But it was time to go.

No goodbyes. No tears. She set her tool near the watercooler and stuffed her gloves in the back pocket of her shorts. She'd need them later. She waited, aware of where everyone was located. As soon as a couple of the boys brought another piece of a large trunk for Bryce to split, she took them all cups of water from the cooler.

"Drink up, boys. You need to stay hydrated."

"Thanks, Kylie," they said between sips.

"I'm heading to the little girls' room. So you fellows are on your own for a minute or two. Maybe even three." She smiled. The smile that teen boys had fallen for so many years ago. She casually bent and retrieved her bag.

"I can watch that for you." Bryce almost touched her arm but pulled it back to the ax handle. Probably remembering this morning's toss to the floor.

"I need what's inside. Understand?"

He nodded and those teenage boys sort of cringed. She giggled at her brilliance and waved to Richard for a lift.

The bathroom wasn't a bad idea. She grabbed a couple of apples from the kitchen counter, a soda and two bottles of water. She couldn't ask for them, so she left a five-dollar bill in the drawer.

With Bryce's gun and phone well-hidden inside the barn, she grabbed Little Bit and walked her to the far side of the house. There would be lots of sunlight left when she reached the north fence. If Bryce tried to follow her, he'd have to drive half an hour to get to the road she was heading to that bordered the far side of the property.

She clicked to Little Bit and didn't look back as she loped away.

Chapter Four

Bryce mentioned he needed a break. Everyone was exhausted so Fred called out quitting time. They all walked up the incline while Fred and Richard rode in the ATV.

He had a very bad feeling why Kylie had been gone so long. His gut told him she'd left, along with his service weapon and his phone.

"Dammit."

"Something wrong?" Martin asked.

"Just slipped. These boots weren't made for climbing."

"Yeah, we noticed. But thanks for coming. You did a lot. You Kylie's boyfriend now or something?"

"No. I live across the street. I'm helping Mrs. Mackey out for a while." Might be longer if he'd lost his Sig to a runaway witness.

The kids gave each other fist bumps when they saw Mrs. Childers arrive with pizza boxes. It was a familiar scene. He'd grown up in a small community. There was just one thing notably wrong… Kylie wasn't anywhere in sight.

For some reason, no one was overly concerned with her disappearance. That bugged him. Was he the only one not in on her planned escape? Did they already consider him the enemy?

The kids were sprawled across the porch cooling off. Proud of their work today, they were inhaling the pizza and soda. Richard and Fred were tallying the stacks of wood to determine which team won. Mrs. Childers and her granddaughters were bringing out cupcakes they'd made for the young people.

And Kylie was nowhere. Not in the house. Not waiting in the truck. Mrs. Childers shrugged and searched a little herself when he asked. Everywhere except the barn.

Still shirtless, because Kylie had taken that along with everything else, he cautiously walked through the barn's double doors. Open, clean, neat. If he hadn't been looking for something out of place, he'd never have caught the shirttail in the hayloft.

Wedged between a hay bale and the rafters, he pulled the shirt free and found his cell, badge and gun. Relief a hundred times over. No words could describe.

Since the gun was hidden, it meant that Kylie wasn't missing…just trying to disappear. Everything in place and with his shirt on his back, he sought out Mrs. Childers for answers.

"Did you happen to drop Kylie off back in town?" He didn't want to seem overanxious, but his insides started to grind like coffee beans.

"Well, if I had, I would have told you when you were looking for her earlier." Lisa immediately turned her back to him but didn't walk away.

"Funny thing about honest folks trying to lie. They don't do it often enough to be good at it." He stood next to her and took the empty pizza boxes from her grip, setting them on the porch swing. "You may not have taken her back to town, but you know what's going on."

"No."

The worry in her eyes clued him in. She'd helped but had no details. "Mrs. Childers, I realize you're friends with Kylie and you have no reason to trust me. I need to show you something." He removed his badge and let her take a long look. "It's important that everyone in town not know who I work for."

"Then why tell me? Are you here to arrest Kylie? Because I won't help you."

"No, ma'am. It's worse. I'm here to protect her." Bryce put his badge away and leaned against the wall. He tried to be as casual as possible, attempting to gain any trust he could.

"If that's true, then why would she leave?" She shook her head, one hand knotting in her apron still dusted with flour.

"She seems to be a very independent woman. Did you give her a ride?"

"No. And that's the truth. She's spending the night with Jan Turner and said she wanted to get to the northeast gate. The only way is on horseback. She said she'd leave the gear there and set Little Bit free. She wouldn't tell me anything else except that it was important for her to leave without anyone knowing. Is she in danger?"

"Thanks. You've helped tremendously." He took the porch steps two at a time.

"How are you going to find her?" Lisa asked behind him.

"With a lot of luck and crossed fingers."

No local PD involvement. At least not yet. He had to try to locate her on his own. Oh, yeah. He could follow tracks. He was a Texas Ranger who had a knack for computers. But at his roots, he was a simple country boy who'd grown up hunting with his dad.

"Richard?" Lisa shouted from the porch. "Will the four-wheeler get back to the northeast quarter of the property?"

"There's still too many downed trees," Richard replied.

"Well, then help Bryce saddle up Tinkerbell. He needs to save Kylie." Lisa's voice held a slight tremor of worry.

"Save Kylie?" Richard asked, but got an elbow in his ribs from Fred. "Whatever you say, dear."

Both men stopped what they were doing and moved to the barn. The one horse in the stall Bryce had seen earlier must be Tinkerbell.

He could approximate how long ago Kylie had left, but not how fast she could push the horse. There was also no way to know exactly how long it would take to catch up with her. The trees were thick in some parts and would make it hard to follow a trail.

"I can saddle her if you show me the tack," he told the men as they entered the barn. He wanted both of these guys to know he wasn't a novice.

"Doesn't make me no never mind." Richard mumbled and unlocked the storage room. "I've stayed married all these years by listening to Lisa. Doesn't make any sense riding a horse where you can drive. I just do what I'm told."

Fred snickered, clearly knowing something Bryce didn't. Then again…

"I appreciate the help, but aren't you guys curious as to *why* I need the horse?"

And there it was as plain as day turning to night. These honest men compressed their lips and dug the toes of their boots in the dirt.

"Did Mrs. Mackey tell you something about me?"

"Tell us what, son?" Fred asked as innocent as a five-year-old with his hand in a cookie jar.

"You know. And you want me on this horse pretty badly. In fact, I'd say you're practically throwing me on it." Bryce looked at the mare and had a bad feeling. "Give me your keys, Fred."

"What's that you're saying?" Fred held his hand, cupping his ear.

"Go ahead, Fred. He won't find her in the dark on his own and we're certainly not going to help him."

"I will not." The older man took a step back.

Richard looped the lead rope over the stall's gate and crossed his arms in defiance. "If we're lucky, he might be stuck out there all night and she'll get clean away."

Bryce opened his palm, taking a step closer.

Fred dug deep in his jeans pocket for the set of keys. He held them in a tight fist, not forking them over. "Maybe I should drive? That old motor gets kind of cranky."

"Thanks, but I think I'll get there faster on my own." Wherever *there* happened to be. "Pick it up at my place tomorrow."

Fred tossed. Bryce caught and hit the dirt running. Already tired, he should have been drinking a gallon of water to rehydrate. A slight headache had begun. Not to mention the idiot burn he had thanks to Jesse's suggestion of taking his shirt off.

He shifted the truck into High and skidded to a halt at the end of the long private driveway.

"Which way?"

His cell had no reception. No GPS. They might have counted on that. But he had the map he'd downloaded of the area. With details. Lots of details.

Kylie was headed to the northeast portion of Richard's property. Why would she go there? He enlarged the map and knew…there was no road that passed from US 281 on the west side of the Richard's place to County Road 238 on the east.

It would delay him to double back toward Hico and try to cut her off.

"Where will I find her?"

Had she made arrangements to be picked up on the country road? Was she just going to hoof it to the next town? It wasn't an impossible idea. But a faster way to disappear would be to hitch a ride. And if she walked the county roads northwest, she'd hit Highway 67 with plenty of traffic.

Everything rested with him making a logical guess.

He turned right instead of left back to town and pushed the truck harder than it had been pushed in a while. It sputtered a bit, but got the job done. The cooler air of twilight passed through the open windows. When he turned again, he could smell hay and cattle.

Working around Mrs. Mackey's house for the past couple of weeks had brought back a lot of memories. The third time he'd called his mom, she'd asked him what was wrong and had kidded him about being homesick.

Homesick? He couldn't wait to leave his family's acreage and pass on his riding lawn mower duties to his younger brothers. They'd all left the house and were spread out across the country now, settled with families or kids on the way. He rested his elbow on the door and tapped a drum solo on the old-fashioned vent window.

Darkness was slowly growing. The moon wouldn't rise for quite a while so it might be harder to see someone walking in the fields. He'd taken the most direct route to the next county road Kylie might be on. He turned right again and kept the truck in second gear.

Reminiscing was fine, but his job was to find Kylie Scott. After he got her back to headquarters in Waco, he'd find out how Fred and Richard had known about his cover. The only person who supposedly knew was Mrs. Mackey. Why would she tell anyone?

It was dark enough that unless Kylie had a flashlight, he wouldn't be able to see her. He continued along the road at a normal pace for the truck. How would he explain this wild situation to Major Parker?

If she disappeared again on his watch, he might not have to explain anything to anyone.

THE DAY HAD already been long and exhausting before Kylie

had started traipsing through uneven fields in her tennis shoes. She couldn't rush. There was no flashlight or even a penlight in her bag. And it was just her luck that tonight there wasn't even a moon.

Hours after leaving the horse, her legs were cramping and she was thirstier than she'd ever been. And hot. There was no breeze to cool the sweat that dripped in buckets down her back. She'd pulled her color contacts and stowed them in her bag.

She'd avoided the roads, but kept them just to her left. No one had driven past her. Or at least she hadn't heard any vehicles. The birds she'd come across had practically scared her senseless.

Each time she'd carefully squeezed between the strands of wire fence from one field to the other, her fingers were crossed that there wouldn't be a bull or something more dangerous in her path. She pulled herself through the last pieces of barbed wire fencing and picked up her bag, straightening and stretching her back.

The hardest part of the hike was done. She could follow this road to the closest thing this area had to a highway— a two-lane blacktop. Then all she had to do was hitch a ride and she was…

She was what?

The word *free* kept trying to finish the sentence. But she wasn't free. If she was free to choose where she wanted to live, it would be Hico. She'd never felt more at home in a community. They accepted that she didn't talk about her time before living there. They really didn't know anything about her.

At least not the *previous* her. The Sissy Jorgenson her. Such a fake. It had taken a while, but Sissy had been laid to rest with all the cool kids she'd hung out with.

Unfortunately, Sissy wouldn't have had anything to do with Kylie Scott. And she wouldn't have waited two weeks to have a fling with the guy across the street. One look at his body and Sissy would have been all over him.

Bryce was nice looking. He was also a Texas Ranger ready to take her back to Austin whether she liked it or not. It didn't matter if she knew about the Tenoreno family business. The attorneys five years ago had offered her protection in exchange for information.

Did they really think she would have walked away so quickly if she'd known enough to put those men behind bars?

Blinding headlights popped on in front of her.

"I was just coming to look for you." Bryce's voice came from next to Fred's truck. "You going to run again?"

"Mind shutting off the floodlights?" Kylie saw his silhouette lean through the window and everything got dark again.

With no place to go and no energy to run, she accepted the setback, but not defeat. Somehow, she'd get away from Bryce Johnson and get on with another new start.

"Want a ride?" he asked with an air of innocence.

"Yes, if you're heading back to Hico."

"It's on the way to Waco." He casually leaned against Fred's pickup.

"How long have you been waiting?"

"At least an hour." Bryce tapped the old green truck. "Did the horse throw you or something during your evening ride? Get turned around finding your friend's house or the way back? I know you weren't attempting to run away. Right?"

She didn't need to answer. He was making fun of her so she glared at him, even though he couldn't see the glare in the dark. She wrapped her arms around her bag, almost afraid he might arrest her on the spot.

"Are you as starved as me? Or did Lisa give you something before you left?" Bryce continued, fingers tapping out an unknown rhythm against the old metal truck.

"I'm actually starved. And parched. Any chance there's a water bottle in there?" She leaned on the warm hood.

"Nope. But it's not far to Hico." He threw his thumb toward the cab. "We can get something to go."

"Nothing is open at this time of night in our little town." The sun had been down a long time. Too long for the hood to still be as warm as it was. "You must be a really lucky son of a gun to choose the exact road I was heading to."

"I like to think of myself as a highly skilled Texas Ranger. Come on, get in."

"Who had his gun and ID lifted by little ol' me," she mumbled.

"There's no reason to get nasty."

"I'll admit defeat when you confess how you found me."

"I had a map. Calculated your foot speed—they teach us things like that."

"And how long have you really been here?"

"All right. I tried several roads before deciding on this one. Satisfied? I got lucky and saw something moving from the road over there. Been waiting about fifteen minutes."

"So you guessed."

"Pretty much." He grinned.

The dark wasn't pitch-black, even with no moon hanging overhead. She could see that he'd found his shirt from where she'd hidden it in the barn. That meant he'd found his gun, too. Bryce could force her to go with him. If he was a dirty cop he could make her disappear. Especially now that she'd told Lisa she had to leave town.

No one would be looking for her.

There was nothing she could do to prevent it. Not here. She had to get back to town, maybe show her face at the Stop-N-Get It. But her instincts told her that Bryce was legit. A good person who believed he was following the law and had her best interests at heart.

Right. That's what they all say.

"If I keep walking down this road…" She threw her chin in the direction behind the truck. "Are you going to arrest me?"

"Don't make me, Kylie."

Her fingers were already wrapped around the handle. She was getting into the truck, she had little choice. But she didn't have to like it. They both got inside and slammed their doors.

"You need someone to look out for your safety," he said softly, reaching for the ignition key.

"No offense, but I think I was doing pretty good without you."

Exhaustion like she hadn't felt in five years hit her like a slow wave as soon as she sat down. It started in her shoulders and crept up her neck, then down her back. She hadn't stopped and had barely slowed, holding a steady pace across those fields. And yet, Texas Ranger Bryce Johnson had been waiting on her.

Just dumb luck? Or was he really that skilled?

Chapter Five

As soon as Bryce had put the truck in gear, Kylie's head sank against the window and she was asleep. Totally and deeply. The mumbles and sleep jerking couldn't be faked. Not that well. A little twitch, then a jerk that should have awakened anyone who was dozing.

Exhaustion had overtaken her. He'd probably have to carry her inside her house when they arrived. As long as there weren't any alarms. *Get a grip.* They weren't staying.

A quick stop to grab water and clothes. That was it. He was taking her to Waco. Tonight. No waiting. No discussion.

The truck was much too noisy to hear the sleepy words escaping her lips. He couldn't see her face, but could imagine the soft worried crease across her forehead. He'd watched her all afternoon. Had suspected that she was up to something and should never have let her leave—especially with his gun.

But for some reason he'd trusted her to realize how much danger she was in. Maybe that was the problem. Maybe she knew and didn't expect him to be able to protect her from the Tenoreno family. He could understand that.

Sort of.

Running had been a logical choice. She didn't know him. He had to respect that she'd had a plan. Been prepared. Five years after she'd disappeared and she'd still been ready to take off with nothing. Smart.

Then again, she'd left his weapon behind.

Crazy woman.

Maybe smarter than he'd been thinking about her for the past three years. Smarter than Sissy Jorgenson had been when she married Xander. Kylie Scott was a completely different person, who didn't mind working hard side by side with teens who needed some guidance.

Why? What had changed her? Besides the near death experience, of course.

They were almost back to town when she mumbled something about getting down. Her head tossed back and forth in a bad dream. Her long legs kicked out, striking the metal of the truck near her feet.

Kylie jerked awake. She looked frantically all around her. "Oh my gosh. We're not home yet?"

"Bad dream?"

"Let's just say that for a short one, it was really intense." She dropped her window farther and dipped her hand in the wind blowing past the mirror. "I wish the Koffee Cup was open this late. I sure could go for some pie."

"The fresh strawberry was really good this morning."

"This morning? You had pie for breakfast?" Her hand fluttered to the door handle.

"Fruit is good for you." He slowed the truck to a stop, very aware that there'd be no way he could stop her from jumping from the old vehicle. She might get a head start, but he'd catch her. She might know her way around town better, but she was also more tired than he was.

"How do you eat pie for breakfast and look that good?" She shook her head. "Never mind. It's a guy thing. I get it."

"A guy thing?" He loved the blue flash of her eyes, even if the look was a little deadly. He really wanted to ask about the "looking good" statement. Maybe the sunburn was worth it after all.

The light turned green and her elbow rested on the window's edge again. He liked the way this woman's brain worked. She was constantly ready. Had distracted him with the pie conversation, yet had thought her choices through before acting rash and running.

"Where are you going? Our street is to your left."

"Yeah, I know." He took a second right into the motel nearest the highway. One car in the parking lot. Sliding the camera app open, he handed Kylie his phone. "Can you snap the license?"

"Sure," she whispered like someone inside the room could hear them. "You sure this is legal?"

"Very. It will give me a heads-up if anyone's here that might be looking for you."

He swung around and they repeated the picture-taking at the other two hotels in town. She was out of the truck before he pulled to a complete stop once they were in front of her house.

"Kylie, wait." He pulled the key and caught up before she opened her front door. He stopped her hand on the knob. "I need to check it out first."

"Go ahead. Where do you want me to wait? Here on the porch all alone? Or just inside where the bogeyman can sneak up on me? Or, I know, out in the woods where the ax murderer is sure to be waiting?"

"The woods are out?" Humor or sarcasm…probably not the best way to handle the situation. Truth it was. "Hand on my shoulder. I go. You go. I stop. You stop. Stay close behind me until we check all the rooms. Got it?"

"Sure." She shook her head and placed her hand on his shoulder with a firm grip.

He drew his Sig and entered the house. If someone was inside, they'd just given them time to secure their position and prepare to overpower them. It was a chance they'd take.

"Stop." She tapped his shoulder. "Alarm." She pushed the code and the light turned green.

Bryce had a feeling that Kylie wouldn't be satisfied just getting a glass of water. He also planned to find her gun of choice that was stowed in the bathroom before she did.

Slowly, he checked out each of the rooms in the small home. One uncomfortable couch, one compact kitchen, two bedrooms, one bed and an empty bath.

"Does it look like anyone's been here?"

"No. Excuse me a minute." She pushed on his shoulder to get him to move.

"Not yet. We need to look in the garage."

"Seriously? My eyeballs are floating."

He resisted laughing and managed to question her with a look. Taking her hand, he placed it back on his shoulder and kept his over it until they were back down the hall and he found the door locked.

"But—"

"Shh. Where's the key?" Not just a dead bolt to turn. He'd assumed that it was extra protection when he'd seen the security lock that morning. Now, with her hesitation, he wasn't that sure.

"It hasn't been messed with so there's no reason to go in there."

"I need to be certain, Kylie."

She stared at him a second. Placed her hands on her hips the next. Then reluctantly pulled open a cabinet drawer without looking. Inside was a small combination box. She rolled the numbers and dangled a set of keys from her fingertips.

"You're going to want to know the whole story behind this and I'm not ready to share it. So can you check out the garage and forget about it for tonight?" He reached for the keys and she yanked them back. "Your word, Ranger Johnson."

"That's asking a lot from a guy here to protect you."

"That remains to be seen." She tossed the key ring, crossed her arms and released an exaggerated sigh.

Bryce opened the door and cautiously stepped down to the garage level. Kylie flipped the light switch causing him to blink. A single set of shelves across from him held some labeled boxes. Christmas decorations, patriotic, miscellaneous, fall theme, Halloween and one that was unmarked.

But taking up all the room in the single car garage was a vehicle covered with sheets. The sheets across the trunk had a layer of dust on them. Unlike the one in front. No one had disturbed anything anywhere in the house, including here.

But he was curious. He holstered his Sig and tugged, letting the sheets slide to a pile at his boots.

In the time that he'd been watching her, Kylie had ridden a bike to work, walked to the store or caught a ride. He'd never seen a car unless someone else was picking her up like today. So the beauty in the garage was a surprise.

"Where did you get this?"

"We can't take it anywhere. It's stolen."

"Can I ask why you kept it then?" He slid his hand along the stylish fin from the '60s and immediately regretted spoiling the clean shine.

"I didn't want that louse to have it." She threw up her hands. "All right. I admit it. I sort of took it to get back at him. I was so angry that he'd taken everything from me that I wanted something of his that he'd miss."

"This belonged to Xander Tenoreno?" The black Cadillac had a fire-engine red interior and was in mint condition. The paint job was still shiny and bright. He stroked the edge as he walked to the front of the garage.

If Kylie hadn't touched the car, someone had. There

was a battery charger near the tire. So he could no longer assume she didn't have a vehicle to drive. He'd bet money that this one would move pretty good.

"Of course it did. Does." She walked to the opposite side of the car, but leaned against the unfinished wall with her hands behind her. "I left the hospital when I knew the family was gone. I wanted my stuff. Anything really. Or maybe some cash to get out of the country. I used what little I had to bribe one of the guards to let me in. The bastard had moved everything. Even the cat. It was like I'd never existed."

"So you grabbed his car?"

"One of them."

"This one's pretty distinctive."

"I know. It was new so I figured it would be missed. I didn't say I was thinking straight at the time. I drove until I ran out of gas."

"To Hico? That's how you got here? How you chose this town to hide out?"

"Not very strategic, right? This gas guzzler coasted to a stop right next to the Billy the Kid statue. The top was down and I put the seat back. I stared at that statue and fell asleep. Fred drove by the next morning and helped me push the car to the station."

"So he talked you into staying?"

"He took me to breakfast. Denise just had a baby and Allison offered me a temporary job right there on the spot. I'm sure Fred had something to do with it. He almost always does."

"If the engine is in good condition, I'm surprised you haven't tried to sell it."

"You heard me say it's stolen, right? It seems so simple in my head—drive the car and I get killed. There isn't a different version. Xander would know I've been living here if this car was discovered."

"Lots of stolen cars are illegally traded. You probably could have gotten enough money to leave town. So why did you stay?"

Why run? He knew that the state's attorney had offered her immunity for anything connected with illegal activity. All she had to do was give them evidence. Anything to help break up the Tenoreno family's crime syndicate. Instead she'd stolen a car.

"If my ex-husband didn't already want me dead, knowing that I've had his precious car all this time would be another reason to hunt me down. It makes me nervous to even look at it. I haven't glanced at it in at least two years. Fred keeps it polished." She reached for the corner of the sheet. "And I stayed in Hico because I like it here."

"You most likely had it off the streets before it was reported missing. We might be able to lay out a trap using it as bait if he loved it as much as you say." He slid his hand over the polished tailfin again. "Man, I'd love to take it for a spin."

"What is it with guys and cars? It's not going anywhere." She dragged the dusty cover over the trunk. "Taking it brought me to Hico, but driving it now will just get us killed."

He grabbed the opposite corner and helped hide the convertible. "We'll take my truck to Waco. I was thinking about later. After you're safe."

"There isn't a later. Don't you get it? I won't be safe. Ever. If I go with you, Xander *will* find me. He's probably already sent someone. Just let me go." She draped the hood and crossed her arms, protecting herself. "You could tell everyone you didn't pick the right road to wait at. It might be a little embarrassing, but we'd both be alive."

"I can't do that, Kylie."

She wanted to be relaxed, cool, act as if none of this

conversation bothered her. It did. Thinking about Xander and the men he had working for him bothered her a lot.

Bryce lifted his arm, waiting on her to pass through the garage entrance to her kitchen. She didn't like the feeling of helplessness. It made her mad. There was nothing in the kitchen to help her overpower this man. Her aikido skills had paid off this morning, but he was prepared for them now. She couldn't outrun him to the bathroom and she couldn't lock him in the garage since he had the door behind him waiting on her.

So she passed in front of him and stepped onto her worn linoleum. He'd already mentioned that he thought she had a gun stashed in the bathroom. If she asked to go, he was the kind of guy who would search it thoroughly beforehand. He might even find it.

"Want a bottle of water?" she asked.

"Been craving something cold for the past hour." Bryce wiped the sweat from his forehead. "But water will do."

"Yeah, I know what you mean." She went to the fridge and grabbed two bottles, tossing one across the room to him as he locked the door. It didn't escape her that the keys to the Cadillac dropped into his pocket.

They both stayed put in the dark and drank their bottles dry. Bryce crunched his to a fistful of plastic and set it on the table. Sixteen ounces of fluid didn't seem to be enough for her thirst so she opened the fridge for more.

"Kylie!"

Bryce dived across the open section of kitchen, knocking her to the floor behind him and dragging her to the far side of the refrigerator.

The window shattered. Milk streamed across the floor toward them. Orange juice exploded sending glass in the opposite direction.

"You okay?" he asked, pulling her around the wall into the living room. "Thank God I saw their sighting laser."

He pulled his weapon but as soon as he stuck his head around the corner things in the kitchen began shattering again.

"Call 911," he shouted.

"No, I won't. These men will kill responding officers without blinking an eye." She was crazy for thinking they could take care of this themselves. His look told her as much, but she didn't want anyone to get hurt trying to save her. "Too many have already died."

He took out his cell and in a quick call told whoever answered what their situation was. "They've got us pinned down." Backup was on its way. "The thickness of the refrigerator on the other side of this wall is the only thing protecting us. Don't move until I come up with a plan."

Her life wasn't worth more than anyone else's. She had to do something. If someone got shot, how would she live with that again? The white gravel lot had been drenched in blood. She barely remembered shooting details and yet, the image was so vivid.

Red on white. Just like Darren lying on top of her.

As much as she hated the memories, she clung to them to remind herself. She wouldn't forget how vicious Xander was or how he didn't value human life. Everything was different...except that.

Bryce had his arm across her chest. She was loosely pinned to the wall where he'd leaned just that morning for support. Something—maybe a clay pot one of the rec center kids had given her—exploded in front of them.

A couple of choice words escaped from Bryce. "Dammit. They've shot a hole through the damn wall. What caliber are they using? When our backup gets here..."

She was paralyzed in place, hearing only half of what he instructed. She caught on to the fact he wanted her to slide her head to the floor and lie flat.

"Kylie? Can you hear me? Understand what I'm explaining?"

"I can...I can do it. But why?"

"Their next approach should be coming through the front. It's wood and glass—easy enough to penetrate with the firepower they have." He bobbed his head when the television screen was pierced by another bullet.

"You're coming, too?"

"I might be on top of you if you're too slow." Bryce extended his legs and pushed her couch across the old wood floor.

A small coffee table blocked a clean path to the door, but she could get around it. She wasn't paralyzed any longer. "Are you sure we shouldn't just get up and run?"

Something glass exploded into a gazillion pieces. She covered her eyes. She didn't want to think it, but it looked like someone had shot through the front door.

Bryce answered his phone. "Johnson. From the southwest. No visual on the north. We're pinned in the front room. Got it." He stowed the phone and covered most of her body. "We're staying put. Three police cars are en route."

"Call them off, Bryce. Please. They'll be slaughtered." She turned to her side. His arm was wrapped around her waist. She tried to scoot away, but he pulled her back to him. She shoved at his chest and he captured her hand.

"We aren't going anywhere and the officers are doing their jobs. They aren't coming in blind. They can handle the shooter. We'll be fine." He patted her back.

Was he shushing her? He pulled her face to his shirt when something else burst behind her. He smelled musky. The good kind after working all day. She could feel the heat from his sunburn through the soft cotton. It was comforting, even if she didn't want to admit that it had been a long time since she'd been held by a man. Or anyone.

But she couldn't let herself be comfortable. She

stretched her neck backward so she could look him in the eye and tell him what he could do with his "shushing."

Glass rained around them as the front windows shattered above their heads. Xander's men weren't leaving anything to chance. She waited for the bullet to pierce her skin. For the second time she knew her life was over.

Chapter Six

Shots were fired outside the house. A multitude of ear-piercing pops. Some single rounds like at the gun range. Some rapid like five years ago. Would the men who had them pinned here run? Could the cops actually scare them away?

Lying there, waiting to be shot, Bryce had rolled her to her belly and shielded Kylie from the shards. The weight of the man on top of her should have kept her from breathing easily. He'd supported most of his weight on his arms to keep from hurting her. It took her a couple of seconds of silence to realize he wasn't moving, but it wasn't the weight of the dead like Darren.

Bryce was still breathing. There was a gap between his arm and the floor where she could see parts of her living room. Or what used to be her living room—war zone was more accurate.

A beam of light broke the semidarkness.

She wasn't in a hurry to be free. She needed to catch her breath and get back to the present. This wasn't a white gravel parking lot. She hadn't been shot. They were alive.

"Police! Johnson? Kylie? You in here?"

She recognized the voice. She'd stood next to Todd Harris at the Chamber of Commerce pancake breakfast last year. He'd told her all about his three kids, especially his son who had hit a rebellious period.

That's how and when Martin Harris had gotten involved in their teen program. He was one of the leaders now. She was proud to have helped that father and teen. And now he was putting his life in danger for her.

"I'm okay." She waited for Bryce to roll. He was slow but finally moved to his side.

"Is the perimeter secure?" He groaned.

"We're working on it," Todd said. "You good here? You shot? Need an ambulance?"

"You're bleeding?" Kylie carefully put her knees in the glass-free zone where her body had been during the attack. She watched Bryce sit, awkwardly limiting his movements.

Todd turned his flashlight behind them drawing her attention. "What the hell did they shoot at you? A cannon?"

The hole in her wall next to where they'd been sitting was indeed the size of a cannonball. Whatever it had been, she was glad the old refrigerator had enough thickness to protect them.

"Sure felt like it. We're good. I got us covered." Bryce seemed a little out of breath as he spoke. "Can you watch the perimeter of the house? We need ten minutes."

"Not a problem," Todd answered and picked his way back to the door.

Afraid that another round of shots would happen at any minute, she kept her eyes on Todd and possible movement behind him. Of course the only light was from the porch across the street. Not much help at all.

"Do you know who did this or think they'll come back?" Todd asked, plainly wanting the Texas Ranger to issue the orders.

"My guess is they didn't want us dead," Bryce answered out of breath. "Otherwise, they would have rushed the house. They'll wait for a second attempt when they can grab whatever they're really after. Might already be out of town."

"Well," Todd drawled, "it won't hurt to look."

Bryce sucked air through his teeth catching Kylie's attention. She turned and caught him pulling a large piece of glass from his forearm.

"Are you crazy?" She slapped his hand away. "Let me get a first aid kit. If they're too deep, you'll need a doctor."

He clapped a hand on her arm. "I'll go with you."

They helped each other stand. He didn't let go of her while he addressed Todd, giving him instructions on how far to set up checkpoints. She'd had no intention to get her hidden handgun, but evidently he hadn't forgotten about it.

Nor did he trust her to leave it there. The glass was lodged mainly in his left arm. He shook off some pieces stuck in the fine arm hair before they left the room.

"Everything's gone. Completely destroyed." There really was nothing left of her cute little home. The curtains were in shreds, everything was cut in half or shattered on the floor.

"We're alive."

"For now," she whispered.

He sat on the toilet lid, covered in a red faux fur that she adored. She went straight to the cabinet, keeping her eyes away from the picture on the wall. Tweezers, alcohol, Band-Aids...she laid everything side by side on the short counter.

"You've certainly been through the wringer today." She took a good look under the bright light.

"These are just scratches, but a couple do look like they need tweezers."

"You should be plenty sore from the sunburn and swinging that ax." She pulled the rod that held the stopper in place. "Hold your arm over the sink."

Bryce did as he was told, hissing as she poured the alcohol across his skin. It had to burn, but he didn't wave at it. She thought about blowing on his skin, but it seemed too intimate. So she poured more alcohol over the tweezers and went to work picking out the shards.

"The Hico police turned out to be more competent than you gave them credit." Bryce winced. "Are you surprised that we're all still alive?"

"What about the next time? Who's going to get hurt then?"

"I'm taking you to Waco and if anyone's watching they'll know it. Then they'll be facing a company of Rangers."

"Or not." She placed the last bandage over the deepest cut, then wrapped his forearm with gauze.

"Why do you keep saying that? Don't you want to get to safety?"

"Of course I do, but I've tried explaining this not only to you but to everyone I spoke with five years ago. I simply don't know anything. I don't have anything worth trading for protection." She backed away from the sink. Thinking over and over again that she shouldn't look anywhere else in the bathroom. She needed to stare at Bryce and forget about taking the gun.

"Would you like some more aloe?" she asked, remembering the warmth of his skin. She put the kit away and grabbed a tube of cream, making the decision for him. "Take off your shirt."

He stood. The bathroom shrank. The result was like washing a cashmere sweater in a hot load of whites.

"Thanks for the offer, but I need to check on our rescue team."

They switched places, hands their only barrier between bodies sliding next to each other. "I really need a drink."

"Not a bad idea." Bryce rested his wrists on top of her shoulders. "Something stronger than water this round?"

"I don't think they shot the top shelf of the pantry. There's probably still a bottle intact." Tilting her face in his direction required as much bravery as sitting petrified while bullets were shot through her walls. "That is, if you're serious."

Bryce tapped her shoulder a couple of times, made eye contact, looked away, then back again. She had a good view of his Adam's apple jumping up and down as he swallowed hard. He was nervous. Because of her? Or was it because there was barely anything left of her house?

"We should…um…wait for another time. As much as I'd love a shot of whatever you have, I need to get you out of here. No way to secure—you know…" He squinted as he looked down the hall.

"Is there something you want, Bryce? I thought you were going to check on Todd."

"Is that his name?" He nodded his head as if agreeing with her. His lips were compressed in a straight line, but still looked inviting.

Honestly, they could have been standing on her porch waiting to say good-night. The moment felt more like that than of ten minutes after someone had tried to kill them. Maybe she was in shock. Maybe she was just tired of fighting the inevitable.

Or maybe in spite of the weird circumstances that had brought them together, Bryce was as attracted to her as she was to him. Maybe. If she was lucky.

She cleared her throat and gently slid his hands from her shoulders. "Todd Harris, father of three teenagers all rooting for rival Texas colleges every Saturday afternoon. He mostly works weeknights now so his wife, Irma, could take the day shift. She's a nurse in Stephenville."

"Sounds like a nice family."

"And I want to keep it that way. Those kids need their father. Don't order him to—"

"Todd Harris has a job to do, Kylie. He signed up for this." Bryce tried to look stern. It didn't work on him.

"Get real. He signed up to make sure people drove the speed limit and to get cats out of little old ladies' trees."

"I think you might need that drink more than you think." He backed his wide shoulders through the doorway and latched on to her hand. "On the rocks or straight?"

"Can I get some clothes? My toothbrush?"

He pulled her into the kitchen. There was a more concentrated destruction path. Her refrigerator was completely ruined. Her free hand began shaking and she couldn't stop it.

The mess was surreal. It registered on levels she didn't—couldn't—comprehend. She did need a drink. Perhaps more than one. But she *hadn't*. Not in five years.

"This is some good stuff." Bryce grabbed the whiskey from the top shelf. Then took a tumbler from the drain.

The bottle was half-gone. He unscrewed the cap, tipped the bottle...

"Wait. I can't. Especially that stuff." She shook her head, matching her hands. "It was in the car, Bryce. It belonged to...to Xander. I don't drink anymore. Can we just go?"

That bottle was a symbol of her past life. It and the car were the only two things she'd kept.

"Sure. I'll grab your toothbrush."

She turned looking at the broken things she'd collected. "Forget it. I need a new one anyway."

The clothes, things, books and even the house would be easy to leave behind. She picked up one of the photos that had been held in place by magnets on her ruined fridge. Fred and Lisa had locked her in the jail in the museum.

"It was a bet about how tall I was." She flipped the milk-drenched photo toward Bryce. "You see, Lisa thought I was over six feet and that's how tall the old cell is. So when I stood inside...she thought she'd won. I didn't point out that my shoes had heels."

Tears. It had been a very long time since she'd cried over the life she'd given up.

Bryce used a scraped knuckle to wipe the trail dry. "You'll see your friends again, Kylie. I promise."

"It's out of your control. You can't keep a promise like that." More scared than she'd been in a while, she could barely whisper.

"She'll see her friends right now."

FRED SNELL HAD marched through the debris, crunching glass, not attempting to be quiet. Bryce hadn't heard a thing. Admittedly, his ears were still ringing from the gunshots. But his focus had been on Kylie instead of on keeping her safe.

"I would have gotten here sooner, but someone hijacked my truck. I had to call Bernie for a lift." Fred angled his back to Bryce and took Kylie in his arms.

"I'll call the officers for an escort to my truck and out of town." Bryce had his phone in hand about to hit Redial.

There was something about the look that Fred shot him. Anger. Disbelief. Defiance. The emotions of a protective father.

"Is that what *you* want, Kylie?" Fred asked, already assuming he knew she didn't.

"I don't seem to have a say in the matter. Fred, Bryce is a Texas Ranger."

"I know."

"I told them this afternoon." But they'd already known.

"I knew before that, son."

"Does everybody in this entire town already know?"

"Probably. Most of them are standing out in the yard waiting to find out what happened here. It's not too often that we have a shoot-out on Pecan Street." Fred crossed to a still-shaking Kylie and hugged her with one arm. "I think you two can use some pie."

"The Koffee Cup is closed."

"Don't mind that little detail. I know the owner." Fred secured Kylie with an arm around her shoulders. His lanky frame was a bit deceptive considering how he'd worked all afternoon. "We'll take my old Chevy and Ranger Johnson there can grab his newfangled vehicle after he straightens out this mess."

"Fred, I can't allow that."

"It's Ranger Snell, retired. She'll be all right, son. I've got a couple of men already on their way to keep her safe."

"There's no way she can stay here."

"Are you arresting her, Bryce?"

"That wasn't the plan."

"Then do what you have to do and know she's safe."

"No, sir." Bryce stopped the older man as he tried to leave. "She stays with me. I think we could both use some coffee, but it'll be at my house. I'm under orders. She's not leaving my sight."

"Good for you, Ranger. Good for you." Fred patted his hand against Bryce's chest. "We're agreed that she needs to leave?"

"Yes, sir. I just need to find Officer Harris."

"He's trying to get people to head home." Fred guided her into the living room. "Come on, sweetie."

"Bryce?"

"Want that toothbrush?" He winked, trying to let her know that everything would be okay.

Nodding to Fred to move ahead of him, he drew his weapon and followed steps behind Kylie. There was a crowd of about forty gathered in front of the house. He looked around and didn't see any unusual people. Most were couples or men he'd seen driving rigs and parking at their homes.

A retired Texas Ranger. Hard of hearing Fred. Who would have thought that? Mrs. Mackey might have told

Fred about who was living in her house as soon as Company F had put the plan into motion. Just his luck that his first field operation had turned into such a disaster.

This wasn't all about him, though. His assignment was about Kylie's safety. Her insistence that she didn't know anything was a problem. Whatever she knew, whatever she had on Xander Tenoreno it had to be big.

Something had kept them alive through that shoot fest. He had no illusions that he'd done anything to keep them safe. He'd walked them right into a death trap.

Whoever had been firing at them had taken their time and what? Deliberately missed?

The big question was why.

Chapter Seven

"Eventually the police will begin a search. They will find you and where will I be? Back at the beginning. The girl will get away and I won't have leverage." Daniel Rosco felt his body tense with the anger pulsing through him. "I have waited five years for this freedom. Do not rob me of it!"

Daniel threw the cell across the room. He didn't care that it burst apart. The burner wouldn't be used again. The dent in the wall might be noticed by his wife's maid, but was easily explained away with a lie.

"They had her, Papa. The incompetents had her and wasted our element of surprise." He spoke to a picture on the mantel. His father and mother had both been executed by the Tenorenos. "I swear on your graves that those bastards will not get away with this."

"Daniel, are you all right? I thought I heard something fall?" Nancy peeked through the door connecting their rooms before coming through wearing nothing but her dressing gown. "Whatever's happened, it will be okay, sweetheart. Do you want to talk about it instead of ruining the paintings?"

She wrapped her arms around him, flattening her breasts against his back. The comforting hug was not enough to assuage his anger.

"I apologized for the Rivera and have replaced it."

"Darling, that's not the point. I don't like to see you

this upset." She rubbed her hands up and down his chest. "Sit on the bed and let me help get rid of all this tension."

He covered one of her hands and brought it to his lips. "You're good to me. But this tension is good. It keeps me on edge."

"It's going to send you to an early grave. What went wrong? Didn't they find where Sissy Jorgenson was hiding?"

"Yes. But a cop is with her now. He saved her life and called the local PD."

"I can understand your frustration about them not completing their job, but you must be happy that the information we paid for is solid. Xander has been hiding her all these years. That tells us she must mean something to him."

"We've lost the element of surprise. They'll be watching for the men and more prepared to fend them off. I've been lying low long enough. It's time to reclaim my heritage."

He spun Nancy in his arms and kissed her hard, pushing open her robe and feeling the artificial breasts she admired so much. He used the frustration he felt to have sex, bending her over the lounge chair. She didn't complain. She'd rather spend their time coupling than talking. It was the real reason she'd come into the room and they both knew it.

Afterward, he carried her to bed, lighting them both cigarettes and pouring his favorite whiskey three fingers deep into two glasses. He'd need it if he was going to take her again. She expected it. He hated that she did and would get what she wanted.

She was propped against the headboard with the pillows behind her. He left the cigarette to burn in the ashtray and threw the whiskey back so it would burn sliding down his throat. Then he lay face down across his wife's legs, allowing her to drag her nails across his skin.

The action soothed him anyway. It was a familiar routine. An action that needed no words. Familiarity that kept him just far enough from the edge that he wouldn't lose it.

He thought of Xander and how much he hated him.

"Daniel, stop. You need to relax, love. Focus on the good. We're close. So close," she whispered. "This setback is a little bump in the road. We'll get our revenge. Don't doubt that."

He controlled his body, keeping it slack. But he let his mind list the ways he would destroy Xander with the retrieval of the flash drive. He'd tease him first with the knowledge someone had betrayed him.

It wasn't enough to kill Xander's ex-wife. He wanted Xander to cry out in pain. To suffer. And Daniel wanted to watch the Tenoreno family fall.

Then—and only then—he'd tell Xander why.

Chapter Eight

Bryce and his self-appointed armed partner cleared the rented house. First phone call was to Officer Harris who moved his three officers closer for a protection detail spanning both houses. The officers hadn't spoken to anyone who had spotted the shooters. After this much time it wasn't likely they'd find anything in the dark.

While the coffee brewed, his second phone call had been to Major Parker. To say the man was unhappy was an understatement. He also verified that Fred had served a distinguished career in Company A before he retired. Backup was on its way. Jesse had texted five minutes ago that he'd been ordered to lend assistance.

He'd be lucky if Jesse hadn't sent a mass email letting the rest of the state know he was coming to Bryce's rescue.

The house was secure. Kylie hadn't been out of his sight. Fred had been standing next to her the entire time. They'd said very few words. The older man watched the backyard and occasionally squeezed her shoulder. The comforting seemed to help her to be patient.

Time for some answers.

"Before you get yourself all worked up…" Fred pulled out a dining room chair, joining Kylie at the table. "I recognized you, Johnson, as soon as you got to town. I read the news and keep up with current events. So no one informed me that you were here. Even without your glasses it would be hard to miss one of the Rangers who helped bring down Paul Tenoreno last spring."

"Why the interest in Kylie? Why do you want to keep her in town?"

"She's our friend and hasn't done anything wrong. It's not a question about keeping her. If she wants to leave, then she can leave."

"Fred," Kylie began, "there's something you should know."

"That you used to be married to a Tenoreno or that he tried to kill you five years ago? I recognized you when you ran out of gas. Hard not to. Everyone thought you'd been abducted and murdered. Your face was all over the news, honey." Fred scratched the white stubble on his chin. "This ain't my first rodeo. I was in law enforcement my entire life. Took me a bit longer to reach Texas Ranger than you, kid. Loved every minute of it once I did. It's not like you just stop because you ain't wearing the badge."

"You never said a word." Kylie looked completely astonished.

"Neither did you." Fred winked and grinned. The old man was having a blast. "We all figured that when you were ready, you'd tell us. After a couple of years, we figured it was better for you if you didn't talk about it."

"Who all knows her real identity?" They both ignored Bryce, continuing their own conversation.

"I can't believe you did all that for me. I was so lost. If it hadn't been for you and Allison at the Koffee Cup, I would have been… Fred, I don't know what would have happened to me."

"You settled in here real good, young lady. We wanted to keep you." The smile on Fred's face was as genuine as his words.

"This is all very inspiring," Bryce interrupted, "but it still doesn't solve our problem or answer my question. I've been ordered to bring Kylie to Austin for questioning by the state attorneys."

"Then I'd like to see the warrant or summons. Sorry, son, but if Kylie doesn't want to go…she's not going."

"We're just talking for now. Nobody wants to issue a warrant, especially if Kylie hasn't done anything wrong." He tried to catch her gaze. He didn't want everyone to know Tenoreno's stolen car sat in her garage. Hell, maybe everyone in Hico already knew. "I need a list of people who know who Kylie is and what happened to her before she arrived five years ago."

"Most everybody thinks of Kylie as someone who the community took in and who gives back to us a hundred-fold. Few know that a mobster tried to kill her."

"I need those names, Fred." He opened a notepad on his phone. "Type them here and I'll check them out."

Fred tapped his pockets. "I don't seem to have my bi-focals."

"Use these." Bryce found his glasses in front of the television. "Squint if they don't work. I need to talk to Kylie."

Fred covered her hand with his own. "I will admit that it's been a challenge keeping you out of the public spotlight, sugar. 'Fraid that's out of our hands now. You should know that your friends decided way back that we'd stand shoulder to shoulder with you if something happened. You're not alone."

He nodded to Bryce to take a chair while he pushed back from the table. He scooped up the cell and glasses and went to stand by the front window.

"I can't believe this." Kylie shook her head, looking as shocked as he felt.

Bryce spun the dining chair and straddled it, leaning on the back but close enough to lower his voice so only Kylie could hear him.

"I think he's sincere. That creates a big problem for

us." He waited until she looked up with a question in her eyes. "A while ago you didn't want to call for help because you were afraid of what would happen to trained officers. What do you think is going to happen if your friends stand shoulder to shoulder?"

"A lot of innocent people are going to get hurt."

"Yeah. I'm not saying that Fred isn't right. He is. I don't have a warrant. Compelling you to testify is something I can't do...yet. But for their sakes I think it's time you told me what you know about Xander Tenoreno that makes him so determined to kill you."

"Bryce, I really don't know anything about his business." She threaded her fingers through her blond hair. "Please believe me."

"I've read the reports of the night you were shot. Didn't you wonder why he wanted to meet in that part of Austin?" He knew the answer, but wanted to hear her personal account, too. "Maybe you'll remember something different this time."

"I went for my cat. Xander is a cruel man...at least he was five years ago when I knew him. I told the police, I never suspected that he would try to kill me. When his alibi checked out, along with all of his closest men, there was nothing anyone could do."

"What about the day-to-day operations of the Tenoreno family?" He noticed that Fred was standing at the window, arms crossed, frowning and definitely listening.

Hard of hearing old man? He doubted it.

"I lived there for a couple of months. I was on photo shoots back then. Or going to movie premieres in LA. Xander went with me everywhere, even to Fashion Week in New York. He seemed to get a high from draping himself all over me. I liked the attention at first." She rested her head on her hands, hiding her eyes from him.

"But?"

She jerked straight, throwing her head back and pushing her hair away from her face. "Do we really have to do this now? I'm a little exhausted. Actually, I'm more than exhausted and need some sleep." She pushed the chair back, grabbing her shoulder bag and standing. "You have a bed, right? I'm using it."

"Kylie—"

"I'll take that cup of coffee now." Fred jumped between him and the woman running down the hall. "She'll be better in the morning. This is a lot to process right now."

Fred's hand was plastered against Bryce's chest. Not necessarily pushing, but if he pressed forward, he'd have to knock the older man to the side.

"You need to back off." Bryce pushed the words through a jaw clamped so tight his teeth wouldn't move.

Fred threw his hands up in surrender, gesturing toward the kitchen. "Want a cup?"

"Let me explain something. You're a guest here. Only here because of your previous service and because I can use an extra set of eyes keeping her safe. We'll reassess the situation when my partner arrives."

"Sure thing. I'll get that coffee." Fred stepped aside toward the kitchen.

Bryce followed Kylie toward the bedroom—there was only one furnished. The door was open and she was lying across the covers, arm covering her eyes. There were still a lot of lights flashing outside even with the blinds drawn shut.

"I need to move you to the middle bedroom. It's smaller, but easier to defend."

"Okay. Do you have a cot or something? I didn't see another bed."

"I'll put this mattress on the floor."

"That isn't necessary."

"Of course it is, Kylie. Don't worry about it."

She picked up the pillows and he lifted the mattress, bedding and all onto its side. She stepped out of the way and he pushed it down the hall to the smaller room.

"Keep the lights off. If someone's watching the house we might fool them as to which room you're in."

She sat on the mattress and leaned against the inside wall, pulling the sheet up to her chin. "I could really use a good soak, but I assume that's out of the question."

He nodded.

"And I don't suppose I'll be left alone?"

He shook his head. "I'll stay right here."

"All right." She plumped the pillows and twisted awkwardly to put her head down. "Is there something else, Bryce?"

"I need to see what you have inside the bag."

"Take it. There's nothing inside. You know all my secrets already." She covered her head with the covers.

He picked up the green bag, slid his back down the wall to the floor and reached for his phone, remembering Fred still had it. A couple of four-letter words went through his mind at the thought of getting back up. Then the smell of coffee got stronger. Fred sauntered his long frame down the hall.

"You know there are chairs in the other room a lot more comfortable than that floor." He handed over one cup and slurped at the other.

"I'm good. Thanks for this."

"Here's your phone and glasses. I'll be right back. My bones are too old to sit without support."

Bryce placed his frames on his face and gawked into the black brew like an old gypsy telling futures with tea leaves. He wanted a plan. Something solid. Or a reason for Tenoreno to have made a move on Kylie today.

"Why now?" he whispered as the legs of a dining chair

scraped the floor. "He couldn't have known she was here. Not that fast. I just made the confirmation today."

"And by confirmation you mean?" Fred sat in the chair at the end of the hall.

"I told Kylie that she was in danger."

"How did you find her? Can I ask that?" Fred tipped the chair to two feet balancing against the wall.

"Yeah, can we both ask that?" Kylie's voice from the bedroom didn't sound interested in sleeping.

Three years of my spare time. "Facial recognition from a picture that appeared with an internet magazine feature. It was about the teen and senior program you volunteer with."

"Runs and created." Fred slurped loudly. "Does a damn fine job."

"The article said it was a community effort. It's impressive, I like what I experienced today. I take it you've been keeping Kylie behind the camera instead of in front of it?"

"I volunteered. I thought I'd convinced everyone it was more about them than me. I can't believe everyone knew."

"Everyone didn't. You've got the two other names besides myself. One's the owner of the Koffee Cup and the other is the woman who runs the Billy the Kid Museum. They were watching the morning news together when I brought a disheveled young woman who didn't weigh as much as a toothpick into the shop. Praise be that those two old women don't gossip."

"Why didn't you turn me over to the police, Fred?"

"It wasn't like you'd broken any law by walking away from everything." He shrugged. "We all thought you'd been through enough. If you needed some peace and quiet, why shouldn't it be here where we could watch out for you?"

"I can't ever tell you how much these years have meant to me. They changed my life."

Bryce could hear the emotional catch in her tone. Kylie was about to cry. He did admire what the people of Hico had done, and everything that she'd done to make her life meaningful. It was much better than the fast lane she'd been in as a teen model.

None of it mattered.

Kylie's location had been discovered and it wasn't because of him. He hadn't had much time to think things through since the firefight. But now that he could…he'd called only the major to inform him. *He* hadn't informed anyone else. The one call he'd received at Kylie's that morning was from the Austin PD telling him they'd lost Tenoreno.

"Fred, have y'all noticed anyone new in town? Any strangers here longer than they should be?"

"You mean besides you? Nope."

"This doesn't make sense."

"What doesn't?" Kylie asked.

"How did they find you? Not only that. How did they find you *today*? It's illogical." Bryce's brain was at home with computers and patterns and logic.

"Did you do anything different today, girlie? Besides trying to lose this fellow across the fields?"

Bryce heard the sheets rustle behind him, then Kylie was at the opposite side of the doorway. Hair tussled as if she'd just awakened and had tossed and turned all night. The house wasn't an icebox. It was more like an old unit that barely put out cold air, yet she still wore her long sleeves and covered up.

"Nothing different. I mowed the lawn, started trimming a couple of dead limbs, talked to Bryce." She finger-combed her hair while she explained, smoothing it back into place. "When he left me alone, I came up with the idea of walking away. I've had plans in place for years. But with him watching the place like a stalker, I had to improvise."

"Looks like the only thing different in this equation is you, son."

They both looked at him. Eyebrows raised. Eyes opened wide. Expecting something that resembled an answer. It wasn't against the rules for him to share what he knew. And they knew most of it anyway.

"The Austin PD has been tailing Tenoreno since Thomas Rosco's death. He shook the car following him today. I told you that this morning," he said to Kylie.

"You're right, though. It's a bit coincidental that someone tries to kill Kylie after all these years. And on the very day you show your hand." Fred smirked.

"Here's the other thing that's bothering me. Why so public?"

"That was an awful lot of firepower for something that could have been handled with a single blade as a home invasion. No offense, Kylie." Fred set his empty coffee mug on the floor and brought all his chair legs back to earth.

Bryce hadn't touched his own coffee. It was cool enough now to just gulp it for the caffeine. Which he did.

"Why would they want the entire town to know I'd been killed?"

"Exactly." He had to ponder the question awhile.

In fact, every question they asked just led to more questions and no answers.

Bryce unfolded his glasses, put them in place and then checked his phone. No messages from Jesse or Major Parker. He'd missed his Saturday afternoon call with his mom and dad. That was it. He sent the names Fred had typed into his message to headquarters in Austin. Same thing with the car licenses from the hotels.

Ironically, if he hadn't been on this assignment, he'd be the one sitting in Waco. He'd be utilizing the information available for the Rangers and collecting data. He'd find out if any of these Hico citizens had a connection to Xander or Paul Tenoreno.

Fred was on his phone. When he noticed Bryce looking at him he said, "Calling my daughter. She might actually be a little worried." He put the phone to his ear and walked toward the back of the house.

"Where's your cell?"

"I don't have one. Just the landline and the laptop." Kylie adjusted her position, sitting cross-legged in the doorway. "The kids instant message me online if they want to talk. Adults call."

"I don't think I've met anyone over twelve that doesn't have a cell phone."

"Believe me. It might have been one of the hardest things to give up. After running away and starting completely over with a thousand dollars in my pocket." She crossed her arms to match her legs and rested her head on the wall. "I used to have two. Cells, that is. One was completely for social media and the press, my agent, my favorite photographers, my publicist. Only my closest friends had my personal number. Even that had to be changed every three or four months when a weird fan would call or post it to the world."

"Do you miss it or ever want to go back?"

"I can't go back if I did want to. My skin is definitely… flawed."

He searched her perfect skin. No freckles, no acne, no discolorations. He reached out to tap the tiny crinkles around her eyes. "Flawed?"

"You're funny. Didn't you say you'd seen my file? Doesn't it have pictures of the gunshots?"

"Oh, yeah. Couldn't you still model, though?"

"I don't want to go back. That life was never real. It belonged to Sissy Jorgenson, my stage name and persona. It turned everyone I ever loved into money-starved…" She had been looking around the room, sort of staring at nothing. Then she locked eyes with his. "I couldn't see what it did to me while I was living it. I was willing to marry Xander because he didn't need anything from me. At least that's what I thought. I was just a dumb kid."

He shook his head, agreeing, letting her assume he knew what she had gone through. But he didn't.

"I have a scar," he threw out.

"You might have some from that burn you got today," she teased.

"It's not much, but it's never gone away." He pulled up his jeans leg and slid off his boot, pushing down his sock. "When I was a kid a rattler got me. See it? Those two white spots."

"No appendicitis? No shotgun blast to your back?"

"Shotgun? Why would you think—"

"From all those husbands and boyfriends chasing you out windows, silly."

Again with the teasing. He was glad she could laugh. Her life had been turned upside down five years ago. If it had happened to him and then began repeating itself, he didn't know how he would have handled it.

"It's just stuff, you know. Everything over there can be replaced."

"Except the Cadillac," Fred said from the corner. "She's a beaut. Am I right? Did you see her?"

"Except the Cadillac," Bryce repeated. "That's our answer. It was the car."

Chapter Nine

Kylie tried to sleep. Her body told her she should. She was exhausted from the day's activities and mentally tired of playing the games she'd run away from so long ago. She was also tired of everyone trying to manipulate her. Even Fred while trying to protect her. If she walked away from the people who had stood by her all these years…

Was she betraying them?

Or protecting them as Bryce had pointed out?

Now sleep was impossible because a total stranger was pacing the halls, tapping on his cell, cursing at whoever he was texting to answer back. Jesse Ryder was Bryce's partner. And yet, he'd walked through the door and Bryce had barreled past him, Fred not far behind.

"They're checking something out on the Cadillac." She tried getting his attention from her protected space. Bryce had reminded her to stay put with a graphic description of what the gun had done to her house. So she was close to the hallway door with her back against the closet. Remembering the hole in the wall made her want to sleep inside the bathtub.

"Where?" Jesse stopped as he walked past the door. "What Cadillac?"

"My house. Across the street and two doors down. There's a flowerpot of marigolds on the front porch—well, there used to be. Come to think about it, I think someone knocked them off. The porch light is on."

"Every porch light is on after what happened earlier." He typed more on his cell. "You shouldn't have made it out of that attack alive. Or was Johnson exaggerating?"

"No, I think he got the details right. The headline will probably read something like Giant Hole in the Wall, Refrigerator Saves Couple. I think there are pictures now."

The new guy barely cracked a smile. He looked like he was in an old spaghetti western, one boot propped against the wall, head down rolling a ciggy. Only instead of a cigarette, he was focused on a cell phone.

"At least you're not trending yet. But you're right. There are definitely pictures." Ever vigilant of his surroundings, he stood straight at the slightest sound. His hand would go to his holster on his hip, then he'd relax against the wall again. "I heard you tried to walk cross-country to get away from him."

"It was the only thing I could think of at the time."

"I can think of a much easier solution...just come back with us. Do you know *why* they had to look at this car?" Jesse asked.

"It's stolen. I know that much."

"You said it was your house. Did you steal it?" He left her to walk to the front room again.

"The official story is that I borrowed it." She spoke a little louder so he could hear her around the corner.

He nodded his head. He wasn't as tall as Bryce, not quite as built through the shoulders. She drew her knees to her chest, trying to stretch her back and get comfortable. It didn't feel right lying on the mattress with the new guy watching. Even if she had all her clothes on, including her shoes.

"I have a question." She waited for him to nod that he'd

answer. "Do they really teach how to calculate walking speeds or something like that in Ranger school?"

His confused expression was all she needed to know that Bryce had been full of it earlier. She silently laughed at herself for halfway believing him.

"So what's so important about the car? I'm guessing that you didn't steal it today."

"Five years ago."

"That's when you— Is it Tenoreno's?"

She nodded. "I told Bryce about it just before they attacked. He had some revelation about fifteen minutes before you got here. Fred argued with him that it wasn't possible. Don't ask me what it is, because they wouldn't tell me. Bryce said he wanted to confirm his suspicions."

"I guess we both wait then." Phone in his pocket, he began his patrol again.

Resting her head and eyes, she could hear his boots walk up and down the hall, pause at the front window, circle through the kitchen and repeat. Silently, she debated the pros and cons of going to Waco with Bryce.

No matter how hurt Fred's feelings might be, leaving with Bryce was her only logical option. What if the gunmen had opened fire on the event earlier today? With that thought, she knew leaving was her only choice. They were under orders to keep an eye on her so they wouldn't let her leave alone. One way or another it had to be with them.

Drifting off, she was yanked back when Bryce and Fred burst into the house, arguing loud enough to wake the block. Well, if anyone had actually gone back to bed.

"I tell you it's not possible. That GPS locator has a short range. They wouldn't be able to pick it up in Austin." Fred yelled.

"Don't you get it? They could have followed her that first night. If it's short range, they just drive until they find it." Bryce yelled back. "Someone's probably known where she was this entire time. It's not a coincidence that I show up and all hell breaks loose."

There was a loud piercing whistle that got the men to shut up. Kylie left the protection of the bedroom, stopping at the edge of the hall. She didn't want to draw eyes back to herself and be sent to her room like a child.

"It can't be right," Fred repeated.

"Can you explain what we're talking about?" Jesse bent the window blinds looking outside.

"It's not good. There's a GPS locater on Tenoreno's Cadillac." Bryce answered him, keeping his back to everyone.

"A tracking system? How strong? Wait. Why didn't we locate her when she stole the car and disappeared five years ago?" Jesse was at attention. Did he realize his fingers had drifted to the gun at his side?

"GPS. Either law enforcement wasn't looking or it wasn't reported stolen."

Kylie could see the tension in the way he was standing. And the way he was looking out the back windows. Did he expect to see another targeting laser pointed at the house?

"You've been driving a stolen car for five years and no one's caught on?" Jesse looked straight at her. The other two men's heads turned, too.

"Don't look at me. I don't drive the blasted thing. It never leaves my garage. I avoid it as much as possible. The engine can't even crank." An eerie feeling was creeping up the back of her neck. There was something terribly wrong with what they were saying. Maybe she was too tired to read between the lines, but even then…

The men's reactions were beginning to scare her.

"I'm the one who charged the battery last week when you got here and made certain it would run. Just in case, you know, she needed it one day soon," Fred said.

"Like tonight?" Bryce said strongly again.

"What if—what if he didn't know about it?" she whispered and searched their faces getting their attention. "Xander hadn't had the car very long. He'd been bragging about winning it. That's why I took the convertible, because he seemed so excited about it. But he was out of the country when I left."

"By the time he got back, I'd disconnected the battery." Fred scratched his scruffy chin.

Why did it all matter, though? How they found her wasn't as important as the fact that they *had* found her. Right?

"I don't understand why this is so important. I'll come up with a new plan after the state attorneys hear my pathetic cry of 'I don't know anything' a thousand more times."

"If the locator drew someone's attention, they found you pretty easily after it was reconnected." Jesse was oh so matter-of-fact with his explanation. "If it didn't, someone's following Bryce."

"Someone? You mean Xander."

"Or the guy he won the car from. Either way, someone out there wants you dead. They just aren't very good at it." Jesse crossed his arms and leaned against the wall.

That can't be true.

"Dammit, Ryder." Bryce moved to her side. "She's as white as a sheet."

"He tried to kill me. I know it was Xander. It had to be." Kylie hadn't experienced a panic attack. There was no time for one, either time her life had been threatened.

Bryce looked into her eyes, forcing her to focus on him. "We should keep all the possibilities open. Do you have any idea who else would want to kill you tonight *or* five years ago?"

Right this very second her pulse raced, her breath seemed to be cut off at her nose and she could barely stand.

She might really pass out. "I'm walking across the room and sitting on that couch. Don't try to stop me."

Nobody touched her. Of course, having her hands splayed in a don't-touch-me position might have warned them that she was serious.

Bryce motioned for his partner to check outside. Jesse walked out the door without a word. Fred worriedly rubbed his chin and took a seat at the table. She could see he was blaming himself for not catching the GPS gadget earlier. His comfort would have to wait.

Right this second she had to wrap her head around an entirely new possibility. Did someone besides Xander want to kill her? Very publicly making a show of hurting the people around her. Who could want that? Do that?

An unknown person who hated her? Five years ago, Xander wanting her dead had been hard enough to live with, but at least she understood. Now she had to think about someone else managing to get close to accomplishing it...twice.

"You have to be wrong, Bryce. I didn't know anyone who hated me like my ex-husband."

BRYCE TOOK A dining chair and set it close to her, straddling it as he had earlier, arms folded over its back. He dropped his right hand to cover one of hers that was resting on the couch.

"I know I'm right. Sure, there are a lot of possibilities. Just trust me. We can't argue any longer." He lowered his voice so Fred wouldn't interrupt him. "I need to get you under the state's protection before there's another incident."

"But—"

"I get it, Kylie. I do. But for your protection and for everybody around you, come with me. Make your deal, talk with the attorneys, have them guarantee it in writing. Then let them decide what you know or don't. It's the only way I can keep you safe."

She nodded.

"He's right," Fred said from the dinette. "I wish there was something I could do."

Bryce stood, offering his hand to help Kylie up. "Get your bag. We're leaving now." He turned to Fred. "There is something you can do. We'll be working with Hico on the crime scene." He removed the Cadillac ignition key from the key ring. "Before anyone gets here, disconnect the GPS tracker and move the car to a safe place. Somewhere no one will get hurt if someone comes looking."

"I know the perfect place."

"Good. Keep it to yourself for now." He clapped the man on the shoulder.

Fred did the same. "We're trusting you with our girl."

"Yes, sir. You have my word."

"I'm ready." Kylie gave Fred a hug. "Stay safe, my friend."

"You betcha. Don't worry 'bout a thing. We'll all still be here when you come home. And I'll get that hole patched just as soon as the cops are done with the place."

Bryce waited at the door during the embrace. Kylie joined him, putting her hand on his shoulder just like they'd done at her house. Hard to believe it had just been a few hours earlier.

"We don't know if they're still out there. If I stop this time, get as close to my body as you can. Become my second skin. Got it?"

"Yeah, I'm good."

"Straight to Jesse's truck."

Through the door, Jesse was at his elbow. He unlocked the doors, taking his place in the driver's seat. When Bryce joined Kylie in the backseat she seemed a little surprised, but scooted over to the other side.

"Keep your heads down, you two. If we're lucky, we're out of town with no incident."

Bryce slumped in the seat, and gestured for Kylie to stretch out across it. There wasn't any hesitation as she leaned on his chest and let him support her on the trip out of town.

Once they passed the east city limit sign, Bryce put away his weapon and tried to relax for their passenger's sake. Kylie sat on her side, but watched the town disappear behind them.

"Don't forget to buckle up, kiddies," Jesse taunted. "Sun's coming up. Going to be a beautiful day."

"Maybe for you," Kylie mumbled.

"Anybody following?" Bryce looked over his shoulder, too. He couldn't distinguish any vehicles that might not be using their headlights.

"Nada. Maybe they weren't watching the house?"

He met Jesse's glance in the mirror. His partner had said that for Kylie's peace of mind but didn't believe it any more than Bryce. Someone was watching her house. They'd been waiting for Kylie to return, so they knew Bryce was with her. So logic followed that they knew where Bryce lived.

"You can grab a nap if you want." Bryce squeezed her hand.

She smiled but her eyes were full of sadness.

"You'll be back, Kylie. I promise."

Jesse frowned and shook his head. Kylie turned in the big seat of the extended cab and withdrew. The hour drive seemed to take as long as all of the previous day.

Uncertainty reared its ugly head. Had he done the professional thing? The right thing? He wouldn't be able to answer that until this situation was resolved. But he was certain about one small piece…he'd done the best thing for Kylie.

Her life was in danger and his gut told him these people weren't about to stop now that they had her in their sights.

Chapter Ten

Austin, three days later

The location was supposed to be secret. Who leaked it didn't matter. On the way inside the first day, Kylie and her attorney had been swamped by the press. She was the story of the hour. The headlines screamed her name—or Sissy's name.

At night in her hotel room, she alternated between glued to the television scanning the news for a mention of her name and handing the remote to the guard posted outside her room. The men guarding her rotated through the night and got a laugh at passing the baton—remote—to each other. All of them were gentlemen.

None of them was Bryce.

Missing her friends in Hico was natural. She'd known and worked with them for a long time. But Bryce? Why should she miss him? He'd told her to trust him and that he'd have a plan in place soon. Then promptly agreed to hand her off to become someone else's problem.

Okay, that was harsh. He hadn't really agreed. She'd heard him arguing with his commander who'd said the men in Company F had been making it a habit of getting too close to their assignments. Whatever that meant. In the end, she'd been given a few clothes, a hamburger and escorted to headquarters in Austin after a phone call to her lawyer.

No phone calls since she'd been here. Not even a phone in her room.

It didn't matter how illogical it was, she had been attracted to Bryce since she'd first met him. And since she'd first admired him mowing that dust bowl of a lawn Mrs. Mackey owned.

Oh well. It wasn't to be. Whatever happened now, she doubted she'd see the tall law enforcement officer again.

Day two in Austin wasn't any better. Everyone wanted to know where she'd been or why she'd been hiding. Did she fear for her life? Were the men guarding her or was she under arrest? She had ignored shouts from the press before. Ignored the many photographs of her taken each time she'd been in public.

It was harder this time. Harder to ignore all the questions because they weren't obnoxious or too personal. Each of them was pertinent. But she couldn't answer them...she didn't know the answers.

In fact, she had more questions today than ever before.

They walked through the front door with her escort— the one that did not include either of the men who had found or rescued her. Their meeting was on the sixth floor and they took the elevator. Two rangers—she hadn't caught their names—crowded the front and refused to allow anyone else to board. She stood next to her lawyer, who had dropped everything to help her the past three days.

Everyone was silent. There wasn't even silly elevator music to help pass the time. Kylie was nervous, but next to her friend and lawyer, she looked like the calm and collected one. Her guards dropped them off at the door and another officer showed them to a conference room.

Lizbeth Reynolds opened her briefcase, took out a yellow notepad and her pen. She straightened them a couple of times after setting the briefcase on the floor. No one else had arrived yet. She poured a glass of water from one of four pitchers on the long oval table.

"Want some?"

"No thanks. I had three cups of coffee watching the news at my motel."

"I saw some of the highlights. You look good and have the sympathy of the people."

Sympathy of the people?

"Oh, Lizbeth. If it was you who told the press that I was back in town, don't ever tell me. You were such a good friend to me. You'll never know how much I appreciate you taking my case on such short notice."

"Don't ever think of me as a friend in the past tense again. I'm not certain why you want me. You'd be much better off with a criminal defense attorney."

Lizbeth patted her hand, but didn't deny being the one to leak the location. It was okay. Especially since she was right. The press and population were on her side. It would be harder for the state to compel her to do anything. And if she had to, she'd meet with the reporters and share part of her story.

Of course, it would also be harder for her to disappear again. One step at a time. She had to power through this particular mess first.

The court reporter took her seat. The attorneys filed through the door. Kylie could feel Lizbeth's legs shaking. The men kept standing while the judge entered.

Everyone was introduced for the record, then the judge said they were going to recess for five minutes, excusing the court reporter from the room. He waved everyone to sit. Confusion followed by an immediate burst of fright hitting her like a tsunami.

"Let's keep this as informal as possible," the judge said.

"If things get out of hand, I'll call Joyce back in here and we'll start from the beginning."

Kylie looked at Lizbeth who drew a question mark on her pad, shrugged and shook her head with no explanation. Kylie sat on her hands not wanting to appear nervous. But she was.

"Truth of the matter, gentlemen," the judge continued, "is that you have no case. Miss Scott has continued to tell you that she knows nothing of her ex-husband's business dealings. She told all those involved five years ago and she's continuing to do so now."

"Your Honor—"

"Yeah, I'm not finished." He shook his head. "In fact, I'm utterly ashamed that you've yanked this young woman away from her quiet life in Hico." He turned and looked at Kylie. "Nice little town, some of the best pie in Texas. My wife and I drive through there to visit our son."

"I'll tell Allison you mentioned it."

"Nice. Real nice." He took off his glasses tossing them to the table. They scooted past the second lawyer who stuck his hand out and caught them. "You see, fellows, you're trying to tell me that you'll drop the charges of auto theft if Miss Scott testifies. This is where your brief lost me. Not only did you *not* find the 1964 Cadillac convertible on Miss Scott's property, you lack a vehicle theft report. The owner claims the car is still on one of his properties."

Kylie's leg was being gripped so hard by Lizbeth she'd be black-and-blue the next day. Then her attorney excitedly smiled and tapped her pen on the yellow pad so fast, Kylie was afraid it would fly and hit the judge in the eye.

"I know you're excited, Miss Reynolds, but again, I'm not finished." He turned to The Three Stooges of attorneys. "I'm advising you to withdraw your request. Now. Once I bring Joyce back in here…well, you don't want to know what I'm going to say."

He motioned that it was someone else's turn to speak.

"If Your Honor would issue the search warrant—"

"There won't be a search warrant for Mr. Tenoreno's property. He has several, including in other countries. Without the car or a theft report…"

"Then Your Honor leaves us no choice but to withdraw all protection from Miss Scott."

"Good. You on the end, call Joyce back inside, please."

The reporter took her position. The charges were officially dismissed. The lawyers put away their papers. Lizbeth was shaking with excitement. And Kylie was utterly stunned.

"Everybody can go," the judge announced. The group stood and the judge tapped Kylie's arm. "Mind staying a minute, Miss Scott?"

"Not at all, should Lizbeth…?"

"No, it's nothing official. I just want to apologize for these jackasses."

"That's not necessary. Really. Everything's fine." She turned to Lizbeth, wanting to leave.

"I'll wait for you downstairs in the lobby." Lizbeth smiled and waved.

"Why don't we go into the office?" He held the door for her.

"I can't believe what just happened. It was all so fast my head is still spin—"

She preceded the judge through the entryway. He gave her a little shove and backed out, quickly closing the door. The term spinning was no longer figurative. She literally spun to the side and into Xander's arms. She pushed and shoved attempting a release, but his grip got tighter and more hurtful.

When she stopped fighting him, he released her.

The aikido that she'd studied had disappeared. None of the auto-defense moves that she'd practiced had kicked in.

She sought a level of calm by smoothing her dress and pretending not to pay attention. Just under the surface of her movements she was aware of her ex's every turn.

Her nerves were jumpier than a magic jumping bean she'd had once as a little girl.

"Dear God, what have you done to yourself?" he spat meanly. "You've gotten fat."

She could handle his harsh words. She'd heard them before, even when she was much under a normal weight and all her bones stuck out. She could take anything he served.

"I see you still employ that wimpy lawyer who lost you everything in the divorce."

"Lizbeth is my friend, and we both know what happened in the divorce. She had nothing to do with it. Why are you here, Xander?"

"It's simple. I want an annulment. We were never married in the church, but that doesn't matter to the church."

"Sure. Do you have the papers with you? Or you can send them to Lizbeth's office and she'll know how to find me. You didn't have to go through these scare tactics to get your way. I'm not that same inexperienced child bride that you married."

"You aren't, are you? But I'm only interested in the annulment."

"Can I go now?"

"I want it done today." He paused, which was unlike him. "The papers are at the house. I, um...so you took the Cadillac?"

"That boat has sailed, partner. No proof. The judge threw out the case." She calculated how long it would take to reach the door.

Which door? The one behind him that she knew led to the conference room or the two on her right? *What if one is a closet?* Would he catch her? *Yes.*

"Unless he has a theft report." He took out a folded

piece of paper from his shirt pocket. "Which I just happen to have."

"I don't know where your car is and I don't care." She inched a little closer to the door with a light under it. "I left it at my house and when the police arrived, it had been stolen. How's that for irony for you?"

He crossed the short distance between them and raised his hand. She'd been on the receiving end of that slap once or twice. It wouldn't happen again. She moved at the last minute and Xander's fist hit the wall.

"Tell me where the Cadillac is." He steadily raised his voice, talking through gritted teeth. "Dammit. I want... my car."

"Then *find* your car. But leave me alone. Send your church papers to my lawyer. You're done in my life. Do you hear me? We're done. You can't hurt me anymore."

Defiant words for the abundance of fright fluttering inside her. Back to the wall, she scooted sideways until her hand felt the door handle.

"You're forgetting that I can do anything I want." He supported his hand, vigorously massaging the knuckles. "Nobody will stop me."

Never taking her eyes off him, she slipped through, closing the door behind her. She wanted to collapse in a ball right there in the hallway. But she had to get away from him. She ran, heels echoing through the empty halls until she found the restroom.

Inside she got into the last stall and slid the bolt. It wouldn't protect her. She knew it, but had to have something between her and Xander. She leaned against the wall and cried.

All because of fear. She hated fear and the way it ate at every level of confidence a person could muster.

The rest of the afternoon was a blur. She might have stayed where she was if Lizbeth hadn't eventually found her. Frantic herself, they held on to each other and got someone who worked in the building to call a cab and let them out the back.

The rangers were gone.

That meant no protection.

Bryce was wrong. He couldn't keep his word and Xander wanted her dead more than he wanted that stupid Cadillac.

Chapter Eleven

Waco

Being called to the head of Company F's office had never felt like a visit to the principal before. The difference this time was that he'd broken some basic rules, not orders. Rules put in place to protect witnesses and officers.

"You're playing with fire, Bryce."

"Sir?"

Major Parker put both palms on his desk and pushed himself to stand, staring Bryce in the eye and not blinking. Bryce was about to be reprimanded, an action he wasn't used to but was determined to accept. Even if he wasn't volunteering information about what he'd done. Or apologizing.

"You know I've been calling in favors to get you back on this case. I understand what it's like to give your word to someone. I explained that the state's attorneys felt it best to remove you from Kylie Scott's protection detail."

"Because she trusted me too much? That makes no sense—"

Parker's stare made it unpleasant enough that Bryce shut up without finishing. How the man stood taller was one of those mystical practices no one wanted to experience. The air got sucked out of the room somehow and Bryce felt ten years old again.

Parker put his hands behind his back and met Bryce boot toe to boot toe. "Did I give you the impression you could speak yet, Lieutenant?"

A question that if answered meant he was in the dog house. Yet by not answering did he look like he didn't understand? Or maybe he did, but Bryce chose to stand at attention, eyes forward not meeting the major's.

"Hacking into the state's records to find out where your girlfriend—"

"Miss Scott."

"—is being held is against every protocol we have in place. You've been suspended for two weeks."

"Suspended, sir? But this is my first infraction."

"And it's a severe one, Bryce."

"But she's not being held anywhere at all, sir. They let her go. Didn't even bother to give her a ride back to Hico this morning."

"I know." The major put his hands on his hips, seeming less stern than seconds before. "We have orders to stay clear of the situation."

Realization hit him over the head. Severe discipline allowed Bryce to keep his word. He could help Kylie without officially involving the Rangers. Two weeks without pay was definitely going to make a dent in his budget, but helping her was worth it.

"Thank you, sir. I guess vacation wouldn't do?" His commander's stern look made him follow up with, "I get it. I completely understand, sir."

"Since our computer expert will be out of the office for two weeks, I'm going to remind you that your access to our database will remain active. You should refrain from using that access." He paused. "At least as much as possible. And then there's the matter of your badge. I think you should have Vivian secure it for you. Damn, I think she's at lunch." He looked toward the empty desk of the

Company's secretary. "Just bring it by tomorrow. You understand what I'm saying, Bryce?"

"Yes, sir."

Major Josh Parker sat behind his desk and picked up a plain number two pencil. He threaded it through his fingers and began his habitual twirling. Bryce didn't think he'd been dismissed. The normal sign that the major was finished was when his feet went to the corner of his desk. The Company called it his thinking mode.

"I gave her my word, too. I'm counting on you to keep it. But if you get into trouble…" The pencil cracked over his knuckles. "I have vacation time."

"Got it. Thank you, sir." Bryce was grateful, but not surprised that his commanding officer was willing to break the rules to help keep his word. That's the kind of man he was. One of the true good guys.

"Turn the files you're working on over to Vivian. One last thing." He stood, palms flat on his desk, the apparent fury of a man who meant what he said behind every word. "There won't be a next time. I don't need men who go behind my back and disobey orders."

"No, sir. It won't happen again."

"Just bring the problem to me, Bryce." He sat again and crossed his ankles on the corner of the old wooden desk. "I usually know what I'm doing."

"Thank you, Major."

Bryce took care of the case files and explained the situation to Jesse. His partner cursed that he'd be working alone and then said he was due vacation time. Bryce spent fifteen minutes convincing him he'd call if he got into a tough spot.

As soon as he was out of the building he called Fred. "Did Kylie contact you?"

"Yeah. Said she was catching a bus to Dallas. Said it was too dangerous for her to come home."

"Dammit, why didn't she call me? I could have picked her up, taken care of things."

"I think that's why she asked me *not* to call you. Repeated the part about being dangerous for everybody and that it was better for her to start over." Fred paused but Bryce knew what was coming. "Alone."

"What bus line and what time did the bus leave?"

"She called right before boarding the nonstop. Should be passing through Waco in about half an hour. I can get to Dallas and drag her back here. Damn, I wish that girl had a cell phone. Would be handy about now."

"I'll take care of it. You said you had her place cleaned up?"

"Everything's set back to rights." Fred's voice perked up. "Everybody pitched in."

"There's one more thing I need you to do. If we're going to catch the person who's after Kylie, it's going to take a lot of cooperation." Bryce got into his truck, the hands-free connected and he headed out of the parking lot.

"I don't think you'll have a problem finding it."

"Yeah, but how do people feel about moving out of their houses for a couple of days?" It was a drastic plan, but he didn't think he had a chance getting Kylie to go along with it if anyone was in danger. And to prevent someone getting hurt…they simply couldn't be around.

"You mean evacuate the block?"

"As much as possible. And we need a system where people around town check in."

"You mean a phone tree? I think the Methodist church and the schools have one for bad weather. I'll get Allison to work on that. What do you think these men are going to do, hold the town hostage?"

"Whatever's necessary. I'm putting a great deal off on you, Fred. I know I'm asking a lot."

"She's a good woman. She deserves to be free of this. You take care of her."

"I will. Don't look for us until tomorrow."

"We'll be ready."

The hands-free disconnected about the time Bryce pulled in front of the mobile phone store. He added a line to his bill and got the phone activated, charging it in the truck. It took longer than he'd anticipated.

The entire time he stood there answering questions he thought about Kylie. If he couldn't find her...

What would he do? What *could* he do?

He had no claim on her. He wanted to help, but if she refused could he catch the person who wanted to harm her? After all the publicity she'd received in the past three days, he doubted she could easily disappear. Then again, she'd done it once just by running out of gas.

Flipping his lights and siren on, he tore past Baylor University and used the on-ramp for I-35. Flying down the highway, he kept his eyes open for her bus. It had to have passed through the city by then. Just past the Lacy Lakeview exit, he got behind a bus and it eased to the side of the road.

The driver met him on the shoulder holding paperwork. Bryce displayed his badge and waved that things were okay. "We're good. Mind if I take a look at your passengers?"

"Whatever floats your boat." The driver tucked his folder under his arm and lit a cigarette, taking advantage of the break.

Bryce climbed the steps, excited that he was about to see Kylie again. Just how much he wanted to see her surprised him, but not as much as looking at all the faces and being disappointed she wasn't among them. He didn't have a picture of her to show and ask the passengers if they'd seen her at the bus station.

"You'll be back underway momentarily, folks. We're looking for a woman, blonde, twenty-six years old, about my height. You might have seen her in the news recently."

He took his time looking everybody over, wondering if she'd used a disguise or had maybe dyed her hair. That's when he saw a man's finger clandestinely pointing across the aisle. Bryce walked as quietly as possible across the rubber floorboards. Whoever was there—Kylie or a criminal—they didn't want him to know they were on the bus.

"What did the woman do?" someone asked behind him.

He was even with the row and recognized Kylie even with her head between her knees. "She didn't trust the right man."

She popped up when she heard his voice. "You can't force me to leave with you. I've done absolutely nothing wrong. A judge already said that and mentioned that further interference in my life might be considered harassment."

"You're right. If you don't come with me by your own free will, you'll just run away again."

"Oh, give him another chance, honey," an older woman three rows in front of her said. "He looks like he means it."

"Don't go if he hit you. They never stop. No matter what they say," a woman who needed to wash stated flatly.

"It's nothing like that," Kylie tried to explain. "We're not a couple. He's a Texas Ranger."

"Snatch him up, girl. Those guys have job security," the older woman said.

"What do you say, Kylie? Let's talk. If you don't want to stay, I'll drive you to Dallas."

"You can't beat that offer," someone in the crowd said.

"Whatever you want, lady, but I gotta get this bus movin' again," the driver said from up front.

"Come on, Kylie." He held out his hand and smiled.

She placed her fingers in his palm and scooted to the

aisle. Her blue bag was hooked over her shoulder. She had a death grip on the overnight bag they'd purchased the day she'd left Hico.

"I'll talk. That's all I'm promising."

The bus clapped.

"It's like a fairy tale."

"Or that movie, you remember…he comes in and whooshes her away."

"That's not romantic."

"We're really not a couple—" Kylie tried. "I barely know him."

One of the younger passengers stuck their phone in the air obviously recording them. He faced the young woman and pulled Kylie to a stop.

"Actually, she took one look at me with my shirt off and couldn't keep her hands off me."

"You were sunburned." She looked at everyone but him. "I rubbed lotion on— What are you doing?"

He put one hand around her waist and the other gently at her throat, then whispered, "Roll with me, Kylie. It's all part of the plan."

"Wha—"

His lips captured whatever she intended to say. There were ooohs and ahhs all around them, he heard more clapping, felt the bus rock a little with the foot stomping. But what he felt…

The softest lips he'd ever kissed were right…there. He didn't want to break free of them. She parted her lips slightly and he took advantage. He teased her tongue into dancing with him, holding back because of where they were. His hand slid to the back of her neck. His fingers spread through her silky hair.

There might have been more, but a firm grip on his shoulder pulled him away.

"Take it outside, pal," the driver said. "You sure you want to go with this guy, Miss?"

Kylie nodded, turned and squeezed by him to get off the bus.

The young woman recording it all dropped the phone in her lap.

"How fast can you post that for me?"

"Couple of minutes," she answered, already typing.

"Would you tag me? Bryce T. Johnson, Waco."

"Sure. Want me to tag your lady?"

It's all part of the plan.

"Great idea. She used to be a model but lives in Hico now. Sissy Jorgenson."

Yep, all part of the plan.

Chapter Twelve

"What the hell was that all about?" Kylie didn't know if she was upset because of the kiss or because the passengers on the bus were tapping on the windows and taking her picture.

Bryce pulled her farther off the road as the bus left.

"Seriously, Bryce. Why did you do that? Why were they taking my picture?"

"It's part of my plan."

"Then kissing me makes perfect sense." *Of course it didn't.* "I thought we were going to talk about your *possible* plan? Talk about it, not just start perfecting it."

"I'll be honest—"

"Oh please, let's."

"—perfecting is real nice." He winked at her. "I've already put the plan in motion. The first part was to let your enemy know where you were and social media took care of that."

"And the first step was making a public statement that I'm heading to Dallas. So whatever plan I had when I arrived isn't any good."

"Did you have a plan once you got there?"

He still hadn't put the truck in gear. They sat on the shoulder with cars and trucks zooming by. It wasn't the safest place in the world, especially to have a discussion or argument. His question was another that she didn't have an answer to. A bus ride to Dallas was cheap, saved money, got her out of Austin and more than anything else gave her time to think.

Shoot. In the two hours on the bus she'd only thought about one person... Bryce. She wasn't even that upset about being ambushed by Xander the day before. She'd slept soundly for the first time since this mess began.

Why? She should have been scared after his threats. But she wasn't when she thought of this man who had come to stop her from running away. He'd raced after a bus because he had a plan. He'd kissed her because he had a plan.

"Maybe we should talk over coffee or maybe something to eat?"

"I can handle that. I'll even buy." He put the truck in gear, left the flashing lights on and passed cars as they slowed on the right.

"I'm not starving, Bryce."

"Hell...I am. Now you got me hungry for Bush's fried chicken. It's a staple here in Waco. Ever had it?"

She shook her head. His certainty about what to do seemed to be wearing off. He fidgeted a little, not much, but enough to make her aware of it.

"Look, I...um...I want to say I'm sorry for not sticking with you to Austin. The guys from headquarters took good care of you, though. Right? I tried to find someone who was on your detail, but I wasn't quick enough. They rotated them with short hours."

"I noticed. They didn't allow me a phone in the room and barely time alone with my lawyer. It's okay. I'm fine." Should she tell him about Xander?

Maybe not while he was still behind the wheel. He wasn't really speeding and when traffic thinned down, he cut his flashing lights off. His chicken place wasn't far off the highway and when he rolled his window down the smell made her glad he'd sped most of the way.

"You're heading through the drive-through? Are we going to talk in the truck?"

"I thought I'd take you to my place. We can hold a conversation and avoid people taking your picture."

"I notice the cut from my house is healing." He didn't have it covered with a bandage any longer. "Are we close to your apartment?"

"We're right around the corner." Bryce ordered enough for a small army, including a gallon of iced tea.

He exaggerated a bit with his claim that his house was right around the corner. Maybe that's how they measured things in Texas, but he lived a good fifteen minutes southwest of the highway. The smell of the chicken was absolutely driving her nuts.

The cul-de-sac on Hidden Oaks Circle had four huge houses. At first, Kylie thought they'd made a wrong turn.

"Bryce, did you forget to tell me something?"

"Like what?"

"Are you married? All this food, this big house… Do you still live at home?"

He laughed and pushed a gate opener. "I live alone. I haven't even got a dog."

"Oh, why not? I'd get one if I could." She looked around the perfectly manicured lawn and porch. Everything seemed to have a specific place, laid out nice and neat.

"You have a great yard in Hico, why didn't you get one?" He pushed a second remote and opened the garage but didn't pull inside.

"I've always wanted a dog but I traveled too much and never had a yard. Then when I started over, I thought I'd have to leave town in a moment's notice and it wouldn't be fair to leave a dog behind."

He put the truck in Park and turned toward her. "A lot of people wouldn't think of that. They'd just get one anyway." Did he want to kiss her again? He hooked her hair behind her ear and brushed her cheek. "And I work too much. Long hours and a lot of weekends. Let's eat."

"Can we eat outside? I've been cooped up in stuffy rooms since Sunday." She walked around the end of the house and another section of the yard opened up with a pool. "Really? That's just a little overkill for a bachelor."

"I got the house for a song and it's a great investment. I needed it for taxes. Let me get some chairs."

"I won't need one. I'm sticking my feet in the water to cool off."

"I'll join you."

They took off boots and sandals, then rolled up their jeans and sat on the edge, feet on the top step, food between them.

"If I close my eyes I can imagine that I'm on a picnic at a lake. That's on my bucket list, too."

"Wait a minute." Bryce looked seriously shocked behind his mirrored sunglasses. "You've never been on a picnic or to the lake?"

"Either. Neither. Whatever word I'm supposed to use." Kylie was seriously tempted to ask for a trip to buy a bathing suit and take the rest of the night to float.

"I have problems believing that." He shook his head and ate another chicken strip.

"I've eaten outside plenty of times. If you can call what I did back when I was modeling eating. We had photo shoots outdoors and I did plenty of rolling around in the surf at a beach. But never a family picnic or camping or riding bicycles...nothing like that."

"That's rough."

"Don't feel sorry for me. My job took me around the world more than a dozen times. I have some fantastic memories. Especially of the people I met and how gracious fans were."

"Now, you've got me on that one. I flew to Oklahoma

City a couple of times. Driven to the surrounding five-state area a lot, but that's about it. Went to school here. My parents took off all the time, but I was the kid who preferred to stay home."

"You haven't traveled at all?"

"Well, I wouldn't say that. Texas is a pretty big place and I travel all over. I worked with DPS before landing this job." He must have noticed her blank stare. "Sort of like the state highway patrol. The Department of Public Safety is the division that the Rangers operate under since 1935. I can't think of anybody who didn't serve there before becoming a Ranger."

"I didn't even know how to drive a car until I married Xander. I never needed to learn before that. When I stole that Cadillac, I didn't have a license. I was horrified I'd have an accident and have to call someone to find me."

"So if you've never been on a picnic at a lake, I guess you've never gone skinny-dipping." He hung his glasses on the side of his boot.

"Of course not. I got paid to skinny-dip in the surf, though. That day was so cold." She shot him a fake shocked look and then splashed water his direction.

"Keep that up and you'll find out what it's like to be thrown into the pool."

"Been there. Done that." She decided to live dangerously and splash him again.

"Keep it up, Kylie. I live for revenge…at least where the pool is concerned. Last summer my nephew learned pretty quick how ruthless I can be and he's only seven."

"You have a nephew?"

"Four of them now. Each brother has one and my sister has two."

"That must be nice."

"At least for my parents. I get a lot of digital pictures.

Oh, I almost forgot. I bought you a cell this afternoon. It's in the truck. Want me to get it?"

"But I don't need a phone."

"Fred and I disagree."

He stood on the first step, ankle deep in water. The compulsion to push him was overwhelming. She rose slightly and pushed against his hard abs almost as if he'd expected her to. He fell into the pool and she hoped his phone wasn't in his pocket. That would be dreadful. Nothing else that had happened mattered at that particular moment. He rocketed from the bottom of the pool and snatched her ankles.

Getting her wet wasn't a pull and dunk. His hand tickled the bottom of her feet until she was laughing so hard she couldn't breathe. Then he inched her under as she held on to the side of the pool. Then he held on to her waist as she surfaced.

"Oh, no you don't. I told you, I take my revenge seriously."

She went under to escape his grasp, but it didn't last long. They bounced around in the shallow end, taking turns coming up for air and darting back under. They slowed a little and were suddenly face-to-face.

"If we were kids my mother would be yelling to quit before someone got hurt," he said, out of breath.

Or at least acting like he was.

"Good thing we aren't kids then."

The heat of the sun and crispness of the water felt good, but she remembered the kiss from the bus. His mouth came closer to hers and she closed her eyes, letting him take her back to that awesome sensation.

No hesitation this time or wondering what his intentions were. She rested her arms on his shoulders and parted her lips. He whooshed her through the water, pulling her body into his. Every muscle was outlined and defined by the cotton. And each one of them was pressed against her.

The water didn't cool them down. The more they kissed, the hotter she got. The pool should have been bubbling. He lifted her in the water to have access to her neck, pushing her outer shirt off one shoulder.

She should stop him. She couldn't take it off...but it felt so good to be touched, to have his teeth nip at her skin, to feel again. She returned the action, tugging at his buttons and pushing his green shirt out of the way.

Mouths back together, it was hard to kiss through the smiles and playfulness, but he did. He wrapped his arms around her and took her below the water, kissing as long as she could hold her breath. When they came up, he caught the back of her long-sleeve shirt and pulled it free as she got away.

Without that protection, she was lost. Her sleeveless tank wouldn't cover the ugly flesh on her left arm. She swam away from Bryce, slicked back her hair and dipped her shoulders below the water.

With her right hand, she waved at Bryce as he set her shirt on the side of the pool tile. "Hey, I need that back."

"It'll be easier to swim without it. In fact, we should take off our jeans, too. My wallet is probably ruined. So what? Won't be the first time."

"No, really, I need my shirt back please."

"Okay." He looked a little confused.

Probably because of the anxiousness in her voice. There was panic there, but as long as he gave her the shirt back, she'd be fine.

"Thanks." She reached out, keeping the scarred side of her body away from him. "Time to get out. No more games."

BRYCE COULD ONLY watch as Kylie turned away and struggled to get her shirt back on. As soon as she had her left arm through the sleeve she was hightailing it out of the water. Game time was definitely over.

Picking up their leftovers, she stuffed everything back into the bag. She slung the string of her bag across her shoulder and walked to the back door, dripping.

He followed. "Why are you so worried about me seeing the scars? I've seen wounds before. You can relax around here."

"I can't relax anywhere. Sorry. Can we just go inside? It's getting late."

The keys were still in the truck along with his cell and her new cell. She stood on the back patio, visibly shivering in the blazing July sun. He wiped the water running into his eyes away. It was important for him to show her she didn't have to be afraid.

Time he didn't have. That's what he needed. Or maybe to have become a part of her life in a different month or year. But he was stuck with today. Stuck in the timeline where someone was trying to kill her.

"I'll grab your travel bag. You'll want your clothes."

He needed a minute to cool off, just leaning against the side of the truck. At the moment he doubted he could get his jeans off without ripping them with scissors. And that might be a little dangerous until all his parts calmed down.

With the bag hanging on the French door handle, she had stopped shaking and was wringing the water from her shirt. Then her hair.

Beautiful. She was just…beautiful.

Of course, she knew it. The whole world knew it. She'd been a model for more than half her life and didn't need to hear it from him. But he'd yearned to say it since he'd first met her. Natural beauty that came from deep within her soul. No scars would change that.

Bag in hand, he put the key in the lock, opened the door

and they were both hit with a blast of cold air. "Want a towel or to make a run for it?"

"I'll follow you."

He darted forward and was halfway up the stairs when he realized she wasn't behind him. She'd stopped to turn the dead bolt. He pretended like he hadn't seen her, slowing his pace. She caught up with him and at the top of the stairs he dropped her small case in the guest room and grabbed extra towels from the cabinet in the bath.

"Are you sure you're not married?"

"Yeah, pretty sure."

"Your place doesn't look like a bachelor lives here."

Bryce shrugged as if he was indifferent. "I have my mom to thank for that. She hired a decorator before they'd come to visit. Told me she was too old to sleep on an air mattress or eat off a paper plate."

Kylie laughed and was still laughing when she locked the door.

Showering eased some of the tension his body had built up, but not all of it. He put away the leftovers while she used the hair dryer. Back in a tank and a light long-sleeve shirt, she looked more relaxed when she came downstairs.

She packed her wet clothes in a plastic bag insisting she wasn't staying the night with him. But then started washing a load of towels she'd used.

While he showed her where things were, it was close quarters in the laundry room. There was an electric current between him and Kylie. Each time he passed close to her he wanted to touch. When he finally did, he might as well have stuck a screwdriver into an outlet. She jumped away from him so fast he wondered if those kisses had affected her in a different way.

"Coffee?"

"Sure. I need to warm up while we talk about this great plan of yours."

"Oh, yeah."

"There is a plan? You weren't lying to get me to come home with you?"

"No. I mean yes, there is. Fred's already set parts of it in motion." He backed out of the room as fast as he could, tripping on a laundry basket. "Why don't you start and tell me what happened with the judge."

"I'm sure you heard it online or somewhere that they dismissed all the charges, along with my protection detail. I'm surprised that you were sent after me to see if I'd co-operate again. The judge was pretty clear…" She slowed to a stop. "There's something you're not telling me."

There was a lot he wasn't telling, but she needed to know it wasn't official. There'd be no safety net other than the people of Hico.

"I guess I should start by letting you know I was offi-cially suspended this morning, but that Major Parker told me this was the only way we could help."

"So you have his unofficial blessing to put together a plan? How's that supposed to help?"

"Since most of Hico will be in on the plan, the state of Texas probably shouldn't be liable if something goes wrong."

"There's one major flaw in whatever your plan is. I'm not going back to Hico. I refuse to put all the people I hold dear in danger like that. And don't even bother telling me that Xander isn't a threat. He ambushed me with the judge's help and said he wanted his car back among other things."

"How did he ambush you?"

"The judge invited me into his office. He said he wanted to talk about—I don't remember. Xander was inside and the judge didn't bother staying."

Bryce wanted to find the judge and make him pay for that. But he also wanted to show Kylie he could protect her. But Kylie closed herself off. It wasn't the first time she'd reacted that way. This time he had a reason—Xander. He wanted two things for Kylie. First to not hide behind her clothes and the second was to not be afraid of the world.

"You okay?"

"Just great. At least I was while I was sitting on that bus putting a safe distance away from my friends. Are you ready to tell me what you're doing?"

"It won't work without you, Kylie." He wanted to hold her, to comfort her. "And you might think you're protecting everyone by running away, but consider a couple of things. Friends don't walk away from friendships. And then there's your ex. He assumes you've hidden the Cadillac in Hico somewhere. Your friends won't be safe until we put Xander behind bars."

Chapter Thirteen

Bryce was going to set a trap for her ex. He was determined to do it without the help of any law enforcement sanction or backup. He wanted her help.

And she didn't think he was crazy.

Or maybe she was just as crazy as he was for wanting to believe it might work.

"You've sort of hinted at this before Bryce. But what if you coming to Hico alerted someone? Then they came searching for me and the car."

"I have thought about that scenario more than once in the past week." Bryce rubbed his chin with both hands. "The plan will work. We'll catch whoever shot up your house. You'll be safe."

His house was decorated as if he'd been married and his wife hated the place. There weren't any real traces of Bryce. No pictures of family, only a rare landscape photograph hung on the wall. The color choice was neutral… everywhere neutral. There wasn't even a sport trophy in the game room where they were sitting.

"I'm changing the subject, Bryce. You said your mother hired a decorator. Did they consult you at all?"

"To make her happy I said she could do what she wanted. I don't spend much time anywhere except this room and the bedroom."

"I can understand why. It's so…"

"Bleak? Old? Stuffy?"

"I was going to say beige."

"Are you okay with the plan, Kylie?" Bryce licked chicken from his fingers then wiped them in a napkin.

There was nothing special about it. Nothing meant to be provocative. So why were her insides fluttering with excitement? He leaned forward on a knee, sort of expecting an answer. What had he asked?

"I, ah…I'm willing to give it a try. I don't know if it will work, but I don't want to leave Hico. I need a life. Not…"

"Beige."

They laughed awkwardly. "Right. It's time to live some bright bold colors."

As long as it wasn't red, but she wouldn't say that out loud. He didn't need to wonder about her commitment to his plan. At least he had one.

He was finishing up another round of chicken. She'd passed on seconds but had nibbled on a roll. She'd gotten to the point that thinking wasn't really helping. A weird sensation of the more she tried, the fewer thoughts were actually in her mind.

"It's bothering me that Xander didn't act like he knew where the car was located. Am I missing something?"

"Fred disconnected the GPS locator and moved it. No one but him knows where it is."

"But Xander reacted like he hadn't known I was the one who stole the car at all."

"Interesting." Bryce's jaw muscles flexed.

"Don't agree with me and just blow off my opinion. I know what I'm talking about. I know what he said."

"No, sorry. I'm thinking it's a legitimate theory. Fred said he hadn't connected the charger until this last week. So whoever had the GPS on the car might have just realized it was on."

"I am totally lost. Explain it to me."

She was lost. But mainly at the thought that someone besides her ex-husband hated her so much.

"Say someone—Xander or an unknown—wanted the car. Let's say they've been looking for you or waiting on you to surface."

"I don't see why, but okay."

"Kylie, I've been looking for you for three years because the state was interested."

"Why? I don't understand."

"The state has been working on a case against the Tenoreno family for a decade. This is the closest they've gotten to bringing their crime syndicate down. You were a piece of the puzzle." He scratched his chin, thinking.

"A missing piece."

"Exactly. So when the picture of you surfaced, I came to check it out. It hasn't been a secret that the state wanted to find you. We didn't broadcast that we had, but we didn't keep it a secret either."

"So it really is quite possible that you alerted someone that I was alive and living in Hico." The wonder of it blew her away, because no one believed that she didn't have a clue about the Tenoreno family's business. Even after all this time... "So you think Xander is lying?"

"Maybe, but we have to be prepared that two different parties might be interested in the car. You know, I don't think whoever fired at us Saturday got to your house before us. So if they did follow me to Hico, then located the car, they still waited for instructions on how to proceed."

"How does that help?"

"The men shooting at us were following orders...not giving them." He nodded his head as if he'd had a breakthrough.

"Well that makes everything perfectly clear for me." She couldn't even laugh about it. Like her brain trying to think everything through to a conclusion and getting nowhere, it seemed her emotional bank was completely depleted, too.

"The plan is a basic one. We move the car back to your place and wait for them to show up. Whoever *they* are, we'll be ready."

"You, Fred and a few other Hico citizens."

"Fred spoke to the police officers and they're evacuating the homes. They'll be ready." He leaned back against the cushions again, more relaxed. "We didn't want to put you or anyone in danger."

"I don't think you're responsible for that particular mistake in my life."

Bryce smiled. "Maybe not. I will be if something goes wrong. The idea is to get to them before they get anywhere near you. That's it."

"And what if Xander or this mystery person doesn't show?"

"I'm thinking of one solution at a time." He leaned forward to pick up the remote. "I'll show you how to use this thing if you want to watch television. I have some stuff I need to take care of."

"Oh, then I'll call a cab to take me to a motel."

He scrunched up his face and cocked his head as though he hadn't heard her correctly. "There's a bedroom upstairs. I'm not spending the night at a hotel watching you sleep."

"I didn't ask you to."

"Kylie, do me this one favor and let's not argue about where we're sleeping. We're safer here than at a motel. I have an alarm. Locks. Bolts. If I hear something, I have lots of protection in my gun safe."

Everything he named off made her feel more secure. She wouldn't let pride or whatever she was feeling put them in jeopardy. "I didn't want to be trouble."

"Will you please stay here?"

She nodded her head and saw lights in the yard. The

pool lights reflected off the six-foot fence and she didn't have to imagine that it was prettier sitting next to it. "Now I wish I'd packed my bathing suit."

"Suits are always optional. You could mark skinny-dipping off your bucket list." He smiled overly wide like an emoticon.

"But it's not on *my* bucket list. Driving through the fall leaves in New England...now *that's* on my list."

"Shame. I could help you cross off something tonight, right now."

He was so cute. But skinny-dipping meant no coverage. She tugged the light long-sleeve shirt into a more comfortable position.

"If you have to work, I guess I should just go on up, then."

"I didn't say work. I was suspended, remember?"

"How could I forget since I was the reason?"

"I need some research. I'm not working for anyone but you. So what else is on your bucket list? Not seeing the world. You've done that several times."

"Having a dog, for one."

"That's cool."

"Really? Most people would think it's too simple."

"Who said simple things couldn't make a bucket list?" Bryce's arm was along the back of the couch and touched her. "I'd like a reason to take a day off and lay around that pool. Maybe meet my neighbors. Have a barbecue. Is getting to a lake picnic on your top ten?"

She forced herself not to react to the simple brush of his finger along her shirt. Everything about the evening had been casual. She wanted to keep it that way. But her insides were doing that flutter thing again. Or maybe they'd never stopped.

"I guess it should be. Mine is really silly. Let's change the subject. I'll watch a movie if you watch it, too."

He grabbed her hand as she reached for the remote.

Maybe they shouldn't be relaxing at all. It was all quite possible everything was about to go to hell in a handbasket or in a 1964 fully restored shiny black Cadillac convertible.

"This thing's crazy. Trust me with the remote?"

"We aren't watching football, right?"

"Not this time of year. What do you like? Suspense, drama, comedy—"

He was looking at the cable guide. "I don't think I could take *The Fugitive* or anything like that. And I'm not too sure comedy would work."

"*King Kong*?" He looked at her and moved on to the next one. "Classic John Wayne. You've got to like John Wayne?"

"All right."

"You don't sound very enthusiastic."

"I just saw this one three weeks ago."

"Then we keep flipping."

"No, Bryce, it's okay. Really. Oh wait, go back." She flipped her fingers until he returned to the right channel. "Is that Fred Astaire? Would you mind if we watched that? I've been on an old movie kick. I was going to set my DVR but—"

"But everything in your house was shredded. I remember."

He leaned back against the couch. "Want popcorn or soda? Maybe a beer?"

"I'm good, thanks."

Bryce leaned his head back on the cushion. Kylie expected him to be snoring before the first dance number. But she didn't mind. Sitting here like two normal adults was ridiculously soothing. And exactly what she needed.

She loved the idea of normal.

That was on her bucket list, too.

It wasn't long and *The End* rolled across the screen.

Bryce had slept through the entire movie. She wanted to turn off the TV and tried but pushed the wrong button in the dark. A DVD began playing and before she could click it off a THX sound check played at practically the loudest level available.

BRYCE SHOT OFF the couch, eyes wide open, realizing exactly what had happened. "Middle top turns everything off."

Kylie pushed the remote but handed it off to him. It took him a second or two. Whatever she'd attempted in the dark had switched a different electronic device on instead of cutting everything off.

"I didn't mean to wake you up, but I had no idea a remote could be so complicated."

"Universal remote." He wiped the sleep from his eyes. "Did you enjoy the movie? Sorry I sort of passed out. Guess our swim had me more tired than I realized. Did I snore?"

She shook her head and yawned. "You didn't, but I might if I stay up any later. And yes, the movie was great. Fred and Ginger—what's not to love?"

"All the dancing?"

"You don't like to dance? That's another thing on my list. I want to learn how to waltz properly."

"All right." He began clicking through the music stored in his system. "I'm sure I put something that had a three-quarter time beat… Mom's playlist. That's it."

He scrolled through and found the perfect song, put it on Repeat and opened his arms.

"What's this?" She looked baffled.

"'Waltz Across Texas.' That's how you waltz with boots on."

"We're both barefoot, Bryce." Her hands were on her hips, the flowy shirt that hid her skin pushed behind them.

Skinny jeans hugged her long legs and the dark T-shirt clung to her, outlining perfect-sized breasts and waistline.

"Perfect." *In more way than one.* He set a hand on her hip and held his palm open for her to drop hers onto. "Barefoot is how I learned."

"What do I do?"

"Follow my lead. My granddad told me to keep the lady's foot between mine and hold her close. Do you mind?" He didn't wait for permission, the song played again and he tugged her to fit against him. "Now don't get any ideas about throwing me to the floor."

Kylie laughed for the first time since the pool. She might be tall, but she was really a tiny thing.

Kylie tried to drop her chin and look at their feet.

"Chin up and trust me, darlin'. I know where I'm going."

He led her around to the back of the couch, keeping them in a tight square. He counted off the three beats in his head. She let him lead completely as if she'd never attempted a waltz before. Had she?

Maybe she had and he'd misinterpreted? "I like these words."

"My grandparents danced to this at least once a week when I was young." *One, two, three. One, two, three.* He needed to keep this right and not mess up. "If it wasn't the first song they danced to, it was the last one. They even played it at their funerals."

"It's nice that you have that to remember, but it's a little sad."

"Dancing made them happy. They passed it on to all of us." His fingers flexed across her back, anxious to get her even closer.

She tipped her head back and stopped moving her feet. "Wait a second, you just said that the thing wrong with the movie was all the dancing."

"Watching other people dance isn't the same as holding a woman in your arms." He secured his arm tighter around her, curled her fingers within his.

She rested her head on his shoulder, her warm breath was calm and regular across his skin. Lucky she couldn't feel his, which was getting more excited with each step. He pulled her closer still and gently nudged his knee between hers to keep them locked together in the waltz box.

Dancing together was close and intimate behind his couch and he felt the heat. He wanted to kiss Kylie, but the repeating voice of Tex Ritter was beginning to wear a little on the mood. Instead, he twirled them close to the amplifier and selected Random.

Mistake. The beat changed to something from the '70s.

"That was lovely, but this..." Her hands went to his shoulders, not pushing, just ready to be released. "I can dance to on my own."

Bryce went to the next song and wrapped her hand back in his, admiring the strength he felt in the slender aikido-filled defense weapons. He hugged her, swaying to the soft band music from the '40s. Kept her close to him through the next '60s song with a faster tempo. Then encouraged her head to rest on his shoulder when Frankie Valli sang "You're just too good to be true."

"You sing pretty good."

"I didn't realize I was." He didn't sing for anyone. It gave him a weird feeling. He hadn't even played drums in high school because he didn't like to perform.

Barefoot. Three feet of carpet either direction. Hand in hand. This time when he kissed her it was different. The edge of not knowing what he wanted was gone. He knew exactly.

Kylie.

Chapter Fourteen

Daniel Rosco was on his back in coveralls wheeling himself under a 1976 Trans Am. He was restoring it himself. The tediousness of working and cleaning every part on the engine was the only thing that calmed him.

As a child, his mother would send him out here when she saw him overly anxious. The garage had been immaculately clean and he'd yearned to get grease on his hands. Paco Valdez had been their driver back then. He'd taught him a lot about engines, but most of Daniel's knowledge came from research and intuition.

Paco was gone now. He'd been gone many more years than his mother or father, who had both been murdered in the past six months. *Murdered! Taken out. Gotten out of the way.*

It wasn't something he hadn't thought about doing himself…especially with his father. He didn't like that the decision had been taken out of his hands. He knew the man responsible. He'd once called him his close friend in spite of the rivalries and competition between their families.

Xander would suffer for standing by and letting his father execute his sweet momma. But he'd slit the throat of the bastard himself for ordering the assassin who left his father to rot in the desert.

Xander's days were numbered. And now that he knew

where the flash drive was located… It was just a matter of time before all his plans became reality.

"Boss?"

Daniel set his wrench on his chest and rolled the creeper from under the car, wiping his hands on an oily rag that put more dirt on them than took off. He carefully placed the wrench among the other well-used tools. All arranged precisely in the order he expected to use them.

Lennon waited. He knew not to ask mundane questions like what Daniel was doing. Otherwise the wrench might land against his head instead of being replaced on the towel.

"Do you have him?" He stood, hopping to his feet, feeling like a teenager instead of someone approaching thirty.

"Yes, sir, but Xander Tenoreno is here to see you."

"Interesting. I didn't expect him until I had the package. How close are we to that detail?"

"The model's house is being watched. The local authorities don't know we're already in place."

"Excellent. Send in Xander. I'm excited to hear what he has to say to me." His back was to the door when Xander entered, but he could see his rival in the small mirror above the sink.

"I guess you know why I'm here. The man you had spying on me said your hired thugs put on quite a show. What the hell were you thinking?"

"The package will be in my possession within twenty-four hours." Daniel dried his hands and shrugged out of his coveralls, tying the arms around his waist. "Then our deal is off."

"You hired men behind my back to take care of our problem. I thought we had a partnership."

"You should have told me your ex had the drive. Trust runs both ways…friend."

"What even makes you think the drive is still in the

Cadillac? Or that you beat me to it? Do you think I would have left it with Sissy all these years?"

"You don't have it." He took the other man's measure, gauging how far to push him. "Just as I knew you did then…you don't have it now."

"What about the partnership between the families? Are we going back to square one, fighting for the scraps that the Mexican cartel will leave?"

They moved around each other, opposite points on a circle they were walking.

"My father was an old man, willing to go into business with yours, and look what it got him. Dead. I'm not old and I'm no longer willing to step aside. I think we both know why."

"Sissy doesn't have any idea what's hidden in the car. If she had the information she would have used it long before now or thrown it in my face yesterday."

Daniel had control over his body. He didn't act concerned at all.

"I wondered if you'd seen her. I suppose you made arrangements with the authorities." Daniel dropped his hand on Xander's shoulder, stopping their dance around each other. "It amazes me you believe that in all these years she never looked at the drive."

"You aren't going to kill her until we know for certain." Xander knocked Daniel's hands aside.

"Of course I am." He moved to the wall of screwdrivers and files, but didn't expect to use them. This was his garage with his men stationed all around.

"I should have killed you years ago, Daniel. But we were friends. I thought we had a plan to take everything from our fathers. Telling you of the missing Cadillac was a big mistake on my part. But it's been your impatience that led prosecutors to my ex-wife. It was your impatience that has involved the authorities and made the entire situation more important. I doubt they'll walk away anytime soon."

"You aren't claiming any responsibility for not finding her during the past five years? If you'd handled this correctly to begin with—"

"No one could have known it was Sissy who stole the car." Xander said matter-of-factly. "I'll deal with it. Back away, Daniel, before you destroy everything we've worked for."

Xander turned to leave.

Daniel's hand closed around the handle of a screwdriver. It could have been thrown like a knife. But…he wanted Xander alive to witness the Tenoreno empire fall. Old-fashioned, yes. What could he say? He enjoyed theatrics. Maybe he'd seen *The Godfather* too many times.

"You go through with your plans in Hico," Xander said at the door, "and we'll have to take extreme measures."

"Are you threatening me?"

The death in Xander's look might have frightened him when he was younger. Daniel knew the look well. He practiced it. He lived it.

Tenoreno sauntered away, thinking he had the upper hand. Seconds later, Daniel's right-hand man—everyone in this business had one—stood in the open doorway ready for the next order. Daniel gestured to send the man in.

"Let's get this over with, Lennon."

The man who had lost track of Xander's ex-wife was thrown through the garage door and left alone with Daniel. Feeling like a man with power, he sat on the workbench stool and retrieved a pistol. He spun, then opened the chamber very dramatically.

"I've got to let people know what happens to men who don't follow my orders."

"I'm sorry, Mr. Rosco, but I didn't know he was going to take her off the bus."

"I. Don't. Care." He dropped a bullet from a chamber for emphasis of each word. Then two more. The theatrics was just that. Fun. Nobody was there to witness the murder. It was just drama and made him feel like the boss. He'd seen his father go through this ritual at least half a dozen times before he was fifteen.

With one bullet remaining, Daniel handed him the pistol.

"This is simple. Pull the trigger on yourself and we're even. Pull it on me and every person you love dies."

The explosion was expected. It was the man's only choice after all was said and done. Lennon came through the door, a moment of wonder wiped from his face as soon as it appeared.

"Sorry about the mess, Lennon. We should have used the drop cloth. Get the body disposed of and send five hundred to his family."

Daniel was tempted again to take care of Sissy himself. He'd only met her a couple of times while she'd been married to Xander. But there was too much heat near her at the moment to make that possible. The men he'd hired couldn't be traced back to him. It was better to stay clear and let them handle it.

They had nothing to lose and soon the little town of Hico would look like a war-trodden wreck. "Who knows? Maybe Xander will want to intervene and get stuck in the middle of it. One can always hope."

Chapter Fifteen

Perfectly shaped lips, effortlessly pink without artificial color. Eyes a beautiful shade of blue with a little definition. Blue? Great detective skills. She'd been wearing dark-colored contacts until today. Bryce left Kylie's lips, skimming her cheek then her jawline to whisper in her ear as he passed it.

"You ready to head upstairs?"

"Why, Mr. Johnson, are you asking me what I think you're asking me?" She skimmed his lips, then sucked his bottom lip between her teeth. "Never going to happen."

He would have believed her if she'd pulled away. Or maybe even if she'd said the "never" with a bounce in her voice. But she hadn't. Her voice was full of sadness—not fright like that afternoon—just sadness and regret.

"I've been afraid to tell you," he whispered, searching her eyes and seeing the hunger he felt. "I think—"

He couldn't blink, connected as he was to her emotional pain.

"Don't think that you know me, Bryce. If you've been searching for Sissy Jorgenson... Well, she died five years ago. I told you that. I have the scars to prove it. I'm not afraid of them, but I don't share that part of me with anyone. They remind me every day that I was given a second chance. Those shots took away a career, security, my friends. But they gave me a family in Hico that I couldn't fully appreciate until this week. For that I'll always be grateful to you."

She turned to leave, slowly. Hesitating. Letting him keep her fingers secured inside his hand.

"Let me ask you a simple question."

"What?"

"Do you *want* to go upstairs with me?"

"There's nothing simple about that question." Her chin dropped to her chest, her free hand covered her eyes.

"Sure there is. I know my answer. And I think I know yours." He pulled her back to him and devoured her mouth. She allowed him access to the curve of her neck, the soft skin across her collarbone.

Answering his invitation without words. Her hands were on his hips bringing him closer and harder against her. Their bodies rocked against each other when Deep Purple's "Smoke on the Water" shot through the speakers. Her tongue danced inside his mouth, darting, demanding.

She was in charge of their fate. And he kept his hands above his head to prove it to her. He told himself he could walk away if she changed her mind. But he sure as hell didn't want to.

She pushed at his T-shirt. Since his hands were in the air, practically above his head, he reached to his shoulders and pulled it free. Her mouth left his, pressing against his chest. Teasing with a mixture of a lick with the tip of her tongue and a playful bite. She worked her way down, her short nails scraping lightly until they reached the top of his zipper, then outlined his erection underneath.

"Let's go," he whispered when she unbuttoned his fly.

"What's wrong with here?" Her fingers drew circles on his abs.

"Kylie." He shook his head, then caught the look in her eyes.

It was back, the fright that he'd seen when her shirt came off.

"I like it right here," she whispered trying to sink to her knees.

He slid his hands to her elbows, stopping her. "I'm not treating our first time together like we're teenagers looking for a fast thrill in a game room. We're not only too old for that, we deserve better."

Dusting her hands like she was done, she hurried away. "Fine. This is all I have, Bryce. All I can do."

He touched her shoulder and she stopped. Did she want him to change her mind? Show her how much he cared about her? "If it were me… If our positions were reversed, and I was the one with scars. What would you do right now, Kylie? Would you let me run away? Continue to be afraid?"

She covered her face. "I am afraid."

He could barely hear her. He asked just as quietly, "Of me?"

"Strangely enough, no. But yes, maybe of you most of all."

"I don't understand."

Kylie faced him, cupping his cheeks, using a thumb to entice his lips—whether that was her intention or not.

"You've been looking for Sissy. I've seen that desire before from the men who admired her beauty. I'm afraid that you'll be—"

"Be what?"

"Disappointed, Bryce. You're going to be disappointed and never look at me like that again." She gulped, holding back tears.

He pulled her in close again, this time for comfort. He wanted to tell her it wasn't true, but something told him to just be quiet. Let her cry. He hated that she was afraid, but there was a kernel of hope buried in there…

She not only wanted him…she didn't want him to just go away after they made love?

He wanted that, too. He wanted a relationship. And she was wrong—Sissy had been a young girl of the world. He was falling for the woman from a small town.

Kylie was warm against his chest. Tiny but not frail. Crying, but catching her breath. He was glad to hold her and wait, trying to form the words he wanted to say.

"Sweetheart, I'm not the person you're afraid of. I have no intention of walking away from you anytime soon. Believe me when I tell you that I have a pretty good imagination about what you look like, and yeah, I saw a lot of your modeling career photos. But none of that will ever compare to the real thing. You have to trust me a little."

"I do, but—I don't know how to get past this."

"Hell, you don't want me to see anything? Just blindfold me." He was joking. She knew he was joking, right?

When he saw the relief on her face, he knew he shouldn't be joking. It was the solution she needed and might be a little fun at the same time. No, this was serious.

"It'll probably kill me, but we'll move at whatever pace you need. Hands wherever you want them." He splayed them, stuck them behind his back, then extended his right. "Deal?"

"Deal." She took it and shook, but quickly grasped his face and kissed him.

And kept kissing him until her hands were moving up his back and it was as though their foreplay hadn't been interrupted. He wanted the first time to be special, but he'd never forget this woman or what was about to happen.

"Dish towel or necktie?" he asked when she nibbled on his neck.

"Tie, I think I'll get a better knot."

"Good."

As tall as she was she still weighed nothing. He picked

her up and bolted up the stairs. He bounced her onto the king bed and pulled dress ties from the closet. Kylie had the comforter and top sheet thrown to the side. She was sitting on her knees in the middle, plumping pillows.

He gave her a choice of two ties he never wore. She pulled the one decorated with four-leaf clovers, sliding it across his palm.

Yeah, he felt pretty darn lucky already.

"You know you don't have to do this, Bryce."

"Believe me. That's no longer an option. I'll be right back."

The package of condoms had been in the cabinet for a while. He took two, just in case, and dropped them on the nightstand next to the bed.

"Feeling ambitious?" she asked moving to the edge.

"More like prepared."

"So how does this work?" She pulled the tie from one hand to the other.

A simple gesture that was anything other than innocent. It fired his imagination. On any other day he could keep his pants on to hold himself back. This one he had to dig deep to find the strength.

All he could do was swallow hard and shrug. "You're running the show."

A split-second look of uncertainty, then the playful Kylie stood and draped the tie around his neck. "I guess I am."

His body thrummed as she slowly ran her hands over his skin again, making him tense each time she dropped a finger down the edge of his jeans. The button was already undone. Just when he thought she'd forgotten about blindfolding him, she backed up and gestured for him to turn around.

Anticipation had his heart racing and pumping the blood through his body until he was almost jittery. And she'd done nothing but touch him. The tie slid to his back, looped around his neck. He closed his eyes, hearing the bed move.

Kylie positioned his blindfold, pulling it tight against his eyelids. She must have been standing on the bed because her lips and teeth tugged at the skin on the back of his neck and across his shoulders.

She didn't ask if it was too snug. It didn't matter if it was. He couldn't object or she might lose her nerve. *He* wouldn't. He wanted her, wanted them together. But more than that, he wanted to give her the confidence to live again.

And making love was part of living.

There was more rustling behind him. The dark surrounding him was absolute. He turned his head, but could only imagine that Kylie was removing her clothes.

"Time to get rid of that denim you're wearing." She patted his butt like a teammate.

"You're not going to help?"

"I think you can manage that in the dark. But here."

Reaching around him, the back of her cooled fingers dipped against his skin, holding his jeans at the top of his zipper. Before he could fully suck in his surprised breath, she'd playfully outlined his erection, then unzipped.

Those same knuckles stroked him again through the last layer of cotton. He reached for the jeans at his hips and she slapped his hands away.

"I changed my mind. This is temptingly fun."

"Or cruel."

"It was your idea. Want me to stop?" She stroked him again, slower this time.

He was breathing through his teeth. He couldn't help it. He shook his head and felt his jaw popping as the intense pleasure of her touch tightened every muscle in his body...*every* muscle.

She tugged the jeans down...one side, then the other.

Back and forth a couple of times until they could slide down his legs. He was grateful to stcp out of them and wished she'd tugged his last bit of clothing along with them.

She slowly spun him around and checked the blindfold. It was still tight. He didn't know what to do with his hands, so he laced his fingers together and rested them on top of his head.

Kylie giggled.

"Having fun?" he asked.

"Not that I would want them or anything, but I imagined handcuffs for a second. I mean…you are standing like you're under arrest."

"Search away."

Vulnerable and uncertain—understatements for the way he felt. The darkness changed his expectations. He listened, trying to picture what she was doing based on the sound. He concentrated on her movements and anticipated every touch. He was still caught off guard when the bed moved and he was suddenly propelled to his back.

"You'll have to scoot to the middle on your own."

He did.

"I kind of like your hands where they are." Her nails created a trail of sensation down his side and across his belly, their tips skirted under the elastic. Teasing yet again.

He took a pillow from above his head and gripped it with both of his hands. His concentration was split between the delicious trace of provocativeness and keeping his word to only do what she wanted, when she said so.

The light skimming across his skin with fingers and lips and bra silk had him bringing the pillow on top of his face. It lasted the barest of moments as Kylie extended her body over his and uncovered him.

Kissing. Nipping. Fully. Sensually. Completely. He was

running out of ways to think about it. He was running out
of the willpower to hold back.

"Honey, if you don't let me touch you soon…"

"Patience," she whispered tugging on his earlobe with
her teeth.

He concentrated on her breasts rubbing across his chest,
still covered by their satin cage. His fingers contracted as
he envisioned them in his hands. Kylie's mouth substituted
for her nipples. She pulled back and he went with her, rising off the bed as she sat across his lap.

He groaned with the pressure. The knowledge that at
some point he'd be surrounded by her had him dropping
like a hard rock back to the mattress. Groaning yet again.

"Kylie." He was breathing hard as though he'd run a
marathon and they hadn't really begun yet. "Sweetheart,
you…are you doing okay?"

As far as he could tell she was fine. He wanted more
right then. He swallowed hard, grabbing the sheets under
his hands as she tugged his underwear down his legs. He
couldn't see but felt himself come to attention.

So aware of everything around him, he heard the cloth
hit the carpet. Heard the short intake of breath as Kylie
saw him for the first time. Felt the hesitation in her fingers
as she explored more of his body.

Bryce was at his limit. Her tentative kiss was his undoing.

He must have died at that point, because he was definitely in heaven.

KYLIE WAS ENJOYING the small bit of torture she was putting Bryce through. But there was only so much she could
manage without torturing herself.

Her desire had been almost unmanageable when they'd
had all their clothes on. Now that his were off… He was
such a gorgeous man. The sunburn from the weekend be-

fore had turned brown. The pale color from his waist down might have been comical if he wasn't so…impressive.

No. There wasn't anything funny about the way he made her want him. All he had to do was lie there and her body trembled.

Aching for him was the easy part.

Was it fair to keep him blindfolded? Literally in the dark where her body was concerned. She leaned forward to remove the lucky tie. Her bra skimmed his chest and another genuine groan escaped from Bryce. She wanted to release him, have him take a turn torturing her with touches and kisses and exploration.

But she just couldn't.

Instead, she used the silk of her underwear, sliding against him until his head shook side to side.

"Dammit, Kylie. Please let me touch you." One of his hands twisted the pillow into a ball, the other twisted in the sheet at their sides. "I'm being honest, sweetheart. This is getting hard."

A burst of laughter escaped. "I am so sorry."

He moaned. "Great balls of fire, I didn't mean that the way it sounded." His ab muscles tightened as he chuckled when she laughed more. "Shoot, I didn't mean *that* either."

"It's my fault. I know I'm not supposed to laugh."

"Why the hell not?"

"Well, won't it sort of deflate your ego?"

"Honey, there's nothing deflating there." He flexed under her.

He was right…nothing was deflating. She kissed him with all her confidence restored. She turned to her side, tugging him on top of her. She was ready. She had to give him a chance.

"Okay."

"Okay I can take the blindfold off, okay?" His hand went to push it away.

Both her hands grabbed his, stopping him in time. "No. I meant that I was ready."

"You might be, but I haven't had my turn yet." He switched to his side, then to his knees. "It's your call, but don't you want me to take a turn?"

"You would have to...touch me."

"That you can count on." His hand skimmed from her stomach to the top of her bra. "You're still dressed?"

Straddling her, he tugged a little on her panties, replicating what she'd done to him. Shouldn't he put a pleasurable end to the need building even higher? Of course he could...but he wasn't.

He touched her like a blind man. Exploring every crevice of one leg and then the other without stirring what was between. Purposefully ignoring her and using his light coating of facial hair to tickle her behind her knees...and then farther.

When he latched on to her hips, his fingertips were so close to one of the scars she thought he glided across it. He touched her intimately, thoroughly, and suddenly she didn't care where he'd touched before.

"Relax, hon, breathe," he whispered.

Had she forgotten to breathe? She certainly hadn't forgotten to feel. Every infinitesimal brush where their skin met was on fire and ready to explode. Breathing she could handle if he would just take her...

Never completing the thought, she fell into a moment of tense nothingness. And then again. She felt like crying for mercy until she realized his hand was on her scar.

The torn flesh was numb to her. No feeling had ever come back. She was both breathing hard from where Bryce had taken her moments ago and holding her breath because of what he'd say.

"Kylie? Is there a chance?" He touched the lucky clover tie. "Trust me."

Whether he really said those words right then or they echoed in her mind from earlier, she didn't know. But she did. She wanted to trust him with all of her and that meant letting him see the scars.

If he was repulsed so be it. But in her heart she knew Bryce was different. There was something in the way he looked into her eyes and understood.

Scooting away from him, she saw his shoulders droop in apparent defeat. He couldn't see that she was heading to him to remove his blindfold. He jerked in surprise when her hands touched his handsome face.

Once she'd pushed the tie onto his forehead, his eyes started to blink. She put her palm across them, keeping them closed before he could focus. They were face-to-face, knee to knee on his giant bed.

He took her hand in his, and kept his eyelids closed hiding the cinnamon brown beneath, but not the attention he gave her or his patience.

"You don't have to be afraid to take this next step or to go the distance with me, Kylie." He cupped his chin with her hand and leaned into it, then kissed her palm. "I won't let you down. Promise."

It was time to share the last bit of herself.

"Open your eyes."

Chapter Sixteen

Bryce opened his eyes and Kylie turned on her left side. It was easier to hide. At least until he made a move to really look. She hadn't paid attention that the bedroom lights had been on, suddenly wishing she'd turned the brighter ones off.

No regrets now. She'd enjoyed looking at Bryce's body. She couldn't deny that most of her life had been around beautiful people and she knew how to appreciate the contours of his body.

She looked up at him, attempting not to be in a rush. Yet, her heart raced and the heat of his stare made her flush.

He gently nudged her to her back. "I imagined your bra as red."

"I don't own anything red. I hate that color."

"I'll remember that. The pink is sexy. Did the underwear match?"

She nodded, biting her lower lip. His grin disappeared when he noticed the healed wound above her hip. His fingers traced it. And like before, she felt his fingertip around the edge but not the actual scar.

"Where are the others?"

She pointed under her arm. "The jagged rip had never been repaired correctly."

"Why?"

"I didn't hang around the hospital longer than I had to. Especially after they pulled the protective detail. When it happened there wasn't time and when there was time, there was no money for a plastic surgeon."

He stretched out along her left, pulling her into the curve of his body. She felt so protected it hurt to realize how much she'd longed for it. He caressed both scars. Seriously caressed.

Over the years, she'd never imagined getting close to someone again. Never dreamed that she'd be intimate. Wondering how a lover would react had always been intertwined with her horrified repulsion.

"Your body was made for me to make love to it." Bryce spread his large hand across her tummy, then up again to her breast.

He teased the flesh at the edge of the satin. Feathery light caresses back and forth from her ear to thigh. Touches that almost said more, teasing her as much as she had him.

Propped on one elbow, he got her excited with one hand. She relaxed into his body and let him push the strap down over her shoulder. His lips and teeth nipped on her skin and then closer and closer to the flesh she wanted him to devour.

Bryce kissed until only skin was between them. Somehow the protection of her bra was gone as he twirled her nipple under his tongue. His movements had been subtle and delicate, then he moved on top of her, cupping both of her breasts into his hands.

His fingers found her last secret, the one she could hide under the bright pink satin. The most horrific reminder of all… He paused only for a second—if that long—raising himself on one arm and forcing her to meet his eyes.

"I've wanted to tell you this since I first met you in Hico." He dramatically paused, no smile, his brown eyes darting to every inch of her face. "You're too beautiful for words."

Kylie threw her arms around his neck, pulling him to her so their lips met. Their hips meshed together and they rocked in a frenzy. Bryce remembered the condom. She watched while his hands shook a little adjusting it into place.

Then they danced for real. A tempo that was faster than a waltz. What did someone call a dance that grew to a crashing crescendo? It didn't matter.

Kylie felt alive. In fact, she felt *everywhere*. The tips of her fingers and toes were electric. There was a buzzing in her ears as the world was blocked out and Bryce spun her out of control. And spun her again until he joined her.

The exhaustion was just like they'd danced the night away.

They lay tangled in each other's arms and legs. She was getting self-conscious and was moving to grab the sheet when Bryce's hand landed on her left breast. His fingers gently caressed the far side and the bullet's path.

"You survived, Kylie," he said into her shoulder. "There's nothing ugly in that."

Bryce was well on the way to another nap. Definitely a nap. She'd let him rest for a moment before she reached for that second package and let him twirl her on their private dance floor again.

The music was still playing downstairs. She heard it while trying not to cry at his simple, beautiful words. Trying not to fall in love with him a little more than she already was.

BRYCE WASN'T USED to eight hours of sleep. Hell, he wasn't used to six hours of sound sleep. The closer the Tenoreno murder trial had gotten, there'd rarely been a reason not to work late, or travel, or bring work home with him.

He was awake with the dawn and strategically getting out of bed without disturbing Kylie. He pulled on swimming trunks and did something rare. He swam laps. Short ones because the pool wasn't designed for that sort of thing, but laps nevertheless.

And during his time in the water he only had time to think. He cared about Kylie and didn't want her to return to Hico. There wasn't any logical reason for her not to. He knew she wouldn't stay away. How could he expect her to agree when all of her friends were going to such extremes setting the trap?

Yeah, she was the bait. But was bait necessary for this fishing expedition? He was an idiot for blabbing the plan before thinking it all the way through. He started the coffeemaker and grabbed a shower downstairs just in case she was still asleep.

There'd been no hesitation making love to him a second time. No hiding on her side or behind a bra. Just wanton sexual satisfaction for them both.

Was it? Not for him.

He didn't just care about Kylie helping with his plan. He cared about her. But he'd already known that.

"Good morning." She practically sang the words through a smile he hadn't seen since she'd told the kids he was buying pizza. "I smelled that coffee while I was in the shower. Is it strong?"

"Strong enough."

"As in standing a spoon in the cup and I should use some milk? Or is it actually drinkable?"

"Milk."

She opened cabinets like he had the first time after his mom had the place redone. Logically looking for coffee cups, closest to the coffeemaker. "Are you grumpy first thing every morning?"

"Not usually. I've been thinking." *And thinking. And thinking.*

She paused with the coffee carafe midair. "Trying to think of a reason for me not to be a part of your trap, I suppose."

"Yep."

"There's only one thing that will keep me out of Hico. Call the whole thing off." She poured two cups, then milk into one.

"I've weighed that option. If I call it off, you'll never be safe. But there is a chance if we go through with the Hico plan. It's up to you whether we take it." He was so mixed-up about what she should do. Had his mind shut down because they'd made love? He honestly didn't know which was better for her. Each plan carried its own set of risks. He didn't like either of them.

"I knew there was something I liked about you."

She set the cups down and was close enough for him to snag then pull into his lap. He didn't have to think long on whether to thoroughly kiss her. "Good morning." Man, oh man, he loved her lips.

"So there's a couple of things I like." She winked.

"Nothing I can say to change your mind? I'm not exaggerating about how dangerous it is."

"You were very clear about that when you were explaining and reminding me how close we came to being shot last weekend. I watched your eyes when the realization hit you that someone might get hurt. It's dangerous for everyone. Even you." She reached for the coffee, changed her mind and kissed him instead. "I know you'll take every precaution. You're moving everyone from the houses around mine, hoping that limits the people involved."

"Someone might get hurt anyway."

"Yes, that's true." She looked as if she drifted into a memory.

"I haven't forgotten your friends in Austin. And I haven't forgotten that your mother-in-law and her friend were assassinated. That's six people in your life who have already died."

"Just don't let the next one be you." She tapped him on the tip of his nose and smiled softly. "I don't know if I can handle that."

The debate he'd been having with himself turned into full-blown doubt. How could he have expected her to face their unknown opponent? She wasn't a professional. She hadn't even asked for his help.

Yet, here she was accepting his plan of action as the only choice she had. She moved to a chair and sipped at her coffee.

"I want you to know that it took all my willpower to let you get some rest this morning instead of making love to you again." He picked up his mug. "Pretty much still true."

"We'll have more time together after this is finished. Want some eggs or do we need to get on the road? Have you talked to Fred?"

"You believe that, right? You're not just saying we'll have more time because it sounds good?" He had a moment of panic that if all things didn't go well, she'd disappear again. She was already good at it and this time she had a town full of reasons.

"Don't you believe it?"

"Well, yeah. But I'm the kind of guy that knows what he wants and goes after it." And when all was said and done...he wanted her.

"So am I what you want, Ranger Johnson? Or am I an assignment you need to finish? Maybe you should think about that before you answer."

He didn't need to think. Realizing that she needed to wait, well, that was okay. He could handle that she needed time. A lot had happened in the past week.

A lot more would happen in the next couple of days.

"How do you like your eggs? I noticed you have some biscuits, too. Those are the two things I can make with confidence. Besides tea, lemonade and sangria." She pushed back from the table. "It's a solid plan. I'm glad you came up with it. And knowing Fred like I do, there's no telling what he would have done otherwise."

"I'll give Fred a call and make sure everything's set. Cook whatever you want. We're not in a rush."

"Famous last words." She gathered her items.

He retrieved his phone, but planned to call Fred on speaker so Kylie could hear. Fred would want to know she was all right. Biscuits were in the oven and she cracked eggs in the bowl. He walked in just in time to catch her fishing out a piece of eggshell.

"Don't laugh at me."

"Oh, I'm not. I'm a terrible cook. If you use a larger piece of the shell, you can scoop it out faster for some reason. Learned that after crunching my own eggs a couple of times."

She used half the eggshell and started whipping the eggs. "Good tip. Where did you learn that? In fact, I hardly know anything about you."

"You know all the important things."

"Right." She nodded her head with an all-knowing smile. "You don't care what your house looks like. You don't like sunscreen, burn and then tan. You have a pool you rarely use. You know how to chop wood. And you're pretty good in bed. Did I miss anything?"

He laughed with her.

"I have four nephews I like a lot. I was raised on a ranch about three hours west of here."

"Really? A ranch with horses and cows, those sorts of things?"

"Yes." He looked toward the eggs, trying to get her attention without jumping up to mix them around the hot pan. She had a list of questions, genuinely excited about visiting a ranch. He lifted a finger pointing to the stove. It didn't work.

"Do your parents still live there?"

If the eggs she scrambled were a burned mess, he'd eat every bite. He admired her effort for trying. He remembered his mom's one or two tries at cooking. She and Kylie would have at least one thing to talk about. Now all he had to do was tell her she'd be meeting them that afternoon.

"I guess you'll find out soon enough," he answered.

Were they hiding their anxiety about luring the shooters into the open by talking about his family? Did he care as long as she remained relaxed and calm?

"Oh, you mean providing we survive this adventure and live to start the next." She finally scrambled the egg mixture in the pan.

"Well, sort of." He checked his text messages. His dad expected them around two and said that the ranch was guest free. "I think those biscuits might be done. Did you set a timer?"

"I didn't see one." She left the pan, pulling drawers open to find a pot holder.

"Want some help?"

"No. Go ahead and call Fred." She waved the oven mitt over the very dark brown biscuits.

"I think I'll wait till after breakfast." *And I'm sure the house hasn't burned to a crisp.*

"What are your parents like?"

He shrugged, wanting to jump up and pull the pan from the burner. "Normal, I guess." He stayed put because he'd never seen Kylie so relaxed.

"Am I being too nosy asking why you let your mother hire a decorator? Why would they want to spend all that money on something you don't really like?"

"Shoot, it's worse than that. She spent my money."

"I thought you said you worked for the Texas DPS Highway Patrol before joining the Rangers."

"I did." He slurped his coffee watching the real question form in her eyes. She wanted to know how he could afford it. "My family's business is, let's say, a successful one."

"Well, that's good. Hopefully you don't have to worry about it while you're working here."

No worries at all. She'd find out that money wasn't an issue when she met his parents that afternoon. It would be safer to hang out there, surrounded by all his dad's security. Bryce intended on taking her yesterday before he'd been distracted in the pool. And other things.

Something was different about her... It was right in front of him. He could see the skin on her arms. She wasn't wearing a long-sleeve shirt. His heart did a backflip. He couldn't make a big deal about it. He wanted to, but his instincts told him no.

He also wanted to destroy the person who had marred her with that scar. Wanted to put them away where they couldn't hurt or kill anyone again. His gut told him that was a strong possibility.

But not now. Today was meet-the-parents day and he didn't know if Kylie was ready for Cheryl and Blackhat Johnson.

Chapter Seventeen

Kylie loved the drive to the ranch. They hadn't been silent because of tension or arguing. Just the opposite. She'd spent most of the ride asking questions about her new phone. They listened to one of his songs and then she'd skip forward until she found one she liked. Bryce looked casual behind the wheel, but there was a layer of tension she assumed was because they had to be on guard.

When they arrived at the gate, the guard on duty recognized Bryce and waved him through. Kylie stiffened in her seat, finally feeling the tension obviously flowing from Bryce.

"This isn't a big deal, right?" she asked. "I mean... there's not going to be twenty questions or anything about how we met? No misunderstanding why I'm here?"

"I explained everything to my dad already and he said we could stay in the guesthouse. It might just be meals?" Bryce shrugged not really committing or answering her question.

They got out of the truck and he tangled their lips together in a deep kiss. It would have lasted longer, but they were interrupted by someone clearing his throat.

"Want me to come back later?"

"Dad!"

"That would be me. Who's this?"

Bryce turned back to her, bringing her close to his side. "Kylie Scott, this is my dad, Blackhat Johnson."

"Pleased to meet you and have you here at the Rockin' J. Cheryl is going to flip when she sees you. Come on to the main house."

"You did tell her that we want to stay in the guest-house?"

"Sure thing. Why wouldn't I?" He shrugged shoulders just as broad as his son's. "Course, she's not standing for that. Main house or the barn. Yeah, I think that's what she said."

"Dad." Bryce stretched the word into three syllables like a kid.

A striking woman almost as tall as Kylie ran across the yard and threw herself into Bryce's arms. She kissed his check with a loud, artificial smack and then pushed him away. It took a few seconds for it to register that it must be Bryce's mother.

"You're such a bad kid to stay away from home like you do."

"Good to see you, too, Mom."

"You know I'm teasing. So this is Kylie? I'm Cheryl and we're so glad to have you visit. Are you sure we can't invite a couple of people over—"

"No one," Bryce interrupted and pulled Kylie back to his side.

Bryce had his arm around her as they passed through the side door. He was quickly tugged away from her by his dad and replaced by his mom. Cheryl escorted her inside and through a ginormous foyer.

"Are you guys tired? Want to retreat to a bedroom, hon? We have plenty of those." His mother ignored the shaking of Kylie's head and waved at a woman cleaning the stove. "Lorie G, sweetheart, can you please make up one of the rooms that opens to the patio? That will be nicer for Kylie in the morning. Do you swim, hon?"

"She just got here, Mom. Can't the interrogation wait a bit?"

"We're all so excited to meet a friend of our son's. And, Bryce Johnson, am I supposed to ignore our guest because she just arrived? How long has it been since you both ate? Johnson! Where is that man?"

"He's checking on extra security, Mom."

"There's more security out there than the President's ranch. So food? Rest? Or just a big margarita?"

"Mom." Bryce sang her title like the kid who had said "Dad" earlier.

"Bryce, go help your father or go see what's in the fridge. Either way…you leave us alone for a while. It's been so long since I've gotten the scoop from anyone younger than me. Especially a woman."

Kylie loved Bryce's mom instantly. She was bubbly and so full of life moving through the simple ranch house— her inaccurate description of the twenty-odd-room house and studio.

Cheryl Johnson had memorabilia sitting around and loved talking about where each piece had come from. The house was one hall after another. The center of everything could be considered a great room with a huge fireplace in the middle. Bryce's mom encouraged Kylie to look around, asked if she enjoyed margaritas and went to the bar to make a pitcher.

Kylie didn't mention she didn't drink. The explanation would bring the conversation back to her own past. She was more curious about Bryce and his family.

"Is the dragon from China?" Kylie wasn't about to pick it up. She'd had a similar very expensive piece in her former life.

"Yes, Johnson brought that back from a tour when I was

pregnant with the youngest. I normally traveled with him back then. That ivory carving of an elephant is something he picked up from the Japan tour for Bryce when he was three. At least I think that was the year."

Tour? It would be insulting to ask what kind of tour. That's something you should know before staying overnight with the parents. Right? She had no clue since Bryce hadn't mentioned it. Or anything other than that their business was successful.

Next to the dragon was a set of drumsticks and a picture encased in crystal. It looked as though it was Bryce's parents and...

"Isn't that Duff McKagan from Guns N' Roses?"

"Yes. Johnson was an emergency replacement for a Dallas concert. It was sweet of him to send us that as a thankyou." She stirred the ingredients.

"He tried to pick me up at a party once."

"I had to keep a close eye on our baby girl when she came to a concert. All four kids performed on stage at one time or another with Johnson, but when she got older, guys would hit on her, too." Cheryl shook her head, tsking under her breath. She poured salt onto a plate then began dipping the glass rims. "We've got all their pictures in the movie room. Go ahead and take a look. I'll bring these in a sec."

It was hard not to want to take a peek. After everything that had happened, Kylie was ready for some normalcy and alone time. If she retreated to her bedroom, she'd break down. She'd rather be curious about Bryce and his life before becoming a Texas Ranger.

The movie room had four sections of wall space dedicated to family pictures. Each featured a different child. Three were performance pics of Bryce's siblings from various ages to adulthood, some with celebrities, some on stage alone. But the ones she was most curious about had one picture with a famous singer and then...horses.

"He was barely five there and such a cutie. I think he wore his hair slicked back for a couple of weeks rehearsing for that show."

"Is that really Frankie Valli?"

"Oh, yes. Johnson has played with just about everybody. It's been a wild ride at times." Cheryl handed her the margarita, then pointed at the back of the stage in the picture. "See that miniature drum set? Bryce played those."

Kylie held the cold glass, but didn't have a real desire to take a sip. That was Sissy's thing and didn't really interest her any longer.

"It was just one song, Mom. And I was so bad, Dad never asked me to do it again." Bryce laughed and took the margarita from her hand, sipping before he pulled her close. "I like the rodeo pictures better."

"You just preferred horses," Blackhat said over his wife's shoulder. "You were never bad, son. Where did you get that idea?"

"There's much more to that story than either of them is willing to tell." Cheryl looked back and forth between father and son. "Seriously, you don't remember, Bryce?"

"I remember it was an awful experience."

"Do you really not remember what happened that night?" his dad asked.

Bryce shook his head. His parents stared at each other.

When no one continued the conversation, she was torn about asking. Kylie was super curious. More than wondering what would happen to the Tenorenos. Not as much as imagining what might happen in her new relationship with Bryce. She could ask Bryce later, but he seemed genuinely in the dark so she wouldn't be able to find out later from him.

"I really don't know what they're talking about," Bryce answered.

"Do you mind if I ask what happened?" She looped her

fingers around his upper arm and tugged him to stay put. Did she have the right? She didn't know. But she wanted it. Since he stayed, she hoped it was willingly because he didn't mind her knowing.

Cheryl looked at Blackhat and he shrugged. "Beats me why he doesn't remember. Maybe he's stared at his computer screen too long and it fried his memory circuits."

Cheryl playfully swatted him, then hugged his arm, weaving her fingers through his. "That oldies benefit was in Austin. Johnson was playing for several artists. Bryce performed and I was waiting at stage left for him. He exited stage right and before I could make my way around to that side, he'd disappeared. He was gone for about half an hour."

"You guys never talked about this." Bryce's muscles tensed under her palms. He looked at her, confused. "It's the first I'm ever hearing about going missing."

"It's why we bought this place," his dad laughed. "Don't you remember getting that badge Mom keeps on the kitchen bulletin board?"

"The toy star?"

"Honey…" Cheryl gave him an all-knowing look only a mother could. "That's the real thing given to you by the man who found you. After that you didn't want to have anything to do with the drums. Like your dad said, we bought this place. You learned how to ride and were focused on becoming a Texas Ranger."

"Where did he go? Did someone try to kidnap him?" Now Kylie wanted the entire story.

"He never told us. He was found several blocks away. Good thing you knew your name. The ranger knew the song you were singing and had a feeling you belonged to someone at the '60s benefit concert. Bryce made it back before the police could begin their search. That's why the papers and television never got the story."

"You've never sung since," his dad said.

"He sang for me," she admitted before thinking much about the importance. All three faces brought the significance to her attention.

"Was it 'Can't Take My Eyes Off You'?" Cheryl asked in a whisper.

"Yes."

"Cool," Cheryl and Blackhat said together. They looked at each other and hugged, shaking their heads. Then Cheryl let out a soft *squeee*.

"Don't read anything into that." Bryce dropped his chin to his chest.

Kylie tried. Really tried not to believe what his parents were implying. But it didn't work. She spent the rest of the night thinking of what could be right with Bryce instead of everything that had been wrong for so long.

KYLIE WAS LYING next to Bryce on the patio listening to music later that afternoon. His parents had left them alone just a few minutes before. She was drifting, letting the hot sun hypnotize her into deep oblivion. Someplace she didn't have to wonder about what would happen tomorrow.

"Still awake, Kylie?"

"If I have to be." She was completely content not to move or think.

"I don't think it's necessary for you to go to Hico and draw these guys into the open. Just bringing the car to the house should accomplish that. It's safer if you stay here with Dad's security. I spoke with my father earlier and he's cool with it."

She couldn't raise her voice to argue. She also couldn't make an argument for or against a plan that he hadn't told her about yet.

They'd been sitting in silence and she'd actually thought he'd fallen asleep. Kylie turned to her side, leaning on her elbow. She attempted to be calm even though her heart was racing ninety to nothing at his out-of-the-blue decision. "If the plan isn't safe enough for me, then call the whole thing off."

"It's still a good plan that could work."

"Then I need to be a part of it."

"But—"

"No buts. No exceptions. I have to do this. I thought you understood that." They hadn't explicitly said the words aloud. But she had thought he understood because she'd been included from the beginning.

"I get it. I just…"

"Last week at my house convinced me that no one is safe around me. Even if I start over in another town, maybe even in another state, I'd be putting people in danger. I have to face whoever tried to kill me five years ago, Bryce. No more running. No more people hurt because of me."

He took her hand in his and rolled to his back. "I had to try."

And so did she…only she needed to succeed.

Chapter Eighteen

The outside walls and windows had been repaired on her house—or Fred's house since he was the one that rented it to Kylie. The inside had been picked up, swept clean of glass and the destroyed items removed. The bedroom was okay and her laptop was safe inside that room.

After the drive, she excused herself and checked on her gun safe. The handgun was still in the bathroom. Either Bryce had forgotten about it, or he trusted that she at least wouldn't pull it on him.

"Officer Harris and Fred made certain everyone was off the street." Bryce told her when she joined him in the living room. "I'm surprised that everyone was so cooperative."

"Why here? Why couldn't we do this at Fred's place outside city limits?"

"We talked about it and agreed they'd think it was a trap."

"But not this? I mean, it's summer and there are no kids on the block. No one driving anywhere."

"We can't have everything."

"In the meantime, we're sitting ducks here. Will the walls hold up if they start firing that cannon at us again? Fred didn't have time to get another refrigerator." She hadn't been thrilled with the idea of trying to trap the men after her. Honestly, she'd agreed solely because she knew Bryce and Fred had already committed to it. The wheels had been put into motion without her.

"It'll be okay." Bryce wrapped his arms around her, hugging tight. "I've been wondering—only a little, mind you—about something."

"What are you wondering only a little about?" She tried to smile at his attempt to cheer her.

"How come there's no Mister Kylie?"

"If you're asking why I'm not married, I didn't want to become involved with anyone with this—" She drew a circle around her. "—situation hanging over my head. It wasn't fair to bring anyone else into the uncertain future I have."

"Had. We're remedying part of that problem today."

She wished. Hoped. Prayed it would be over. "How about you? Why aren't you married yet instead of just uncle of the year?"

"Haven't met that right person. My dad once looked at my mom and told me to fall in love completely. Not halfway. I can't tell you how many times he said not to expect the person you love to fill you fifty percent. 'It's all the way or not at all.' One hundred percent all of you…that's love."

"Those sound like song lyrics."

"Probably. My dad is a drummer, remember?" He shrugged. "I've never been that much in love with anyone. But I figured if it worked for my parents, maybe I should wait for the real thing."

Bryce's phone buzzed and they separated for him to look at the message.

"Fred just texted. He just got to town. He stopped at the Koffee Cup to buy pie."

"Nothing like setting priorities."

"Good move. We get pie and somebody might see the car since the shop is on the corner." Bryce rubbed his hands together in a greedy motion.

"You better tell him to get coffee, too. The coffeemaker was shot to pieces."

Bryce typed a text and looked up. "I'm going to open the garage so he can drive inside." He pointed to the folding chair and what lay on top of it. "Time to put that on."

"You're not wearing yours."

"I will be. The vest is the only way I can protect your heart." He left through the front, stopping on the porch to tap on his phone.

The bulletproof vest was heavy. Bryce had already adjusted it to fit her. She assumed one of the police officers had borrowed it for her since HICO PD was printed across the front and back.

It was only a few minutes until they had plastic forks in one hand and pie containers in the other. Bryce stood next to the front window, Fred at the back. She sat in a folding chair in the hallway.

"I can't believe I didn't know about this pie. I've driven through Hico a lot over the years to get to the ranch." Bryce put another mouthful of banana blueberry cream into his mouth, then another. He looked guilty. What had he said? Was he afraid Fred would frown on his background?

"Your parents never stopped either?" Fred asked.

"No, sir. They don't drive much."

"I thought you said they traveled a lot and you stayed home."

"I did. I mean, they did travel. Do. My dad's a pilot. They own a sweet Piper Cherokee that they take to major airports." He scraped the bottom of his container. "My dad's threatened to fly and get a gallon of milk before. The Rockin' J is a long way from everything."

"Wait a minute. Your parents own the Rockin' J?" Fred asked like everyone knew what that meant. "Blackhat J is your dad?"

"I knew he was a drummer and has played with some

famous people." Kylie quirked an eyebrow in his direction. "They never implied that people would recognize his name."

"Kylie, Blackhat J has played with the best rock and roll bands in history. He's in the Rock and Roll Hall of Fame. You met him?"

"I stayed there the past couple of days."

"It's no big deal. He's just a drummer." Bryce supplied reluctantly, shrugging. "I'd be happy to change the subject now. And would appreciate it if you kept this info to yourself, Fred."

"If you insist." Fred looked a little sulky.

"So he and your mom traveled and you stayed at home?" She reminded him of one of the few things he'd said about his family. "You don't fly much?" Sarcastically adding.

"Not commercially. And I did stay home, traveling made me sick as a kid. When I was a teen, I had commitments at school. My siblings didn't feel the same way and traveled all over the place. But I knew what I wanted and the only way to get it was to stay in school, go to college."

It was the first time she'd seen Bryce flustered, embarrassed, talking too fast. He didn't seem to enjoy his parents' status and looked uncomfortable.

"How come the Rangers didn't play up who your daddy was? They make big deals of politicians and military grads all the time." Fred finished his pie and took a long gulp of his coffee.

"I didn't tell them." Bryce's pie was set to the side as he looked through the blinds. "Changing the subject, we're sure all the houses were cleared?"

"Yes. Harris and I checked in with everyone."

"Even the house on the corner that normally has the big rig out back?"

"That would be Grant Fenley's place. No one was home

early this morning. His wife has a sister in Meridian. Want me to have somebody follow up?"

"It may be a ceiling fan or something, but the curtain keeps fluttering."

"I can have Harris check it out again—"

"Let's wait." Bryce interrupted and stared out the window. "Something just doesn't feel right."

"You guys told me the plan for getting here. So what happens now?" She was curious, of course. But were they really just going to wait around for an attack? "What do you think those men plan to do?"

"We thought they'd…well…try to get you." Fred scratched his stubble whiskers.

"Even after my confrontation with Xander in Austin?"

Fred plopped all four legs of his chair back to the floor. "What's this? You talked to Tenoreno?"

"He wanted me to sign annulment papers. I got away before he could do anything threatening. You don't need to get upset, Fred." Kylie stood in the hallway, able to see both men, feeling the weight of the situation as well as the bulletproof vest on her shoulders. "Oh, and he acted like he hadn't known I had the car all this time."

"So he didn't think you had the Cadillac? You know, Bryce, that's always bothered me. From the time Kylie drove that classic convertible into town I expected to find a stolen vehicle report on it. That's why I was so fast to believe Kylie was the intended target."

"If they aren't looking for Kylie, then what are they…?" Bryce nodded his head "The car? They actually want the Cadillac. What's inside it? I'm assuming you checked it out?"

"Didn't let her park it here until I did. But there's nothing. Trunk is clear. I searched for blood, debris, drugs. No papers, nothing in the glove box except a bottle of whiskey that I gave to Kylie."

"I didn't know you did all that, Fred."

"Darlin', we might have wanted to play the Good Samaritans when you arrived, but I couldn't have lived with myself if I let you bring drugs into town. I hung up my badge, but not my good sense."

"Why wouldn't Tenoreno report it stolen? If he was after Kylie it would have been the fastest way to find her." Bryce rubbed his forehead as if he was tired of thinking about all the possible whys.

"Unless, he really didn't know I had the car. He said as much in Austin." She'd been trying to piece it together in her mind throughout the morning. "There's one thing Xander didn't mention. The shooting. He didn't smirk or brag or anything like that. Which actually says more. He's the kind of guy who would have pointed out how unsafe it is without him around."

"If the police had picked you up with a stolen vehicle, they could have searched it. So something has to be inside."

"There's nothing in that car," Fred said with more conviction.

"Nothing obvious." Bryce left his window. "Can you get Richard to watch the Fenley house more closely? Kylie, come with me. Fred? Key?"

"There ain't nothing in that car," Fred mumbled, tossing the key. "I'll tell Richard."

Kylie followed Bryce into the garage. He slipped the Cadillac key back onto the ring she'd grabbed from the Tenoreno rack so many years ago.

"What do you hope to find?"

When she got near, he stole a lingering kiss. "I've been wanting that ever since Fred arrived. And have I told you how sexy you look in that vest?"

"Why are you buttering me up, Ranger Johnson?" Kylie smiled at him. Who wouldn't want that smoldering kiss?

"Is it because now that we've *slept* together you think you can ask me to hide and I will?"

"I didn't say a word." He held up his hands as if he was defenseless.

"You're thinking it. Open the trunk and start looking." She raised her voice to be heard inside, "I think you're a very thorough man, Fred. I bet you looked under the seats."

"Yes, ma'am. I think I spent the quarter I found."

"So there's no reason for me to look there." She took a flashlight off the shelf. "I'll slide under the car and see if anything's noticeable."

"I'll do that." He lifted the flashlight from her hand. "You take the trunk so you don't have to take off the vest."

Bryce was under the car before she could think of a response. There was nothing inside the black carpeted area. The ridges were still there from being vacuumed.

She stared into the darkness. It was one of those moments where she really couldn't think of what to do next. Fred had searched the car but she agreed that Xander's interest in the car was unusual. Something had to be here.

"A car doesn't seem like a very safe place to hide something important enough to kill over. It would have to be secure and other than taking the car completely apart, how would we find it? Xander could have bought a safe or rented a safety deposit box. His father had a safe. Why use an old car he rarely drove?"

"We don't have time to unscrew every screw. And I would imagine he wanted to keep it away from everybody or this was a temporary place."

"Except the other person shooting at us. Don't you see? At least two people knew something was hidden. The man shooting at us last week seemed to know about the car, too."

Bryce scooted his head from under the back. "You're right."

"Are you through with the flashlight?" She took it from his extended arm. As soon as he was free from the undercarriage, she crawled in the trunk. "I don't think Fred did this."

She lay on her back and aimed the beam of light into all the nooks and crannies of the car. The light reflected off something shiny stuck way back in the corner toward the seat. She used her feet to push herself closer and found a small lock.

"The key ring that you have, Bryce. Does it have a small one on it like for a lockbox?"

He put them in her hand, fingers around the smallest. She slipped the key into place and turned.

"A safe made for a car?" Fred asked from the doorway.

"Looks like it. Anything inside?" Bryce asked.

"Just this magnetic hide-a-key thingy." She handed it and the flashlight to Bryce. "Wait for me."

Once out of the car, they all stared at the tiny box as Bryce slid the top off. "A flash drive."

"I wonder what's on it?"

"Something to kill for."

"Okay, let's get the hell out of here." Fred whooped on his way up the step.

"Leave? Don't you want to catch those men? You've gone to so much trouble." Kylie dropped the key ring in her jeans pocket hoping they wouldn't listen to her. It was the one time she was playing devil's advocate and not wanting to be right.

"We have what they're after. We leave. Take this drive to Company F and find out what's on it in Waco. There's no reason to hang around here and risk our necks." Bryce stuck the drive in his jeans pocket.

"Fred?" The radio hanging on her friend's belt squawked. "Grant Fenley just drove up to his house. He has his kids with him."

Richard had been watching the street.

"Dammit," the older man said through gritted teeth. "Who let them through? Shoot, it doesn't matter. We'll come up with a plan B."

"It's okay, right?" she asked.

"Get in the car." A confused, worried look overtook Fred's face as he pointed to the convertible.

"No. I can shoot. For gosh sakes, Fred, you taught me how."

Bryce shrugged.

"Sorry, darlin'." Fred took that shrug as Bryce's agreement. "The car's the safest place for you."

"Oh, don't you 'darlin'' me with that sweet cowboy drawl." She tried to march past Bryce but Fred blocked her and shut the door in her face. She heard the dead bolt turn. "I cannot believe you just locked me out of my own house!"

The garage was locked on the outside. No window. At least the light was on. She had the new cell that Bryce had purchased. Those guys weren't going to answer and they weren't going to change their minds. She was definitely stuck.

Chapter Nineteen

"You think she's safe in there?" Bryce asked the retired ranger and received a nod.

The radio walkie-talkie Fred held squawked again. "You want me to stay here or do something? Reckon those curtains are moving because someone's looking through them?" Richard surmised from Bryce's house.

"Tell him to stay put. I'll check it out."

"You guys have to let me out of here!" The shout was faint through the door.

"Forgive us, Kylie. We'll be right back." Fred turned to him. "I guess we should have, like, a knock or something so she'll know it's us."

"Or we could just call out to her. She'll probably recognize our voices."

"Kylie, we'll tell you it's us. If someone opens that door before we get back…find a shovel or something." Fred tapped on the door, indicating his departure. Then the older man turned to Bryce. "I'll keep watch in the backyard while you check things out. No one will get inside here."

If there was a shovel in the garage, Kylie would probably take it to both of their heads when they got back. Bryce motioned for Fred to go out the back door.

"Just in case it's not a fan blowing those curtains, you take the long way and approach Fenley's house from the north. I'll give you a couple of minutes since you have the longer ground to cover." He tapped the radio. "We work together."

"Got it. Put on the vest, son."

"Heading for it now, sir." Bryce had a moment…just a moment where he wanted to say something poignant, but he couldn't think of a thing. They nodded at each other and split. "No matter what happens, keep Richard inside. I'll give Harris a call and tell him the trouble we were expecting may have showed up."

Fred darted to Kylie's big tree in the back, then through the back gate of the privacy fence. He must have removed the locks earlier since there was no pause in the stealth of his journey.

But locking Kylie inside wasn't a great idea. He just didn't have time to explain himself. Bryce did an about-face and unlocked the garage door. Kylie jumped up from the step, dipped her head and marched into the kitchen.

"It's a good thing you came back here, bust—"

Bryce pulled her body to his, capturing her lips and shushing her lecture. "I didn't want to argue with you or Fred. The door is ready for you to open if you need to get out of here fast. Wait." He covered her tender lips with his finger. "*If* things go wrong. Drive straight to the police station. Don't try to outrun them to anywhere else. Got it?"

"This is my fight, I don't want to run."

"Promise me. I need to know you'll be safe."

"I promise. Don't get shot or worse. We have whatever they're looking for now. We can—"

"First we have to get the Fenley family out of there." He saw the panicked look in her eyes, heard the sudden intake of breath as if she was about to make a speech. "I know what you're about to say. That this is your problem and no one else is supposed to get hurt. I want to be clear. Exchanging yourself for them won't help. So don't think about it."

"So you want me to stay here and twiddle my thumbs?"

"Yes. And stay alert listening to the radio. We need you to talk to Hico PD, keep them up-to-date on what's happening. I got to get going."

"Bryce." She sandwiched his face between her palms and kissed him. "Don't be long. We have things to do."

"Yes, we do. Go grab that handgun from behind your picture in the bathroom." He winked at her split-second of astonishment before heading to the front door.

Staying close to the house, he searched the vicinity for guns pointed his direction. He wanted to check out the Fenley house and find everything perfectly normal. They'd evacuate the family and everything would be back on track. But his gut told him this was it. Tenoreno's men had been waiting on them instead of the other way around. He pulled the bolt on the garage so the door could be raised from the inside.

Taking off down the driveway, he pulled the Velcro tight at his ribs and drew his Sig, wishing it was a shotgun. He was better with a shotgun. Easier to hit his target. In this case, the better scenario would be that he wouldn't have a target at all.

Walking in the street, he passed the rooster and hen belonging to Kylie's neighbor. A cat watched them from the bottom limb of a mimosa tree. How the chickens were still alive…no idea.

"Hey, Todd." He kept the phone on speaker. "Things might get hairy around here in a minute."

"I'm at the end of Pecan by the statue."

The Fenley family had two kids, eleven and eight. The rig that Grant drove was out back where it had been absent that morning. A two-foot cement wall outlined the property. A small pink bicycle was safely parked by the front steps.

Porch swing, chairs, small table, birdhouses, plants and

a cow-shaped message chalkboard all worked together to make the place look lived-in. The house itself was long and not too wide. The curtain dropped, covering whoever was behind it.

It wasn't a ceiling fan.

Three or four more steps and he could dive next to that rock wall. He heard the crack of a glass pane and he hit the ground. The street was peppered with bullets just behind him.

The small pieces popped up hitting him in the back, pinning him with his face in the dirt. Small glass-like rocks dug into the back of his left hand. His right still held his Sig close to his chest. When a pause came in the shots, he retrieved his phone and called Todd Harris.

"Shots fired out west window. I'm pinned at the street. Fred's coming from the north, can you approach from the east?"

"Got ya covered."

Bryce was about to signal Fred on the radio, but the shots began in earnest again and stopped just as suddenly. He readied his Sig and risked a look over the wall. The porch screen door was kicked open, bursting the spring and slamming shut. He watched a booted foot toe the door open.

A thirty-something man was pushed forward, stumbling onto the porch, immediately getting to his knees. "Don't shoot! You can't shoot! Please don't shoot!"

"Drop to the ground, Grant," Todd called out.

Bryce couldn't see where the officer was from his position at the wall.

"I can't," the guy on the porch said. "I have to stay here or they'll…they'll kill my kids."

"You okay, Bryce?" Fred asked on the radio. "The shades are drawn. I have no target from my position."

"I have eyes on the porch, but I'm blind for the rest of the house."

"Johnson? Bryce Johnson?" Grant called.

"I'm here."

"They said all they want is a woman named Sissy and a car." Grant turned a bloodied ear toward the door. "I mean the Cadillac. It has to be a Cadillac. Then they'll let my kids go."

"Bryce," Kylie broke in on the radio.

"Out of the question," he shouted, wanting to stand to let them know who was in charge. But his instincts kept him beside that wall.

Behind him he heard the garage door go up. "Kylie, no!" Half into the radio and half down the street, he roared to get her to listen to him. He caught himself. Screaming wouldn't work, he had to reason with this woman he'd come to care about so much.

"We can't trust them, Kylie," Fred said.

"Trust me," he pleaded into the radio.

It was too late. The car was rumbling on the street and she wasn't responding to the radio pleas. She drove slowly. He could have easily run alongside if he'd been across the street.

He rose, ready to move. Shots from the house hit the street just behind him.

"Don't do it, Johnson! God, I'm begging you please. They've got a gun to my son's head." Grant was weeping.

Kylie rolled the window down. "It's my turn to fix the problem, Bryce. I can't let those kids get hurt."

"Johnson," Grant called for his attention. "They want you to throw down your guns. Kylie's supposed to drive. What?" He turned back to the door and reached into the dark room.

Grant Fenley's hands were zip-tied together as he

walked down the porch and sidewalk. "Sorry, Kylie. I need to lock you to the steering wheel."

"I'll be okay, Grant. Don't worry about it." She placed her hands on the wheel again and Grant did as he was instructed then returned to the house.

"I can't just let you drive to your death." Bryce was close enough he didn't have to raise his voice.

"I'm not. I'll meet you in Austin." Her eyes looked toward his pocket. "You still have bargaining power."

He couldn't answer before two masked men—backs together—moved from the house. One carried the little girl. One held a gun to the eleven-year-old's head. Grant wasn't near them.

Both of the kids were blindfolded. Bryce couldn't let this happen. He got to his feet, resting his Sig on the wall and raising his hands in the air.

"We don't want any trouble, Ranger," the one holding the girl said, spinning a little away from his partner.

"Take me instead of the kids."

"No offense," the other man said, "but you won't keep your partners from shooting at us. These guys will."

Bryce didn't move. He didn't even shake his head or look anywhere except into the cocky one's eyes. "Come on, man. Where do you think you can drive this car and not be seen? The State Troopers will have you in their sights or a helicopter will be on your tail by the time you pass the city limits. Why don't you hand over your guns without anybody getting hurt? You tell us who hired you and why, and I'm sure we can make a deal."

"Stay back, Ranger."

"I'm back, I'm back," Bryce answered as calmly as his racing pulse could manage. "But if you take the kids, there's nothing I can help with. You catch my meaning?"

The men's backs were a little farther apart now, inching

their way down the sidewalk. Bryce wanted to rush them himself. He'd have to step up on the two-foot wall and hit the ground running again. He was too far away to use the border wall to his advantage and launch himself from it.

No, he didn't have options. Hands in the air, gun on the rocks, girl cuffed in the car, kids with barrels to their temples. He'd lost.

Or definitely lost control of the situation.

The gunmen were almost at the car and didn't look like they had any intention of releasing the kids. Fred and Todd were within sight. The other police officer sirens were close. He was out of ideas. The situation was about to turn from worst possible scenario to completely—

"You can take me to Xander, but those kids are staying here," Kylie commanded, revving the engine on the Cadillac. "I'm serious. And the only ride you've got."

"Kylie—"

"No one else gets hurt because of me! Does everyone hear that?" she yelled.

"You don't call the shots, bitch. We're in charge."

Bryce closely observed the body movements of the men. One had a looser grip on the boy, but the other shifted the girl and held her tighter.

They weren't letting her go.

Everything happened in seconds…

Two police cars blocked the street running north and south. The mouthy one shoved the boy to the ground. The gunmen both broke into a run, the girl squirming and crying. Bryce scooped up his Sig and aimed. The men ran around the trunk.

The boy was yelling for his father. Grant was screaming from the doorway. The gunmen were fast enough and smart enough to turn in circles, keeping the girl between them and most of the cops.

Multiple gun barrels pointed at the Cadillac.

No one had a shot.

If anyone fired...people would die.

"Hold your fire!" Bryce shouted, pointing his Sig to the clouds. "Hold your fire!"

"Smart choice, Ranger man!" one of them shouted as he jerked open the door and shoved his partner and the girl inside.

Bryce could only stare as they forced the little girl to crawl in the wide back window and both men sank low into the seats. He connected with Kylie as she sadly looked his way, but gunned the engine.

Tires spun on the edge of the road. No vehicles would block their exit past the Billy the Kid statue at the end of the street.

Bryce ran after them. There was no shot to take. They couldn't shoot the tires. If the car rolled the little girl would be killed. If they shot at the men, they could easily kill the girl or Kylie.

"You had to let them go, son. No choice." Fred said, looping an arm across Bryce's shoulders.

Where had this all gone so wrong?

He turned to Todd. "Get on the phone. Company F, police, troopers, statewide bulletin, everything. Do your job and find that car!"

Bryce ran up the street to his truck.

The radio squawked, "They turned east toward Meridian."

Squawked again, "Don't let them see you following!"

Richard and a couple of others stood in the front yards with shotguns and rifles on their hips. They'd tried. They'd all tried. But this was on him. His mistake. He'd let Kylie and the Fenley girl down.

"They really took Darla, too?" Richard asked.

Bryce didn't have time to acknowledge him. He started the pickup, tore out of the driveway and down the street after Kylie. He pressed his contacts for Major Parker. No answer.

Cursing, he banged the steering wheel with the edge of his fist. He was three minutes behind them. He pushed the truck to the max. Six miles out of town. Seven. Eight. Still no sign of them.

"Where the hell did they go?"

Chapter Twenty

The men had used plain zip ties to lock Kylie's wrists to the center of the steering wheel. She could barely turn a corner, but managed. Minutes past the city limits sign, the masked man next to her grabbed the wheel and yanked hard to the right. She thought her arms had cracked as she fell sideways.

Sitting a quarter of a mile away, hidden from the road, was a semi-trailer truck and trailer. That's how they planned on getting away from the police who would be looking for the Cadillac.

"Hand me your phone," the man next to her commanded. "Line up with the ramps."

"I can't turn." He sliced through one of the plastic ties with a pocketknife and got out. She took the phone from her pocket, then lined the car up and was about to kill the engine when he reached through the window and pulled the switch for the top.

While the electric top folded into place between the trunk and backseat, he removed the phone's battery and threw the pieces into the brush. Her hope of Bryce following her with that bit of technology was tossed like the phone. She'd have to be more inventive. But she would get them free.

"Darla, honey. Climb over the seat to sit next to me."

She cooed to the crying girl, trying to calm her until

the men had the top secured and motioned for her to pull onto the ramps. Once inside, a man who'd been waiting in the trailer squeezed along the edge of the car with more zip ties and a roll of duct tape.

Remembering some of the defensive research she'd allowed herself over the years, she flexed her wrists, making them as wide as possible. This man seemed to be younger and didn't realize her little trick would allow her to squeeze free.

Hopefully.

He tore a strip of tape to cover Darla's mouth.

"Please don't. She won't be able to breathe. We won't scream. Right, Darla? Promise him, sweetheart."

"Don't matter. I got orders," he said, reaching toward Darla who shoved herself to the far side of the vinyl seat. Her screams were those of a young child being yanked from her father and used as a human shield.

Kylie wanted to scoop the girl to her side and protect her, comfort her. But her hands were secured. The man pushed Kylie forward into the steering wheel, leaning across her back to reach Darla. The little girl screamed more and at a higher pitch.

"Tell her to shut up!" he yelled.

"Please. Can't you see how scared she is?"

Kylie needed Darla free. Just in case she couldn't slip out of the zip ties, she needed the little girl to help. She saw the hesitation in the younger man's hands. He raised them, then dropped them again.

"Tell her to come over here and I'll do it real loose so she can get it off easy and breathe."

"Darla, did you hear? We can play a game, okay? He's going to put tape over our mouths and then we'll see if you can get yours off first. Okay? Can you do that?"

Darla nodded, looking terrified. But she got to her knees and hesitantly scooted closer. When she locked her hands around Kylie's upper arm, the guy looked somewhat less threatening as he placed the tape first on Darla and then on her. Now, if they'd leave them alone in the trailer…

The two men who had kidnapped Darla came on either side of the car. They yanked on her hands, testing them, and pulled the tie closer to her skin.

If her mouth hadn't been taped shut, she would have cursed like a sailor.

"Tape the kid's hands."

"She's just a kid. What's she going to do?" the younger one still holding the roll asked.

"Don't backtalk me, boy. Just do what I say."

"Yes, sir."

The one giving orders left the truck. Kylie watched him in the rearview mirror. He closed the first half of the double doors shut, bolting it into place. It was the first time in a very long time that hearing a secured lock didn't give her a feeling of elation and comfort.

"You ready, boy?" He began swinging the second door and the light inside their giant box began shrinking.

Darla's body shook next to her. The one referred to as "boy" jumped into the backseat and flipped on an electric camping lantern.

"Got it, sir."

The doors shut.

"If you move, I'll tape your hands and make you sit with me. Got it?"

Darla nodded her head, whimpering beneath the tape.

Kylie couldn't make her feel secure or at ease. All she could really do was breathe deeply through her nose to try to calm the racing of her own heart. Eight years old or not, Darla had a grip. Her fingernails were cutting into her flesh. Kylie hummed.

The lullaby "Mockingbird" immediately popped into her head, more from seeing it in movies than personally hearing it. She hummed, saying the words in her head. There was no way she could slide her hands through the smaller loops around her wrists. Getting free now would involve Darla.

The kid bounced the car a bit as he stretched out. She heard the heels from his work boots hit the side of the car. The big rig lurched forward. She heard a click and they were plunged into darkness. Darla screamed behind the tape.

The one great thing about the horrific afternoon heat was that the inside of the big rig immediately began sweltering. Normally this wouldn't be a good thing. But today it made her upper lip sweat. And sweat helped loosen the tape across her mouth.

Boy, as the guy in charge referred to him, would soon be snoring. The rocking of rig, heat and darkness made it a perfect place to nap. But not relax if you were a captive, headed to a Mafia family to be killed.

Using her shoulder, she rubbed the corner of the tape, peeling it back slowly. Not waiting for it to dislodge from both sides, she lowered her voice, "Sweetie, can you pull the tape off now? It might sting a little. Be brave, little one, and don't cry. Can you do that?"

Kylie had to trust that the little girl was doing as instructed. No light seeped into their traveling box at all. The pitch-black made everything more frightening.

"I ain't asleep so stop trying to put one over on me." Boy clicked on a small penlight. "You both need to chill. We're gonna be here awhile."

Kylie saw Darla blink, then rub her eyes, between her own rapid adjusting. She couldn't see Boy's face, but one arm was relaxed across his belly. The other up and out of her view in the mirror. He was still stretched from window to window.

At least they weren't in the dark any longer. He'd said

they were going to be there awhile. Did that mean Austin or somewhere no one would find them? The truck had been moving slowly and now seemed to be picking up speed.

There were three distinct noises she could hear—the truck, the almost panicked breathing from Darla and the deeper relaxed breathing from the backseat. She leaned forward and pulled the remaining tape from her skin.

It wasn't hard to catch Darla's gaze, she'd latched on to her again as soon as the light had come on. "Shh," she whispered. Kylie used her head to indicate for Darla to come closer.

"Sweetie, I need your help. You've got to be very careful and quiet as a mouse."

"Okay," she whispered as well as an eight-year-old could.

"See that shiny button over there? I need you to get me the knife that's inside."

Darla immediately shook her head.

"I know you aren't supposed to play with them, but this isn't playing. We need to hurry before he wakes up."

Darla hesitated and crawled to the glove compartment. Kylie pulled the steering wheel to the right, trying to turn the wheels and getting there inch by painful inch. Talking the little girl through how to release a zip tie…where was she going to get the descriptive words?

She wished there was a screwdriver, but she hadn't grabbed one from the garage. Just the very sharp utility knife Darla now had in her hand.

Chapter Twenty-One

"What about the cameras we set up on Main Street? They've got to show some traffic. We obviously didn't stop all the vehicles in and out of town. Grant got through." Todd gave instructions over the radio to the other Hico PD.

Bryce was alone in his truck, waiting at the apex of downtown Hico, listening to the radio chatter. All he needed was a direction and he was hightailing it after the Cadillac.

"When Grant got to the road block we instructed him to stay out of town. He agreed to head to his in-laws' place."

"Where is he? Has anybody had eyes on Grant Fenley? I want to talk with him." Fred interrupted inserting his own agenda.

"We're losing time," Bryce broke into the conversation. "Every minute that ticks by is another mile she's away from me. Gone. Got that? Now give me something. Have the additional roadblocks been set up?"

"Nothing's come through Meridian. Over."

He'd missed them. Trying to catch up with the Cadillac, he'd missed that they'd detoured. "They must have pulled off someplace, changed vehicles and come back through town. Todd, have you got that camera footage yet?"

"We let five cars past all with families. One semi rig no markings headed northwest. One semi transporting milk headed northwest. And Grant's red tractor and trailer heading south toward his family's place. Over."

"Somebody better find Grant Fenley. Something's fishy, Bryce. That red tractor couldn't be his. I'm looking at the rig he parked at his house." Fred's curse words broke off. "I think we need to switch to cells. Somebody's probably monitoring police frequencies."

Dammit. His phone buzzed on the seat next to him.

"You think Fenley's in on this?" he asked Fred.

"Yeah. Do you have enough resources to commit to the roads northwest and south?" Fred's voice shook.

"It'll take time to get additional men and roadblocks. And that's what they're counting on. So they're probably closer than we think." Then why did he feel like everything was lost?

"That's my guess, too." The older man sounded resigned as if the same lost thoughts had crossed his mind. "Wherever they take her it'll have plenty of cover, might even be a building."

"A building will be more secure. They could switch rigs that way. Got anyplace around here that fits those parameters?"

"There's a couple of private airstrips in the area if they're planning to take Kylie out by plane."

"Fred, they don't need one. Just a field to land a helicopter and a building to hide the truck from the air."

"True."

Based totally on his gut, Bryce took off to the northwest. "Find Fenley. He's got to be involved, especially if we can track a rig just like his heading south."

"You think that's where they've taken our girls?"

"I can't know for sure, but I'm heading northwest. You head south following Fenley."

"Then you think it's a decoy." Fred sounded reluctant to chase down the least possible route.

Meaning the older ranger thinks they're heading this direction.

"Yeah. Be sure to take Richard with you. I'll call Todd and have him pin down where Fenley's wife could have gone."

The call to Officer Todd Harris was short and to the point. He was already solving the problem of the missing family. If Fenley had cooked up a deal with the kidnappers it didn't include his mother-in-law or his wife, who had her laptop tracing Grant's phone.

The family used a program showing where they were so the kids could find their dad on a map when he traveled across the country. Harris texted the coordinates. Bryce punched Find and never slowed down. Fenley's phone was fifteen minutes ahead in Dublin.

"Fred," he called. "Did you get Todd's text?"

"We've already turned around, but we're probably twenty-five behind you."

"I'll let you know what to expect. If not..."

"None of that, son. Everybody's coming out of this safe and sound. No exceptions."

Dublin PD were notified to watch the area but hang back until Bryce arrived. The call to Major Parker went as expected. The Rangers had been called in as soon as the Fenley girl was kidnapped. Rangers were on their way from different companies. All headed to Dublin, but none of them would get there sooner than him.

The sun shone through the windshield. It was a cloudless, deep blue sky. It would have been beautiful if he hadn't been racing to save the woman he loved. He hated having time to think about what they might be doing to her.

He had time for one more phone call. His stereo flashed Dialing. There was a gravelly hello through the speakers.

"Dad? I need a huge favor."

KYLIE WHISPERED INSTRUCTIONS to Darla, guiding her through sticking the tip of the utility knife in the release square—or whatever it was called—of the zip ties. It wasn't easy. In fact it was as scary as trying to remain undetected while they got it done.

The man guarding them remained asleep, but he could have jerked awake with any of the bumps from the truck. Maybe he'd been awake all night or something. It would explain why he never moved when the knifepoint stuck the back of her wrist and Darla gasped an "I'm sorry."

With one wrist free, Kylie could work the second one herself. The truck was slowing. Was it just for another small town or would they be opening those doors?

Hands free, she moved Darla into the passenger floorboard. "Stay quiet and as small as possible. No matter what happens. Promise?"

"Promise. Sorry I cut you."

"You did great," she whispered, then flipped over, scooted to stretch out until she could search under the driver's seat for the extra key. The tiny thing had stayed wedged where the seat was bolted to the floor. She slipped the key into the change pocket of her Wranglers, then thought better of it.

If someone searched her…she stuck the key back in its secure spot.

It was a long shot, but might get them both out of this mess…or at least be used for bargaining Darla's freedom. But first, she couldn't just wait to talk with Xander or even risk that begging for her life would satisfy him. Even waiting for a Texas Ranger wasn't the smart thing. She had to try to rescue herself.

She drew a deep breath, sitting behind the wheel. Boy had his gun wrapped between his arms and his chest. He was moving like someone about to wake. And the truck was slowing, turning, slowing more.

They'd arrived.

Kylie moved. Climbed. Planted her backside on the top of the front seat with one leg stretched across to the back. She balanced. Breathed. Prepared. She remembered the words of her instructor. Didn't let the importance of what she was attempting freak her out.

And most important, she remembered Bryce's caring touch that calmed her. His confidence made her whole. She had to do this for Darla, for Bryce…for herself.

The truck inched to a stop.

At the same moment she placed her boot heel on the man's throat, she plucked the handgun from his chest. Darla screamed. Boy startled awake, his hands going to her leg. She pulled the trigger over her head. The noise blasted her eardrums and the kickback of the weapon almost toppled her. She regained her balance by throwing both arms toward her captive.

"Let go of me." She removed her foot and straddled the seatback.

The doors opened with at least three guns aimed at her.

"Get up and get behind the wheel," she told Boy. If she could get out of the truck and the parking lot, she'd push this guy from the car and just keep driving until she found the police. "Start the car."

A slow clapping—just one person—started off to the side and joined the men at the back of the truck. All the men deferred to him. He was definitely in charge. And he was definitely *not* Xander.

"Very commendable, Sissy. Or should I call you Kylie now?"

Well-dressed, but in casual cool for Texas heat. He stood shorter than the rest of the men, so that meant shorter than her. He obviously knew who she was, but she didn't recognize him. It fit Bryce's theory that someone unknown to them wanted the car and her.

"Better think twice about your next move, Kylie," he said, hands on his hips. "I already have what I want." He waved his hand toward the Cadillac.

"Let the girl go and I'll do whatever you want." She barely glanced at Darla in the floorboard. "I'll let your man go as soon as I'm around a corner."

This lunatic would never let her drive away.

"You're mistaken, thinking I care about either of them. Again…" He waved a finger and the guns were aligned with her heart once more. "I already have what I want. You're only a bit of insurance."

He stepped from the area that she could see and spoke in a low grumble. Two additional men pulled the ramps over to a loading dock. Even if she could get the car out of the semi, she'd be stuck inside some sort of warehouse.

"What could you possibly want? There's nothing in this car. We've looked."

"Did you know that I restored this beauty? I lost her in a spur of the moment bet with your husband. The kind where I drove up in the Caddy and was left on a street corner before I could remove my belongings."

"Please just let us go. We have nothing to do with this."

"Bring him."

Bryce? Her heart dropped. Had he followed them as they left Hico and been caught trying to rescue her? His face was backlit by a warehouse light. She couldn't tell. The clothes were wrong. Tennis shoes, not boots. Bryce was still out there.

There was still hope if her ploy didn't work.

"I'm sorry, Kylie. They took my family," Grant Fenley said.

She might not be able to see his face, but she could see the gun pointed at his head. Without being told she dropped the weapon outside the car and watched it bounce underneath. Boy hopped over the door and she sank onto the seat, extending her arms for Darla to crawl to her lap.

"Don't get the idea that you bargained with me, Sissy," whatever his name was said. "If Xander had treated you the way I suggested, putting you in your place a couple of times, he would never have had you as a problem."

What?

This egotistical bastard thought he could have told Xander how to put her in her place five years ago. So he had been a part of her life back then. More importantly, he knew what was locked in that hidden safe.

What would happen if he realized the flash drive in the safe wasn't the right one? How was she going to protect Darla then?

Chapter Twenty-Two

"Kylie isn't heading to Austin. It's not Xander threatening her, although his involvement can't be completely ruled out." Bryce parked the truck as far as he could from the deserted grocery store where the Cadillac had been taken. "Fenley is a hostage. There must have been a third gunman in the house who forced him to drive the rig they put the car into."

"Wait on us, Bryce," Fred said over Richard stating something similar. "Don't rush in there on your own."

Kylie's ex-husband's path had crossed many times with the man giving the orders on that loading dock. Bryce knew everyone involved in the Tenoreno family dealings. Crime boss Daniel Rosco was considered a family friend.

Both the only sons of the Texas Mafia. Raised to be cruel and ruthless. He'd seen the file of accusations that should have had this man in prison a decade ago. Rosco's father had been brutally murdered by an assassin most likely hired by Xander Tenoreno.

So was this a revenge killing on the ex-wife? Or was something on the flash drive currently in his front pocket?

"I don't have eyes on Kylie or the girl yet. I need to get closer to see what's going on." And find out if Kylie was okay. He'd heard her name yelled by Fenley, but couldn't see past the semitrailer.

"Bryce—"

He disconnected. There wasn't any choice. He was the only person who could identify the kidnapped girl and Kylie. The Dublin police weren't equipped to deal with a hostage situation.

Hell, he wasn't either. There was just no choice.

Reversing the truck, he parked in front of the Dublin cop who became his shadow as soon as he'd hit town. Bryce could swear the young kid barely looked old enough to drive. The local PD had spotted the truck, notified him and retrieved a key to the building from the owner.

Bryce verified his phone was on Silent and grabbed his weapons. He handed the flash drive to Officer Trent Dawson, who knew enough of the story to copy the files onto his laptop. Bryce was most concerned about the kid opening them and becoming more involved. It was a risk he had to take. The state needed to see whatever was there, but Bryce needed the drive on his person for leverage.

Trent returned the drive and Bryce issued instructions that would be passed along to the other locals. They'd also be relayed to Fred and anyone else who showed up to help. Then he took off for the opposite side of the store-front, used the key to enter and began to snake his way through the empty aisles, reaching the back hallways to the warehouse.

"You would rather I hurt this beautiful little girl and her father? Come on, Sissy. Just hand over the key."

"The keys I had to that car were in the ignition. I don't know anything else about keys or secret safes. I took half a bottle of whiskey from the glove compartment and—"

Bryce heard the slap. Open palm flesh hitting her cheek.

"Beating me, or any of us, won't change the facts. If there's a lock, can't one of your thugs pick it?"

Bryce inched around the corner.

He had a side view of what was going on. Rosco had

father and daughter off to the side. They'd faced the girl against the wall, wearing headphones and playing a game. Her father was taped to a chair next to her. Kylie was leaning against the open car trunk.

He wanted to rush in, guns blazing…okay, gun, he only had one, which wouldn't go far.

Plain and simple…the hostages would be killed.

A confrontation before backup got here…he'd be overpowered, they'd search him, they'd find the drive and he'd be left with no bargaining power.

There was no way to let Kylie know he was there. No way to warn her or the others. Maybe that was Fenley's phone his daughter was playing on. The headphones would keep any notification sound silent. But what if it wasn't?

Rosco turned and opened his palm. Wordlessly, a gun was placed in it. He swiveled and pointed it at Kylie's forehead. Bryce gripped the edge of the corner, ready to spring forward. He'd never get there in time. He raised his Sig and took aim.

KYLIE DIDN'T REMEMBER Daniel Rosco. She searched her memory but couldn't come up with anything. A friend of the Tenorenos or maybe even an enemy. Whoever he was, there was something dead in his eyes that was more frightening than she'd ever experienced.

His gun was about three inches from her eyes. She'd never stared down a gun barrel before. It took a lot of willpower to stand there and not move. One of his men stood next to her ready to keep her in place.

"I don't have it. I don't know what you're talking about," she lied.

"Say I believe you. Someone has checked that car. It's been polished, vacuumed. Who?" Rosco asked, shrugging and dropping the barrel to point at her toes. "Bring him. Take the girl to my car."

Once Darla was outside, he turned the gun toward Grant. She didn't doubt that Rosco would pull the trigger. He inched closer and closer.

"All right. Stop. It's me. I'm the only one that knew about the extra key." She held her hands up as Rosco's gun pointed at her face again. "I hid it under the driver's seat just before I was abducted by those monsters."

Don't antagonize them. She could hear Bryce's voice in her head even though she was certain he'd never said those exact words before. She didn't really have a choice. She couldn't let him hurt Grant or Darla.

"That's closer to the truth. Get the key." Rosco used the barrel as a pointing stick toward the car.

"Mr. Rosco, you want us to check around the building? Make sure everything's secure?" The one who had ridden in the back asked, shifting from foot to foot.

"Stay put. I don't want to draw any attention to this place. No one knows where we are or even *who* we are."

Except Grant, Darla and me.

She took her time, not about to rush anything. The slower she moved the more time Bryce had to find them. She stroked the Cadillac's fin-shaped fender. "So when did we meet, Daniel? It couldn't have been at the Tenoreno Christmas party. They only invited friends to that."

"We were invited, but didn't attend. Xander and I ran into each other at a club opening. He had you draped on his arm."

Kylie took a deep breath seeking a calm place before she opened the passenger door and stretched across the seat to find the key. She knew exactly where it was, but stalled a little and took her time.

"Kylie?" Grant sounded frightened.

She looked over the edge of the car, scooting to her knees. The gun was back against Grant's temple. She held the key up. "I found it."

"Let's get something straight, Sissy. I've had some restless nights recently and I'm ready to head home. No more delays."

She tossed the key at his feet. "What incentive do I have to comply? Aren't you going to kill us anyway?"

"Oh, God, not Darla! You can't—" Grant got a face full of metal for his outburst. He fell to the warehouse floor.

Kylie searched the room for a possible place to run. And that's when she saw Bryce. He'd found them. He signaled to keep stalling. Hopefully that meant there were more officers coming. She had to trust him and get close to Grant so she could let him know. She hurried to her neighbor's side.

"Open the safe, Sissy. Don't play games," Rosco said, kicking the key toward her. "I know you've already been inside."

He really believed there was no one following his men to this place. "Are you okay, Grant?" She leaned closer, checking his head. He tried to rise, she pushed him back down. "That's a deep cut." She lowered her voice. "Help is here. Stay low and take cover when the rescue happens." Then louder, "Are you okay to sit?"

"I'm just a little woozy."

They worked together, moving him closer to the wheel of the car. He could roll under it or even make it to the semitrailer. It would make it easier on their rescuers if they stayed together.

"Now that you've taken care of your boyfriend—open my safe."

Should she keep up the pretense? She tried not to look toward Bryce, but she did anyway. She wouldn't climb into the back of that car and potentially be caught inside—or even locked inside.

She held up the key and leaned over the edge. She found the keyhole with her fingertip and guided the key inside.

Then she felt around for the magnetic hide-a-key, freed it and tossed it to Rosco.

"That's what you wanted. I don't know why I had to retrieve it for you."

"Don't you?" He slid the compartment open and removed a flash drive. It looked close to what he'd put there five years ago.

Kylie prayed that he couldn't remember the differences. "No." But she did. "If you're afraid that I shared the information with the police, the fact that I'm not under their protection is proof that I didn't. They let me go. And getting involved now is the furthest thing from my mind. I haven't plugged it in or looked at any part of it."

"On the other hand, she did give me the real one." Bryce swaggered around the corner like he was walking down Pecan Street trying to get her attention. Hands toward the ceiling, no weapon in sight, no sign of a bulletproof vest… he tossed a flash drive—hopefully not *the* flash drive—in the air. "I don't know what's on that thing you've got, but I do know what's on this."

He stopped when all the guns in the room turned toward him.

"Now, do you think I'd waltz in here without backup?" Bryce tossed the flash drive into the air like a ball, caught it and shoved it in his pocket. "You're done, Rosco. So are your friends, including Xander Tenoreno."

Rosco tipped his head toward his men.

She stood next to a seated Grant urging Bryce to start moving.

Two smoke grenades bounced across the concrete floor, leaving a trail of gray mist in their wake. Bryce darted behind a wooden crate as the guns close to her began firing.

In other words, all hell broke loose.

Chapter Twenty-Three

Chaos. A man ran past him, but that wasn't his objective. The hostages were. There was a plan in place and he had his role. He wasn't physically prepared for the tear gas, although he knew it was coming. Bryce didn't have time to cover his mouth and nose. He held his breath and waited for the cover of smoke before heading to the Cadillac.

Trent shouldn't have fired the gas into the warehouse until they had the little girl out of harm's way. The Dublin police, Fred and Richard were waiting outside to grab the five men helping Rosco. Bryce needed to find Fenley and Kylie.

"Run!" she shouted.

It wasn't to him, so she must be instructing Fenley. He ran toward her voice, toward the door at the loading dock. Someone, severely coughing, staggered through the opening and then down the first couple of steps. Fred was there and lowering his shotgun.

"Grant, where's Kylie?" Fred asked, burying his face in the crook of his elbow.

"He got her. She told me to run. I couldn't see. I came to find Darla—I thought you were still in there to help her." Grant Fenley looked at Bryce with his explanation for leaving Kylie.

"Two men unaccounted for, Bryce!" Fred yelled after him as he re-entered the building.

He instinctively knew that Rosco was the snake who had Kylie. He pulled his shirt over his nose and mouth to avoid the smoke now rising and clearing. Something moved in the direction he'd come through earlier. He followed, gun at the ready.

Bryce approached and rounded the corner he'd hidden behind. No one was there, but he heard something crash. He followed through the front and out the door, ducking back when shots ricocheted off the solid door and hit the glass window.

"Rosco! All I want is Kylie." Bryce couldn't tell where the shots had been fired from. He ducked to the ground and belly-crawled through the door.

He listened, trying to hear anything other than the shouts on the other side of the building. Then he heard it, scuffling, gravel hitting the steps to his right.

Staying low, then smashing himself against the building, he got closer into position. He turned ready to fire. But Rosco had Kylie in front of him, covering his body like the kidnappers had used the little girl.

"Ranger, I swear I'll put a bullet in her brain. I want a car to take me back to my plane. Then…"

Rosco talked. Bryce's gaze met Kylie's. She spread four fingers across Rosco's forearm that held her captive around her neck. Then three. Bryce barely nodded acknowledging that he understood. She was going to do something at the end of the countdown. He just didn't know what.

"Tell me this, Daniel," she said. "Was it you or Xander who shot my friends?"

Rosco's gun was aiming at him, then at Kylie. "You aren't calling for a car, Ranger."

Down to two fingers as the gun moved. Now he had the timing.

"Answer her question." Bryce pulled his phone from

his pocket and dialed Fred. "Might as well let her know it was you."

Rosco took small steps back. Bryce couldn't tell if he was dragging Kylie along or if she was forcing him onto the gravel where he could lose his footing. One finger.

Bryce was ready. The gun swung away from him and he moved forward at the same time Kylie bent the fingers around her neck toward his wrist and made Rosco tilt back and away from her.

She fell to the ground, hitting Rosco's knees together.

It didn't work. She stared into eyes that looked prepared for her attack or defense. But Bryce was there. She flattened herself to the ground, ready to roll out of the way.

Bryce sent a double punch to the man's gut, then another to his jaw. The gun flew. Kylie scrambled to her knees to capture the gun and keep it from Rosco's hands. Bryce took a couple of punches to his body, but sent an uppercut to the other man's jaw. Rosco fell backward hitting the gravel.

Fred came running around the corner. Kylie was in the older man's embrace while Bryce rolled Rosco to his stomach and yanked his arm behind him, pinning him to the ground.

"That didn't look like much of a fight," Fred stated.

"Not much of an opponent. That's what happens when they get arrogant." Kylie sniffed and wiped her eyes from the tear gas.

"Good enough to put bullets in you," Rosco spit into the gravel.

"Want me to take him off your hands?" Fred asked.

They exchanged places and Bryce took Kylie around the corner. The adrenaline wore off and she broke down in his arms for a couple of minutes. Real tears on top of the watering eyes from the tear gas.

"It wasn't Xander. I won't wonder anymore who killed my friends. It's over. Really over."

"Everything except the paperwork." He grinned at her and gave her a brief kiss. "It's going to get crowded around here with all the law enforcement headed this direction, but I don't want you out of my sight."

"Yes, sir. Ranger, sir." She playfully saluted. "Don't worry, I don't plan to leave your side."

"COME WITH ME." Bryce tugged a little on her elbow to get her moving. The sun was sinking and he wanted to slip away without a lot of questions.

"Don't I need to hang around or be whisked off for a more formal interrogation? I know they're going to accuse me of something else."

He looked over his shoulder to see if anyone was following. "That's what I'm trying to avoid."

"Okay, I was joking, but you clearly aren't. Are they going to accuse me of knowing about that flash drive? You were with me. You know that—"

He spun her around and sealed her lips with his. "You scared me to death, woman. I thought I'd be identifying your dead remains somewhere. Try not to come to anybody's rescue except mine. Will ya?"

Their lips tangled in a deep kiss that would have lasted longer but was interrupted by someone clearing his throat.

"Want me to come back later?"

"Dad!"

"That would be me. Nice to see you again." His father took Kylie's hand between his.

"My dad's taking you to his ranch until most of this blows over. You'll be safe there while I get things straightened out." Bryce wanted to move them along, but he didn't know which direction his dad had come from.

"I'm not going anywhere without you."

"Thing is, if you stay here, you'll probably have to and there won't be anything I can do about it. Trust me on this."

"You're in just as much trouble as me." She crossed her arms and he knew she was stubborn enough to go to jail if need be.

"She has a point, son. I can fly you to Waco tomorrow. Just tell them you'll be back." His dad shrugged like it was no big deal.

"Yeah, tell them you'll be back, Bryce," Kylie echoed.

He could swear he could hear her toe tapping on the road. "What are you driving, Dad?"

"Hickson let me borrow his Chevy at the airport." He pointed to an old brown rust bucket. "Got me here. Should get me back."

"I'll meet you around the corner in ten. If I'm not there…" He gave his father a look that meant he was to take Kylie with him no matter what.

"Be there." She pulled his face toward hers and kissed him. She looped her arm with his dad's and they strolled down the street. "Did you know your son, the big bad Gunslinger, took down the bad guy without firing a shot?"

Bryce wanted to hear the rest of that conversation. Instead, he found Fred and Richard to make arrangements for his truck. He found Major Parker who was inside the warehouse accepting the appreciation of the police chief for loaning a Texas Ranger to his team.

"More than happy to be of service," Parker answered, shaking hands with all around him. When they'd walked away, he turned to Bryce. "You managed to get everybody out of this alive. Good thing I never put your suspension papers through."

"Yes, sir." The surprise probably made him look like a wide-eyed rookie. "We got the flash drive open. It's full of old border crossing maps and has some photographic evidence that the Rosco family was involved in exactly what we thought. You name it, they smuggled it. I think it'll help the state's case against Tenoreno if we can prove they worked together."

"You know you were lucky you came out of this unscathed," his boss said.

"One riot, one ranger. Right, sir?" Bryce hesitated waiting for a shoe or handcuff to drop somewhere. "So I'm going to head out then. See you tomorrow?"

"Why don't you take vacation? I've already called headquarters. They're going to interview Miss Scott next week. Then you won't have to look so guilty about hiding her."

"Yes, sir. That should work out great."

"Yeah, I bet it will." Parker stuck out his hand. "Good job, Bryce. Thanks for keeping our word to the lady."

Bryce shook his major's hand and ran to catch his father and their flight to the Rockin' J.

Chapter Twenty-Four

Less than two hours ago, they'd been involved in an abduction and shoot-out. Kylie had to take a moment to breathe.

Bryce had whisked her off to a private airfield where they'd climbed into his father's tiny airplane. The ride had almost been straight up and straight down, arriving faster than Bryce could explain why they were coming. He didn't really have to. She knew. She needed to be stashed someplace safe until all the hoopla had blown over and the Austin state lawyers decided how important she was or wasn't.

This visit, Bryce's mom was unusually quiet as they entered the house and showed Kylie to the same bedroom she'd slept in before. Instead of following her into the kitchen, she spread out on the bed with a wet cloth across her eyes to help with the stinging from the tear gas. The door opened and Bryce leaned against it.

"Do you really think my ex-husband had nothing to do with this?"

"If he does, we'll find the connection. But my gut tells me that Rosco tried to kill you for his own perverted reasons. Maybe vengeance? Or even to get into Tenoreno's good graces. I think if your ex had any knowledge, Rosco would have brought him down when he bragged about it to us."

"You're probably right."

"You doing okay, Kylie?"

"Honestly, I don't know how I should feel. For five years I've thought Xander hated me enough to kill me." Kylie dropped her arm over her eyes, shutting out the ceiling, the bloodstained gravel and the confession of her friends' murderer.

"There'll be an investigation that might take a while. We have time to find out the truth." He left the door, standing next to the bed. "Hey, my parents turned in early. Let's go stick our feet in the pool."

They left their shoes in the bedroom and silently raced to the pool, sticking their feet in the cool water. She could hear music from across the patio and saw a silhouette of a couple dancing.

"Your parents are cool." She grinned from ear to ear hearing the music of Frankie Valli. "So what's the story on you singing to me?"

"That's a family joke. Strictly need-to-know basis."

She really wanted to know. In fact, she had a theory and needed to discover the inside story of the person she loved.

Yes, loved.

There it was…she said it—or thought it. There was something about Bryce that she'd fallen in love with from the moment she watched him jerk his shirt over his head and get it caught on his ear.

She hoped it meant he cared for her, but she let it go. "You have a nice family. I'm looking forward to their jokes."

"Good thing, since you'll be staying with them awhile." Bryce splashed the water. It didn't seem to matter that the bottoms of their jeans were getting soaked.

"I don't want to be a bother."

"That will never happen. They'll love the company. You'll be lucky if the entire family's not here within a couple of days. Which means I should probably stick around to protect you from any and all accusations thrown your direction."

"I'm looking forward to getting that family secret out of them, but why would they come?"

"I've never brought anyone home before. Ever. Now I've done it twice in a week. They'll be curious." He reached into the water, splashing it on her face.

Cool. Refreshing. Playfulness. She wanted it all, especially him. "Maybe you can let them know this is for work and head them off."

"Kylie." He tangled his foot with hers, reminding her of when he yanked her into his pool. "If you want this to stay professional, then I need to take you to Company F tomorrow and hand you off to someone else. I want you to be safe, but I didn't bring you here just to protect you."

"What a relief." She laughed and lay back against the tile. "I was hoping this wasn't all one-sided."

The man she'd fallen so fast and so hard for cupped her cheeks with his cool palms. Tilting her head to look past her eyes into her heart.

"Is it too soon to say I love you?" he whispered before devouring her lips.

She wanted to fall into the pool with him and mesh their bodies as close as possible. She almost did just so he could get her out of her clothes, but a look over Bryce's shoulder revealed his parents watching from their patio door.

Wait. The word repeated in her head while she kissed him. But she didn't care if his parents watched. She didn't care that someone else was discovering Rosco's motive or that Xander might have been involved.

Nope. All she cared about was kissing Bryce. She was a little frightened to stop capturing the sweet taste of his mouth. If she stopped, he might answer his own question. Might say it *was* too soon to talk about love. Then again…they'd come so close to losing each other before ever being together.

"Damn, you are so beautiful. Inside and out. I see my soul tangled with yours when I look into your blue eyes."

"And I see my future in yours. I wouldn't have had one if you hadn't come looking for me. I'm so happy you did."

That was all the encouragement he needed. She wrapped her arms around him and planned to end each of her days there for the rest of her life.

Epilogue

Four years later

Kylie sat under an umbrella on the porch watching Bryce mow the lawn. Four years with him and it still felt strange to go sleeveless and not cover the scars—even if they had been smoothed a bit by surgery. His confidence and effortless love for her is what made it possible.

The spring air was warm and she couldn't wait to get the pool stabilized and running. Fred and Richard had the teens come by for some work. The men taught them how to put in a small fence. Babyproofing the yard for their godchild had been on their minds all winter. Now it was done and Bryce was determined to get everything ready for the barbecue baby shower next weekend.

That is, if they made it to next weekend. The baby kicked and her muscles tightened. "Shush, baby. Those silly Braxton Hicks contractions are getting to me, too." She smoothed her tummy, receiving another kick for her efforts. "You are going to be just as demanding as your daddy."

Even through her sunglasses she could tell he was getting red. It was the first time he'd been in the sun this season. They went through the same thing every year. She waved at her husband and got his attention. "Bryce, hon.

Come and let me put sunscreen on your back and shoulders before it's too late."

"I'm nearly done."

"Bryce, come on. I came outside to put this on you and have been waiting. We haven't bought any aloe yet. Don't come to me when you're blistered and suffering. I'm not running to the store at midnight."

He shrugged and continued mowing. He'd done all the yardwork without a shirt and without sunscreen. She'd come out to sit in an uncomfortable chair to spray his back. But when he'd switched lawn tools she had been inside making lemonade. She shifted in the cushioned swivel chair attempting to get comfortable.

It was impossible.

The mower's buzz hushed and Bryce joined her, plopping tiredly into the chair next to her. The false contraction came again with a wallop. The baby was demanding attention, acting crowded.

"This chair was a lot more comfortable when we bought it last year. Or maybe I just fit it better then. Along with my clothes, my shoes…I even think my toothbrush fit better then."

Bryce laughed, then tipped back the lemonade she'd brought out on the same serving tray she'd used when they'd first met. What else could he do but laugh? She was the grouchy one. Even though the false labor had them both on edge, he still grinned at her. Braxton Hicks contractions for weeks. Two practice runs to the hospital had made them both feel like overanxious beginners.

"Ow." She rubbed her belly. "Seriously, I don't know how much more of this I can take."

He set the glass on the tray next to the pitcher. "Probably all of it. You're going to be a great mom."

"You know just what to say."

He leaned forward and talked directly to the baby. "Hey,

little man. You're giving your mom a hard time. I think you both need a nap." Then looking up at her. "What do you say? Is it—Wow. Was that a real contraction for once?"

"Just one of those silly Braxton Hicks. They've been coming all day."

"As in every couple of minutes all day?" He looked at his watch.

"No. Or I don't think so. I try to ignore them." Now that she was thinking about it, the pain was a little more in her lower back. "Owwww. Okay, that was pretty close to the other one."

"Too close. How do you feel about having a baby today?" He didn't sit back. Instead he spread his hands across the baby and kept them there, waiting.

"But it's three weeks earlier than they thought."

"It's not an exact science, Kylie. I think we should go."

"You don't want to call the doctor? Ask an opinion? Wait to see if it's just indigestion?" She smiled at him, trying to get him to smile. He looked too dang serious for either of their sanity. "Come on, Bryce. Both trips to the hospital, they said my water would probably break. That hasn't happened. I don't want to be sent home again."

"Hon, I can do a lot of things, but delivering my own baby is not one of them." He popped up from the chair. "You stay here. I know where everything is."

"Babe, my bag is already in the truck. You put it there two days ago."

"Right. Do you want to change clothes or anything? Should I? I should since I probably stink. Do we have time for that?" He was taking a step toward the house, then back to her and then toward the house.

"Are you okay? You look really nervous." Kylie laughed, ignoring the discomfort.

"I'm, ah…yeah, I'm fine."

"How about a sho—wer. Oh boy, that was rough." She

wanted to huff and puff her way through it. "Maybe you're right and we should sort of hurry."

"That was about a minute and a half after the last one." He helped her to her feet. "Let's go. I'll call the doctor's service on the way."

"Sweetheart, you really do need to change."

"I'll be okay."

"But I won't. I'm not going through six hours of labor with you standing next to me smelling like a wildebeest."

He raised his arm—just like a man—and sniffed. "I guess I do smell sort of rank. I don't want to put this off."

"At least grab some clean clothes, hon. Please? I'll wait for you in the truck."

Bryce took one more sniff and unbuckled his shorts, dropping them on the way to the pool, hopped over the three-foot fence and jumped into the icy water.

Kylie watched, sort of in shock, until another contraction hit. Dripping freezing water, Bryce came back to her at the end and helped her limp to the truck.

"What made you think of a wildebeest?"

"We took the boys to the zoo and there was that awful smell." Kylie leaned on Bryce to get in the truck. No choice there. She wasn't only nine months pregnant, she was also midcontraction.

"That was a skunk, babe."

The contraction was tighter and lower and following more quickly. "Uuuh…just hurry with those clothes."

Then the smell of fried chicken permeated her nostrils. She looked in the back and sure enough, there was a sack. Bryce had a habit of leaving his lunch bones in the truck so Honeybear couldn't find them in the trash.

The smell in the truck, the pool, the stress, the worry… it all brought back the reminder of how far they'd come in four years. The first time she'd had Bush's chicken she'd been falling a little bit more in love with the man she couldn't live without now.

The Tenoreno family couldn't hurt them anymore. Daniel Rosco had been prosecuted for the murders of her friends. His confession and the evidence on the flash drive sent him to prison for life. He'd taken a video of their bodies as proof he'd completed the job. Then lost the Cadillac in a bet that she would die. She shivered, not wanting to think about it again.

On a happier note, the teen and senior program she'd begun in Hico had an interim director while she'd be home with the baby. And on their last trip for pie, they'd run into the Fenley family. Darla was doing well and had tried to stretch her arms around Kylie's growing baby belly—something Bryce joked about being unable to do all the time.

"We've had such a wonderful life already, baby boy. You are going to make it completely full. Oh…goodness." That contraction felt a little more intense. She leaned her head out the window. "Bryce! Hurry!"

He came barreling under the garage door as it started to close. Shooing Honeybear back underneath with his socks and boots in his hands.

"I'm using the lights."

She grabbed her stomach, breathing hard. "I think you should."

He pushed his hair back out of his eyes, looked through the pile he'd dumped on the seat and found his glasses. Then put the truck in gear. "I love you."

Each time he told her it was special. Each time he made her feel like it was the first time he'd ever admitted that he loved anyone.

"I love you, babe. Now get this truck moving." She squeezed his hand and flipped the flashing lights on herself.

Bryce grinned and ran the first stop sign. "Time for baby Johnson to make his debut."

* * * * *

Don't miss the next book in Angi Morgan's
TEXAS RANGERS: ELITE TROOP *series*
when HARD CORE LAW goes on sale next month.

He walked up to Andrea, careful to come at her slowly and from the side so he didn't sneak up on her in any way.

"Hi." He kept his voice even, calm. "What are you doing out here? Everything okay?"

She looked at him, then back at the parking lot. Without being obvious about it, Brandon withdrew his weapon from the holster at his side. Had she seen something to do with the case?

"Andrea." His voice was a little stronger now. "What's going on? Is it something to do with the murders? Did you see something or did someone threaten you?"

She kept staring.

"Andrea, look at me."

She finally turned to him, hair plastered to her head from the rain, makeup beginning to smear on her face.

"I need you to tell me what's happening so I can do something about it."

MAN OF ACTION

BY
JANIE CROUCH

First Published in Great Britain 2016
By Mills & Boon, an imprint of HarperCollins*Publishers*
1 London Bridge Street, London, SE1 9GF

© 2016 Janie Crouch

ISBN: 978-0-263-91910-3

46-0716

Our policy is to use papers that are natural, renewable and recyclable products and made from wood grown in sustainable forests. The logging and manufacturing processes conform to the legal environmental regulations of the country of origin.

Printed and bound in Spain
by CPI, Barcelona

Janie Crouch has loved to read romance her whole life. She cut her teeth on Mills & Boon Romance novels as a preteen, then moved on to a passion for romantic suspense as an adult. Janie lives with her husband and four children overseas. She enjoys traveling, long-distance running, movie watching, knitting and adventure/obstacle racing. You can find out more about her at www.janiecrouch.com.

To Anu-Riikka, because you talk me down from the ledge with almost every single book. Thank you for listening to me for hours on end and for offering a fresh perspective when I can't see clearly any longer. You're the greatest buddy a writer could have.

Prologue

Andrea Gordon huddled inside her car in the bank parking lot as pandemonium reigned all around her. Cops, SWAT, ambulances and other emergency vehicles she didn't even recognize flooded the area. Blue and red lights flashed in a rhythm that drummed brutally against her eyes. Officers pointed assault rifles toward the building. People ran back and forth.

Just behind the roped-off section, news crews formed the next layer of people, their lights and cords and equipment adding to the chaos.

Beyond that were the witnesses, the gawkers, hoping to catch something exciting. Andrea wasn't sure what would pacify them. A chase? Bullets? A dead body? Smartphones recorded the scene from every angle.

Three men had taken sixteen people hostage after an attempted robbery had gone wrong in a bank just outside Phoenix, Arizona. Andrea would've been one of those sixteen, but she had seen the signs on the robbers' faces when they'd first walked in.

Danger. Violence.

Andrea was only nineteen years old, but she was an expert at spotting the approach of danger. Maybe she should be thankful for all the times she'd had to discern it in her uncle to avoid his fists. Either way, it had gotten her out of that bank before the trouble went down.

The men hadn't come in together, but they were definitely working as a team; Andrea had immediately seen that. It was obvious to her that they weren't afraid to hurt, even to kill. Simmering violence was a vibe she was very attuned to.

Two of the men fairly buzzed with it. Excited about taking money that wasn't theirs and maybe taking a life, too. But it was the third man, who stood completely still and broadcast almost no outward emotions at all, that scared her the most.

She'd waited a minute longer, studying them while pretending to fill in a deposit slip, in case she was wrong. The two hyped-up guys were making their way back toward the bank manager's office. The other man, the scary one, stood against a side wall, a briefcase in his hand. He caressed it with a lover's touch.

He felt her eyes and turned to her, giving a smile so dark, so full of violence, Andrea had turned and nearly run out of the bank. She'd felt his eyes follow her as she left.

She'd been the last one out. Not two minutes after her exit, shots had been fired inside. The robbery soon turned into a hostage situation. Once out, Andrea had hidden in her car, parked in the back of the bank lot, and watched as the police arrived minutes later, then observers, then press.

Andrea would've been escorted back with the observers if anyone had known she was in her car. She'd been so scared at the third man's evil smile, she had literally melted herself into the driver's seat of her vehicle, curling into a ball and protecting her head and face with her arms.

She'd learned long ago that position didn't stop pain, but at least this time it had kept her away from anyone's view. The uniformed officer who had been in charge of security and taping off the parking lot had walked right by Andrea's car without even seeing her in the dimming hours of twilight.

Unfortunately, now she was trapped here since the lot was blocked off by police vehicles. There was no telling how long the showdown could continue with the three men inside. She would need to go find someone who could let her out if she wanted to leave this evening.

Andrea exited her car, kept her head down and walked toward the action, planning to talk to the first relatively nice cop she could find. She didn't want to draw any attention to herself, just wanted to get the help she needed and get out.

When she got to the front line of police officers, Andrea started looking around more. There was a lot of excitement in most of these cops. Some were nervous, a few downright fearful. A couple were bored.

She was easily able to spot the man in charge. He exuded self-confidence and self-importance, even without a radio in each hand and people constantly asking him questions. When he gave orders he expected them to be followed, and he was definitely the one giving orders in this situation. Another man and woman were standing with him. Everything about their faces and body language also suggested confidence, but they were respectful, caring—not power hungry. They stood back slightly, observing.

Drawn by the situation even though she didn't want to be, Andrea made her way toward those people in charge. She was careful not to get in anybody's way or do anything to draw someone's scrutiny, although she expected to be stopped at any moment. When she got close enough to hear the leaders, she stood beside an unmarked sedan, watching them studying and discussing the bank.

She heard the man and woman—the observers—arguing with the man in charge.

"Lionel, deadly force isn't necessary yet," the man stated, quiet but emphatic. "Plus we don't know the exact situation. We have no inside intel."

"This isn't your operation, Drackett," the man named Lionel snapped. He wasn't interested in anyone else's opinions. "Omega isn't in charge here—the Bureau is."

"We're not even sure how many perps are in there, nor how many hostages," the woman said, her voice as calm as Drackett's had been.

"We've got eyes on the building. There's obviously two gunmen holding a room of seventeen people. They've got everyone in one location to keep them in line."

Lionel was wrong. There were *three* men involved. But Andrea imagined the third one with the evil smile just looked like one of the hostages if he hadn't made any obvious threatening moves. With his briefcase and suit he'd blend right in.

And he meant to kill everyone in the building. Everything in his body language and his emotions had screamed violence.

"Neither of those guys have hurt anyone yet. Let us get our hostage negotiator down here to talk to them. Matarazzo is a whiz in this type of situation—you know that." Drackett again. "He can be here within the hour."

Lionel shook his head. "No, I don't need your rich wonder boy. I will handle this the way I see fit. The two gunmen have left the back of the building ripe for our entry. They are obviously camped in the front. They're nervous. I'm not going to wait until they kill someone before I make my move."

Although their expressions changed for only the briefest moment, Andrea could feel the waves of frustration coming off Drackett and the woman he was with. Whatever was going on, it was personal. Lionel all but hated Drackett.

That disdain was going to get everyone in the building killed. She could hear Lionel getting a SWAT team ready to breach the back door.

She was afraid when they did, the third man would make his move. She had to tell the police leaders what she knew. She didn't know if it would make a difference, if they would listen to her at all, but she had to try.

She walked over to Drackett and the woman before she could let herself chicken out. She didn't try to talk to Lionel; she already knew he wouldn't listen to her.

"Excuse me, Mr. Drackett? There's a third man inside that bank. Someone more deadly than the other two you can see."

Drackett immediately turned his focus to her, as did the woman. It was a little overwhelming. Andrea wasn't used to people actually listening to her that intently.

"How do you know?" His voice was clipped but she knew it was because they were running out of time, not because he didn't believe her.

"I was in there. I saw them come in. I'm—I'm pretty good at reading people, their expressions. I could tell something was not right with the three of them. Those two guys." She pointed at the bank doors where the two men could be seen. "And another one you don't know about."

Drackett and the woman met eyes and stepped closer to Andrea. She could tell they had Lionel's attention also, although he didn't turn toward them.

"I'm Grace. Tell us everything, as quickly as you can." The woman touched her on the arm. Andrea fought the urge to flinch even though she knew the woman meant her no harm.

"The two men, the ones with guns, are excited, a little shaky. They're thrilled about a big payoff and perhaps about having to shoot their way out of the situation. They will kill if they have to, but that's not their primary intent."

"And the third man?"

"Evil." Even in the Phoenix evening heat, Andrea felt cold permeate her bones. "He'll kill everyone. *Wants* to

kill everyone. I think he wants to take as many people as possible down with him."

Drackett whispered something to Grace and she eased back and disappeared into the crowds of law enforcement. She was gone too quickly for Andrea to get a read on whether she believed Andrea or not.

"So help me God, Drackett, if you tell me we need to listen to what this child is telling us…"

"This young woman has more actual intel than anyone else here. I'm not asking you to stand down, Lionel, just to listen and make sure you have all the facts before making any big move."

"I'm not going to wait for these gunmen to kill someone before we move in. SWAT will be ready to storm the back door in three minutes. We go then."

Everything about Lionel screamed determination. Andrea didn't even try to convince him; he wasn't going to listen to her.

She took a step back. She had done all she could do. Things inside the bank would play out the way they would play out.

She was about to fade back even more when Drackett looked down at a message on his phone. He turned and walked the three steps so he was standing directly in front of her.

"You. Name. First and last."

"Andrea Gordon." He wasn't angry with her but the abrupt statement had her giving her real name rather than a fake.

"Just wanted to know the name of the person who's going to cost me my career if you're wrong," he whispered. "Go stand back there with that uniformed officer. All hell is about to break loose." He motioned for the officer to come get her.

Andrea walked back with the cop, but when he becamc distracted with something else, she slipped away. She eased into the crowds. She'd come back for her car another time.

She heard and felt the chaos behind her a few moments later. A shot fired then a bunch of people yelling. She just kept walking, not looking back.

ANDREA WASN'T SURE what had happened in the bank that evening. She'd watched the news the next day and it seemed as if the men had been stopped without any problems. One of the gunmen had been wounded in the raid; the other had surrendered without a fight. All the hostages had left the bank unharmed.

The third man was never mentioned or shown by the media. Andrea accepted that maybe she had been wrong; maybe he hadn't had anything to do with it. But then she thought of that evil smile the man had given her in the bank. Even now it had the ability to make her stomach turn.

Andrea hoped Mr. Drackett and Grace hadn't gotten in trouble because of what she had told them. She'd probably never have any way of knowing, so she put it out of her mind.

Until they both walked in to Jaguar's a couple of hours later.

Andrea was immediately self-conscious. She wasn't on-stage dancing—thank God—but she was serving drinks, and even though the waitress outfits were more concealing than whatever the dancer was wearing, it still left very little to the imagination.

They were obviously here for her. Jaguar's rarely got customers in business suits. Especially suits that screamed law enforcement.

It was too dark for Andrea to read their expressions and body language as well as she would like, but anger radiated off them. This had to be about the bank. They must have gotten in trouble. And now they were here to let Andrea know. She wondered if she was about to be arrested.

"Harry, I need a break. I'll be back in fifteen," she said to her manager.

Harry leered at her the way he always did. "Any more than that and I'll dock your pay." He stepped closer, grasping her chin. "Or we can work out our own way of you paying me back."

He didn't see that Drackett and Grace had made their way up behind him, overhearing his words. Drackett cleared his throat.

Harry pegged them as cops as soon as he turned around. "And by paying me back, I mean working extra shifts," he muttered, going to stand farther behind the bar, glaring at the suits.

"Andrea, could we talk to you outside for a few minutes?" Grace said over the thump of the music.

"Am I about to be arrested?"

Drackett's eyes narrowed. "Why do you say that?"

Andrea shrugged, very aware of how much her clothes revealed. Her skimpy bra was clearly noticeable through the mesh of her top. The short pleated skirt she wore barely covered her bottom, and men often took it as an invitation to run their hand up her thigh.

Andrea had stopped slapping their hands away once Harry threatened to fire her.

She was used to men gawking at her body, but Mr. Drackett's eyes hadn't so much as left her face once since he'd arrived.

"You're angry," she said. It wasn't terribly noticeable in his expression, but she could tell.

Grace was surprised. "I don't think Steve is angry, Andrea." She turned to him. "Maybe we're wrong about her."

Steve shook his head once. "No, she's spot-on. I'm

pissed as hell that she's working in a place like this." He stepped closer to Andrea and she couldn't help but take a step back. He froze. "I'm not angry at *you*, I promise."

Andrea believed him. "Okay."

"But do you mind coming outside with us? This will only take a few minutes."

Andrea grabbed her lightweight jacket and followed them out the side door. "I can't stay out here very long. I'll get fired if I do. I need this job," she said in the quieter, cooler air of outside. Finally she felt as if she could breathe again.

"You were right about the third man in the bank." Grace smiled at her. "You probably saved a lot of lives yesterday. He had a briefcase full of explosives and was just waiting to use them. Was waiting for SWAT so he could take them down, too."

Andrea closed her eyes in relief. At least no one had gotten hurt and these two people hadn't gotten fired.

"Andrea, I'm going to cut right to the chase." Mr. Drackett kept his distance so she wouldn't feel uncomfortable. "We believe you have a gift at reading people's emotions and microexpressions, even when they're only available for a split second."

Andrea wasn't exactly sure what microexpressions were, but she knew she was good at reading people.

"Maybe." She shrugged, clutching her jacket to her chest. "So?"

"I'm Steve Drackett. Grace and I work for Omega Sector: Critical Response Division. We're law enforcement, sort of like the FBI, but without as much red tape."

"And smarter and better looking," Grace chimed in, smiling again. "We're based out of Colorado Springs."

That was all fine and good, but what did it have to do with her? "Okay."

Drackett crossed his arms over his chest. "We'd like you to come work for us."

"What?" Andrea wasn't sure she was hearing right. "Doing what?"

"What you did at the bank. What you seem to be a natural at doing, if we're not mistaken. Reading people."

Andrea's gaze darted over to Grace then back to Drackett. "You don't even know me. Maybe I just got lucky at the bank."

Steve tilted his head to the side. "Maybe, but I don't think so. There are some tests that can help us know for sure. We'll pay for you to fly to Colorado Springs and for all your expenses during testing."

Andrea grimaced. Tests, books, schooling were not her strengths. The opposite, in fact. She looked down at her feet. "I'm not too good at tests. Didn't finish high school."

"It won't be like math or English tests you took in school," Grace said gently. "It's called 'behavioral and nonverbal communication diagnostic testing.'"

Now Andrea was even more confused. "I don't know what that means."

Grace smiled. "Don't worry about the name. The testing will involve a lot of pictures, or live people, and we'll see how accurately you can pick up their emotions and expressions."

Okay, only reading emotions, not words. Maybe she could handle it, but she still wasn't sure. What if she failed?

"Andrea!" Harry yelled from the door. "Time's up."

Steve looked at Harry then back to Andrea. "There are no strings in this offer," Steve said, his voice still calm and even. "You can check us out before you get on the plane, make sure we're legit. Read up about Omega, so you feel safe."

Andrea studied them both. There was no malice in either of them as they looked back at her, just respect, concern and a hopefulness. They legitimately seemed to want her to join them.

"What if I can't do what you want? If I'm not as good as you think?" she whispered.

"Then you'll be paid handsomely for the time you've spent doing the testing," Grace said. "And we'll fly you anywhere you want to go. It doesn't have to be in Arizona."

"Andrea." Harry's voice was even louder. "Get your ass back in here. Now."

"And we'll help get you started in another career. It may not be with Omega, but it doesn't have to be here. This is not the place for you. Why don't you leave with us tonight?" The compassion in Steve's face was her undoing.

She looked back at Harry. He was livid, wanted to hurt her physically, emotionally, any way he could. It seemed as if there had been someone wanting to hurt her all her life.

But Steve and Grace didn't. They wanted to help. She just hoped she didn't disappoint them.

Andrea slipped her jacket all the way onto her body. "Okay, I'll come with you."

There was nothing worth keeping her here.

Chapter One

Four years later, Andrea stood in front of a bathroom mirror inside Omega Sector headquarters. She smoothed her straight black skirt and made sure—again—that her blouse was tucked in neatly before checking her reflection in the bathroom mirror one last time. Blond hair, cut in a sleek bob—the most professional haircut she'd been able to think of—was perfectly in place. Makeup tastefully applied and nothing that would draw attention to herself.

She was about to be fired from her job as a behavioral analyst at Omega Sector's Critical Response Division.

Why else would Steve Drackett be calling her into his office at ten thirty on a Monday morning?

Actually, she could think of a half dozen reasons why he would be calling her in: a new case, a new test, some assignment he needed her to work on or a video briefing where her analysis was needed. But her brain wasn't interested in focusing on any of the logical reasons he wanted to meet with her.

"Steve and Grace both know your background and still want you here," she told her reflection. The scared look didn't leave her eyes. She forced herself to vacate the bathroom and head down the hall. If Steve was going to fire her, there was nothing she could do about it.

No one said hello to her as she walked through the corridors and Andrea didn't engage anyone. She'd utilized this keep-to-herself plan ever since she had realized exactly how important Omega was and the caliber of people they had working here in the Critical Response Division. Ever since Steve and Grace had officially offered her a job four years ago after six weeks of testing.

She may have a gift of reading people, but Andrea didn't think for one minute that she was the sort of person Omega normally hired.

She'd known from the beginning she needed to keep her past a secret. Announcing to her colleagues that she was a runaway, dyslexic high school dropout who—oh yeah—*used to be an exotic dancer* would not inspire much confidence in her. So she'd made it a point not to tell anyone. Not to ever discuss her past or personal life at all. If it didn't involve a case, Andrea didn't talk about it.

Her plan hadn't won her any friends, but it had successfully worked at keeping her secrets. She could live without friends.

Andrea pushed on the door that led to the outer realm where Steve's assistants worked. One of them stood, welcoming and walking her to Steve's office door and opening it. The clicks of Andrea's three-inch heels on the tiled floor sounded more like clanging chimes of doom in her head as she stepped through.

"Hey, Andrea, good to see you," Steve said from behind his desk, looking up from a stack of papers.

She supposed he was handsome, with his brown hair graying slightly at the temples and his sharp blue eyes, but since he was nearly twenty years older than her, she'd never even thought of him in that way. She respected him with every fiber of her being. Not only for getting her out of a dead-end life back at Jaguar's in Buckeye, Arizona, but because of how fair and respectful he acted toward all the people who worked at Omega.

But he was tired. Andrea could tell. "You need a vacation, boss. Some time away from this circus."

Steve put his elbows on his desk and bridged his fingers together, grimacing just the slightest bit. "You know why I don't invite you in here very often? Because you see too much." But his words held no fire. He knew what she said was right.

Andrea nodded.

"Sit down, Andrea. I'm afraid what I have to say might be a little difficult to hear."

Oh my God, he is *going to fire me.*

Andrea took a breath through her nose and tried not to let her panic show. She had known this was a possibility from the beginning. Not just a possibility, a *probability*.

She tried to mentally regroup. Okay, she wasn't the same girl who had left with Steve and Grace from Buckeye. She had managed to successfully complete her high school equivalency degree and even had two years of college under her belt. Yes, her dyslexia made some classes difficult, and she had to take them at a slower pace than most people, but she was making progress.

She could get some other job now. She had money in savings. She didn't have to go back to Jaguar's and let those people paw at her again.

"Andrea."

Steve's tone made her realize it wasn't the first time he'd said her name. She finally forced herself to focus on what he was saying.

"I don't need to have your gift to see that you're panicking. What the hell is going on in that brain of yours?" She could feel waves of concern flowing from him, and it was easily readable on his face.

She rubbed her skirt again. "Steve, I understand if you need to let me go. I've always known that was a possibility—"

"Andrea, I'm not firing you."

"But you said this may be difficult."

"And it probably will be, but why don't you let me finish before you jump to conclusions."

Now Andrea felt the reprimand. She sank back a little in her chair. "Yes, sir."

"I need you for a case."

He really wasn't firing her. "Okay."

"It involves a serial killer. He's been striking in the Phoenix area, with the last woman found dead just outside of Buckeye."

Her hometown. Now his concern made sense.

"And you want me to go there." It wasn't a question.

"I think your ability as a behavioral analyst, plus your knowledge of and history with the area, makes you one of our best chances of stopping this guy as quickly as possible."

She was glad she wasn't being fired, but Steve was right—this was hard. She didn't want to go back to Buckeye. When she'd left there that night with Steve and Grace, she'd never returned. She'd gone back inside Jaguar's to collect her personal belongings and her tips and had told Harry she wasn't coming back.

She'd been glad to have Grace, obviously a cop and obviously carrying a weapon, standing behind her as she did it, because she didn't think Harry would've taken it so well otherwise. As it was, his face had turned a molten red, small eyes narrowed even further. But he hadn't stopped her.

She'd never really explained it all to Steve, but Jaguar's was really just the tip of her iceberg of bad memories when it came to Buckeye. The situation she'd lived through the years before she'd run away from her aunt and uncle's home had been much worse. She still bore a few scars to prove that.

"I know this is hard for you." Steve was studying her carefully from behind his desk.

"Buckeye is not somewhere I'd choose to visit." The understatement of the century.

Steve came around to sit on his desk, closer to her. "Andrea, you're not the same person Grace and I met in Buckeye four years ago. You're stronger, more confident, able to handle the stress of this job, which isn't a light matter."

"Yeah, but—"

"I know you feel like you don't have the same educational background or experience of most of the people actively working cases at Omega. But you have a natural talent at reading people that continues to be honed."

"But—"

Steve wasn't really interested in her arguments. "I can think of a dozen cases, just off the top of my head, where your assistance provided the primary components needed to allow us to make an arrest."

Andrea took a breath. She knew that. Intellectually, she knew all that Steve spoke was the truth. But it was so hard.

"You've got to stop thinking I'm about to fire you every time I call you to my office. I'm not, trust me. I can't afford to lose such a valuable member of the Omega team."

Steve radiated sincerity. Of course, he always had. And she did believe she was part of the team. A noneducated, ex-stripper part of the team, but part of the team.

Okay, she could handle this. She could handle going back to Buckeye.

"Of course, we won't be sending you alone. You and Brandon Han will be working together."

Andrea smiled through gritted teeth, glad that Steve wasn't as skilled at reading people as she was. Brandon Han, as in *Dr.* Brandon Han, with something like two PhDs and an IQ higher than Einstein. They called him "the machine." He was considered the best and most brilliant profiler at Omega.

Not to mention he was hotter than sin. Tall, black hair, with a prominent Asian heritage.

"Do you know Brandon?"

Besides when she'd fantasized about him? "Um, I've never worked any cases with him, but I've met him a couple of times, briefly."

She wasn't sure he would even remember meeting her.

"Great. He'll be here any minute. Then we can go over details and get you guys going today."

BRANDON HAN WAS running a little late for his meeting with Steve but knew his boss would understand. Brandon had just come from visiting the widow and kids of his ex-partner.

Brandon didn't get by to see them as much as he liked, but he knew there were other Omega people checking in on them, also. David Vickars had been a well-liked and respected member of the team. He'd had the backs of many agents over the years, and the Omega family didn't forget their own.

David had died a year ago from a foe even Omega couldn't fight: cancer. He'd worked active duty until a month before he died from an inoperable tumor, then spent his last weeks with his wife and kids.

Brandon and David had been partners for seven years and had been friends for long before that. Brandon hadn't been interested in working with a partner since David died.

But he knew the minute he walked into Steve Drackett's office and saw beautiful, blonde Andrea Gordon sitting in a chair, body language screaming nervousness, that he was about to get partnered again.

Damn it.

Brandon had become quite adept at working alone. He

liked the quiet. He liked being able to work at his own pace, which—no conceit intended—was often quite a bit faster than everyone else's.

"Hey, Steve," he greeted his boss. He nodded at Andrea, but she'd looked away. Par for the course for her. She'd looked away every time he'd ever been in the same room with her.

Drackett stood from behind his desk and shook Brandon's hand. "Let's go over to the conference table to talk about a case."

Steve was moving them to neutral ground, not wanting to pull rank from behind his desk if he didn't have to. He wanted Brandon to agree to whatever was about to be asked without having to force him. If Brandon wasn't mistaken, his boss's friendliness had to do with Andrea. A protectiveness maybe.

"Sure," Brandon agreed amicably. He might as well let this play out.

Andrea stood and joined them. Brandon held out a chair for her, waiting to see if she was one of those women who got offended by the gesture. That would tell him a lot about her.

But she just looked surprised for a moment before taking the chair he held out. He helped slide it in as she sat.

Okay, not afraid of her own femininity and didn't feel that every situation needed to be a struggle of power.

"You've met Andrea Gordon?" Steve asked, glancing at them.

"Yes, a couple of times. Good to see you again."

"Yes, you too," she murmured, voice soft. Sweet, even.

"We've got a serial killer working in the Phoenix area. Three dead so far." Steve handed them both a file.

"Confirmed serial?" Brandon asked, glancing through the file.

"Pretty much as confirmed as these things can get. All

three were women in their early twenties. All were found covered in some sort of white cloth and holding a lotus flower."

"Purity," Andrea muttered.

"What?" Steve asked.

Andrea shrugged. "Lotus flowers are the symbol of purity in some cultures."

"She's right," Brandon said. "And so is the white cloth. Almost like a cleansing ritual."

"Okay, that's something to go on. I'll need you two to leave tonight. The local police department is expecting you."

"Steve, since David..." *Died.* Brandon found it difficult to say the word even now a year later, so he just didn't. "Since David, I've been working alone. That's been going pretty well for me. I think I'm more productive that way."

Brandon turned to Andrea. "I mean that as no offense to you whatsoever."

Some emotion passed across her face but was gone before he—even with all his training—could read it. Frustrating.

"I understand," she said, nodding.

"Brandon, the last murder took place inside the town limits of Buckeye, on the outskirts of Phoenix. That's where Andrea is from. With ritual killings like this, we both know it's usually someone from the area."

Brandon grimaced. He couldn't deny that. Having someone familiar with the area—especially someone with a stellar skill set like Andrea's—would be invaluable.

But still, Brandon didn't want to work with her. Didn't want to be in forced proximity with her for an extended length of time. He glanced over at her but she wasn't looking at him, again. She was studying the pictures in the file, as if she couldn't care less about the conversation going on around her.

Brandon's eyes narrowed. No, he did not want to partner with this woman for a case. He'd discovered over the past year that he liked working alone, but it was more than that.

He didn't trust Andrea. The woman had secrets. Secrets tended to blow up in everyone's faces at the most inopportune moments.

David had kept his illness a secret from everyone for as long as he could. Brandon didn't want to be around secrets anymore.

He especially didn't want to be around a stunningly beautiful woman with secrets. The kind of woman who made him want to toss out his never-mix-business-with-pleasure rule. The kind that made him want to find out all her secrets.

He didn't trust her and she was distracting. She damn well had distracted him every time he'd seen her the past few months. Including today. Her perfect legs in her perfect suit with her perfect hair and makeup. It all distracted him.

He was not a man who liked to be distracted.

Brandon could kill a man a dozen ways with his bare hands, but it wasn't his strength or speed he relied on to get ahead of criminals. He relied on his intellect, his education, his experience to stop the worst of the worst bad guys.

Having Andrea Gordon's distracting presence around him during a serial-killer case was just not going to work.

He leaned back in his chair and feigned a casualness he didn't have. "I just think it's better for me to work alone on this case."

Because he wasn't sure he'd be able to work at all otherwise.

Chapter Two

"She has secrets, Steve. Something she's not telling people."

Steve had already excused Andrea from his office and had told her—much to Brandon's vexation—to go pack for the trip to Buckeye.

"We all have secrets." Steve had moved himself back behind his desk. Evidently time for neutral ground was over. Steve was reaffirming that he was in charge.

"Do you know what they call her around here?"

Steve raised one eyebrow.

"'The ice queen.' She never talks to anyone, never engages anyone. Nobody knows anything about her."

"Just because she's not the life of the party makes her an ice queen? I thought better of you, Han."

Brandon didn't know why he felt the need to so quickly defend himself, but he did. "Not me. I didn't say that or think it, nor any of our inner group. It's just what I've heard some other people say."

"She's damn good at what she does. Next time someone wants to talk trash about her because she's not all touchy-feely, you be sure to tell them that."

"We all know she's good. She's a natural reader. I've never seen anything like it." Brandon held a PhD in interpersonal communication and still couldn't read people's expressions and body language to the extent Andrea could.

"But?"

"No buts about that. All I'm saying is she has secrets."

"She has a past, Brandon. We all do. Hers is a little more bleak than most of ours. If she's got secrets it's because she wants to not live in that past."

Brandon had to admit there was nothing wrong with that.

"I know it hurt you when David didn't tell you about his cancer. To find out then lose him so quickly was tough. It was for all of us."

Brandon got up out of his chair and walked over to the window. "I want to say this isn't about David, but of course that's not true."

"I know he was your best friend too, Brandon."

Brandon nodded without turning around. David had been his best friend since long before they worked together at Omega. David had been his anchor when the darkness of wandering inside the minds of killers had become too much.

"Andrea's the top person for this case, just like you're the top person for this case. There's somebody out there murdering young women and he needs to be stopped before he kills again."

Brandon knew Steve was right.

"Andrea's young, only twenty-three," Steve continued. "She's unsure about her abilities and where she fits in here."

Twenty-three? Something inside Brandon eased. She *was* young. Brandon was only thirty-one, but twenty-three seemed like a lifetime ago. He'd been more unsure about himself then too, so he couldn't blame her.

"You know me, Steve. I like having all the facts going into anything. She's an unknown variable and it gets my hackles up."

"I know some of what she keeps to herself, and although

I am not at liberty to share, what I know about her makes me respect her more, not less. But some of her secrets she's never shared with me. May not have shared them with anyone. That's her choice."

Brandon nodded. As Steve said, everyone had secrets.

"She's damn good at her job and she'll help you find that killer."

Brandon ran a hand over his face. "Okay, you're right. I'll go pack."

"Han, thank you," Steve said as Brandon turned for the door. "I know this isn't easy."

"Like you said, the important thing is getting the killer off the street."

"Going back to that town is not going to be easy for her. I'd appreciate if you'd just keep an eye out for her emotional well-being."

"Anything in particular I should know about?"

Steve shrugged. "It's where she grew up. Faster than most, I would venture."

Somehow Brandon got the feeling there was a huge chunk of information Steve was leaving out, but he let it slide. "Okay, I'll keep an eye out for her as best I can. Is that it?"

"Actually, no."

Brandon didn't even try to refrain from rolling his eyes. "There's more?"

"It's probably nothing, but I wanted to make you aware of it." Steve's tone had turned from concerned to downright serious.

Brandon walked back toward his desk. "Okay."

"Damian Freihof escaped from federal custody thirty-six hours ago."

Brandon filtered his mind for the information, finding it. "He was the guy who planned to blow up those people in that bank in Phoenix, right? What, three years ago?"

"Four. We also think he was responsible for two other bombings, but we weren't able to prove it."

"Do you suspect he's in Buckeye?"

"No. But like you said, the bank he tried to blow up was in Phoenix, pretty close by. He blames Andrea for his arrest."

"Why? Was she even there?"

"She was there, and she was the one who led to his capture, although she was not in law enforcement at the time."

Yeah, because at the time she would've been nineteen years old, if Brandon's math was correct.

"Did you tell Andrea about his escape?"

Steve's hesitation was minuscule, fleeting. Brandon would've missed it if he hadn't been trained to see it. "No, we chose not to tell her. When Freihof went to prison, Andrea was not yet working for us. Plus with two life sentences we didn't figure he would be getting out until he was at least eighty. He escaped during a transfer."

"You think keeping her out of the loop is wise?"

Steve shrugged. "Freihof was mad at pretty much everyone during his case and sentencing, so we didn't—and still don't—give his threats against Andrea much credence. We're not even sure how he got Andrea's name since she wasn't involved in his arrest or trial, but I doubt he's after her now. All she really did was let us know there was a third man in the bank. I don't think she had any idea he planned to blow everyone up and that her info thwarted his attempt."

Another secret. Another potential problem.

"All right." Brandon nodded. "I'll keep my eyes peeled for any extra psychos while we're chasing down our current one."

Steve smiled. "Remember, she's not an agent, just a full-time consultant. She has some physical training, but not nearly as much as you do."

"Okay. I'll keep that in mind."

Steve shook Brandon's hand. "Good hunting. Keep me posted."

Brandon nodded and headed toward the door. This was already more complicated than Brandon liked it. And he knew it was just going to get worse.

BRANDON'S ARRIVAL AT the Colorado Springs Airport three hours later to discover the flight to Phoenix had been delayed due to mechanical issues did not make him feel any better about the start of this case. They were flying commercial since the two Omega jets were occupied with other missions.

Andrea showed up, still looking chic and cool in her skirt and blouse. The ice queen. Brandon wondered if she ever let herself get rumpled. His fingers literally itched with the desire to be the one who did it.

Rumpling Andrea Gordon was such a bad idea.

Brandon had noticed her around Omega for years—it was difficult not to notice someone who looked like Andrea—but he'd been very careful not to allow himself to study her. Not to try to figure out what made her tick and what made her smile or frown. With two advanced degrees in human behavior and communication, not to mention one in law, figuring people out was what Brandon did.

But with Andrea that had seemed a dangerous path to start down.

Then for the past year he'd been so involved in his own issues—David's death, learning how to work alone—that his attraction for Andrea had gotten pushed to the back burner. But now it was sitting down next to him in the airport chair, unavoidable.

"Hello." She smiled briefly at him. "Ready for this?"

Andrea wanted to be professional. Everything about her suggested it, from her prim clothes, to her tasteful makeup, to her perfect hair. Brandon would answer in kind. Professional was better for both of them.

He nodded. "Not quite up to speed yet, but getting there. We're scheduled to meet with the Phoenix and Buckeye police tomorrow. Evidently Buckeye's department isn't equipped to handle a homicide investigation, so Phoenix is helping out."

"Buckeye is small. They don't get many serial killers."

"Let's hope we can stop this one before he kills again."

He found her studying him as he took some files out of his briefcase, her expression a little bemused. "What?"

"Nothing." She shook her head. "You're just…complicated."

Brandon's eyes narrowed. Quite the interesting observation. "Why do you say that?"

She shrugged. "Most people only have one or maybe two main emotions transpiring inside them at the same time. You have more." Her lips pursed. "And they're complex."

He did have more. Brandon knew that about himself. Knew that he compartmentalized in order to be able to get more done, to think about different things without actually dwelling on them.

It was part of what made him a good profiler. His subconscious brain was able to continue to work on certain aspects of a case while his conscious brain focused on something entirely different. Part of it was his own natural ability and intelligence. Part of it came from years of training his brain to do what he wanted.

He also had darkness in him. He could admit that, too. A side of him that knew he could use his intellect and training and experience to commit crimes if he really wanted. And would probably never get caught. It was never too far from the surface, although he never shared it with anyone.

Brandon had never had someone—especially someone

who didn't really know him well—sense the complexity of the emotions inside him. It was disconcerting, particularly because he didn't want her to be able to read him so well.

"Oh." Andrea looked away from him.

"What?"

"Annoyance just swamped out pretty much everything else." She folded her hands in her lap and looked at them.

She thought he was annoyed with her, when really his annoyance stemmed from not having as much control over expressing his emotions as he thought he had. That was the problem with naturals, with people who were just gifted behavioral analysts rather than those who had studied human psychology and nonverbal communication to become experts. The naturals could read the emotions but couldn't always figure out the context.

"Let's just focus on the case, okay?" He handed her a bundle of files. "We pretty much need to be completely familiar with all of this before we meet with the locals tomorrow."

Andrea grimaced. "Okay."

So she didn't like to do her homework. She wouldn't get far solving cases without it. No amount of skill reading people could offset having a good understanding of the particulars of a case.

Brandon began reading through the files. He often found that insight came after the third or fourth read-through, rarely the first.

It didn't take him long to realize Andrea wasn't reading. She was looking at the photographs—the postmortem shots of the women as well as the crime-scene photos—but not actually reading any of the information that went along with them.

When she slipped on headphones and began listening to music or whatever, Brandon felt his irritation grow. Did she need a sound track to make it more interesting? Was death not enough?

Brandon knew different people processed information different ways. Some of his best friends at Omega often got insight on a case while in a workout room or in the middle of hand-to-hand sparring with someone. He should cut Andrea some slack. If she wanted to listen to music and just study the pictures, that was her prerogative.

But damn if it didn't piss him off. It didn't happen often, but she had fooled him. Who would've guessed that under the professional clothes and standoffish attitude rested the heart of a slacker. Brandon took a deep breath and centered himself. It wasn't his fault or his problem if she lacked motivation and self-discipline.

He'd told Steve he preferred to work alone. It looked as if, despite Andrea's attractive packaging, he'd be getting his wish.

Chapter Three

This whole thing was a terrible idea. Going back to Buck-eye? Terrible. Going back with the likes of Brandon Han? Even worse. The plane hit some turbulence at thirty-five thousand feet, as if nodding in agreement with Andrea's conclusion.

Brandon didn't want to work with her on the case. He'd made that abundantly clear in Steve's office. She wanted to assume it was her fault, that he knew about her short-comings and lack of education as an Omega consultant, but forced herself to stop. He'd mentioned liking to work alone. She could understand that, too. Andrea liked work-ing alone, but for different reasons.

Brandon's irritation had been pretty tangible when she'd sat down next to him at the airport. It had just grown as they waited for their flight, first when she'd mentioned him being complicated, then when they were both look-ing through the case files.

By the time they got on the plane, about an hour after their scheduled departure time, Brandon was hardly even talking to her. He was mad—she had no idea why—and she was awkward—as usual around someone she was so attracted to. Good times.

Andrea tried to pretend she was reading the files when he handed them to her, but she wasn't. She knew better than to even try. Her dyslexia made reading simple books difficult, although she had learned some exercises to help with that. But reading handwritten notes and case files often written in different fonts and sizes—that pretty much just led to a headache and frustration.

She'd had an extra hour at her apartment, so she'd used the special software on her computer to scan a few pages so they could be converted into audio clips. She'd found that listening worked much better for her than trying to read. Unfortunately, she hadn't had enough time to scan all the files as she normally would.

Listening to the files on audio clips had just made Brandon more irritated. Andrea had no idea what to do about that, so she ignored it. She would listen to the clips she had, then spend this evening—all night if she had to—reading through the files in her room, when she was alone and it was quiet. She refused to go into that meeting with the local police tomorrow unprepared.

She didn't want to go back there at all. If it wasn't for Steve asking her to go, Andrea wouldn't have done it, serial killer or not.

Maybe they wouldn't run into anyone she knew. Or maybe the people in Buckeye wouldn't recognize her. She'd gone to great lengths to look nothing like the girl who had worked at Jaguar's. Her blond hair was shorter, cut in a flattering bob; her makeup was tasteful. She'd learned how to dress and present herself in a professional manner.

She doubted her own aunt and uncle would recognize her. Not that she planned to drop in on them. She hadn't seen them since the last time her uncle, in a drunken stupor again, had awakened her with a backhand that had sent her sprawling from her bed to the floor when she was seventeen. Another punch had sent her hurling into a glass table. She'd gotten away from him and hidden that night, wrapping her cut arm in a T-shirt.

The next morning she'd told her aunt, who'd looked the

other way *again* during all the commotion, that she was going to school.

Andrea hadn't gone to school. And she hadn't gone back home. Ever again.

She hadn't gone far, just to the other side of the town she'd only ever known as home, but they hadn't come looking for her. Had probably been relieved that she'd left.

So yeah, no joyous homecoming in Buckeye.

Andrea withdrew into herself as they landed at Sky Harbor Airport. She let Brandon take the lead as they rented a car and headed west on I-10 out of Phoenix, stopping to get something to eat on the way. The stark, flat lands of Arizona were a huge contrast to the backdrop of the Rocky Mountains in Colorado Springs, where she'd spent the past four years.

Coming here was a mistake. Andrea was convinced of it. If she'd been alone, she might have turned around and gone back home.

Home, Colorado Springs. That was her home now.

"Hey, you doing okay?"

Andrea struggled to hide her shock at Brandon's hand on her arm. She didn't think he was going to engage with her for the rest of the trip.

"Yeah. I just… This is hard. I don't think I want to do this."

She could feel his annoyance or coolness, or whatever it was he felt toward her, ease.

"Going back to the place where you grew up can be hard. Is there anyone you'd like to see while you're there? Friends? Family?"

"No, I don't think so. I don't think anyone here will remember me."

He didn't push it and she was thankful. They drove on in silence from the airport west on I-10 before turning south on smaller Highway 85. A couple of miles down they passed her old high school, Buckeye Union. Before thinking it through, she pointed it out to Brandon.

"What year did you graduate?"

She didn't want to tell him that she hadn't graduated, so she told him the year she'd stopped going. Then she realized it might make it sound as if she'd graduated early or something, so she changed it to the next year.

Brandon looked at her with one eyebrow raised, but fortunately, he didn't say anything else about it.

Before she knew it, before she could *stop* it, they were in Buckeye. The town hadn't changed much. They passed the dollar store, one of the town's grocery stores and Buckeye Auto Repair.

She actually remembered Buckeye Auto Repair pretty fondly. They had quite politely not mentioned that it looked as though everything she'd owned was in her car when she'd had to take it in for repairs when she was seventeen.

That was because everything she'd owned *had* been in the car. She'd been living in it at the time. Before she got the job at Jaguar's and made enough money to move into a sparsely furnished, run-down studio apartment.

She was pretty sure the owner of Buckeye Auto Repair hadn't charged her the full price for the repair.

She and Brandon pulled up to the town's one decent hotel. There were a couple of others on the rougher side of town—ones that were rented out by the hour, or the opposite, used to house multiple illegal immigrants in one room. This was a much better choice for law enforcement.

Brandon checked them in, getting rooms right next to each other on the first floor. They grabbed their bags and headed through the lobby and down the hall.

"I'm going to call it a night," Andrea said, slipping the key card into her door. She needed to be alone, away from all her thoughts and feelings about this town. She also needed to begin the painful process of studying the case files before tomorrow's meeting.

"Okay, I'll see you tomorrow. We'll leave at eight o'clock." Brandon turned to his door. "Are you okay?"

Andrea nodded. "Good night." She shut the door behind her without another word, away from Brandon and his brown eyes that saw too much.

Because she wasn't all right. Being back here was worse than she'd thought it would be.

This whole thing was a terrible idea.

THE NEXT MORNING at the Maricopa County Sheriff's Department office, Brandon and Andrea waited in the conference room for the local officers who would serve as their liaisons. The sheriff's department was just a mile or so on the outskirts of Buckeye.

When Andrea had seen what building they were arriving at, her eyes had nearly bugged out of her head. Her skin had turned a concerning shade of gray. Brandon had reached for her hand, and she had clutched his, almost automatically. Her skin was cold, clammy.

A sure nonverbal tell of fright. This building frightened Andrea.

She'd taken a couple of deep breaths and gotten herself under control, releasing his hand. She'd smiled over at him, an expression nowhere near touching her eyes, so nowhere near real. Something about that fake smile nearly broke his heart.

Maybe the whole idea of bringing her back to Buckeye had been a mistake. Her input would be valuable, sure, but Brandon had solved a lot of cases without having an inside person.

Maybe the price of doing this was too high for Andrea. Whatever judgments Brandon had made about her began to dissipate a little. Maybe she just wasn't ready to deal with this.

"Andrea." He'd turned to her from where they sat in the parking lot. "Perhaps this isn't a good idea. It's okay if I need to go in alone."

"No, I'm fine. I just didn't realize we'd be coming *here*, to this building, that's all."

What was here that made her so upset? "You have some history here?"

She took a deep breath. "Not really. This whole town just sets me on edge."

"Are you sure you're okay?" He didn't want her to get inside then panic.

"Yes, I'm fine. I promise." The smile she gave him was at least a little stronger than the shadow of one she'd given him a few moments ago. He touched her hand. It was closer to normal temperature again.

But she looked tired, despite makeup that carefully covered it, as if she had been up most of the night. Maybe she had if the town had this sort of effect on her.

But except for the telltale signs that he was sure only he would notice, looking at her from across the conference table now, she looked like the consummate professional. Andrea wore sharp trousers and a matching blazer, managing to be attractively feminine and coolly businesslike at the same time. The high heels she wore everywhere were the perfect complement to the outfit. Not a hair was out of place in her chic bob.

She may have been scared out in the parking lot, but she was determined not to show it in here. Brandon's respect for her ratcheted a notch. If only she was as prepared for the case as she looked, which he knew she wasn't. Maybe he could help her out if she got stuck, save her any embarrassment.

Two men entered the room, one in his midfifties in a

sheriff's office uniform, one in his early thirties in a suit. Both looked a little tired, frazzled. The older man took the lead. "I'm Lance Kendrick from the Maricopa County Sheriff's Department. Since all three murders took place—or at least the bodies were found—in Maricopa, I'm taking the lead."

"I'm Gerardo Jennison with the City of Phoenix Homicide Unit. We're providing investigative resources for anything which the sheriff's department may not have."

"I'm agent Brandon Han from Omega Sector, as you know. This is Ms. Andrea Gordon, one of our behavioral analysts. She'll be consulting as needed."

As Jennison shook Andrea's hand, Brandon could see his appreciation of her as a woman. Lance Kendrick, on the other hand, studied her pretty intently. Andrea had looked at him when they shook hands, but then glanced away.

Andrea recognized Kendrick.

That wasn't impossible or even improbable. Andrea had lived here her whole life. She probably would've run into members of the sheriff's office from time to time. "Have we met before?" Kendrick asked Andrea.

Her expression remained smooth although she shifted just slightly in her chair. "Maybe." She smiled at him. "Omega works a lot of cases."

A very nice side step. She wasn't offering up that she used to live here or that she recognized Kendrick, so Brandon didn't, either. Her comment seemed to pacify the sheriff's deputy, although Brandon knew that wasn't where they knew each other.

"We have three victims so far," Kendrick said, tone bordering on bored. "All Caucasian females between the ages of twenty to twenty-five. Cause of death was strangulation with a thin rope. The ligature marks were quite clear. All had been restrained—marks on their wrists were obvious, but there was no sign of any other assault, sexual or otherwise. And they all were found outside a church. Different one each time."

Putting the victims outside a church corresponded well with the purity theme he and Andrea had batted around yesterday.

"Any known connection between the victims?" he asked.

"They didn't seem to know each other, as far as we can tell. All lived in Maricopa County, but different parts."

"But two had been arrested for something in the last year or two," Andrea interjected.

Brandon glanced at her discreetly. So she *had* studied the files.

Kendrick nodded. "Different charges, but yes. Brought here for holding, actually. One was arrested for solicitation, one for underage drinking. Neither of them were ever booked or went to trial."

If Brandon hadn't been looking over at Andrea, he would've missed her slight flinch. Had there been some trouble with the law in her past? Was that what made her nervous about this building?

"Occupations were not exactly upstanding, either. Two of them worked at exotic dance clubs somewhere in Phoenix or the surrounding areas. One worked at a diner that is known to be a hot area for solicitation." Jennison grinned slyly at Kendrick.

Kendrick chuckled. "Yeah, I offered to do some undercover work at the clubs, but somehow couldn't clear it with my boss, much less my wife."

Brandon ignored the jokes. He wasn't surprised about the women's occupations. Quite often an arrest record accompanied such jobs.

"What exactly have you done concerning the investigation?" Brandon could hear the tightness in Andrea's tone.

"We've done our due diligence." Kendrick sat up a little

straighter in his chair. "We interviewed employers, canvassed the area for witnesses, ran DNA and searched for any prints."

Jennison interjected. "Look, we appreciate Omega sending you down here, and if you come up with any insight we'd love to hear it. We don't want a killer wandering around loose. But the fact is, none of these women seem to have anyone who cares about them, two have an arrest record and all have employment that is a bit questionable."

Kendrick shrugged. "So basically, we'll do all we can—like Jennison said, nobody wants to let a killer go free—but we're not getting any pressure from the higher-ups to put major resources into this investigation. Unfortunately, these women were pretty much nobodies."

Chapter Four

These women were pretty much nobodies.

No family who cared. Arrest records. Questionable employment.

If the killer had been around four years ago, Andrea might have been one of the victims. Every part of that account described her when she was nineteen, before changing her life at Omega.

She wanted to, but she could hardly blame the cops. Law-enforcement funding was limited. Unfortunately, without family demanding justice, these murders, if not easily solved, would just get pushed to the side.

The only reason Omega had been called at all was because it was obvious the three kills had been performed by the same person. Otherwise Andrea didn't know if the locals would've put any true effort into finding the killer.

They were on their way now to The Boar's Nest, one of three bars here in Buckeye, where the latest victim— Noelle Brumby—had been known to frequent. It was two o'clock in the afternoon, but evidently Noelle had hung out here in the afternoons since she worked nights.

Andrea's weariness pressed against her—reviewing the case files had taken her most of the night—but she pushed it aside. She had made it through talking to Lance Kendrick, who had thankfully not remembered her from her brief run-in with the sheriff's office for underage drinking years ago. She could make it through this.

Walking inside, she thought The Boar's Nest looked just the way someone would expect a small-town bar to look in the middle of the afternoon: dingy, run-down, pathetic. Night hid a lot of sins of this place that sunlight brought out.

The Tuesday afternoon crowd wasn't the most upstanding. Anybody who had a white-collar job, and even most of the blue-collar ones, would not be in this place at this time. The people patronizing The Boar's Nest now worked nights or didn't work at all.

Andrea heard a low whistle as they walked in, but didn't know if it was for her looks or because they were obviously law enforcement. Nobody ran for the exit or stopped any activities suddenly, so at least it didn't appear that anything illegal was happening.

She felt Brandon step closer to her and could see him looking around, obviously checking for any danger. Cops were sometimes not welcome in places like this, although that would not stop her and Brandon from their questioning. Brandon had a weapon, but Andrea didn't. Hopefully he wouldn't need to use it.

Two pool tables lined the far end of the room, with three guys playing on one. A bartender unpacked boxes and put glasses away behind the bar, and a couple sat at a table sipping beers in the corner.

All of them were looking at Brandon and Andrea.

Brandon touched her gently on the back—she knew it was an unconscious habit more than anything else but it still sent a slight shiver through her—and they headed toward the bar.

The bartender looked at them without halting his motions. "Lost or cops?"

Brandon chuckled. "Can't be thirsty?"

"Yeah, you can. And I'll gladly get you something, but I'm still pretty sure you're one of the other two, also."

"You're right—the latter. We're investigating the death of Noelle Brumby."

The bartender stopped putting away the glasses. "Yeah, that was a damn shame. She was a nice girl. Friendly. I'm Phil. I own this bar."

Andrea studied Phil while he talked. He seemed very sincere about liking Noelle.

"Can you tell us anything else about her?" Brandon asked.

"She worked at a...er, gentleman's club closer in to Phoenix."

Allure. They already knew that and would be interviewing people there soon, even though Kendrick and Jennison had also spoken with them.

"Why didn't she work at Jaguar's, do you know?" Andrea was hesitant to bring up her former place of employment in front of Brandon, but understanding why Noelle would drive farther to work at a club rather than work at the strip club here in town might have some bearing.

Both the bartender and Brandon looked a little surprised at her question.

"You from around here?" Phil asked. "You've never been in this bar before. I'm pretty sure I'd remember you."

"I've driven through town a few times." Better to just keep her past out of it.

"Noelle didn't like the owner over at Jaguar's. Had heard some bad things about him. Harry Minkley's his name."

Yeah, Andrea already knew Harry's name. And she was glad Noelle had the good sense not to work for him. Although in the long run, it hadn't helped her.

"Noelle came in here a lot?" Brandon leaned one arm against the bar so he had a better view of the whole place.

"Mostly during the week in the afternoons. Weekends were pretty busy for her, as were a lot of evenings. She hung out with those guys over there. The tall, skinny one's named Corey. Big one next to him is Luke and the other is Jarrod." He pointed back to where the three guys were playing pool. "They knew her better than me."

Brandon and Andrea both turned toward the men. "Thanks for your help," she said over her shoulder.

"Thank you for trying to find the killer." Phil turned back to his unpacking. "I wondered if anyone would bother."

The three younger men—all in their early to mid-twenties—continued to play pool as she and Brandon made their way over. But she could tell they were quite aware of her and Brandon as law enforcement and of her as a woman.

"Hey, guys." Brandon's tone was friendly but firm. "We'd like to talk to you about Noelle Brumby."

Andrea tried to watch all three as closely as she could. Two, Luke and Corey, immediately tensed, but she wasn't sure if that was because of their relationship with Noelle or because they just didn't like cops. The other one, Jarrod, definitely expressed some guilt at Noelle's name, but mostly couldn't seem to get his attention off Andrea.

Andrea tried to classify in her mind the reactions of each man. She wished she could record them and study them multiple times later, but she didn't have that luxury in this situation.

"What makes you think we even knew her?" Luke asked, now holding the pool cue with white knuckles.

"Phil said she hung out with you three a lot."

"Yeah, well, maybe Phil should keep his mouth shut," defensive guy number two—Corey—muttered, not looking up from the shot he was making.

Brandon walked around the pool table so he was stand-

ing against the far wall. Andrea understood why he did it,
to get a different angle and perspective for reading these
guys, but she felt more exposed without him next to her.

"We're trying to find the killer of someone who was
your friend. I'd think you'd want to help with that." Brandon was watching Luke and Corey as he made the statement—one meant to cause a reaction. Andrea turned her
attention to Jarrod, only to find him overtly studying her,
so she looked back at the other two men.

"Some sicko killed Noelle," Luke said. "We don't know
anything about it."

Corey was looking more and more uncomfortable.
"What's your name?" she asked softly even though she
already knew.

"You don't have to answer that, Corey." Luke wasn't
too smart.

Jarrod laughed from where he stood against the wall.
"You just told her his name, Luke. Dumb ass." Of course,
he'd just done the same thing.

"Corey—" Andrea took a step toward the other man
"—do you know something? Anything that could help us
find Noelle's killer?"

"No." Corey shook his head, not really looking at her.
"I don't know anything."

Andrea was about to press further with Corey when
Jarrod interrupted.

"Oh my gawd, are you Andrea Gordon?" Jarrod all
but gushed. "It is you, right? You were in one of my math
classes in high school. I'm Jarrod McConnachie."

Damn it. Andrea knew she might be recognized at some
point, but hadn't thought it would be by some guys in a
bar in the middle of the afternoon.

Luke tilted his head to one side. "Oh yeah, I think I remember you. You were pretty quiet. But always hot." All
three men snickered.

Oh God, had they come to see her dance when she worked at Jaguar's? She'd always worn wigs and enough makeup to give herself an entirely different appearance, but the thought they might recognize her and announce it made her absolutely sick.

"I thought you'd moved away your junior year," Jarrod said.

She hadn't moved away, really just to the other side of town. But she'd dropped out of school. "Yeah, something like that."

"But I still kept seeing your mom and dad around. So then I didn't know what happened to you. A couple people thought you'd died and they just hadn't announced it."

It was good to know a few people noticed she was gone.

"It was my aunt and uncle I lived with, not my mom and dad. But yeah, they stayed here when I left." They'd never once tried to find her, thank God. That last time when she'd fallen through the table, they had probably been afraid they might go to jail. Looking for her wouldn't have been in their best interest.

Andrea should've gone to the police. She knew that now. Knew there were good officers out there—Omega worked with them all the time—who wanted to help. Who would've believed her or at least have thoroughly investigated. But at the time she'd been young and scared and thought all cops were the enemy.

The exact way these guys thought of them, too. She needed to get the questions back on track but had no idea how to do so.

"Well, you sure cleaned up nice," Jarrod said, moving slightly closer. "And you're a cop. I'd be happy to let you cuff me to anything you want."

The other guys chuckled.

"How about if I cuff you and throw you in a cell with a couple of long-term criminals?" Brandon interjected, coming to stand next to Andrea again. "Would that work for you?"

"Look, man—" Jarrod backed off "—I was just trying to say hello to an old friend."

Brandon's eyes narrowed. "Instead, why don't all of you tell us where you were on Friday night between midnight and 4:00 a.m.?"

The body had been found Saturday afternoon, but the coroner put the time of death as late Friday night or early Saturday morning.

"I was at home with my wife," Corey said. Brandon marked it down in a notebook.

"I was in Phoenix at a bar with a bunch of friends," Luke said, giving its name. "We started home after last call." He glanced down before looking up defiantly at Brandon and Andrea.

There was definitely more to that story. Luke's emotions weren't necessarily guilt in a specific sense, but a sort of overall vague sense of shame.

"I was at my house sleeping, after walking home from here. I live off Old Highway 80," Jarrod said, still staring openly at Andrea.

"You live alone?" Brandon asked.

Both the other men snickered. Brandon raised an eyebrow. "What?"

"No," Luke said. "He lives with his mother."

Jarrod turned away, grimacing. "Thanks, Luke."

Andrea couldn't help but smile a little at Jarrod's comeuppance. Especially since his desire to bed her practically oozed from his pores. He wasn't even trying to hide his craving for Andrea.

"Your mom can vouch that you were at the house?" Brandon asked Jarrod.

"Yeah, man. She's always at home. Gets so angry at me whenever I go out."

Probably pretty angry that Jarrod didn't have a job, either, but Andrea didn't mention that. Didn't want to draw the attention back to herself.

She watched all three men as Brandon got their names and contact information. He explained that, at this point, they were eliminating suspects. Telling the truth now would save them from more trouble later. Although none of them were thrilled at giving the info, none of them resisted.

Jarrod tried to talk to her while Brandon spoke with the other men, but she wouldn't engage with him. She'd had plenty of practice being standoffish over the past few years. Shutting him down was easy.

Plus, she wondered if he wasn't trying to get on her good side because he was hiding something.

One thing she knew for sure as she and Brandon left the bar, waving to bartender Phil as they went—all three men they'd interviewed today had secrets. All of them had lied or withheld information in some way.

Chapter Five

They spent the entire next day traveling around Phoenix and Buckeye, checking alibis, talking to the employers and colleagues of the women.

As the detectives had said, none of the victims had family who had spoken up. It didn't seem as if they had many friends, either. The killer had chosen well: women whose deaths would go relatively unnoticed. Only the ritualistic placement of the bodies and the symbolic items found with each victim even clued in law enforcement that it was the same killer at all.

The killer probably hadn't been able to stop himself from placing the symbols of purity around the women, even if he'd intellectually recognized that it could lead to his demise. The purity rituals had been just as important to the killer as the kill itself.

The killer was calm, sure of himself—almost definitely a *he* based on the nature of the crimes and the fact that the victims were all females. These murders hadn't been done in rage. There had been no mutilation of the bodies, no bruising beyond the restraints on the wrists and the rope marks around the throat.

If he let himself, Brandon could perfectly envision the rope tightening around the victims' throats. The killer most certainly would've had them on their knees—an act of repentance, needed before one could be deemed pure.

The killer hadn't been interested in the women sexually—or perhaps he had and wouldn't let himself act on it—only in freeing them from their evil. Cleansing them.

Brandon had been sitting in his hotel room for the past hour, looking blankly ahead. To most people it would've seemed as if he was staring out into nothing, but really he was giving his mind a quiet place to sort through all the data he'd been processing for the past forty-eight hours.

Letting his mind get into the head of a killer.

It wasn't a comfortable place to be, and since David's death, Brandon didn't let himself get in that dark place too often.

Brandon was aware of the dark side of his intelligence, of his nature. Was well aware that immersing himself deep into the thoughts of a killer could leave him tainted by that darkness.

And now there was no one to drag him back but himself. No one to warn him when he was getting too close to the abyss. It was one of the things he missed most about having a partner he trusted.

And speaking of partners, it was time to meet his temporary one. When they'd arrived back at the hotel, Andrea had all but fled into her room. She'd said it was because she wanted to look over some notes from today's interviews, but Brandon knew that couldn't be it. She hadn't taken any notes all day.

She was an enigma. Her work ethic seemed impeccable—she was punctual, attentive and focused—but then she'd do something completely unprofessional like refuse to take any notes.

Even Brandon took notes. He realized a long time ago his brain—all brains—were capable of great things, but they were never infallible. Evidently Andrea thought hers was the exception.

He should be thankful for her flaw. For her reminder

that he didn't want someone like her as a partner. Because if he woke up one more time, his body hard and wound up, dreaming about her—about kissing her and removing all the professional clothes she wore like armor—he was afraid he would act on it.

He needed to keep his distance.

Pulling rank and forcing her to have dinner with him was not helping with that plan. She'd wanted to camp out in her own room all evening, grab some crackers, go over what they'd found. He'd told her they needed to eat real food and could discuss the case while doing so. She put up a bit of an argument, but he hadn't listened, just threatened to bring dinner to her hotel room so they could work there.

That got her agreement.

He moved into the lobby to meet her. They were going to walk a few blocks down the street to the mom-and-pop Italian restaurant. He saw her as she walked in the lobby just moments later. He had changed into jeans and a T-shirt, but she still wore her pants and blazer from the interviews earlier. She looked nice, no doubt about that. But definitely not casual or comfortable. He wondered if she ever looked casual or comfortable, if she ever just let herself relax around anyone.

He couldn't seem to make himself stop looking at her. Damn, he wanted to peel her out of those clothes. To see if there was any fire underneath and disprove the ice-queen theory. To show her that it was okay to *let go* with him. To protect her from whatever demons she was fighting. The sudden overwhelming thoughts caught him off guard.

"What?" she asked at his continued stare.

"Nothing. Just hungry. Ready?"

After walking to the restaurant and ordering, Andrea immediately brought up the case, obviously wanting to offset the chance of talking about anything personal. That was fine with Brandon. He hoped to use this time not only to go over the case, but to give her a lesson in law enforcement about the need to take notes. He wanted to point out how many things she missed by not taking notes and trying to keep it all in her head.

"So what do we know about each of the victims? Let's make sure we haven't missed any details," he said as the waitress brought their salads and they began eating.

Andrea nodded. "Victim one, Yvette Tyler, found two weeks ago. Twenty-one years old, brunette, five feet five inches, 115 pounds. No family. Place of employment—Diamond Cabaret Strip Club in Phoenix."

Her lips pursed the slightest bit with that sentence. Evidently she didn't approve of that career choice.

Brandon continued. "She was arrested last year for drunk and disorderly, and underage drinking, but since she had no record the charges were dropped."

"Yes. Victim two, Ashley Judson, found six days ago. Eighteen years old, worked at a diner west of here in Tonopah on I-10."

"That truck stop is known to be a place for truckers to pick up women, and women to pick up rides, literally and figuratively."

Andrea smiled a little at that and speared another bite of her salad. "Judson had also been arrested for solicitation, no surprise there. Spent a couple of nights at the Maricopa County lockup, too. Charges were dropped because of some technicality."

"And we have Noelle Brumby."

"Yes, twenty-three, blond. Worked at Allure in Phoenix."

She knew her facts better than he'd thought. Maybe he'd misjudged her at the airport when he'd thought she was just skimming over the files.

The waitress brought their main course. Andrea had

ordered chicken Alfredo; Brandon had gotten lasagna. He had to admit, it smelled delicious.

"So give me your opinion of Noelle's friends, the guys at the bar yesterday. Jarrod and the other two."

"Luke and Corey," she murmured, taking a bite.

Hmm. That had been his first attempt to catch her, to use as an example later of why she should take notes. Guess that wouldn't work.

"They're all hiding something," she said.

"Something about Noelle's death?"

She shrugged. "Tied to it, probably yes, although I don't think any of them are the killer."

Interesting. "Okay, tell me what you saw and what you concluded."

"Corey looks most guilty at first glance. Or at least he feels guilty about something."

Brandon had noticed that, also. "Go on."

"I think he was either having an affair with her or was in love with her or both. His guilt probably stems from a lot of things—failure to help Noelle, his feelings about cheating on his wife, not being able to do anything about it now."

"I agree."

She nodded. "And he's scared. That's what initially made me think he might be the killer, but I think he's scared that his wife is going to find out. That the investigation will uncover the affair."

"What about the defensive guy, Luke?" He took a bite of his lasagna. It tasted as good as it smelled. "You think he's hiding something, too?"

"He definitely has no love for law enforcement."

Brandon chuckled; that had been clear enough for a blind person to see.

"He also didn't want us looking into his alibi at the bar."

That was interesting. Something he hadn't picked up on.

He slowed his chewing. "Okay, why do you think that? His alibi checked out today."

She shrugged. "He definitely had a vibe, something he didn't want discovered. After talking to the bartenders today, I think it was probably that he and his friends drove home drunk. They were definitely drinking enough to be drunk, and then according to his own testimony he drove himself home."

A good insight.

She took another bite. "Or his guilt may have been about some sexual shenanigans they got into. Maybe he seduced some girl in the bathroom and feels a little bad about that—I don't know." She couldn't quite keep eye contact with him as she said it.

She couldn't look at him when talking about sex. Maybe he wasn't the only person affected when the two of them were together. Maybe Little Miss Professional wasn't as buttoned-up as he thought.

"Okay, interesting theories."

"But not pertaining to the case, so not important." She frowned and stabbed her pasta with more force than necessary.

"I didn't say that. Understanding—getting inside their heads, their desires—can lead you to the right path. It's not always a direct route, but it almost always helps."

She shrugged. "Only if it's the actual criminal. Otherwise you're wasting time."

"Eliminating someone isn't a waste of time. It's one step closer to the truth."

"Well, I don't think either Luke or Corey are our killer. I think they're up to no good in at least some part of their lives, but not killing."

"And Jarrod?"

"I didn't really get a read off him, one way or another.

He was embarrassed to still be living at home, I know that."

Brandon had gotten a read off Jarrod. Not because of his skill as a profiler, but because he was a man.

Jarrod wanted Andrea. It had pretty much consumed the man's thoughts. That neither cleared him nor made him guilty. His mother had told them that Jarrod was home when they talked to her today, but she had to admit, she hadn't actually been in the room with him during any of the hours in question.

Jarrod could've come home then sneaked back out.

Of course, nothing about Jarrod matched the profile Brandon was developing in his mind. Jarrod wasn't methodical or meticulous like the killer, so Brandon wasn't looking at the younger man as a true suspect yet. However, Brandon still might find reason to arrest him if he kept making moves toward Andrea.

"So did you know Jarrod well in high school?" Brandon wasn't sure why he'd asked, but he knew he wanted to know.

The fork that was carrying food to her mouth stopped and returned to the plate without the bite being eaten.

"No. To be honest, I don't remember him at all."

"He said he was in your math class."

She shrugged, fidgeting slightly in her seat. "A lot of high school was just a blur for me. You know how it is."

Brandon wanted to know more about her. "What clique were you? Sports? Nerd? Punk rocker?"

A ghost of a smile passed her lips. "None, really. I pretty much kept to myself."

Like the way she pretty much had kept to herself the past couple of years while at Omega?

She was pushing her food around on her plate now, not really eating it. Okay, she didn't want to talk about high school. Maybe she had bloomed more in college. That happened. For some people high school had been a miserable experience. Brandon's own high school experience had been nothing fantastic.

But now Brandon found he wanted to know something about Andrea. Something about her as a person. Not about her abilities as a behavioral analyst—hell, he was already completely impressed by just about everything she'd done concerning the case. His plan to teach her about note-taking had just proved fruitless; she'd taught him a lesson about her abilities instead.

But what did he really know about her? Name, occupation, age. Brandon made a living getting inside the minds of others, but he'd be damned if he'd been able to do so with her.

Brandon eased back into info and tactics he'd learned in his basic psychology classes way back in undergrad: get someone comfortable with you if you wanted them to freely share information. The best way to do that was a compliment.

That was easy with Andrea. Her skills were impressive.

"I think everything you've said about the guys tonight is spot-on. You caught a few things I missed." He wasn't faking any sincerity when he said it. "And I like to think I don't miss very much."

He could see the tension ease out of her torso even from across the table. She really didn't want to talk about high school. Maybe it was just being here in town; maybe it was something she never wanted to talk about. Brandon wouldn't push.

He smiled at her. "Steve was right about your abilities. It's impressive."

She smiled back at him, obviously basking in his praise. That was something for him to file away. It confirmed what Steve had told him in his office on Monday. Andrea still wasn't sure about herself and exactly where and how she belonged in Omega.

Which was a shame. Someone with her abilities should rest very comfortably in them. It would make her a better analyst if she wasn't constantly second-guessing herself. Brandon found himself wanting to help her with that.

To make Omega a stronger law-enforcement entity, of course. It had nothing to do with getting closer to the woman sitting across from him, with seeing more of her smiles, seeing her relax and ease into her own abilities.

He forced himself to tear his eyes away from hers and eat the last bite of his food.

He would start on neutral territory.

"So, where'd you go to college? Did you decide to study criminal science or end up going with psychology?" It had been a question he'd had to choose, but had found he couldn't decide, so he'd ended up studying both.

"I, um…I—"

Brandon looked up from his plate and found all of Andrea's tension back. More. She was biting her lip and pulling at her blazer sleeve.

Evidently the subject of college was even worse than high school.

"Andrea—"

She stood up, her chair scraping loudly on the floor. She flinched. "Brandon, I'm sorry. I have to go. I'm not feeling well."

"Just wait and I'll—"

"No. I'm sorry, no—"

She was gone, hurrying out the restaurant door before he could stop her.

Chapter Six

Brandon paid the bill a few minutes later, trying to figure out what had just happened. He replayed the conversation in his mind to see if he'd said anything that could be construed by Andrea as offensive or threatening.

All he'd really done was ask her about high school and college.

Brandon had been studying people long enough to know her behavior signified more than just a desire not to talk about herself. It came back to what he had argued about with Steve in his office.

Andrea Gordon had secrets. And they had to do with this town.

What Brandon didn't know was if he should press or not. Her secrets, whatever they were, didn't seem to get in the way of her doing her job. He had no complaints about the insights she was bringing into the case.

But the man inside him—his basic, most primal man— could not abide that she was hiding things from him. That she had pain, that she needed help, and she would not share that with him. He wanted to force her to tell him so he could fight the battle for her.

Brandon grimaced as he sat back in his chair. He knew himself well enough to know there were parts of his psyche that he didn't allow to break through very often, but were still quite strong inside him.

The part of him he called the warrior.

The warrior kept things very simple, saw only in black and white, right or wrong. Not the shades of gray that his intellect wandered in all the time. The warrior inside was who kept Brandon from becoming a criminal himself.

The darkness and the warrior combated each other.

God knew he came by the warrior honestly. He had literal fighter's blood flowing through his veins from his ancestors on both sides: Japanese samurai from his father's side, Scottish clansmen from his mother's.

The warrior wasn't interested in profiling or studying nonverbal cues. He wasn't interested in what was politically correct or even polite. He was interested in fighting for what was *just*. What was *his*.

Brandon didn't let the warrior side of himself come to light very often. He preferred to use his intellect and reasoning abilities to get things done.

But when it came to Andrea, the warrior kept pushing his way forward.

Well, that was too damn bad, because Brandon wasn't about to let his Neanderthal self run roughshod over this entire investigation. Brandon had to work with Andrea. She was his partner, for however long this case lasted. He would not go demanding answers from her.

Demanding kisses from her.

But he would go find her and make sure she was okay. Let her know he wasn't going to push her to talk about things she wasn't ready to share.

The warrior inside all but growled, but Brandon ignored him, pushing him back down.

Brandon exited the restaurant and walked back up the block toward the hotel. And, just his luck, it was starting to drizzle hard enough to be an annoyance.

He almost didn't see Andrea.

Of course, he wasn't looking for her to be standing on

the edge of the parking lot since she'd left the restaurant ten minutes ago. But she was, staring at a car—an old beat-up Chevy—parked close to the hotel's front entrance.

She wasn't moving, just standing in the rain. Frozen in what seemed to be terror.

Brandon's first thought was that it was Damian Freihof, the would-be bank bomber. Had he found Andrea here? But then he realized Freihof wouldn't be sitting in a car and Andrea wouldn't just be staring at him if he was.

He walked up to Andrea, careful to come at her slowly and from the side so he didn't sneak up on her in any way.

"Hi." He kept his voice even, calm. "What are you doing out here? Everything okay?"

She looked at him then back at the parking lot.

Without being obvious about it, Brandon withdrew his weapon from the holster at his side. Had she seen something to do with the case?

"Andrea." His voice was a little stronger now. "What's going on? Is it something to do with the murders? Did you see something or did someone threaten you?"

She kept staring.

"Andrea, look at me."

She finally turned to him, hair plastered to her head from the rain, makeup beginning to smear on her face.

"I need you to tell me what's happening. Is there danger? Did you see something having to do with the case?"

Andrea's eyes finally focused on Brandon. "N-no. No, there's no danger. I just…I just thought…" He waited but she didn't finish her sentence.

Okay, not an immediate danger and nothing from the investigation. Something from her past, then. He holstered his weapon. There wasn't danger, but she needed help. Especially since she didn't seem capable of taking care of herself at the moment.

"Let's go inside, sweetheart." The endearment slipped out unbidden. "Let's get you out of the rain."

She stiffened. "No, I can't go inside." Her attention narrowed again on the old car parked near the front entrance, under the hotel's overhang. It looked as if someone was sitting inside, but it was too far for Brandon to get any details.

He and Andrea couldn't stay out in the rain—even the desert of Arizona was cold in March. Andrea was already shivering.

The car seemed to be the center of her terror, not the hotel.

"What if we go in the side door?" Brandon pointed to a door nearer to them. It wasn't close to their rooms, but it would at least mean not having to go in the main entrance through the parking lot.

She looked over at the door he referred to and nodded. Brandon wrapped an arm around her slim form and led her to the door. Once inside he kept her in his grasp as they made their way down the hall. She was still shivering.

Warrior or not, there was no way Brandon was letting Andrea out of his sight right now. He wasn't even sure he could let her out of his arms.

He stopped at his room and got his key card out of his pocket. He knew Andrea was in bad shape when she didn't protest him bringing her into his room.

He shrugged off his jacket and threw it over the chair, then helped her take off her soaked blazer and eased her down to sit on the edge of the bed.

He left her for a moment to go get a towel from the bathroom. When he came back she hadn't moved at all, was still sitting, huddled into herself, where he'd left her.

His heart broke a little bit at her flinch when he put the towel around her and began gently drying her hair.

"Shh. I won't hurt you. I just want to make sure you don't get sick." He took a corner of the towel and wiped it across her cheeks in an effort to dry them and also re-move some of the makeup that had run down her cheeks. Her green eyes just stared out at him.

Brandon left the towel wrapped around her shoulders and grabbed a chair so he could set it right in front of her. He sat so they were eye to eye.

"Who was that in the car out front?"

He heard the tiny hitch in her breathing. "You saw it?"

"No, I could just see that *you* saw whoever it was."

"That's my aunt and uncle's car. They raised me after my mom died when I was ten."

"And you don't want them to know you're here?"

A shudder racked Andrea. "No. I don't ever want to see either of them again."

She looked away and began rubbing her arm, repeat-edly. He looked down and saw scars, multiple small lines all around her elbow. He'd never seen the scars before but then realized it was because he'd never seen her without a long-sleeved shirt or blazer.

Her professional wardrobe was not just an emotional barrier between her and the world; it was a physical one.

As he looked down at the scars again, at her coun-tenance, her posture, a rage flooded him. She had been abused.

He immediately tamped down his anger, knowing she would read it and could take it the wrong way. She needed support right now. Gentleness. Caring.

"They hurt you." His voice was barely more than a whisper, but it wasn't a question.

"They're alcoholics. And whenever they drank… My uncle mostly. My aunt just locked herself in her room."

A tear rolled down her cheek as she looked away from him out the window. She was still rubbing her arm.

"I know they can't hurt me now. I'm older. Stronger. Not the same person who lived in their house."

"All of that is true. Every word."

"And you could arrest them if they tried anything."

She was obviously trying to give herself a pep talk.

He nodded. "I wouldn't hesitate to do so."

"I was so young and stupid. They didn't want me after my mom died, but I didn't have anywhere else to go. I tried to stay out of their way as much as possible. But in a way, I guess I should be thankful for them."

Brandon couldn't think of a single reason why an abuse survivor should be thankful for what she'd been through.

She shrugged. "It's because of my uncle that I learned to read people so well. The situation at home forced me to really study nuances of expressions."

"So you could stay a step ahead of his fists."

She nodded. "But it didn't always work. Sometimes you knew what was coming, but you couldn't escape it."

She was referring to her situation in second person instead of first—distancing herself. It was a coping strategy.

"The situation at home may have helped you hone your skills at a younger age than you would have otherwise," he agreed. "But I imagine your gift at reading people still would be there. You would've always been an extraordinary behavioral analyst—you just wouldn't have known about it until later in your studies."

Suddenly some of her earlier words and actions clicked into place for Brandon. Her defensiveness about college, the reason she had given him two different graduating years for high school.

"You ran away, didn't you?"

She flushed, embarrassed. "Yes. I was about to turn seventeen. My uncle came in, drunk, and pulled me from a sound sleep, throwing me off the bed before beginning to whale on me. I got out, after falling through a glass table. But I never spent another night in that house."

Rage coursed through Brandon. The temptation to go

out there and give her uncle just the slightest taste of his own medicine almost overwhelmed him. But he ratcheted his temper under control.

Andrea needed him here.

"Good for you."

She rolled her eyes. "Sure, except for the fact that I had to drop out of high school. I was never any good at school anyway." She seemed to shrink into herself. "I'm dyslexic, so reading was—still is—hard for me."

Brandon grimaced. Dealing with dyslexia was a challenge for any child. And a child who had no academic or emotional support at home? A setup for failure. He thought about how he had mentally criticized her for not reading the police file at the airport. Now he knew why. Reading it would be difficult enough for her; reading in a crowded place with a bunch of distractions would be nearly impossible.

"Steve Drackett and Grace Parker, the head psychologist for Omega, met me in Phoenix when I was nineteen. I helped them with a bank hostage situation."

Brandon nodded, leaning closer to her and taking the hand that was still rubbing at her scars. He gently ran his fingers along her knuckles, not sure if he was trying to soothe her or himself. He knew about the bank, or at least about Damian Freihof. At this moment Brandon completely agreed with Steve's decision not to tell Andrea about Freihof. Buckeye was hard enough on her without adding the possible threat of a madman.

"They had me do some testing, because Steve was sure I had a natural ability at reading people."

"Behavioral and nonverbal communication diagnostic," Brandon murmured, not letting go of her hand.

"You know it?"

"I'm familiar with it." More than. He'd helped develop the latest, most thorough version of it when he'd been in grad school ten years ago. She'd taken the test he'd helped create.

"So you ran away to escape an impossible home situation and had to quit school. Steve and Grace realized how naturally gifted you were and brought you into the Omega fold."

She glanced down for just a second before looking at him again. "Yes, pretty much."

There was other stuff she wasn't telling him—glancing down rapidly was almost always a tell of hiding something. Amazing that she could read so clearly the emotions and microexpressions of others, but couldn't control them in herself.

But mostly what she felt, what every nonverbal element of her body language and facial expressions spoke for her, was shame.

"I'm not really your typical Omega caliber person, right?" She smiled crookedly, not quite looking him in the eyes. "No education, no training. Can't even read right. Afraid to face an old couple in a car."

Those sentences explained so much about her and her behavior over the past few years at Omega. She wasn't standoffish or an ice queen; she was an abuse survivor. She'd been keeping herself apart so her colleagues wouldn't find out about her past, afraid they would consider her unworthy of being part of the Omega team.

Brandon couldn't stop himself. He let go of her hands to cup her face, gently wiping her still-damp hair back from her cheeks.

"A few people might have thought that at first, but no one would think it now, given your track record with cases."

She just shrugged.

He trailed his fingers down her cheek. The warrior in him happy to have her close, to finally know some of her pain so he could try to protect her. "You have a *gift*. Steve recognized it so thoroughly that he brought you—an unknown teenager—into Omega. And he has never regretted that decision, I'm positive."

"But I don't have any education. Any training."

"You can get both of those if you want it—you have plenty of time. Hell, if I could naturally do what you do? I would've stopped going to school when I was ten."

A ghost of a smile, but at least it was a *real* one. Brandon wasn't sure he'd ever seen anything so beautiful. He got up and sat next to her on the bed so he could put his arm around her. He had to be closer to her.

"I did get my GED a couple years ago," she murmured, leaning into him. "And have taken a few semesters of college courses. But the dyslexia makes it hard."

"Of course it does," he said against her hair, pride running through him. "But you've persevered. You'll take it slow and finish as you're able. With your abilities, getting a degree is no big rush."

Brandon slid them back so they rested against the headboard of the bed. He kept his arm around her for support, but also because he couldn't seem to force himself to put any distance between them. She didn't seem to want it, either.

He wondered how long it had been since someone had just held her like this.

If ever.

He could feel her relaxing into him. Tension easing out of her body.

"I suppose I should go see if my aunt and uncle are still out there. I shouldn't be surprised they heard I'm in town. Gossip runs pretty freely around here." She shrugged. "I don't want to see them. Don't know why they would want to see me. But I guess I've got to face them sometime."

He tilted her face from where it rested on his shoulder

and kissed her. Gently. Tenderly. His passion was there, just below the surface, but he kept it under tight rein—his passion was not the emotion he wanted her to pick up on. She didn't need that.

"Yes, but not tonight. You face them on your time, when you're ready. Not a minute before."

She sighed sinking back into him, nodding. Brandon wrapped his arms more tightly around her, wanting to keep her safe from anything that would ever cause her harm.

Chapter Seven

Andrea woke up with a start, eyes flying open. It was dark. She always slept with a light on, mostly because she didn't want to wake up like this: panicked, braced for violence. She didn't move, but held her body tense, ready to shoot off in whichever direction would get her to safety.

Slowly realization dawned. There was no danger here. The opposite, in fact. She was lying on top of the bedcover, wrapped in Brandon Han's arms.

They'd shifted a little in their sleep; he pulled her more closely to him so that she was draped nearly all down his side. Her leg was even hooked over his thighs.

Like lovers.

The thought of Brandon as her lover sent little explosions of passion barreling up and down her spine. She could think of nothing she wanted more.

She'd told him about her home situation. About not finishing school. About not having the education or background to really be a part of the Omega team. None of it had seemed to matter to him.

Of course, she hadn't mentioned she'd also been a stripper for a period of eighteen months—the worst eighteen months of her life. Some of those girls had thrived on being onstage, being the center of attention, driving men wild. For Andrea it had been an exercise in agony every time.

It was a part of her life she'd just as soon forget. And

she couldn't think of a reason why she would need to tell Brandon, or anybody at Omega, about it.

She wanted to stay here in his arms, to sleep with him, to wake up with him and kiss him in the way she'd dreamed of. And much more than that.

Now that her eyes had adjusted to the darkness, she could see his chiseled features illuminated by the cloudy moonlight floating through the window. Black hair, prominent cheekbones, soft lips relaxed in sleep.

Despite his earlier, gentle kiss and the fact that he held her in his arms even now, Andrea didn't think Brandon was interested in her sexually. He was a colleague, perhaps could even be a friend. His emotions last night had radiated concern and sympathy for her, and even anger directed at her past.

Not passion.

Andrea eased her way back from him slowly. She should leave now. There was no need to have an awkward morning-after when they hadn't really had the fun part of the night before.

She worked herself away from him and out of the bed without waking him. She grabbed the shoes she'd taken off and her blazer from the chair. With one last look at his sleeping form, she slipped out the door.

A FEW HOURS LATER, in the hotel's dining room, Brandon slid into the chair across from Andrea. It didn't take any special reading ability for her to see he was pretty irritated.

"You snuck out in the middle of the night," he said as he added a creamer packet to his paper coffee cup.

Andrea would've thought he'd be relieved, not mad.

"Yeah, I woke up and thought it would be better if I went to my own room."

He tilted his head to the side and studied her.

"What?" she asked.

"I'm surprised you were able to get out without me waking up."

She shrugged. "I'm good at moving very quietly." A skill she'd picked up when not waking her drunk uncle had been a priority.

He still didn't stop staring at her. It was making her uneasy.

"Did you sleep okay?" he finally said. "Yesterday evening was a pretty rough one for you."

Her discomfiture came rushing back. She never should have told him all that stuff about herself. Sure, last night he'd been supportive, but this morning... Maybe this morning he realized what a fraud she really was.

He reached over and grabbed her hand, squeezing it just short of being painful. "Hey, whatever is going on in that mind of yours right now, stop."

"But—"

Now his eyes were mad. "I mean it. The only one thinking bad things about you at this table is *you*. So stop."

"Okay." She took a breath. He was right. She needed to learn to stop her self-sabotaging thoughts.

"So I'll ask you again—did you sleep okay?"

Did he mean before she left his room or afterward? She had slept amazingly in his bed. In his arms. But she probably shouldn't announce that, since he might think she was trying to get an invitation to do it again. Once she'd gotten back to her room the bed had seemed too big, too empty. She'd slept, mostly from the sheer exhaustion of having stayed up nearly all night on Monday studying the case files, but not nearly as well.

"I slept fine. Thanks." Seemed like the safest answer.

She had gotten up a little early to make sure she had time to do her hair and makeup perfectly. She was wearing the suit she knew she looked most professional in. After what had happened yesterday, Andrea had felt the need to show she was as competent and proficient as possible. To Brandon and herself.

"So what's our agenda for the day?" she asked briskly.

Brandon's eyebrow rose at the question. Andrea knew she was probably being a little too sharp, but she had to find a way to get them back on neutral footing.

Thankfully Brandon took her cue.

He sat up straighter. "We need to talk to the rest of victim number two's coworkers at the diner. See if any of them remember Ashley talking to someone in particular, not only that night, but the nights leading up to her murder. Find out if she had any regulars. That might be more difficult since none of them want to admit they're turning tricks on the side."

"It's probably not a regular who killed her since—"

Her sentence was cut off when both of their phones started vibrating.

"Damn it," Brandon muttered, looking down at the email message that had popped up on his phone. "Maricopa Sheriff's Department found another body. Another girl has been murdered."

They were in the car and headed toward the crime scene five minutes later. Brandon called and updated Omega as they drove, promising to give more details as they became available. They didn't have far to drive. The body had been found just on the outskirts of Buckeye, again in front of another church.

Andrea glanced at Brandon. "Just so you know, I don't do crime scenes very often. My talents are with witnesses."

He nodded. "Yeah, I guess dead bodies don't give off many nonverbal cues for you to read."

"Honestly, I haven't really been around any." This was just another example of how untrained she was.

"Hey, a lot of agents try to get out of crime scenes—especially those with a dead body—any way they can. You know Liam Goetz, right?"

Andrea had worked with him and his pregnant soon-to-be wife, Vanessa, on a human-trafficking case a few months ago. He was head of Omega's hostage-rescue team—and had proved his skills rescuing a group of young girls who had been kidnapped and were about to be sold into sexual slavery.

"Yeah, I know Liam." She didn't know him well, but liked the big, muscular man and how caring he was with petite Vanessa, who was now huge with the twins she was carrying.

"He'll be the first to tell you that he doesn't mind putting bad guys in body bags—that man loves his guns—but he will keel over every time he's in a coroner's exam room or there's a body at a crime scene he has to attend."

Andrea laughed just a little at the thought of it.

"Yeah, go head, laugh," Brandon continued, smiling. "You're not the one who has to drag two hundred pounds of pure muscle over to the side to get him out of the way. We've started requesting he not attend any situation where there's a body being examined."

"So I guess you're telling me it's okay if I don't go into the crime scene with you."

"That's up to you. All I'm saying is that there are Omega agents who choose not to. We don't think any less of them for it."

Andrea did appreciate Brandon trying to put her at ease.

The parking lot of the church where the body had been discarded was completely blocked off by police—both Maricopa County and City of Phoenix officers. There was a buzz of excitement in the air.

With a fourth victim, no one could deny this was a serial killer, not that Andrea had any doubts before.

Brandon immediately walked over, showing his Omega

credentials, and began speaking with the coroner. Lance Kendrick and Gerardo Jennison were here also, talking to each other and Brandon.

Andrea hung back. She didn't want to do something stupid like pass out from being too close to the body. Although the thought that Liam Goetz did so made her smile.

Andrea could still see where the dead woman lay from where she stood. Like the others, she was covered with a sheer white fabric and a lily had been placed in her hands. Andrea couldn't tell, but she would guess the woman had been strangled like the others.

Officers were moving all around her, canvassing the area for any clues that might have been left on the ground. Another two were attempting to get fingerprints from nearby surfaces.

When he saw her, Kendrick excused himself from Brandon and Jennison and walked over to her, purpose in his eyes. He'd remembered her; she had no doubt about it. She wanted to run, but knew it was no use.

"You're Andrea Gordon, Margaret and Marlon's kid."

His expression wasn't hostile or even condescending. If anything, it was sympathetic.

"Actually, they're my aunt and uncle, but yeah, my guardians."

"You looked so familiar, but it was so vague I thought it was a case, like you'd suggested."

Andrea shrugged.

"You look a lot different than your mug shot," Kendrick continued.

Andrea clenched her teeth. Was this it? The end of her career? Would Kendrick tell Brandon? Could someone with a criminal record even work for Omega?

"Once I saw that picture I knew where else I'd seen you. Coming in with your mom—well, I guess your aunt—to pick your uncle up after he'd been thrown in holding when he was too drunk to find his way home. Must have happened a dozen times."

Andrea shrugged again, turning away slightly.

"Uncle was a mean drunk, if memory serves. Maybe those nights we threw him in holding we were doing you a favor, I'm thinking now."

They'd been a much better night's sleep, that was for sure, but Andrea didn't say anything.

"There were a lot of screwups where you were concerned, Ms. Gordon. I'd like to offer Maricopa County's apologies, my personal apologies, for that."

Andrea turned back to Kendrick, surprised.

He looked at her solemnly. "Sometimes you can't see the full picture, except in hindsight. The system failed you. But you seem to have done all right for yourself." He gestured at her outfit.

"You mean despite having a record?"

Kendrick smiled at that although there was still a lingering sadness in his eyes. "You don't have a record, Andrea. You got brought in for underage drinking, but were never formally charged. I think the arresting officer just did it to scare you into going straight."

"It worked. I still can hardly drink anything without feeling some panic."

The officer smiled. "Well, there's no official record of your arrest, outside our storage room. So you don't have to worry about that. I'm just sorry no one ever looked further into your situation earlier, before you ran away."

His regret was so authentic it was almost painful.

"Like you said, I did okay for myself. I have a good job where I make a difference."

"And you're very well respected, if Agent Han is anything to go by."

Andrea looked over at Brandon to find him gazing at

her, concern in his eyes. She smiled at him to offer reassurance.

Lance Kendrick made his apologies once again and expressed his happiness to be working with her. Then he left to go deal with things pertaining to the dead woman. Not long after, Brandon made his way over to her, the notebook where he wrote everything down open to details about the case.

"Everything okay? I saw Kendrick over here."

"Yeah, he remembered me. He's a good cop. A little rough around the edges, but he cares."

Brandon nodded. "I got the info about the victim. Twenty-two years old, from here in Buckeye." He flipped a page in his notebook. "Her name is Jillian Spires and she's another stripper. Worked at a club called Jaguar's."

Chapter Eight

Andrea had wisely hung back as Brandon had examined the body with the coroner. As he'd told her, there was no need for her to get close unless she wanted to. If she wanted to get more thorough in investigating, he could ease her into that later when they were back at Omega in controlled circumstances. It didn't need to be while she was standing around a group of people she didn't know.

Or maybe one she did. Brandon saw Lance Kendrick come up to Andrea and had kept an eye on them as they conversed. Now that Brandon knew more about Andrea's past, what she'd survived, he found himself much more protective of her. The warrior was protective of her, as was the intellectual man.

Not even to mention how angry *both* were when he awoke to find her gone. It had been all he could do not to storm down to where she was and demand her return to his room.

To his bed.

But he'd gotten control of himself. An icy shower had helped. By the time he'd made it to breakfast he'd been able to be civil. He'd gotten the warrior tamped down, buried.

But he hadn't been able to stop himself from keeping a close eye on her all morning.

Andrea's conversation with Kendrick had been civil.

Whatever the older man had to say, she hadn't been upset by it.

Or so he had thought. Because when he came over to give Andrea the details about the dead girl, all the color had drained from her face. The police had told him the dead woman had a local address, and she was close to Andrea's age. Maybe Andrea had known the woman personally.

"Hey, are you okay?" He stepped closer and cupped her elbow, moving her so she was blocked from the eyes of the other cops. "You look shaky. Did you know Jillian Spires?"

Andrea closed her eyes briefly. "No. I didn't know her. She must have moved here after I left."

Brandon's eyes narrowed. Her statement was odd. Wouldn't you automatically assume you just hadn't run in the same circles? Buckeye was a small town, but not *that* small. There would certainly be people you didn't know. Why would Andrea assume Jillian had arrived after she'd left?

"Are you sure you're okay?" he asked again.

She shrugged. "Yeah. I'm fine. I'm just— These women are my age. Some of them younger. They may not have a lot of family, but they don't deserve to die like this."

Brandon agreed although he was sure that wasn't the entire situation going on inside Andrea's head.

"Maybe this one will have family. Kendrick will do a more thorough check as soon as they get back to the office."

"So what's our next step?"

"We have a home address and a work address for the club, Jaguar's, where she worked. I figure we should probably start with the home. See if we get any known associates from there."

Her nod was just a little too exuberant. "Yeah, her home is probably our best bet."

Brandon's eyes narrowed slightly once again. There was something off in Andrea's behavior. She was hiding something. He almost started questioning her about it, but then stopped himself.

It could be about what had happened between them last night. Or about being back in this town that held so many painful memories. Or about being at her first homicide crime scene.

There were a lot of reasons Andrea could be a little off. He'd cut her some slack.

"The locals will also be there processing the scene at her home, so it'll be crowded. But we'll see what we can find. Besides, I would imagine her place of employment isn't open at ten thirty on a Thursday morning."

She didn't say anything, just turned toward the car with him. The ride across town to Jillian's apartment was mostly in silence, also. Generally Brandon didn't mind silence. He preferred it to someone filling the car with inane chatter. But he couldn't help but feel as though Andrea was not talking in order to deliberately withhold information.

Privacy was her way, ingrained over the past few years of having to keep totally to herself. Just because he knew about her abusive past didn't mean she was automatically going to start sharing every thought that came through her mind. Which was fine.

Except there was something else going on, he knew it.

They worked through lunch, examining Jillian's apartment. She hadn't been a neat freak, for sure, which made going through her personal belongings more time-consuming. They did find two glasses on the cardboard box that doubled as a coffee table, one rimmed with lipstick, one without. That meant someone besides Jillian had been in here relatively recently. The locals would run prints.

If anything, Andrea got more quiet as they looked through the girl's apartment. Brandon knew this wasn't her area of expertise—objects rather than people—so he didn't really try to draw her into the investigation. She looked around, staying out of the crime-scene team's way. Brandon did similarly.

There were two boxes full of stuff—notes passed in high school, a yearbook, pressed flowers from dances, a few stuffed animals and other knickknacks. Obviously items Jillian cared too much about to give away, although none of it held any value. Andrea picked up the yearbook and began looking through it.

"She graduated four years ago. She's from Oklahoma City." She held out the page that showed Jillian's senior high school picture.

Young, smiling, very much alive.

"That gives us something to go on." Brandon took a picture of the picture with his phone. "She looks different now, but we can still use this picture when questioning people."

"Maybe she has a family." Andrea's face was pinched.

"Maybe. Kendrick will definitely start inquiring there."

After they finished with the apartment, they hit a fast-food place for a very late lunch. As they were finishing, Kendrick called to say the Phoenix coroner was almost ready to go over the body with them if Brandon wanted to attend in case he had any questions. Brandon agreed.

At his words, the heaviness that had befallen Andrea since the discovery of the body seemed to lift a little.

"Um, I don't think I'm up to seeing a dead body twice in one day," she said. "What if we split up? You can head into Phoenix. I'll walk up to Jaguar's—it's only a few blocks from here—and start interviewing the girls as they come in for work."

Brandon nodded. "Yeah, that's a good idea." He trusted Andrea's ability. At the very least she could narrow down who they should talk to more. "They're probably more willing to talk openly with you."

She paled. "Why do you say that?"

Brandon tilted his head to look at her. Why was she reacting so strongly to his statement? "Because you're a woman. You're young. I would think you pose much less of a threat to them."

Andrea smiled, but it didn't reach anywhere near her eyes. "Yeah, absolutely. Good thinking."

Brandon stood. "Okay, I'll text you when I finish at the coroner's office and we can touch base."

They both walked out the door. "I'll just give you a ride, okay? No need for you to walk. The extra two minutes won't make any difference to Kendrick." There was no rush. A dead body wasn't going anywhere.

She tensed for just a second before shrugging. "Sure. Thanks."

Brandon drove the few blocks to the gentlemen's club, *gentlemen* being quite a loose term in this situation. At night he was sure it didn't look quite so run-down and cheap. But right now it just looked like a warehouse that nobody cared about. He felt bad that Jillian had worked here. Felt bad for any women who worked here.

Andrea was staring at the building with as much contempt as he was. Her lips were pale with tightness and her hands pressed against her stomach. For a moment he thought she wasn't going to get out of the car.

"I'm sure the front door isn't open yet. I'll go around to the side. Text me when you're done, and we'll make a plan like you said." Her voice was tight. She didn't look at him.

She was out of the car before he could check that she was all right. She stopped a few feet away, then turned and waved, giving him a slight smile.

Obviously code for: *I'm okay. I can handle this.*

Brandon pulled around and out of the parking lot. Four

days ago he wouldn't have left her here alone. Wouldn't have trusted that she could do the job. Wouldn't have believed she wouldn't miss something. It was that knowledge that kept him driving toward Phoenix. He needed to show he trusted her professional abilities.

But everything in his mind insisted this situation was wrong. That he was missing something obvious. Andrea hadn't been okay all day since they'd arrived at the crime scene.

No, actually, she seemed to have done okay with that, too. It was not until he had told Andrea the dead girl's name that she'd totally withdrawn into herself. Had she known the woman? Her statement about Jillian moving into town after Andrea had left still struck Brandon as odd.

But Andrea had been right, according to the girl's yearbook. Jillian had obviously been in Oklahoma City four years ago, and that was when Steve had brought Andrea to Omega.

So she didn't know the girl.

Then what was the cause of Andrea's reaction? Her *continued* reaction all day, because she certainly hadn't bounced out of it. It had only gotten worse.

Brandon tried to think of exactly what he'd said when he told Andrea the victim's name. As he figured it out, he cursed. Violently.

Andrea hadn't been reacting to Jillian's name. She'd been reacting to the other information he'd given her: Jillian's place of employment.

Jaguar's.

He spun the car around at the first available safe place on the road. He put his phone on speaker and dialed Kendrick.

"This is Lance Kendrick."

"Lance, this is Brandon Han. I have some stuff I'm

looking into and will need to miss the meeting with the coroner."

"No problem. I don't think there's anything much different than the other women. I'll email you his full report."

"Thanks."

"You need help with your lead?"

"No. I'll let you know if we find anything. Andrea and I are headed to Jaguar's now to interview Jillian's coworkers."

"We'll keep each other posted, then."

"Absolutely." Brandon ended the call. Right now he just wanted to get back to Andrea. To figure out what was going on there. Fifteen minutes after he'd left her—pale and tense—in the parking lot at Jaguar's, he pulled back in.

She'd known there was a side door and where it was.

Brandon cleared his mind from every thought. He didn't want to come to the natural conclusion Andrea's actions pointed toward. He walked toward the side door she'd mentioned and entered the building once he found the door propped open. He stood back in the shadows, close enough to hear but not easily be seen.

There was Andrea, surrounded by four different women, all of them crying and hugging her. They all talked over each other, about Jillian's death, the state of the club, how much they'd missed Andrea and how mad they were that she'd just left without telling anyone.

Brandon couldn't force the thoughts away any longer, his brain turned back on full force.

Andrea had been a stripper at Jaguar's.

Chapter Nine

Walking back into Jaguar's had been the most difficult thing Andrea had ever done. She was thankful Brandon hadn't been here to witness it because there was no way she'd be able to explain the terror that swamped her as she made her way to the side door from the parking lot.

How many times had she come through the door in the late afternoon just like this? Her apartment had been only a few blocks away, so she had walked most of the time, a bag full of skimpy outfits, wigs and makeup thrown over her shoulder.

The eighteen months she had worked at Jaguar's had been some of the worst of her entire life. She had hated every second of it. But after being attacked while living out of her car when she couldn't afford anything else from what she made working at a gas station, Andrea had decided her safety was worth more than her pride.

Working here had at least gotten her off the streets.

She hadn't expected anyone to remember her when she came back, or perhaps they would just be able to vaguely place her. After all, she'd pretty much kept to herself here, too. The instant recognition and warm greetings—hugs, in fact, from three girls—had definitely not been expected. A fourth girl, who didn't even know Andrea, didn't want to be left out and jumped into the fray.

At first they'd just held on to her and cried. They'd heard

about Jillian's death and were sad, scared. Then they'd had questions. They all, just as Andrea remembered—one of the few fond memories she had of this place—talked over each other.

"You just left without saying goodbye."

"Oh my gosh, you look so fancy. Like a lawyer or something. Gorgeous."

"Do the cops know who killed Jillian?"

"You're not coming back to work here, right?"

Andrea tried to answer the questions as best she could when they were being fired so rapidly she couldn't figure out who was asking what.

"I work as a consultant for a law-enforcement agency called Omega Sector. We're looking into Jillian's death with the local police."

"You were always too smart to work here." That was Lily. Andrea remembered her. She was kind, sort of scatterbrained.

Andrea shrugged. "I don't know about that. I didn't even graduate from high school. Dropped out."

"You may not have been book smart, but you definitely had an awareness of people. Could tell what they were thinking and feeling. Downright spooky sometimes. I'm not surprised the cops scooped you up to work for them."

That was Keira. She wasn't in the hugging/crying circle, didn't have time for that sort of nonsense. She was two years older than Andrea and had been the closest thing Andrea had had to a true friend while working here.

Keira may have been the closest thing Andrea had had to a friend, ever.

Andrea removed herself from the circle of women and walked over to Keira.

"Hey," Andrea said softly. "I'm sorry I didn't say goodbye all those years—"

She was shocked as Keira pulled her in for a tight hug.

"Don't apologize for taking your chance to jump this ship," she whispered in Andrea's ear. "If you had come back after having a chance to get out, I would've kicked your ass."

Keira grabbed Andrea by the forearms and pushed her back. "Let me look at you. You cleaned up exactly like I imagined you would." She put her forehead against Andrea's. "I'm so proud of you. So happy for you."

"Thanks, Kee. I have a great job."

"And a man who cares a great deal about you."

Andrea laughed. "Um, no. Unfortunately, the job didn't come with that accessory."

"You sure about that? Because there's one tall drink of water over there who can't keep his eyes off you. And his suit says law enforcement, too." Keira gestured toward the side door with her chin.

Andrea felt her stomach lurch and swallowed rapidly. Brandon was here?

"He's just a man, honey. Don't forget that. Ultimately, we hold the power," Keira whispered in her ear before turning to the other girls. "Ladies, I'd like to see you at the bar so we can go over tonight's set. You can talk to Andrea later."

The women murmured disappointment, but followed Keira over to the bar. Andrea finally forced herself to turn around. When her worst fears were confirmed, she closed her eyes.

Brandon stood, the shadows from the doorway casting a bleak hue over his already-dark features. There could be no doubt in his mind that Andrea used to be employed here. There was no other possible interpretation of what had just happened with the girls.

"Andrea."

She opened her eyes, surprised to hear him directly in front of her now. Almost within touching distance.

But not quite.

"You should've told me."

What could she say to that? She just shrugged.

"I thought you were going to Phoenix."

"Kendrick is going to email me the info instead. I had a feeling there would be more action back here."

Andrea gave a short bark of laughter that held no amusement whatsoever. "You definitely got that right."

"How is it even possible you worked here four years ago? I'm not licensed to practice law in Arizona, but I imagine the legal age has to be twenty-one."

Not licensed to practice in Arizona? That meant he had to be licensed to practice in some other state. Plus two PhDs? Andrea rubbed her eyes tiredly with her hand.

"I had a fake ID. You could dance at eighteen, but couldn't serve drinks. I soon discovered I could make a lot more money if I waited tables between my dances. The owner wasn't one to look too closely at the IDs we showed him."

Brandon's lips pursed. Disapproval all but radiated off him. Andrea wrapped her arms around her waist. She couldn't blame him for disapproving. She should've just told him everything up front last night. At least now he understood why she really could never be part of the Omega team.

She'd always known eventually someone would find out about this. She looked around the club, the deep bucket seats around the tables where girls gave individual dances, the stage shaped like a T with three poles. With all the lights on there was nothing sexy about it. Just coldness, hardness, crassness.

Yeah, she'd always known eventually someone would find out about this—the truth Steve Drackett and Grace Parker had always refused to see—and would know Andrea wasn't meant to be part of Omega Sector.

It looked as though Brandon Han had just become that person.

ANDREA LOOKED AS if she might shatter into a million pieces at the slightest touch.

He wanted to wrap his arms around her, to hold her, to assure her that everything would be okay. But the tension in her body language suggested she would reject the physical contact. So he took one step closer, but went no farther. Even then she looked as if she might bolt.

He shouldn't be surprised that Andrea had worked in a place like this, given her history. But try as he might, he couldn't imagine her on the stage. He'd been to his share of bachelor parties, and hell, *college*, so he'd been to strip clubs before. Andrea definitely had the looks and physique to be a dancer.

But nothing he knew about her personality or temperament suggested to him that she would've wanted to work at this place. Not like, say, the friend she'd been talking to, who seemed very comfortable in her own skin and able to easily manipulate the stage and men's desires. Not that it mattered either way.

The psychiatrist in him wanted to fire off a bunch of questions, to understand her psyche, to understand all the circumstances surrounding her working here. Although a lot of it he could probably piece together himself.

"You needed money after you ran away."

She nodded. "I was living in my car, working at a gas station. When I was almost attacked one night while sleeping, I knew I had to do something else. I happened to meet Keira and she told me about this place."

"It's understandable, Andrea. No one would blame you for that choice."

"Yeah, right." She slid by him to walk out the door but stopped when a man entered. Andrea backed up.

"What are you doing in here?" the man—big, greasy, gruff—asked. He turned toward the bar and yelled,

"Keira, what are customers doing in here before we're open, damn it?"

He turned back to Andrea. "We're not open, so you'll have to come back lat—" His eyes bulged and a nasty grin spread over his face. "Wait a minute—I recognize you. If it isn't little Drea all dressed up."

"Hi, Harry." Andrea's voice was small. Her shoulders hunched, and Brandon could see her arms crossed over her stomach in a protective huddle.

This man frightened Andrea.

"You come back to work for old Harry, sweet girl? I hear we have an opening."

Brandon gritted his teeth in distaste. He wished he could arrest Harry for something right now. He hoped he could keep himself from pummeling him into the ground, this man who so obviously threatened Andrea.

The warrior stretched inside him.

"No, I—I..." She was having difficulty getting the words out. Getting any words out.

Brandon stepped up so he was flanking Andrea. His chest was right at her shoulder and he placed his hand on her hip, making sure she could feel him. She wasn't alone in this.

"I'm agent Brandon Han with Omega Sector. We're investigating the death of Jillian Spires. You, of course, are one of our prime suspects." That wasn't true, but Brandon felt no qualms whatsoever about the lie. "We'll need you to provide a detailed written analysis of where you've been for the past seven days."

Harry's mouth fell open, but he stopped leering at Andrea. That had been Brandon's ultimate objective.

"I, um." Harry blinked rapidly and turned his attention to Brandon. "For a whole week?"

Brandon nodded, using his hand on Andrea's hip to guide her behind him. "That's right. Every place you've been. Written down. We'll be back to get it tomorrow and maybe to bring you in for questioning."

Brandon had no doubt that if Harry contacted a lawyer, his counsel would tell him that he didn't need to do any of this. That unless law enforcement was going to formally charge Harry with a crime, he didn't have to do jack squat to cooperate.

But Brandon had a feeling that Harry, with his thinning hair made even more evident by the way he slicked it back, was too cheap to call a lawyer. So let him spend the rest of his evening stewing and writing.

Brandon looked over his shoulder to Andrea, relieved to see at least a little color coming back to her face. "Would you mind telling the ladies that we'll be back tomorrow to interview them? Ask if they could come in early afternoon so we can talk."

Andrea nodded and walked toward the bar.

Harry evidently decided to try the buddy-buddy approach with Brandon. "Even all buttoned up, you can imagine what that one looked like on the stage, can't you?" His grin was slimy. There was no other word for it.

"She's my colleague." Brandon clenched his fists.

"Well, let me tell you, there was something about her up there." Harry had no idea how thin the ice he skated on was. "She wore wigs and makeup, but you couldn't hide those big green eyes. Like a deer caught in headlights every time she was up there. Everybody loved it. Not that they were looking at her face once her ti—"

The warrior inside Brandon broke free. He was in Harry's face in less than a second.

"That woman over there is an important member of a prestigious law-enforcement agency. What she did when you hired her—illegally, I might add, since she was a teenager—holds no bearing whatsoever to her ability to do her job now."

Harry swallowed hard. Brandon barely refrained from grabbing the other man by his dirty T-shirt.

"If I hear one disrespectful word come out of your mouth again about her, I will personally see to it that every person you've ever hired, every license you have to operate and every code involved in running a business like this is investigated. And if there are any problems or discrepancies, you will be *shut down*."

Harry nodded.

"Okay, I told them." Andrea returned and touched Brandon on the arm. He took a step back from Harry. "They'll be ready tomorrow."

Brandon turned to smile at her. He knew she would be able to pick up what was going on between him and Harry and wanted to assure her it was okay. "Harry and I got some things straightened out, too. Isn't that right, Harry?"

"Um, yes, sir. We're all clear. I'll have what you need by tomorrow. Anything to help catch Jillian's killer."

Brandon took Andrea's arm and led her out the door.

Chapter Ten

Andrea was huddled against the car door, as far away from him as she could get in the small rental, as they drove back to town and the hotel. Brandon, despite his training, wasn't sure what to say to her. But he knew it had to be something.

Finally she solved the problem by speaking first.

"I should've told you I had worked at Jaguar's." Her voice was small. Tiny. Ashamed. Part of his heart broke.

Brandon shrugged. "Maybe you should've this morning after we found out Jillian worked there. But before then it was pretty much irrelevant."

She rolled her eyes. "Right. Because no one at Omega would care that I was an ex-stripper."

He pulled the car into the parking lot of the hotel and shut off the engine, turning to her. "If I had been a carpenter or a janitor when I was twenty years old, would it make you think any less of me as an agent now?"

"That's different."

"How is it different? Most of us had a life—some of us had completely different careers before we worked for Omega."

"It's not the same." She clenched her fists.

"Why?"

"I took off my clothes for money."

Brandon took a breath. Damn, he was pissed. And he

knew she would be able to feel it. But his anger wasn't directed at her. He wanted to make sure she understood that.

"What you did was survive a situation most people never have to live through."

"Nobody at Omega is going to care about that."

Maybe it was time for a little tough love. "No offense, but nobody is going to care either way."

That got her attention. She spun her head toward him. "What?"

"You do your job well. That's all anybody at Omega cares about. You are an intelligent, gifted behavioral analyst."

"What I am is a runaway high school dropout, ex-stripper."

She got out of the car, so he did the same. Thankfully the parking lot was mostly empty. She stared at him across the hood of the car. At least there was some color in her cheeks and fire in her eyes. She didn't need sympathy and gentleness. That just encouraged the vulnerable side of her. She needed someone to tell it to her straight.

A friend.

Brandon wasn't sure she'd ever had one. Definitely hadn't had one at Omega. Well, he could be one for her.

He may be a turned-on friend, but he could be a friend.

"You forgot dyslexic."

Her eyes bugged out of her head. *"What?"*

"You're a runaway, dropout, *dyslexic* ex-stripper. Throw in an unfortunate shark attack and you've got yourself a pretty tragic tale there."

Now her eyes narrowed to slits. "Do you think I'm trying to get you to feel sorry for me?"

"No." Although God knew there was plenty to feel sorry for. "But I'm trying to get you to see the truth."

"That my past doesn't matter." Her lips tightened into a line. "You'll have to forgive me if I disagree."

She turned and began walking toward the side entrance of the hotel they'd used last night. Neither of them wanted to have this conversation coming through the main lobby. He jogged a few steps to catch up with her. Amazing how fast the woman could walk, even in heels.

"Of course your past matters. Everybody's past matters."

"That's easy for you to say. Your past is filled with schooling and degrees and graduations. Mine is filled with thongs and sleeping in my car and getting beaten by my uncle."

Brandon stopped her at the door. "Like it or not, our pasts are what make us who we are. But when it comes to Omega, you only want to concentrate on the bad parts of your past."

"That's because they're the most important parts."

"Says you. And you're stuck in your own head."

She started to reach for the door, but Brandon grabbed both her arms. He was gentle, but there was no way she was getting out of his grasp until he was ready to let her.

"You know what else is in your past? Four years of helping Omega solve cases. Saving many lives and assisting in putting a number of criminals behind bars."

She shrugged, looking down. He put a finger under her chin and forced her face back up, ignoring the heat coursing through him.

"Not to mention you dropped out of high school but then got your GED, so I think you can stop using the dropout title. Plus you're actively going to college. At twenty-three, it's not like you're some grandmother going back to school."

He could tell he was getting through to her. Her posture was relaxing, her body angling more toward him.

He wanted her; he could feel it in the tightness throbbing through his body. He wanted to sweep her up in his arms and carry her down to his room like a grand romantic movie. Wanted to make love to her for days until neither of them had strength to move.

But more than that he wanted her to see the truth about herself. How much she brought to the table.

He released her chin when she nodded. She opened the door and they both walked into the hallway.

"It's hard for me to get past. Hard for me to think anyone else could get past it, either, especially at Omega. Best of the best and all that."

"I would argue that your talent, your ability to read people, makes you one of the best. And your past—even the part when you worked at Jaguar's—helped make you into who you are now and what you can do."

"I just wouldn't know how to tell anyone about it."

"Why would you have to? Have you ever been in a briefing where we all sat around talking about our complete history? No. Because that's not what matters. Tell people you waited tables. That was true, also."

"Yeah, I guess so."

He wanted to shake her. Or hug her. Or definitely kiss her, but knew it wasn't the time for that. "You have a natural gift. Everybody knows it, and no one questions it. You don't have to have an origin story to tell everyone."

She laughed a little. "That's good, because I'm not a superhero."

They were at her door. He wanted to say the most important thing before she left. "You don't have to tell anybody anything about your past. Most people won't ever ask, and hardly anyone would care even if they knew all the details."

She nodded slightly.

"But the true issue here, I think, is not even about what judgments people might make if they knew about your shark-attack past and the rest." He tried to keep it light, before making his ultimate point. "The true issue is that if you embrace your past and own it, you'll be forced to stop treating every good behavioral analysis choice you make like it's a happy accident."

Her head jerked up to look at him.

"Embracing, or at least accepting, your past means accepting your present and your future at Omega. It means having to trust people. Not about knowing your past, but about allowing you to make mistakes in your future and not hold it against you."

He kissed her forehead gently, although he wanted to do much more than that. "You hold yourself away from everybody to try to make yourself perfect. Being real, being part of a team, means showing others you're not. And giving them a chance to accept you in spite of that."

He stepped back from her. "The past doesn't have to control your future anymore."

Brandon turned to walk to his room. He heard Andrea's door click and hoped he hadn't said more than he should.

WAS BRANDON RIGHT? Had she kept her distance from everyone these years at Omega not because she was afraid of what they'd think of her past if they knew, but because of her refusal to take the responsibility of her job as a behavioral analyst?

How many times had she called herself a fraud? Too many to count. Was it because it was easier to think of herself as a fraud who got lucky with some of her analyses?

She'd certainly lived in fear the past four years of doing something majorly wrong and getting fired. Of getting fired for no reason at all.

Either way, maybe it was time to stop letting her feelings about the past control her every action. It had stunted her growth professionally, for sure. But it had also stopped her from making any friends.

From having any intimate contact with anyone at all.

All the stuff Brandon had said, she was going to have to sort through. It would take a while. Some of it wasn't correct, but some of it was dead-on.

Especially the part about not letting the past control her future anymore.

She'd hated seeing Harry today. Hated even worse seeing the stuttering idiot she'd become around him. The same with her aunt and uncle in the car yesterday, afraid to face them.

These people were from her past and didn't have any control over her unless Andrea gave them that control.

She was tired of giving control over to anyone or anything else but herself. She'd lived without things she wanted—friendship, companionship—for too long. Let her fear convince her to give them up.

She wanted sex and she wanted it with Brandon Han.

She shot off from where she'd been sitting on her bed, the fading evening sun shining on her through the window. She was out the door and knocking on his before she could let herself overthink it too much.

"Hey," he said to her, his eyes traveling all over her face. "Are you okay? I was afraid I said too much, that I overstepped my bounds—"

Andrea grabbed his tie and pulled his mouth down to hers, stretching up on her toes to meet him. She didn't have far to go in her heels.

She thought for a second he might pull away, refuse, but he didn't. Instead he wrapped an arm around her waist and pulled her rapidly, fully, against him. He spun them around, getting her out of the doorway so he could shut it.

The heat was instantaneous. Overwhelming. It seemed to pool through her entire body. The fact that Brandon obviously felt it too just made the heat increase.

She'd wanted this man for years. She'd been afraid to

show her attraction, to move on it, because of her past, of what he might find out.

But now he knew. And beyond that, damn her past and the hold it had had over her for so long.

He backed her up until she was against the wall, their bodies pressed so close against each other there was no room for anything else. Still, her hands gripped his waist, tugging him closer to her before sliding up his back to link behind his neck to capture him. The heat of his body against hers thawed something that had been frozen in her for far too long.

His lips were the perfect blend of firm and soft. Her eyes slid closed as his large hands came up to cup her face, to take control of the melding of their mouths. Andrea was glad to give over the control. She wanted him to give her whatever it took to ease the hunger that clawed at her every time she saw him.

Brandon kissed his way across her jaw and over to her ear. She couldn't stop the quiet gasp that escaped her when he bit gently on her lobe.

"Are you sure this is what you want, Andrea?" he whispered. She could feel his hot breath against her cheek.

More than anything else she'd ever wanted.

"Yes," she murmured, her eyes still closed, her arms sliding to his shoulders, trying to force his big body closer to hers.

But he held firm. "We can wait. It doesn't have to be tonight."

Her eyes flew open. Had she misread him? Did he really not want her? How could she have been so wrong about something like this?

"Is this not what you want?" She choked the words out.

"Oh, it is very much what I want." He stepped his body up against hers so there was no space between them whatsoever, leaving her no doubt that he did want her. "I'm just trying to be a gentleman."

"I don't want a gentleman. I want you."

He smiled. A wicked, hot smile that had her insides melting.

Then his mouth was instantly back on hers, the kiss harder, more urgent. He licked deep into her mouth and they both groaned. He slid his arm around her waist, pulling her off the wall, closer to his chest, so he could ease her blazer down her shoulders. He tossed it over on the small table where his also lay.

He brought his lips back to hers and began unbuttoning her blouse. "You cannot imagine how many times I've wanted to get you out of the perfectly professional suits you wear."

She smiled against his mouth. "I've had a few similar thoughts about you and those shirts and ties."

"Well, then." His brown eyes were so clear she couldn't look away. "I think we've delayed gratification long enough."

They made quick work of getting rid of the rest of their clothes.

He reached down and crooked an arm under her knees, swinging her up in his arms as though she didn't weigh anything at all and carrying her over to the bed. He laid her gently on it and reached down to devour her mouth again as if he couldn't bear to be away from her lips for another second.

A hot ache grew in her throat as his lips moved down her jaw to her neck and bit gently; her fingers slid into his thick black hair. His lips grew more dominating as his hands moved downward, skimming either side of her body to her thighs and back up, before pulling her tightly to him in a raw act of possession.

He hoisted himself up onto his arms for a moment so he could look down at her body then back up to her face.

"Mine," he whispered fiercely, and she almost didn't recognize him as the controlled, intelligent being he usually was.

It ignited something inside her. A burning she knew only he could ease.

Andrea pulled him closer and forgot about the past, forgot about the future, forgot about everything but the heat and desire between them.

Chapter Eleven

He caught her trying to get back out of bed in the middle of the night. To sneak back to her room.

"Not this time," he murmured, reaching an arm out to hook her waist and pull her back into bed next to him. "No sneaking off."

"I should probably go back to my own room," she said.

"In the morning," he said, snuggling into her neck. "Sleep now."

He held her close, her back to his front, running a soothing hand slowly up to her shoulder, then back down, catching her waist then following the line of her body down to her hip and outer thigh, then back up again.

He wanted her to rest, to relax, to get the sleep she needed. Even before the mind-blowing sex they'd just had, it had already been a pretty overwhelming day. Hell, the whole week had been stressful for her.

The warrior in him wanted to protect her, to keep her in his arms until she got the rest—the peace—she needed. He wanted to hold her and keep her safe from anything that would harm her. But even more he wished he could go back and protect the girl she had been. The one who had been forced to work for the likes of Harry Minkley at Jaguar's just to survive. His teeth ground thinking about it—about her on a stage she hated with men leering at her—but he forced the hand that touched her to remain calm, soothing.

He soon realized she was not relaxing under his touch and definitely wasn't going to sleep.

"What's going on in that head of yours?" he asked against her hair.

"I've never slept with someone before. It's weird. I can't relax."

Brandon tensed. "What? You've never..." Had he heard her right?

"Well, I've...you know...had sex before. A couple times in high school. But it was a quickie and never in an actual bed. At night. Ugh."

She pulled the cover up over her head, embarrassed.

It made sense that she hadn't been with anyone since high school. She'd kept herself so apart from everyone else at Omega, there couldn't have been much chance to find someone she was attracted to.

It hurt him again to think of her alone for all those years. Especially when she hadn't needed to be.

He pulled her in closer to him and wrapped an arm around her waist. He slid his other arm under her pillow so her head rested on it.

"There's nothing to it. You just take a few deep breaths and let your eyes close."

"Sometimes I have nightmares."

"About what?"

"Mostly my uncle. That he is attacking me, hitting me, before I can really get awake and away from him. That was finally the reason I left home. Because I knew eventually he would kill me."

"Somebody should've helped you. A school counselor, a doctor, somebody."

He felt her shrug against him. "I was good at being invisible. And terrible at asking for help."

"The trouble asking for help is still a problem, I see. You need to get better at that."

"Yeah, probably. I'm still pretty good at being invisible. I don't think anyone knows me around Omega."

Brandon laughed outright at that. She turned toward him. "What? I don't ever really talk to anyone."

"That doesn't mean they don't notice you, sweetheart. Most are just too scared to start up a conversation with you. You're known as being…" He cut himself off. He didn't want to hurt her feelings.

"What?"

"A loner. Not someone who wants to socialize with others."

"That's pretty much true, I guess."

"Not anymore. Not once we get back to Colorado Springs." He felt her stiffen. "But we don't have to talk about that right now. Right now you just practice the task at hand."

"Oh yeah? What's that?"

"Learning how to sleep with my arms around you."

"Okay, that I can do."

Brandon held her until he felt the tension ease out of her body and her breathing take on the deeper evenness of sleep. But it was a long time before he could sleep himself.

ANDREA STILL SNEAKED out a little before dawn. She wasn't trying to make Brandon angry. She wasn't even trying to get away from him. She just needed to be by herself. To regroup before seeing him again.

Before seeing his gorgeous brown eyes and striking cheekbones. His thick black hair she didn't know if she'd be able to stop her fingers from running through next time she saw him.

Everything about last night had been perfect. And she wasn't running now. Wasn't scared. Or at least wasn't scared of being close to Brandon. It was just that being close to him—being close to *anyone*—for that long was hard for her. She'd spent a lifetime keeping people at arm's length. That habit wasn't going to change overnight.

Not that Brandon had given any sort of indication that he was interested in anything more than just last night. She wished she had more experience with this sort of situation. She'd known one thing: if he'd awakened this morning and she'd sensed regret from him, it would've broken something inside her that couldn't be fixed.

So maybe she was running a little bit.

After putting on jeans and a shirt, for once not feeling the overwhelming need to look immaculately professional, she headed out to the hotel's small dining room as she had yesterday.

She was hungry. She and Brandon hadn't had much dinner and had expended considerable energy during the night. But first things first: coffee.

The lobby was deserted; she couldn't even see someone working behind the counter. The little dining room was also empty.

But for some reason Andrea felt like someone was watching her. She spun all the way around, but couldn't see anyone, just the shadows from the sun starting to rise behind the clouds. It cast an eerie light in the building.

But she could swear she could feel rage, violence, hatred pointed in her direction. She'd felt them enough from her uncle over the years to recognize the emotions.

Was her uncle here?

She was about to go back to her room, to lock herself in, but stopped. No. There wasn't any reason to be frightened. No reason to go hide somewhere.

There was no one here. Just her own imagination—coupled with not getting enough sleep—that was messing with her mind. This *town* messed with her mind.

And if her uncle and aunt were here, she would deal with it.

She forced herself to get the coffee she wanted, then sat down at the corner table. Her back was to a wall and she could see everything that happened in both the dining room and through the glass into the lobby.

She felt better a couple of minutes later when three guys came walking—albeit quite unsteadily—into the lobby. Maybe that was whose presence she had sensed, although it seemed unlikely. They were all laughing so hard she would be surprised if they didn't wake sleeping guests.

They'd obviously been out all night, were barely sober and were highly amused with themselves. They were college-aged, a little younger than Andrea. Clean-cut, good-looking guys.

"Top of the morning to you, miss," one of them said as the others made a beeline to the coffeepot.

Andrea raised an eyebrow. *Top of the morning?* These guys were definitely still drunk. Normally that would have made her tense, but, although she was wary, she found herself too relaxed after last night to jump back into full tension mode.

"Looks like you fellows had a good time. I'm hoping you didn't drive here just now."

"Oh no," another one said, holding up two fingers. "Scout's honor, we took a cab."

"But we do have to drive home in just a few hours." All of them groaned at that. "They're going to have to send security to drag us out of bed at checkout time."

The third one added a ton of sugar to his coffee and grabbed a Danish. "We've got to pace ourselves, you guys. We're never going to make it through the pilgrimage if we keep having nights like last night."

They all smiled. "But what a night."

"Pilgrimage?" Andrea shook her head. "I'm almost afraid to ask what pilgrimage you guys might be on that has left you in a state like this."

Guy number one eased himself into the table next to her, wincing at the sunlight beginning to come through the lobby windows.

"We went back to a place we heard about on the Devils and Angels Pilgrimage."

Andrea had no idea what that was.

"We go to Arizona State," he explained.

"The Sun Devils," Andrea said. Anyone from around here knew Arizona State's mascot.

"Yes!" The guys were all inordinately pleased that she knew that. They got distracted and started talking to each other about their school's latest basketball endeavors. Evidently the Sun Devils were doing well.

Andrea just went back to drinking her coffee; she wasn't interested in basketball statistics. Honestly, she wasn't interested in these guys at all, but knew they'd leave of their own accord soon.

Finally they remembered she was there and that they'd been in the middle of telling her something.

"Sorry. Anyway, Devils and Angels Pilgrimage. One of the local DJs decided he was going to travel all over Arizona to find the best…" The guy stopped, looking at Andrea, unsure how to continue.

He was embarrassed. Andrea could feel it radiate from him. One of the other guys leaned down and whispered something in his ear.

"The best exotic dance clubs," the first guy continued, obviously relieved to have found a more neutral phrase. "All over the state. Some fraternities are taking part in the pilgrimage, including ours."

"So, what, a different club each week?" she asked.

"Yep." He got a bent postcard out of his pocket and slid it to her. "See, we've done the first six and now have three more to go."

The postcard wasn't too difficult to read since it was

just a list of clubs and dates on one side. A picture of a scantily clad she-devil and angel sitting on the shoulders of DJ Shawn "Shocker" Sheppard on the other.

But what caught Andrea's attention was three clubs on the list. Three of their four dead girls had worked at three of them.

"Do you mind if I keep this?" she asked.

"Sure," the guy said, sitting up straighter and looking at her more carefully. "Hey, are you interested in going to any of the clubs with us? There are always a few women there, even straight ones. I'm Pete. We'd love to have you. It would be a lot of—"

"She's not interested, but thanks." Brandon's deep voice came from behind them. "Or if she is, I'll be the one to take her."

He slid into the chair next to Andrea, kissing her on the way down. "Good morning."

"Morning," she murmured against his lips. Brandon pulled back, but kept his arm around Andrea's chair. The message that she was off-limits was more than clear.

"Yeah, well, we've got to get some rest," the college guys said, instinctively backing away from the threat they could feel in Brandon. "The information on the postcard is also on the DJ's website. It's a whole big thing where people vote and they talk about it on the show. It's pretty wild."

The guys grabbed a few more things to eat and then headed up to their room. Pete winked at her over his shoulder and Andrea couldn't help but smile.

"Things are getting progressively worse with you," Brandon told her as he stood to get a cup of coffee. "Yesterday you sneak out of the bed. Today you sneak out of the bed and have three boyfriends by the time I get to breakfast."

"If it helps, I think only Petey wanted to be my boyfriend." She smiled, a little shocked at herself. She wasn't sure where this ability to make light flirtation was coming from, but it was pleasantly surprising.

Brandon turned and leaned against the counter, crossing his arms over his chest. "I might have to start handcuffing you to the bed so you don't escape."

She grinned. "I believe that would be improper use of your restraints, Agent Han."

The heat in his eyes caused her to blush. The thought of being handcuffed to Brandon's bed sent explosions throughout her body.

She liked knowing this man—with all his brains and degrees—wanted her.

He stood there for a long moment just looking at her. The heat in his eyes never went away, but a soft smile formed on his lips as he studied her.

"What?" she finally asked.

He came back to the table and sat across from her this time, leaning close. "You know, I've seen you in your suits, dressed impeccably professional, and totally naked. Nothing in between."

She felt her face burn. "Oh."

"So seeing you in jeans and a shirt is nice. Relaxed."

She leaned into him. "I feel nice. Relaxed."

And she did, amazingly. She didn't have to worry about her secrets being found out; Brandon already knew them. Even the earlier uneasiness about someone watching her had fled. She was here with him and she was relaxed.

She didn't know how long it would last, but for the moment she was willing to just enjoy it.

Chapter Twelve

"So, what did your boyfriend give you there?" Brandon asked between bites of his cereal.

A number of couples and families were around them now, the romantic mood that had engulfed them broken, but not the easiness.

"Something I wanted to check into. See if the dates lined up." She slid over the postcard with the dates the DJ would be visiting the different clubs. "I noticed they were at Jaguar's three nights ago and at Allure last week."

He took the card to study it. "And at Diamond Cabaret two weeks before that, which would be right around when the first victim was found."

"I know the dates don't correspond with their deaths, but I just thought it was interesting that it was the same order."

Brandon nodded. "Very interesting."

"Do you think this DJ Shawn Shocker has anything to do with it?"

"I doubt he is our culprit. Purity doesn't really look like his thing."

She looked at the back of the card with the picture of the DJ and the angel and she-devil on his shoulders. No, Andrea wouldn't peg him as the killer, either. "So maybe it's someone, like Petey and his friends, traveling around on the 'pilgrimage' with DJ Shocker."

Brandon nodded. "Definitely a possibility. Actually, this could be the biggest break in the case we've had so far. Good job."

She smiled, then looked at the paper again. "It doesn't explain about victim number two, Ashley Judson. She didn't work at a dance club at all, one on or off DJ Shocker's list."

"You're right. But also, there was no one killed from the club that the DJ visited that week."

"What does that mean?"

Brandon shrugged, looking at his notebook. "Let's follow this thread all the way out." He lowered his voice so their conversation wouldn't be overheard by the few people eating breakfast. "Let's say it's a DJ Shocker groupie who's committing our crimes. Someone who is following Shocker from club to club, picking a woman and killing her a day or two later.

"Okay, victim number one, Yvette Tyler, was killed one day after Shocker's stop at Diamond Cabaret. There were no reported deaths after Shocker's stop at Vixen's the next week."

"But victim number two was killed where she worked at the truck stop."

Brandon nodded. "And we know she moonlighted as a prostitute."

"Shocker's group headed to Allure the following week. Noelle Brumby was found dead two days later." Andrea used sugar packets to provide a graphic representation of what she was saying. "And then Shocker was at Jaguar's on Tuesday and Jillian Spires was found yesterday, so killed Wednesday night."

Brandon stood. "Definitely fits. We need to get this to the sheriff's office."

SITTING IN OFFICER Kendrick's office two hours later, Andrea back in one of her professional suits, Brandon could feel frustration pooling all around him. They weren't going to get any help from the locals.

Kendrick had pretty much been ordered to let the case go and release it to the City of Phoenix homicide department. The Maricopa County Sheriff's Department had neither the resources nor the manpower to continue the investigation.

And honestly, except for Kendrick, Brandon wasn't sure they had much of a desire.

The conference call with Gerardo Jennison with the City of Phoenix PD hadn't offered much hope, either. They would offer their labs, coroners, crime-scene investigators and even continue to be a liaison, but they couldn't afford to put much detective and officer manpower on it. Phoenix and Maricopa County in general had bigger problems than the deaths of four women on their hands: they were dealing with unprecedented biker gang wars all along Interstate 10.

Unless something drastically changed, he and Andrea were on their own when it came to investigating. The sheriff's office promised to send out a notice to the owners of the exotic dance clubs in the area, asking them to warn the women working there to be extra cautious.

But that was it. No one else was working full-time on trying to find the killer.

He could feel Andrea becoming more agitated, so Brandon wrapped up the conference call and meeting pretty quickly. He'd been around red tape long enough to know that sometimes you just worked around it instead of trying to go through it. He led Andrea back out to the car.

"They don't care at all," she said, barely out the door. "The deaths of these women mean *nothing* to them."

He walked with her toward the parking lot, stopping by a tree that was at least a little bit away from the main entrance. "I know it seems that way, but I don't think that's true. Money and manpower are finite resources. The department wants to put them both where it's going to help the most number of people."

Andrea ran her fingers through her blond hair. Brandon had never seen her this aggravated before.

"If it wasn't for us, *nobody* would be looking into their deaths. Trying to figure out what happened. Trying to stop it from happening again."

He ran a hand up her arm. "The locals want to help, too. They just don't have the funds."

She turned away from him, looking off into the desert that surrounded them. "What if DJ Shocker had decided to do this stupid tour four years ago? I could've been the one the police found yesterday. And just like those four other women, nobody would've cared about my death. No family members would have stormed the sheriff's office demanding the killer be caught."

Although he knew it was probably the truth, everything in Brandon tightened in rejection at the thought. The thought that she could've died without his ever knowing her.

"Andrea—"

"I care about these women, Brandon. I don't know them, but I care."

He turned her around and folded her into his arms, thankful that she didn't pull away. He needed to have her close to him right now, to know that she was okay.

"I know you do."

"I will stand for them. Find the killer. Stop this from happening to other women. No matter what choices they made in their lives, they didn't deserve to die like that."

"Together. We will stop this guy together."

He could feel her nod against his chest before she took a step back. "I have a plan."

"Okay."

"It involves us both stepping outside our comfort zones a little."

Brandon grimaced slightly. He wasn't sure he liked the sound of this. "Okay."

"We've got four days until DJ Shocker's next club appearance. We'll talk to him, talk to his production crew, see who the groupies are, following from club to club."

He nodded. "Okay, good. I already have an appointment lined up with him this afternoon."

"We'll need to interview those people. See what we can figure out from them."

Brandon nodded. "Yes." So far none of this was out of their comfort zone.

"We know that Club Paradise, on the northern side of Phoenix, is where the party is heading next." She took a deep breath, then continued in a rush. "I'll go undercover. Get a job there as a stripper. Try to lure the killer o—"

"No." The word was out of his mouth almost before his brain had processed what she was saying.

"Brandon, it's a good plan—"

"No."

He could feel the warrior inside him rising up and fought to keep hold of the logical, reasonable side of his mind.

There was no way in hell she was getting up onstage naked in front of strangers and trying to lure out a killer.

No. And no.

He couldn't drag her away and lock her in a room to keep her safe—and away from prying eyes—so he fought to find the logical words to make his case.

"First of all, you're not a trained agent. You don't have the skills or experience to work undercover. Not to mention, what if the killer *does* come after you? You don't have the hand-to-hand or weapons defense training you need to protect yourself."

"But—"

"Not to mention, as someone who holds a doctorate in psychology, I cannot even begin to list the ways it would damage your psyche to go back into a situation like that. To put yourself back into the club scene where you were objectified by men could have a truly damaging effect on your state of mind."

Brandon began pacing back and forth.

"You're just beginning to come out of your proverbial shell, connect with other people—me in particular—and to place yourself back into the exact situation where you found such shame and—"

"Brandon."

"Fear will only set you back emotionally, which is not what…"

"Brandon." She said his name again, but this time she stepped in front of him and touched his cheek, stopping his pacing.

He stared down at her clear green eyes. There were no shadows in them now, as there had been so often in the past. No fear. Just determination.

"You're frightened for me. I can feel it."

He wanted to deny it, to argue that he was just being reasonable—especially if she couldn't seem to be—but he knew it was the truth.

He was terrified at the thought of her doing this. Of the damaging effects it could have on her on multiple levels.

"Thank you," she continued. "For caring enough to be scared for me."

"It's not a good idea for you." He put his forehead against hers. "It will hurt you in ways you're not really considering right now."

"I know it's not the best plan for me. But right now I need to think about whether it's the best plan for Jillian

Spires and Noelle Brumby, and the other women who will come next if we don't stop this guy."

Brandon straightened. Objectively speaking, for the case and stopping the killer, it was actually a pretty good plan. But he still didn't like it one bit.

"But what about you not having training?"

"I was a stripper for a year and a half. I think I have all the training I need."

"No, law-enforcement training. Self-defense training."

"I have some. Drackett required me to have some."

Brandon planned to make sure she had more. Not just for this case, but because Andrea needed to know she could take care of herself, that she never had to be a victim again.

"*Some* is not enough in a situation like this. Especially when you're trying to capture the attention of a killer."

Brandon could feel another plan formulating in his brain. Within just a few seconds he had run a dozen pros and cons mentally and had come up with some plausible alternates to her plan.

"I need to do this, Brandon. It's the best way. You know that."

He held up a finger to get her to wait a moment more as everything fell into place in his mind.

"Fine. But you don't go undercover as one of the main performers. You go under as a waitress. One of our victims wasn't a dancer at all, so that can't be the only link. You'll be able to get up close with the patrons, especially when DJ Shocker is there. See if you can get any readings of anything unusual."

Andrea nodded slowly. "Okay."

"I will also be in the club at all times when you're there. I'll come in as a customer, but under no circumstances are you to leave with anyone except me."

"Okay, that's probably for the best."

"And I'm going to call Steve and tell him we need out

of the hotel and into a rental house. One that has a lot of space in the living room."

"Why?"

"Because if you're going to set yourself up as bait for a killer, I'm going to make damn certain you know more than just *some* defense tactics. We have four days. Anytime we're not interviewing suspects or investigating the case, you're going to find yourself going hand to hand with me."

Chapter Thirteen

"Can't you arrest him for something?" Andrea leaned over and muttered under her breath to Brandon. *"Anything?"*

They'd been in the lobby of DJ Shawn "Shocker" Sheppard's radio station for the past thirty minutes. Unfortunately, because DJ Shocker was doing a live show, they hadn't been able to question him yet. They'd also been forced to listen to his show.

Distasteful would be the most polite word for it. Less polite terms would be *vulgar*, *juvenile* and *ridiculous*.

"Unfortunately, being an idiot is not currently a crime in this country. So, no, I can't arrest him." Brandon looked as disgusted as she felt.

The radio program catered to college students—men in particular—and the humor was rowdy and raunchy. At least one word every second would have to be bleeped out over normal airways, although most of the audience was probably listening to the station over the internet, where no censoring was needed.

Andrea had listened for the past half hour, teeth grinding, as DJ Shocker had attempted to make a case for the banning of all women's sports bras. He'd used every obnoxious tactic from "that's how God would want it" to trying to compare the bras to illegal performance-enhancing drugs.

The entire premise was asinine, but that was the point. DJ Shocker wanted to live up to his name.

They could see him through the large window that separated the waiting room from the radio booth. DJ Shocker wasn't a bad-looking guy. Probably in his late thirties, way too old to be saying the ridiculous stuff he spewed. His show was on the air three hours a day, five days a week. And it was not only one of the most popular radio talk shows in Arizona, but a top-twenty across the whole country. People couldn't wait to hear what he would say next.

Andrea couldn't wait for him to shut up.

He finally did, tying in the topic du jour with his Devils and Angels pilgrimage tour. He invited everyone out to Club Paradise in four days. It would be the focus of much conversation in next week's shows, he promised. Not something any red-blooded Arizonian would want to miss.

The On Air sign finally flipped off. DJ Shocker was finished for the day. He took a moment to talk to his production crew, who'd gotten him through the past three hours. When an assistant came up to him and said something, pointing at Andrea and Brandon, he looked over.

"Hi. I'm Shawn Sheppard," DJ Shocker said as he walked out of the large radio booth, his voice sounding different than it had on air. "Megan told me you're law enforcement?"

"I'm Brandon Han." Brandon shook the hand the DJ offered to him. "I'm with Omega Sector: Critical Response Division. This is Andrea Gordon."

Andrea shook his hand also, although she really didn't want to. At least he didn't come across quite so obnoxious in person. Although he was much shorter than she would've thought. Shorter than Andrea's five feet eight inches. *Much* shorter than Brandon's six feet.

"Has there been another threat against my life?"

Brandon looked over at Andrea. She hid a snicker in a

cough. It was no surprise to her at all that someone would like to get rid of DJ Shocker permanently.

Brandon shook his head. "Not that we're aware of, Mr. Sheppard. Do you get a lot?"

The man shrugged. "Please, call me Shawn. I get a couple a year. Most of them we don't take seriously, although my lawyer has reported them all to the police."

Andrea watched him closely as he said it. He didn't seem to be hiding any fear about the threats.

"No, we're not here to talk about that. We'd like to ask you a few questions about the Angels and Devils Pilgrimage."

Shawn opened a bottle of water. "What about it?"

"Who came up with the idea for a strip-club tour?"

He answered as he led them down the hall toward his office. "My producers and I last summer. Something to do this winter where we could announce the best club around spring break—the end of March. College students make up my primary audience."

Andrea was content with letting Brandon ask the questions. She would just watch and try to gauge Shawn's feelings.

"Would you consider it a success so far?" Brandon asked, sitting in a chair next to Andrea. Shawn sat on a sofa.

"Yeah. Enough that we might do it again, or something similar, next year. The clubs seem to love it—I'm bringing in a lot of extra revenue for them. And I can't complain about the gig." He smiled at Andrea as he said it. She didn't smile back.

"Have you had any problems? Anything weird?"

The DJ's eyes narrowed slightly. "We've had a rowdy bunch sometimes. Once or twice it's gotten a little out of hand. A couple fights. A couple of guys getting a little too fresh with the dancers. Cops were called."

"Were any of these women involved with those situations?" Brandon laid out the pictures of the four victims, shots of them before they'd been killed so Shawn could see how they really would've looked. The DJ studied them.

He definitely recognized the first, Yvette Tyler. Andrea caught his slight change in breathing as well as a stiffening in his posture.

"What's this about?" Shawn asked. "Are these women suing me or something?"

"Do they have reason to sue you?" Brandon asked.

Shawn sat back and rolled his eyes. He was now aware that he was being accused of something here, rather than potentially being the victim as he had first thought. His posture became more defensive, less open.

"Have you heard my show? I offend everyone. I'm surprised there's not a lawsuit every week. Of course, I do have the First Amendment on my side."

"Do you recognize these women?"

"They're all dancers at the clubs, right? But I don't know which was at which. It's all become a blur of pasties and pole dances."

Andrea pointed at Yvette's picture. "But you definitely know her, right?"

Shawn fidgeted. "Look, yeah. She was at one of the clubs a few weeks ago. Cute girl. Sexy. Great dancer. She cornered me in the hallway when I went to use the bathroom. Wanted to do some private dancing with me at home, if you know what I mean."

"And did you go home with her or vice versa?" Brandon asked.

"No. This was business for me. I was a celebrity. Leaving with her publicly wouldn't have been a good idea."

"What about leaving with her privately?"

"No. I didn't leave with her at all. She was irritated at

the time, but when I saw her later after closing, she had moved on to some other guy. Was all over him at his car."

"Did that make you mad? Make you think she was some sort of slut or something?" Brandon asked.

"No. Honestly, I didn't care. I get a lot of women who throw themselves at me, if you know what I mean."

He glanced sideways at Andrea as if he expected her to do just that at any moment. She rolled her eyes.

"You're safe from me," Andrea said.

"What is this all really about? Not me going home with these women."

"No," Brandon said. "Unfortunately, all of these women are dead, Shawn."

"What?" He shot back against the sofa, eyes wide.

As far as Andrea could tell, the shock flowing off DJ Shocker was completely authentic. He had not known the women were dead.

Brandon looked over at her and she gave him a slight nod. He nodded back, agreeing.

"When— What— How did they die?" Shawn looked back at the pictures.

"They were all murdered. Within a day or two of your Angels and Devils tour stopping at their place of business."

Shawn's face lost all color beneath his ginger hair. "Oh my God, are you serious? I'm sorry if I was flippant before. I had no idea they were dead. I swear I didn't have anything to do with this."

Brandon nodded. "We'll need your whereabouts at certain days and times, but we believe you. You're not actually a suspect, although at this time we're in the process of successfully eliminating as many people as possible."

"Okay." He buried his head in his hands. "Sure, sure. I'll provide you with whatever you need."

"Thank you."

Andrea leaned a little closer toward him. Now that he

wasn't acting like a complete jerk, it wasn't so difficult. "Were there any people you remember seeing at all the clubs that showed a lot of interest in these women?"

"There's a number of guys, mostly from competing fraternities, that have come to most, if not all, of the tour stops."

"Do you remember anyone in particular?" Brandon asked.

Shawn thought about it for a long time. "No. I'm sorry. The clubs are pretty crazy and I just wasn't paying attention. More focused on other things." He started to move back into sleazeball shocker mode, but stopped himself. "There were a lot of people around. A lot of women. A lot of guys. I don't remember anyone in particular. I'm sorry."

"Okay. Thanks for your assistance."

"Do we need to cancel the tour?"

"No. As a matter of fact, we think your tour is our best chance at catching the killer."

"Oh. Okay."

Brandon stood and Andrea followed suit.

"We're probably going to be at all your club appearances, from now on. We'd appreciate it if you didn't draw anyone's attention to us."

"Yeah, sure. Whatever will help."

Brandon shook Shawn's hand. The other man looked pretty shell-shocked. Andrea didn't blame him—it was a lot to take in. They left him and walked back out the way they'd come.

"He seemed pretty legitimately surprised," Brandon said, once they were outside.

"Yeah. I think he was definitely authentic about that. He's not our killer unless I'm way off."

"I agree."

They were almost to the car when Andrea turned back toward the building, sure that Shawn or someone from inside was calling them. But she didn't see anyone in the doorway.

But she knew someone was studying them.

"What's wrong?" Brandon asked, coming up behind her.

"Nothing. I don't know. I thought—" She looked around. That feeling from this morning was back. As if someone was watching her.

"What?" She felt Brandon's hand slide down the arm of her blazer. Having him near helped her shake it off. She was overtired. Had been bombarded by too much over the past few days.

Andrea shook off the feeling and leaned into Brandon. "Nothing. I thought I heard someone call me from back at the building. Must be the lack of sleep getting to me. You know any reasons why lack of sleep might have been a problem for me last night?"

Brandon smiled down at her. "Hmm. Maybe. Can't promise that won't happen again tonight."

Andrea hoped so. She would take a repeat of last night any way she could get it.

But there was a lot of work to do before either of them could think about sleeping—or not sleeping.

"We need to go back to Jaguar's so I can talk to the girls. See if they know or remember anything. Warn them to be careful."

"If the killer follows the pattern and keeps going with the tour, then the other women at Jaguar's should be safe," Brandon said.

"Well, we already have one discrepancy with the pattern. Victim number two wasn't a dancer at all. So I don't want to take any chances that the pattern gets changed and the killer comes back to Jaguar's."

He squeezed her shoulder. "Absolutely. Drackett is already making sure that the club owners are aware of the

issue. He knows the local police department is also noti-
fying them, but maybe hearing it from two different law-
enforcement sources will make sure everyone is taking
it seriously."

"Yeah, that's good."

"Are you sure you're okay?"

Andrea looked around again but didn't see anything
that made her suspicious. The only thing she needed to
be suspicious of was her tendency to see the boogeyman
everywhere she looked.

Chapter Fourteen

At nine o'clock the next night Brandon was almost ready to exit his car and enter Club Paradise. Somehow he doubted very much that was what it would turn out to be.

Andrea was already inside, had been there for the past two hours working as a waitress. They'd cleared it with the club manager, "Big Mike," who'd been happy to keep the women who worked for him safe as well as have free help during the Saturday-night rush.

Big Mike, despite his name, was considerate and businesslike, the opposite of Harry Minkley at Jaguar's.

Brandon had been happy to spend a couple of hours putting the fear of God and law enforcement into Harry yesterday as Andrea talked to her friends.

Brandon hated the shadows that overtook Andrea's eyes whenever they were near Jaguar's. The shadows worsened around Harry. There were a number of scenarios Brandon could envision that would make Andrea react that way even four years later. None of them good.

So putting pressure on Harry, even though he wasn't really a viable suspect, was no hardship for Brandon. The man was sweating every corner he'd ever cut—and there were many—by the time Brandon left. Oh, and Brandon said they would have constant surveillance on Harry and Jaguar's for at least the next year.

Brandon rolled his eyes at the thought of how much of

a misuse of funds that would be, how ridiculously expensive, how it would never get approved. But Harry didn't need to know that. Every time someone came in looking slightly uptight, Harry would wonder if the person was undercover law enforcement. Good.

Brandon had watched Andrea interacting with the dancers of Jaguar's—some she'd known before, some she hadn't—and just kept his distance. The women, rightfully, had questions about Jillian Spires's death and Andrea answered them as best she could without giving away important details about the case. DJ Shocker was not mentioned by Andrea, although all the women said how crazy the night had been. Busy, especially for a Tuesday, not normally a great night. They'd all made a lot of money, which had made everyone happy.

None of them could remember any particular guy hanging around Jillian. Of course, there had been men everywhere because it was so busy.

Andrea warned them all to look out for each other. To walk to their cars at least in pairs. To carefully vet anyone new in their lives before trusting them. The women listened to Andrea in a way they never would've listened to Brandon. She was one of their own.

Keira, the woman Andrea had been so friendly with the day before, had come up to them after Andrea was finished and the other girls had left.

She told them that Jillian had been mentioning a new guy in her life. She hadn't given a name, just that it was someone she'd known for a while and that their relationship had recently taken a turn toward the romantic.

It was something to look into and Brandon assured her they would.

"Hey, you won't leave town without coming to say goodbye, right?"

Keira had gorgeous wavy black hair that fell to the

middle of her back. She was shorter and more voluptuous than Andrea's tall slender build. The two of them standing side by side made a striking pair.

"No, the case is far from over."

"Well, I want you to catch this sicko, but no just taking off like last time, okay?"

"I'm sorry, Keira. You were a good friend to me and I shouldn't have done that." Andrea looked down, and Brandon could see her begin to withdraw into herself.

Keira pulled Andrea to her in a huge hug. "Oh, honey, once I found out you'd left with those two cops and you weren't in any trouble, I was thrilled for you. This was never the place you were meant to be."

Andrea wrapped her arms around Keira, also. "You either, Kee. It's time to move on."

Keira slid back and winked at Andrea and smiled over at Brandon. "It's not so bad for me. I know how to work the stage, the whole place. But I got a plan, don't you worry."

"I'm going to be moonlighting over at Club Paradise for the next few days," Andrea told her. "Undercover type stuff."

"Dancing?" Keira's eyes got big.

"No, just waiting tables. We've got reason to suspect the killer might target someone from there next."

"You be careful." She turned to Brandon. "You'll be there looking out for her?"

"Absolutely."

"Good. She's going to need it. She's all tough now, but she won't be feeling so tough when she's in the club. Even working the floor can be brutal. Sometimes more so with the wandering hands."

Brandon felt his own hands clench. The thought of drunk, sweaty men—of *any* men—pawing at Andrea had the warrior clawing to get out. He had to take a deep breath to calm himself.

Keira gave him a knowing smile. "Yeah, you're going to have to keep that under control if you want this undercover mission to work. She can handle it. She handled it for months when she worked here. Can you?"

Brandon hadn't known, still didn't know, as he was walking into the club now.

Club Paradise was nicer—more high-end—than Jaguar's, but in the end it was the same general principle: almost-naked women making themselves pseudo available.

These clubs sold a fantasy—a private dancer fantasy—where it didn't matter what a guy looked like, how short or tall, fat or skinny, skin tones or hairstyles: he got the girl.

For a price.

And only for a three-minute dance.

Although he'd been to a few for parties over the years, strip clubs had never been his thing. He had always found them to reek of desperation from both the men and women, although you could easily ignore it if you wanted to. And obviously many people wanted to.

A woman's naked body, although he could appreciate it, was not ultimately what turned him on. He found a woman's mind, her emotions, her ability to converse, infinitely more attractive.

Take Andrea, for instance. He couldn't deny he was attracted to her blond hair, green eyes, the delicate lines of her face. Her slender body, curved in just the right places, definitely turned him on.

But it was the other things: her obvious intelligence despite having to overcome her dyslexia, her shy smile, her ability at reading people. Those were the things that really attracted him to her.

The thumping sound of the music permeated the entire building. Brandon passed two bouncers who were actively surveilling the club, making sure none of the girls needed to be rescued from any of the men. Their job would get progressively more difficult as the night—and drinking—went on.

It was Saturday night, still relatively early for a place like this, but there were already men sitting around the main stage, where a dancer worked the pole with strength and skill that would rival an acrobat.

A topless acrobat, but still.

Big Mike had reserved a small table for Brandon in a strategic location in a corner near the bar. It wasn't the best seat if you wanted to be close to or watch the dancers, which was fine since Brandon didn't, but it was excellent for watching the rest of the club without looking as if he was doing so.

DJ Shocker's show would be here in three more days. Brandon and Andrea wanted to use her time working here leading up to that to try to identify regulars and people who could potentially pose a threat. Both so they knew who to watch and who they didn't really need to worry about watching when Tuesday rolled around.

Brandon would study behavior patterns: men who looked as though they were observing the girls with a more nefarious purpose in mind. Andrea would use her skills at reading body language and emotions to do the same thing, but from a stripper's point of view.

Sitting at his table, Brandon ordered a vodka tonic from a waitress who came by, smiling. He wouldn't drink it; he needed all his facilities firing at full speed, not dulled by alcohol. Next time around he'd switch it out for a club soda. It would look the same to anyone who happened to be observing.

He hadn't seen Andrea yet, but it was a big place. Big enough that he couldn't watch everything at one time. He had to constantly be looking around in order to see everyone, much like the bouncers. But he had to be much more subtle about it.

He wasn't wearing a suit, of course. Nobody in here was. He was wearing jeans and a black T-shirt, since he knew Club Paradise would just get warmer as the night went on and more bodies were packed inside.

His waitress brought his drink back, smiling, and Brandon paid, tipping generously. Drackett was not going to be thrilled when Brandon's Omega expense report included drinks from Club Paradise.

Brandon saw Andrea as she came out of a room from behind the bar. At first he could see only her shoulders and the side of her head through the crowd. Then a group of laughing guys moved and he could see her completely.

He picked up his drink and gulped it all the way down, alcohol be damned. If he'd had another he would've done the same thing.

This was Andrea as he'd never seen her, hell, would never even have been able to picture her in all her professional button-down suits.

Her shoulders were bare, her breasts cupped in a red corset bustier that cinched her already-small waist. Her black skirt was short, loose, not even reaching to midthigh. He couldn't tell what shoes she wore from where he sat, but knew from the way she towered over everyone that she had to be in heels.

Her hair that had always been perfectly tidy at work was now sexily, skillfully mussed. Her dark makeup gave her eyes a smoldering look.

Brandon wasn't the only one who noticed her. The group of guys that had parted so he could catch a glimpse of her soon saw the gorgeous waitress and made their way over to order more drinks. One put his hand on her waist; another played with a little piece of her hair.

Andrea laughed at something one of them said, then showed them to a table near the stage. All of them were staring at her legs as she walked away to get their order.

When her back was turned to them, one made a crude gesture to another, obviously about what he'd like to do to Andrea.

It took every ounce of willpower Brandon possessed to stay in his seat. What was he going to do, go punch some twentysomething guy in the face because he'd made a suggestive gesture?

Besides, look at what Andrea was wearing. Could he really blame the punk?

Brandon realized that was just as unfair a thought. Andrea was dressed the way all the waitresses here were dressed. It seemed to be a uniform of some sort: corset bustier and flirty skirts. All the girls had them on in different colors.

He hadn't even really noticed the outfit when his waitress had brought him his drink, but he sure as hell noticed it on Andrea.

He leaned back farther in his seat and forced his eyes away from her at the bar. He was here to study potential suspects, for anybody acting out of the ordinary. Not to act out of the ordinary himself.

But he couldn't stop himself from looking as Andrea brought the drinks back over to the guys. As she leaned down to put them on the table, all of their eyes flew to her breasts, hoping, he was sure, that there might be a happy accident with her top. One guy rubbed his hand up and down the back of her knee. Not going far enough up to be trouble, but certainly more intimate than he had a right to be.

Andrea just smiled and shook her head at him, as if scolding a toddler for being naughty. The men paid and she walked away. Their attention turned back to the stage.

Brandon sat back in his chair.

When he had found out a couple of days ago that Andrea had been a stripper, had worked at a place like this, Brandon had thought he was okay with it. He knew how quiet and reserved she was, plus the abuse that had occurred in her past, the desperate situation that had led her to it.

It had made for a very tragic figure in his mind.

What had he thought, that she had just cried all the way through every night she'd worked there? Sobbing and pushing away every man who came near her?

Obviously that hadn't happened. She'd worked the scenario to her advantage. Worked the men. She might have even enjoyed it all, if how she looked tonight—all smiles and flirtation—was anything to go by.

This jarring close-up of her scantily clad past made it a little harder for him to accept.

Brandon sat up and looked away from her again, from her laughs and flirtatiousness with seemingly every man in the room. The warrior snarled, demanding that he remove her from this situation, get her out of here. Prove—to all these men *and* her—she was his and only his.

But Brandon refused. His intellect ruled him, not his body and definitely not his emotions. Not the warrior. He had a job to do. He ignored the darkness that seemed to be waiting like a cavernous pit for him to fall into. And possibly never crawl back out.

No, he would do this job. Find and stop this killer.

Maybe Andrea wasn't the woman he'd thought. The partner, in more ways than one, that he'd been subconsciously hoping for. He'd survive.

Chapter Fifteen

"If a man comes up behind you and has you in a grasp you can't escape from, the most important thing is not to panic," Brandon had said yesterday evening as they went through self-defense moves in the large living room of the house Omega had rented for them for the rest of their stay here.

"Actually, not panicking is always the most important thing," he'd said, then continued to show her how to throw her arms up and then reach behind her attacker in a sweeping motion with her leg to take him down.

"It's not about size—you're never going to get attacked by someone smaller and weaker than you—it's about staying calm, focused and moving quickly."

It was some sort of jujitsu move, he'd told her. He had a black belt in it, as well as Tae Kwon Do. Andrea had always known about his intellectual prowess, but had no idea about the physical. Although she should've guessed after seeing his rock-hard abdomen and well-defined chest while in bed with him.

They'd practiced over and over, Brandon taking the brunt of the fall each time, until Andrea could do it naturally, without having to think about the different steps. Then they'd practiced more because Brandon said it needed to become muscle memory.

She'd finally stopped him by rolling on top of him after she'd swept him to the ground and kissing him.

"I don't think this is how you're going to want to behave during a crisis," he muttered against her lips, but she could feel his smile.

He'd slipped his arms under his head as she'd sat up, straddling his hips, and pulled her shirt over her head. She'd loved how his eyes had narrowed and his breath hissed out of his lips.

"I think I've got that particular attack crisis taken care of. There are some other one-on-one moves I'd like to work on now, if that's okay with you."

"Um…"

She reached back and unhooked her bra, throwing it to the side, and looked down at him, eyebrow arched. "Got any other moves we can commit to muscle memory?"

"I can definitely think of a couple."

Andrea held on to those memories of yesterday evening as the hours dragged on at Club Paradise. The memories of making love with Brandon with her on top, then in the shower, before he'd tenderly held her while they slept. She was getting used to having his arms around her, snuggling into him while sleeping.

She could use his strong arms around her now. It was nearly midnight, she had two more hours to work and the Saturday crowd was getting more rowdy.

Her first steps out the backstage door onto the club floor had brought back memories, all of them bad. The feelings of being exposed, being watched, being thought of as a piece of meat.

The hands that touched her, sometimes innocently, sometimes much less so.

The bouncers were great here, much better than at Jaguar's. She'd already seen one step in at just a look from one of the waitresses. A guy who had pulled her down in his lap didn't want to let go. The bouncer made his way over, and without a word, he offered the waitress a hand to help her out of the guy's lap. He gave a pointed look to the man, again not saying a word. The guy had apologized to the waitress and everything had been fine.

Other waitresses, Andrea noticed, didn't mind the wandering hands of customers. Provided better tips. The bouncers seemed to know who was who.

Andrea still hated everything about it. Being down on the floor was almost worse than being up on the stage. At least onstage there was a distance—you were a performer. Here you were in the middle of the fray.

She'd seen Brandon sitting over at a corner table. She'd wanted to go over there, but didn't. She didn't want to encroach on another waitress's table, plus Brandon seemed to be deep in the study of the club. His face was pinched and focused, almost angry.

So, although she could desperately use a friendly smile from him, she forced herself to look away and do her job.

Survive this night, which had been her motto when working at Jaguar's, was not her job now. Now her job was doing what she could to find a killer.

It was difficult to get a reading of anyone in here. It was too chaotic; her own feelings were too chaotic. Lust was the primary emotion, followed by guilt and greed. Alcohol caused everything to be hazy and people to have emotions they might not normally feel. She felt as if she was trying to filter through solid walls.

She tried to focus and find the emotions of anger, judgment, condescension. The ones the killer was most likely to have. It didn't take her long to realize the biggest place all three were coming from was Brandon's table.

She had to be wrong about that. Maybe Brandon was just using those emotions, channeling them almost, in order to try to find them in other people. Looking for nonverbal clues. She knew he wasn't the killer, but he definitely wasn't happy.

Andrea turned away from Brandon. She had to focus on what she was doing, not on how he seemed to be behaving.

Instead of trying to feel out general emotions for the whole place, Andrea decided to take it table by table.

She carried her drinks, trying to stay a little longer at each table to get a read on the men there.

The killer was icily controlled. What had been done to the women had not been done in a rage or burst of passion. It had been planned. The killer would study his victim. That was what Andrea was hoping to catch tonight. Someone who just didn't quite fit.

The emotions would be cold, not hot. Andrea needed to look beneath the heat of the lust and general rowdiness. She took a breath and centered herself.

The rest of the night went by more easily. She blocked everything from her mind besides trying to find the coldness of the killer. She thought of it in terms of color. Almost everything in the club was red and she was looking for blue.

Once she focused, the things that used to bother her so much when she worked at Jaguar's faded away. The hands that grasped at her leg or waist she ignored. She wasn't here to make tips; she was here to observe. She didn't need to flirt or smile in a suggestive manner. She froze them out and concentrated. These men were nothing to her. She could leave at any time.

She never found what she searched for. She wasn't able to pinpoint any source of contempt or cold calculation. Everything in here just seemed to be what someone would expect from a strip club: drunkenness, rowdiness and a lot of lust.

A little before 2:00 a.m. Big Mike yelled out for last call. Andrea made her way to the back room, taking her tips and splitting them among the other waitresses, slipping the money into their lockers. Her job was done for the night.

She was exhausted.

The last six hours had taken everything out of her. Getting past her fears, getting past the men, getting past it all and focusing despite her feelings. All for nothing.

She wanted Brandon. Wanted his arms around her. Wanted to go to their little house and leave this all behind her. At least until tomorrow night.

The plan was to exit separately so no one would think they were leaving together. Not that she thought anyone was watching her. But it never hurt to be sure.

Andrea stepped out the back employee door to discover it was storming. There were no windows inside Club Paradise, of course, and either the storm had just come up or Andrea had been so focused on finding who might be the killer that she hadn't even noticed if people had started coming in with wet hair. Either was possible.

She stood alone under the small awning covering the door, but it didn't offer much protection from the rain. Brandon should be here soon to get her. He would drive the car, even off the club parking lot if necessary, to make sure no one was watching him, then swing around to pick her up. She wasn't sure how long it would take.

She stood, huddled under the awning, trying to ward off the chill. The doorway was well lit, but the parking-lot lighting here in the back wasn't great, and beyond the lot seemed to be a vast darkness. She shivered.

That feeling was back. The feeling of someone watching her with anticipation and violence, but she was finally coming to realize that feeling was based on her physical exhaustion and emotional turmoil. Like her past, she wouldn't let it control her.

But she couldn't shake it.

She happened to be looking in the right direction—

across the parking lot into the group of trees and cacti
that surrounded the outer edge of Club Paradise—when
the lightning struck.

She could see the outline of a man in the bright flash.
Big, powerful. He wore a black rain jacket with a hood
and the water flowed down it. Although the hood hid his
features, she knew he was staring right at her.

This man intended to harm her. She had no doubt about
it.

She immediately turned back to the door but found it
locked. Damn it. Big Mike had told her they locked it from
the inside after 9:00 p.m. to keep anyone from sneaking
in that way. She rammed her fist against the door heavily,
hoping the music was off and someone might hear her.

She turned back to where the man was. He was the
killer. He had to be. She couldn't see anything in the darkness.

Was he almost on her? She strained her eyes but couldn't
see anything. Dressed in black as he was, it would be difficult to see him in the lot. Lightning flashed again.

He was closer. Oh God, he was closer. He must be walking, taking his time. Which somehow panicked her even
more. He was playing a game with her. Was that a knife
in his hand?

She pounded again. Nothing. She was afraid to keep
her back to him. What if he started to run and pounced?

Should she leave, try to make her way around to the
front door? That would require running through some
darkened parts of the parking lot around the edge of the
building, but it seemed better than sitting here alone with
her one jujitsu move and no one opening the door.

She turned, almost certain she would find the big man
right behind her, but didn't. Her breath sawing in and out of
her chest, Andrea jumped down the side of the small door
ledge, keeping her back to the wall so the killer couldn't

sneak up on her. She was about to run when she saw Brandon's car pulling around the corner.

It stopped, a beacon of safety standing between her and whoever was out there in the darkness. When Brandon saw she was standing in the rain he got out.

"What's going on? Are you okay?"

"The k-killer." She could barely get the words out and pointed toward the lot where she'd seen the man. "I think he's out there. I saw him when lightning flashed."

Brandon immediately pulled out his weapon. "What? Are you sure?"

Andrea nodded, still trying to get in enough breath to calm her racing heart. "I know he was there."

"I'm going to check it out. You stay by the car."

"No!" There was no way she was letting him go alone, or staying here alone, for that matter. "I'll come with you."

"Andrea, you're not an agent—you don't need to do this."

"Yeah, well, I have a pair of eyes. I'm not letting you go out there with your back exposed."

Brandon nodded. "Fine. Let's drive the car that way so we at least have the headlights helping us."

They got in the car and he reached into the glove compartment, pulling out a gun. "This is a Glock 9 mm. Are you familiar with weapons at all?"

"Some, but only at the range."

"That's better than most." He handed it to her. "Just don't shoot me on accident."

They drove over near where Andrea had seen the man during the first flash of lightning. Brandon spun the car slowly in a semicircle to provide light on a wider area, but they didn't see anything.

"He seems to be gone now. Where did you see him?"

Andrea pointed. "At first it was over near those trees.

Then I was trying to get back inside and when I turned around again he was in the middle of the parking lot."

"That rain is coming down pretty hard out there, but let's see if we can find anything."

She didn't want to go. She wanted to stay inside the safety of the car. She wanted him to stay inside the safety of the car. She reached for his hand and was surprised when he pulled away as if she'd burned him.

She turned to him, but he didn't look at her.

"You can stay here if you want—that's okay."

She shook her head, not understanding exactly what was going on, the emotions that were radiating from him. Maybe, like inside the club, he was just focused. "No, I'll come, too."

They didn't find anything particularly useful. The rain was washing away everything too fast. Brandon did find two footprints right around where the man would've been watching her the first time she saw him. Brandon took a picture with his phone.

"There was definitely someone standing right here since the rain started. A perfect place to be watching the door when the women exited after work."

Andrea felt chilled to her very bones, as if she would never get warm again. The rain had both of them sopping wet, but the cold she felt came from the inside.

"He was coming for me, Brandon. I'm sure of it. I could feel him getting closer. I was about to make a run for the front door when you drove up." She managed to get the words out without her teeth chattering.

Brandon was only two feet away from her but he might as well have been a million miles. He finally turned and looked at her. She felt a slight softening from him before his walls rammed back up in place.

"Let's get you home."

ANDREA TOOK ONE look at herself in the bathroom mirror once they got home and understood some of the reason why Brandon was keeping such a distance. She looked like a drowned rat with too much makeup on.

The dark colors she'd used on her eyes to give herself more of a smoldering appearance at the club were now running down her cheeks. The carefully tousled hair now lay flat against her head in knots.

If she was Brandon she'd stay far away from her, also.

He was on the phone with Omega, or maybe the Phoenix police; Andrea wasn't sure which and really didn't care.

She definitely couldn't deny any longer that something had changed in Brandon since earlier this afternoon, when they'd made love for hours, and now, when he couldn't even seem to look at her.

It didn't take a genius to figure out what had happened. He'd seen her in her "natural" habitat. Had figured out what her life had really been like before. And it hadn't been pretty.

Andrea almost staggered under all the weight she could feel pressing down on her.

This was what she'd known from the beginning. Why she'd always tried to hide her past from everyone at Omega. Because ultimately it was ugly and seedy and lewd.

Brandon had thought he was okay with her past until he'd come face-to-face with it tonight. Obviously, now he wasn't. He hadn't touched her once of his own accord since she left Club Paradise. She couldn't hide from that fact any longer.

He now found her distasteful.

She felt something deep inside her shatter at the thought. Pieces she knew she would never be able to put completely back together.

She couldn't bear to look at herself in the mirror any more. She stumbled over to the shower and turned it on.

Once inside she found she didn't even have the strength to stand up. She just sat down and let the water pour all over her. She knew it would wash away the cold, the ruined makeup and the mud.

But it would never wash away her past.

Chapter Sixteen

The next morning Brandon was at a loss for what to do or say. It was new for him and not pleasant.

None of what he was feeling was pleasant.

Andrea sat quietly at the table, eating cereal. Was totally engrossed in her cereal as if she'd never eaten it before and it was the most fascinating thing she'd ever seen. Which he was sure had nothing to do with the cereal and everything to do with not having to talk to him.

Cold professionalism from them both.

By the time he had finished reporting the man Andrea had seen to the local police, she had been out of the shower and had enclosed herself in the smaller bedroom.

Not the one they'd slept in together the night before.

He told himself that was better, that they needed the space apart. That it would've been ugly if they'd had a confrontation right then. But part of him wanted to get it out in the open, fight it out.

Part of him wanted answers to how she could seem to enjoy dressing so scantily and flirting with dozens of unknown men all night.

The reasonable part of his brain nagged at him: Hadn't that been the plan? For her to blend in, do the job, get close enough to be able to read the emotions and nonverbal behavior of these men and see if any were acting out of place?

Just why the hell had she needed to seem to enjoy it so much?

Intellectually Brandon could see the unfairness of the direction of his thoughts. But the warrior couldn't. Couldn't seem to get past the short skirt and heels and hanging all over other men.

So he'd left her alone last night. Gotten hardly any sleep himself. And now they ate in silence.

She was dressed in her professional suit once more: pants, a cream-colored blouse and a blazer. Not a single hair was out of place, her makeup tame and tasteful.

But Brandon knew what lay beneath it.

Hell, just about any guy who'd been at Club Paradise last night had a pretty good idea of what lay beneath it.

He was struck again by the unfairness of his thoughts, but damned if he could stop them. He got up for another cup of coffee. He was going to need it to get through this day.

THE ICY PROFESSIONALISM and silence from both of them continued through the morning as they looked over the parking lot and surrounding area of Club Paradise. The local police had met them there to help search the wooded area, but besides a couple of footprints, nothing had come of it.

But standing where the man would've stood showed Brandon that he'd had an excellent view of the back door of the club. If it hadn't been for the lightning, Andrea might never have seen him at all. If he had kept to the shadows, he could've been on her before she'd even been aware of his presence.

It reminded Brandon once again that Andrea wasn't a trained agent and wouldn't be able to fight off an attacker. What he'd taught her hadn't nearly been enough. He needed to show her more, but that seemed highly unlikely given that they weren't even talking to each other at the moment.

They were now headed back to Jaguar's. Keira had called them; she'd found a note she was sure was in Jillian Spires's handwriting. It had some initials on it and part of a phone number.

Keira was waiting for them inside the empty club and gave Andrea a hug.

"How'd it go last night?"

Andrea rolled her eyes. "It was a Saturday night at a club. Some things haven't changed."

"Get any useful info?"

"No," Brandon said.

Keira stepped closer to Andrea, picking up on the tension between the two of them, touching her arm. "How are you doing? Was going back to it as hard as you thought?"

Andrea shuddered just the slightest bit. "Worse in some ways. But I had a job to do and that gave me something to focus on."

"You never should've gone back there." Keira angled her body so she was standing between Andrea and Brandon.

Brandon realized the shorter woman was trying to protect Andrea.

From him.

The thought was preposterous. Why would Andrea need protection from him?

Andrea's smile was soft and gentle as she looked at her friend. "I won't lie. It brought back a lot of the old memories and old fears. But at least I didn't have to call you to come bail me out this time."

Keira hugged Andrea tightly to her, almost motherly. "Well, you know I would have."

Brandon didn't know what the two women were talking about, but he could feel a weight beginning to sit in his chest. Looking at Andrea now with Keira, he realized the icy professionalism she'd had with him since they'd awakened this morning wasn't actually her true feeling. There was pain in her eyes, in her voice, in her posture that he'd missed before.

Missed because it hadn't been there or missed because he'd been too busy with his righteous anger to see it?

All he knew was right now Andrea definitely wasn't the same confidently flirtatious woman who used her body to get what she wanted that he'd seen with the men last night. Nor was she the consummate professional who'd greeted him coldly this morning, then went about her business.

Right now she just looked young. Haunted. Clutching a friendly hand because she desperately needed someone to hold on to.

The weight in his chest got a little heavier.

"But anyway, I got through it," Andrea told Keira. Neither of them were looking at him. "We didn't really gather any useful intel, but hopefully now I should be more ready for tonight and especially tomorrow when DJ Shocker is there. That's what's important."

"You don't have to do it, you know," Keira whispered. "I'll come do it."

Andrea hugged the woman. "Thanks for the offer. But I can't teach you how to read people the way I can. It's just something that clicks in my brain."

Keira shrugged a delicate shoulder. "Okay. Let me know if you change your mind."

"So what did you find of Jillian Spires's?" Brandon asked.

Keira turned so her back wasn't to him and he could be included in the conversation. But he noticed her eyes were neither warm nor friendly when she looked at him, the way they were when she looked at Andrea.

"A note from last week. Evidently someone had given

it to her and she had stuffed it in the drawer by the server's station."

"Why would she do that?" Brandon asked.

Keira rolled her eyes. "Our outfits—even when waiting tables—don't tend to have a lot of pockets or places to stuff paper."

"What did it say?" Andrea asked.

Keira walked a few steps to the bar where she'd placed a napkin that had been folded. "Here."

She handed it to Andrea, but Andrea looked at it briefly and handed it to Brandon, looking embarrassed. "It will take me too long to decipher that."

Because of the handwriting and water stains, the note would be hard for anyone to read, dyslexic or not, but Brandon couldn't find a way to reassure Andrea of that.

Trust me, I can give you a lot more thrills than DJ Shocker ever could. Text me when you get off work tonight. J

It had a phone number, but the last four numbers were unreadable because of liquid that had hit the napkin.

"That was given to Jillian the night DJ Shocker was here," Andrea said.

"Or maybe the night after," Brandon agreed. "Either way, this person would fit our MO. We know he was here for the DJ Shocker show and we know he wanted her attention."

"Will the phone number help?" Andrea asked. "The area code is local for Phoenix."

Brandon nodded. "It gives us something. We'll also get the police department to run this napkin for any forensic evidence, although at this point it's highly doubtful."

"Do you remember her with anyone, Keira?" Andrea asked softly.

"No. I'm sorry. The night with DJ Shocker was crazy. There were a ton of locals here, plus people we'd never seen before." Keira's distress was obvious.

"It's okay, Kee. You can't keep track of everything and watch over everyone. Even though you try." Andrea wrapped an arm around her.

"She was a nice kid." Keira shook her head. "Wasn't shy, like you. She was outgoing. Didn't mind flaunting what the good Lord gave her, if you know what I mean. Even down here waiting tables, she still had a lot of sass. And tended to go home with men from the club, even though we all warned her that was a bad idea."

"Everybody has to go their own way, Keira. You can't be mother to us all."

Keira, of course, wasn't old enough to be mother to any of these girls, was hardly old enough to be mother to a baby. But age had nothing to do with mothering instincts.

Keira gave them a crooked half smile. "I always try."

It was getting late in the afternoon. Andrea said her goodbyes to Keira, both of them needing time to get ready for the night's work. He left them so they could talk privately.

The thought brought the weight back to Brandon's chest. Everything he'd heard from Keira about Andrea did not mesh with the conclusions he'd drawn for himself after seeing her last night.

Maybe he needed to talk to her, to clear the air. To tell her what he was feeling.

Hey, I didn't like that you pranced around for a bunch of men while being so scantily clad last night. I know you were undercover but you didn't have to look like you were so comfortable with it.

Yeah, he didn't come across as a jackass with that thought. The weight in his chest got heavier.

"You ready?" she asked, joining him at the door. He turned and stared down at her.

"What?" she finally asked.

"Nothing. I—" Not knowing what to say, he stopped himself and held the door open for her. Should he try to explain?

He was about to try as they walked outside, even knowing that it probably wouldn't come across well. But she stopped abruptly just a few feet out into the parking lot.

"What's wrong?" he asked, about to reach for his weapon.

"It's my—" She cleared her throat and started again. "It's my aunt. I don't see my uncle."

Brandon took his hand off his sidearm, but didn't relax his guard. He saw the older woman now. She was standing next to the same car that had been parked in front of the hotel on Tuesday.

Despite any coldness between him and Andrea, Brandon knew he would protect her from this.

"You don't have to talk to her," he told her, stepping closer. "We can just leave. Or I'll go talk to her if you want."

He could see the tension outlining Andrea's body. "No, like you said, they can't hurt me anymore. I don't know what she wants."

As Andrea walked toward her aunt, Brandon stayed close to her side. The older woman took a few steps toward them as they got closer to the vehicle. Andrea stopped about ten feet away.

"Hello, Margaret."

No title or anything to insinuate they were family.

"Andrea. You look so beautiful." The older woman moved closer but stopped when Andrea visibly flinched. "So grown-up."

"I have grown up since I was seventeen and left your house in the middle of the night, scared for my life."

It was Margaret's turn to flinch. "Andrea, I'm—"

"Where's Marlon?"

"Your uncle passed away two years ago."

Andrea nodded, obviously not curious how Marlon had died. She relaxed just the slightest bit. That man truly could never hurt her again.

"I don't expect you to forgive me for not stopping him from hurting you. But I am sorry. Sorry I wasn't stronger and didn't stand up to him."

Andrea nodded again. "Thank you for coming by."

Andrea began to walk away but her aunt stopped her.

"One of the ladies from church told me you were in town and working for law enforcement. She said you knew some people here."

Margaret just stared at the building for a moment. He wondered if she knew Andrea used to work there.

The older woman brought her gaze back to Andrea. "I knew I needed to come and make my apology face-to-face while I could. I didn't think you'd talk to me on the phone."

Everything about Andrea's stance clearly said her aunt was right.

"Well, it was nice of you to make the gesture." Andrea turned to their car, obviously finished with the conversation.

Her aunt reached out. "I also have a box of your things. Letters you received and a few items that were in your room that you left behind." She opened the door to the backseat of her car and took out a box that wasn't much bigger than a shoe box. "You used to like horses and collected a couple figurines."

Andrea stopped and turned back to her aunt, her eyes narrowing. "Yes, I remember those."

"They're in here. Please, honey, I know you don't want

anything to do with me, but I wanted you to have these things."

Andrea hesitated for a moment, but then walked over to her aunt. When she reached out to take the box, Margaret put her hands over Andrea's.

"I stopped drinking. Marlon did too a few months before he died. Both of us realized what damage we'd done to you, and I'm so, so sorry. I know we'll never be family again, but I hope someday you'll be able to forgive me."

Andrea nodded again, but didn't say anything. Margaret held her hands so long Brandon took a step closer in case he needed to force Margaret to let go. Brandon's action caught Andrea's attention and seemed to pull her out of whatever place in the past she'd gone.

"Thank you for getting these to me." She gestured to the box while stepping backward, breaking the contact with her aunt.

"I'm so glad you've done so well for yourself," Margaret whispered. "That you were able to overcome everything and rise above it."

Andrea looked at her aunt, then at Brandon. "I'm learning that the people who hurt you are ultimately the ones who make you stronger."

Chapter Seventeen

The people who hurt you are ultimately the ones who make you stronger.

Andrea's words still rang clearly through his head hours later when he sat at the corner table of Club Paradise again.

He and Andrea had left her aunt, returned to the house, and Andrea had gone into her small room. She hadn't said anything to him besides the most basic of answers to his questions about food and particulars of the case. He'd left her at the house to take the napkin Keira had found to the locals for analysis.

When he'd come back Andrea had still been in her room, although there had been evidence that she'd fixed herself dinner. The box her aunt had given her lay unopened on the kitchen table.

They still hadn't said anything but polite phrases to each other as he took her to Club Paradise to get ready for her shift.

The weight in his chest hadn't gotten any less heavy, either.

She'd looked right at him when she'd said the words: *the people who hurt you are ultimately the ones who make you stronger.*

It was now nearly eleven o'clock and he'd been watching the men in the club—watching Andrea—for more than an hour and a half from the same table as last night.

Despite the weight in his chest, he still couldn't stop his anger, his distaste, at seeing her flirt so easily with the men. At seeing her dressed so skimpily again, at knowing *others* were seeing her show off so much skin.

"How you doing there, Agent?"

Brandon's eyes flew to the petite form, dressed in high heels, jeans and a tank top, who plopped down in the chair across from him.

Keira.

Brandon sat back. "Hi. Didn't expect to see you here."

"Thought I'd come out, give a little support to our girl. I know she needs it."

Brandon looked over to where Andrea had crouched down near a low chair so a man in his midforties could give her his order. He noticed the man never took his eyes off her breasts cupped in the bustier. Andrea didn't seem to mind at all that the guy was salivating.

"She seems to be doing just fine on her own," Brandon said to Keira.

Keira's eyes narrowed, but she didn't say anything. A waitress, with *Kimmie* on her name tag, came over to take her order, and when she brought the drink back, Keira took a twenty-dollar bill, rolled it up and stuck it between the other woman's breasts—also visible from the bustier she wore. Keira winked at the waitress and she winked back.

"You into girls?" Brandon asked.

"No. Not that way." She took a sip of her drink. "Just like to support my sisters who work damn hard for their money then a lot of times are rushing to a second job or a family or something else that also requires their time."

Brandon hadn't necessarily thought about it like that, but guessed it could be true.

"Let's take our waitress, Kimmie. She's Andrea's age or a little younger. Maybe twenty-one."

Brandon nodded. "Probably."

"Maybe Kimmie got knocked up by someone who took off. Or has a husband who can't get a job. Or hell, maybe she's always dreamed of being a stripper. Whichever. She finds a job here. Any of that make you think less of her?"

"Not really."

"She comes in every night, smiles at all the guys. It's not hard for the good-looking frat-boy types. Maybe a little more difficult for the old ones or fat ones or ones that sneer at her. But she still does it, because, well, that's how you make a living at this job. Think less of Kimmie now?"

Brandon knew where Keira was going with this, but didn't stop her. "No, I don't think less of her."

"She gets up onstage and takes her clothes off and smiles. She works down on the floor serving drinks and smiles. She smiles. Because this is her job. Giving men something to look at is her job. And she does it well."

Brandon held a hand out in surrender, but Keira continued.

"There are some girls who have to use drugs in order to do it. Kimmie isn't one of those. There are some girls who make some extra money by going out in back and having sex with guys. But Kimmie doesn't do that, either. Because Kimmie's just trying to live—support her family or whatever—off the money she makes at this job. She doesn't give guys come-ons. Doesn't tease them. She just dresses up her admittedly beautiful body in a somewhat revealing outfit and smiles. Nothing more."

Brandon looked over at Andrea. She was smiling. But she wasn't touching any of the men, leading them on in any way. Like Kimmie, she was just doing her job.

Keira leaned over the table toward Brandon. "You got a problem with what Andrea's doing here tonight? What she did four years ago?"

Brandon shrugged. "I didn't think so until I saw her up close and in action. It's hard to watch. Hard to accept."

"Whose hang-up is it?" She gestured toward Andrea. "That sweet girl right there? I don't think so."

Keira took another sip of her drink. "Do you know why she was so popular onstage? Because everyone could tell she didn't really want to be there. Made her seem untouchable yet available at the same time. Guys ate it up."

Brandon shook his head. He didn't want to think about Andrea onstage, and thinking about her being up there when she didn't want to be was even worse, but Keira wouldn't relent.

"You see me? I am what I am. I go up onstage and I'm confident and strong and hot. It's not every guy's thing, but it's enough that I'm pretty popular. Do you think you could make me feel bad about myself?"

Brandon began to answer but she stopped him.

"Let me help you—no. Nothing you could say to me about my chosen profession would make me feel bad about myself. Because I am how I dance—confident and strong. I own my choices and I don't second-guess myself."

Brandon raised his glass in a sort of salute. Everything Keira said was obviously true.

"But you know what I'm not, Dr. Han? It is doctor, right?"

"Not medical, but PhD, yes."

"I'm not kind. I'm not willing to put myself on the line to help other people. I'm not willing to fight through hardships and claw my way up from the holes life tries to throw me in."

"I'm not sure life would be able to throw you in a hole." And he didn't think the other part was true, either.

She shrugged a delicate shoulder and glared at him. "One thing I know—I sure as hell wouldn't be willing to go back and do something that sickened me about myself, that broke my own heart, because it might help a complete stranger."

She pointed across the club where Andrea was talking to another group of men. "But I think we both know someone who did. Who *is*."

Brandon stared at Andrea for a long time. Finally Keira stood up, her drink empty. "It's time for me to get going. I have responsibilities having to do with stuff not here."

"I'll walk you out."

She put a hand out. "I'll be fine."

She walked a few steps before turning back to his table. "I don't know Andrea well. She doesn't let anybody know her well because she's afraid they'll hurt her. But I've seen the way she looks at you. She respects you, has opened herself to you."

Brandon couldn't deny that. Andrea had opened herself to him, in more ways than one.

"Knowing you were here had to make this even harder for her. That you might judge her. Hurt her like other people had. And then you did."

Brandon couldn't deny it. Keira was right.

She continued. "Andrea will eventually come to terms with the fact that she was a stripper. In the greater scheme of things, who the hell cares? It's in her past and it got her through. Someday she'll look back on her past and realize she has nothing to be ashamed of. I doubt when you look back at how you've treated her that you'll be able to realize the same."

HAVING THE FACT that you were a hypocritical jackass pointed out with such crystal clarity was pretty painful.

The image of Andrea, smiling and flirting with other men in a skimpy outfit, seeming to enjoy it? It burned into his mind.

Another image tried to fight its way in, one of Andrea in the rain, cold, needing him. But he pushed it out.

He could admit to himself it was easier to deal with

anger and disgust over stripper Andrea than with the feelings that swamped him over kind, talented, reserved Andrea.

Those feelings scared the hell out of him.

And it wasn't as if he'd said anything to Andrea about how seeing her at the club had made him feel. He wasn't that much of a jackass.

She was in the shower now. It was nearly 3:00 a.m. He was listening to a message left for him by Gerardo Jennison at the Phoenix police department with a report of what they'd found in the woods around Club Paradise today. It hadn't been much.

He sat down on the couch, realizing he'd been pacing. He pushed all thoughts of Andrea away and concentrated instead on the man she'd seen in the storm.

There'd been no sign of him tonight, and neither Brandon nor Andrea had found any persons of interest in the club. If the storm guy was the same one who had killed the other women then his MO seemed to be changing. He wasn't waiting until DJ Shocker's visits to pick his victims; he was hunting before.

Of course, he'd also killed Ashley Judson, victim number two. She hadn't been a stripper at all, just a waitress, although she'd had a reputation for serving up herself for truckers who stopped at her restaurant and were willing to pay the right price. That could certainly seem just as "impure" as the other women, who took their clothes off to make money.

But coming after Andrea didn't really make sense, since it was her first night and she hadn't really done anything "impure," unless the actual women he killed didn't matter, just someone who worked at a strip club.

Brandon sat back and let his mind work, doing what he did best, thinking of all the possibilities. Maybe the storm guy wasn't the serial killer at all. Maybe it was

Damian Freihof. Brandon took out his phone and speed-dialed Steve.

"Damn it, Han, do you know it's three o'clock in the morning?" Steve asked by way of greeting.

"Sorry, boss. We've had a slight update." He explained the situation and what had happened to Andrea.

"Do you think the killer has turned his sights on her?" All traces of sleep were now gone from his boss's voice.

"Not unless he's changed his MO. I was wondering what the latest update on Damian Freihof was."

"It's still an active manhunt, but he was last seen near Midland, Texas."

"That's not out of the realm of possibility for arrival in Arizona."

"True. But it's also a direct route to Mexico, which is a logical place for him to be headed if he wants to get to South America. Plus, we still don't have any reason to think he'll actually come after Andrea. He hasn't had any contact with her since she's been at Omega."

"All right. Sorry to wake you. Keep me posted if anything changes."

"You'll be my first call. How has the undercover work been going?"

"Fine. Andrea jumped back into it like she'd never left. Seems like wearing next to nothing and flirting with total strangers is second nature to her."

There was a long silence on the other end.

"What?" Brandon finally asked.

"You're telling me that Andrea looked like she was having a good time while working at the club?"

"Yeah. She was fine. Happy, even. Why?"

"I must have misunderstood the nature of the club you were infiltrating. This club must be different than Jaguar's, more like a restaurant."

Brandon all but sneered. "No. It was a strip joint. Maybe

a little higher rent than Jaguar's, but there were still mostly naked girls dancing on the stage. And the waitresses' outfits weren't much better. Drunken guys. Groping. You know the drill."

"And Andrea was all right?"

"More than. I'll bet she made a killing in tips. Looked perfectly at home in a bustier and heels. All smiles."

Brandon couldn't get the image out of his mind. It wasn't even the outfit that bothered him so much. He'd gladly have watched her all day in that skirt and top. Would've loved to have peeled her out of it. Under much different circumstances.

It was her actions. Her flirtations, friendliness. The smiles she'd given other men. Touches she'd allowed.

He felt the warrior clawing his way up. He wanted to go and beat down all the men who had dared to touch her. Then pin her to his side and make love to her until she was never even tempted to smile at another man.

Steve interrupted his thoughts. "Wow. She must be better at undercover work than I would've thought. Good for her, for fighting through it to do her job."

"She didn't look like she was doing a job."

"Brandon, if you could've seen her at Jaguar's when Grace Parker and I picked her up there four years ago, you'd be amazed that she could even function tonight, much less do her undercover work well."

"What do you mean?"

"She was all but broken. She hated every minute she worked in that club—it was destroying her piece by piece. Going back into a similar situation has to be overwhelming for her, probably terrifying."

Brandon could feel something clench in the pit of his stomach. Again.

"I'm proud of her for just facing it," Steve continued. "Even if she had only made it for ten minutes, I still would've been proud. To hear that she did so well? Be sure to pass along my official and personal congratulations for a job well done."

Brandon murmured something; he wasn't quite sure what.

"I hope this will help you guys find the killer. Because I'm sure Andrea paid a high personal price getting out there the last two nights."

Brandon managed to say the correct words and end the call with his boss.

That feeling in his gut still hadn't gone away. Still felt like a heaviness pressing down on him. How heavy was the weight?

The exact weight of a judgmental, hypocritical ass.

Someone who had acted completely unprofessional the past two nights and it hadn't been the unseasoned consultant with no undercover experience. She'd done what she was supposed to do. Make nice with the locals and try to get a reading on anybody who might not fit in.

All Brandon had been able to see was the short skirt, revealing top and sexy makeup. Not the capable law-enforcement figure underneath.

Or the very vulnerable woman who had probably needed support from him. Possibly during her time at the club. Definitely afterward.

He'd turned away. Deliberately.

The shower had long since turned off. He realized Andrea hadn't come through the living room at all. Not that he expected her to come say good-night, but she hadn't come to get any food from the kitchen or even a glass of water.

Regardless of her outfit, she'd worked very hard for the five hours he'd watched and some time before he'd arrived. That tray probably would've gotten heavy after a while, and her heels were even higher than usual. That couldn't have been easy on her feet.

Brandon rubbed a hand down his face. She had pre-ferred going to bed hungry and thirsty than to walk by him to get what she needed.

He headed back to one of the two bedrooms this house contained, looking at the one he and Andrea had slept in together two nights ago. They'd fallen in bed after show-ering, both exhausted by the hours of training and love-making. She'd slept in his arms the entire night, and he'd smiled when he'd awakened to still find her there. No run-ning away this time.

But she wasn't in that bed now. It was empty, covers of the king-size bed still undisturbed. He walked over to the other, smaller room that barely fit the single bed, dresser and desk.

There was Andrea sound asleep.

The light in her room was on. Her back was pressed all the way against the wall the bed sat against, one arm rest-ing halfway over her head in a defensive position. Even in sleep she was prepared for someone to strike.

Brandon knew he had added to her psychological need for that posture by his actions. The thought shredded him.

He pulled out the chair from the desk and sat in it, watching her sleep. He wanted to wake her up, to apolo-gize.

He hadn't said anything that an outsider would consider cruel. Hadn't done anything that would seem unforgiv-able. But Brandon knew how sensitive Andrea was, the emotions she could sense and decipher. She'd known how he felt. His disapproval, his anger. The distaste he'd felt.

God, he would take it all back if he could.

Given some time to process it now, and with the help of both Keira and Steve, he realized he hadn't really been prepared to see her like that. Hadn't really come to grips that she had taken off her clothes for money when she was younger.

But now, sitting here, watching her, he realized he had no right to judge her. He'd been raised by two loving parents, surrounded by two brothers and a sister. He'd been a challenging child, acting out in his younger grades, on a route to trouble. His parents had loved him enough, known him well enough to realize the problem was he wasn't being challenged sufficiently. They'd moved him to a gifted academy, one that allowed him to excel at his own pace.

The course of his life had been set. He'd flourished from there.

Who'd been around to see that Andrea flourished? No one. The opposite, in fact.

She shouldn't have to apologize for how she had chosen to survive. The important fact was that she had. She was already ashamed of it.

He had added to that shame. What did that make him?

He reached toward her to wake her up, tell her all these things, beg her forgiveness, but dark circles under her eyes stopped him. She needed rest. She'd been working hard for days and hadn't been getting enough sleep. The things he needed to say could be said in the morning. They were his burden to carry.

He wanted to at least pick her up and carry her to the bed they'd shared. He wanted to hold her during the night. Be close to her.

But he had to face the fact that she might not want that anymore. She was sleeping peacefully now. For once he would make an unselfish decision concerning her and leave her alone.

She'd scrubbed her face completely clean, making her look so young and innocent and vulnerable that it was almost painful to look at her.

He realized she was exactly those things. Even when she had on a skimpy outfit and a ton of makeup and platform heels, she was still those things: young and innocent and vulnerable.

She had to go back there again tomorrow night—hell, it was so late, it was tonight—but this time he planned to make sure she understood that she wouldn't be going in there alone.

If there was one benefit of having an IQ as high as his, it was that you learned from your mistakes and you learned *fast*.

Chapter Eighteen

Andrea slept later than she had been, but not enough to wipe the exhaustion from her body. Her sleep had been plagued by nightmares. First ones that hadn't bothered her for a while, of her uncle and her life in Buckeye. Then ones of the past two nights, groping hands and the man she'd seen in the lightning.

Her heart began to thud just thinking about him.

She forced the thought of it out of her head. She had to admit she'd been so emotionally piqued getting off work in the storm that it was possible she'd imagined the whole thing. Not the man. She had definitely seen the man. But maybe he hadn't meant her any ill intent at all. Maybe he'd just been a guy walking across the parking lot and it just got all spooky-out-of-proportion because of the lightning.

She also didn't want to think about Brandon and how he obviously now felt about her. She noticed he'd left her where she was for the second night in a row, sleeping alone in the small guest bed. He hadn't wanted to be near her. Hadn't touched her at all since he'd seen her at Club Paradise.

She threw off her covers and got out of bed, still fully dressed in sweatpants and a T-shirt. She even had a bra on. She knew sleeping fully clothed was something she did when she felt nervous or uncomfortable. A habit from the days when she'd had to run in the middle of the night from her uncle. Sometimes she fought the urge. Last night she hadn't.

She was surprised to see Brandon already awake, pulling out the beginnings of breakfast in the kitchen. She stopped in the doorway.

"Hi." His black hair was tousled and his chest was bare. Andrea fought the urge to lick her lips. It was totally unfair that she was this attracted to him when he obviously wasn't attracted to her lately.

"Want some coffee?" She nodded and he smiled at her before turning to get a mug and pour her some.

Her fingers touched his when he handed her the mug. At least this time he didn't jerk away as if he couldn't stand to touch her.

"Thanks." Her voice was husky with sleep. She didn't know what else to say to him.

"I'm going to make some breakfast, okay? I don't think you ate anything last night and you worked pretty hard." He smiled again. "Then we can compare notes, see if we come up with anything."

Andrea was confused by his behavior. This was different from the cold and distant Brandon she'd experienced for the past day and a half.

He was being professional, she realized, something in her sinking. He knew they still had to work together even though he found her distasteful. Their personal relationship was over but he was at least making an effort to make the situation less awkward. She could do the same.

It wasn't the first time she'd put back together the shattered pieces of her emotions. They might not be without cracks, but she knew the glue would hold. Later, after they'd stopped this killer and made sure no more women died, when she was back at Omega and no one was around, then she could fall apart.

While watching him cook, Andrea wondered if Brandon would suggest to Steve that she wasn't Omega material. That he'd seen her in action and she just wouldn't be a good fit long-term.

Maybe it was just time for her to move on altogether.

He brought a plate filled with eggs, bacon and toast and set it in front of her.

"Eat up," he said. "We've got a full day. And night."

She took a bite of her toast and realized how famished she was. He set his own plate down and began eating, also.

Her plate was nearly empty when he asked about last night. She was glad she was nearly done because her food became tasteless. She didn't want to think about last night. Didn't want to face him as she talked about it, knowing what he thought about her. His disgust.

"I wasn't able to pick out anyone in the club who seemed to be acting odd," he said as he took a sip of the coffee. "But then again, I didn't think the killer would actually be there."

"Because you think he follows DJ Shocker in. That he's in the club for the first time that night."

"Maybe not in the club for the first time, but picking his victim then. I was working on a profile last night."

Andrea wasn't sure if he meant while he was at Club Paradise or later while she was sleeping.

"Except for victim two, the truck-stop waitress, all the murders have occurred between twenty-four and forty-eight hours after DJ Shocker's appearance at the club," Brandon continued. "I think the killer picks his victim that night, perhaps the one who is acting the most overtly promiscuous, and comes back to kill her later. But he might come in before, since DJ Shocker's events are so well advertised, to check out potential victims."

"Okay, that's sick, but logical."

"Have you gotten anything over the last couple of nights? Anyone who has seemed out of place?"

She took another sip of her coffee to fortify herself, then looked back down at her plate. She didn't want to eat another bite, but at least it gave her somewhere else to look besides at Brandon.

"It was pretty tough, at first. Filtering through… everything." The barrage of sounds and sights. The unwelcomed touches of men who thought she was cheap. "The first couple of hours of the first night, honestly, I was just trying to survive. Wasn't sure I was going to be able to do it."

"And then what happened?" Brandon's voice was hoarse, almost anguished. She could feel the unhappiness coming from him, but couldn't bring herself to look at his face.

"I don't know. I just had a suck-it-up talk with myself. I had a job to do, and if I didn't, another woman was going to die."

"Sounds like a pretty professional way to think."

For a stripper.

He didn't say it, and she had to admit she didn't even know if he was thinking it. But *she* was.

She still didn't look up from her plate. She took the last bite of her toast that now tasted like cardboard in her mouth.

"Not surprisingly, the overwhelming emotion in the club was lust. Drunken euphoria was a close second. I colored all those in my mind as red and then just ignored them. Guilt—I'm sure more than a few married men were in attendance last night—I colored as green, because I thought that might be worth looking into. Anger and disgust, the key emotions I thought might come from the killer, I tried to color as blue."

"Using colors, that's smart. Did you see any blue?"

"A little." She finally looked at him. "But not from anyone I thought was the killer."

He was too smart not to know she was referring to him. "Andrea—"

She didn't want to talk about his disgust with her. She was holding on by a thin enough thread as it was. She stood up, grabbing their plates.

"You cooked. I'll do dishes. Thanks for breakfast, by the way."

He stood up too and grabbed her wrist gently. "Andrea."

She looked at him, but his face was so intent with something to say she had to look away. She could not do this right now. Not if she had to make it through the entire day and night beyond.

"Brandon, I can't. Not right now. You felt what you felt. Whatever we have to talk about, can we just do it later?"

"Fine. But I'll do the dishes. You go sit. You'll be on your feet enough today. Plus we have another self-defense lesson in fifteen minutes."

She thought about what had happened with the last self-defense lesson, how they'd ended up in bed all afternoon. "Are you sure that's a good idea?"

"As long as there's a killer around, it's a good idea."

That wasn't what Andrea had meant, but she didn't press it. She just left him to do the dishes and went to sit on the couch. The next thing she knew, Brandon was shaking her awake, gently.

"Come on, lazybones. Nap break is over. Time to do some work." She found his face close to hers, smiling, as she opened her eyes.

She touched his cheek before she remembered she wasn't supposed to. But he didn't pull back as she expected. Instead he leaned forward and kissed her on the forehead.

"I must have fallen asleep for a few minutes," she murmured.

"Try two hours."

Her eyes flew open at that. "Are you serious?"

He smiled again. "It's okay. You needed it. But now it's time to work."

He stood and held his hand down to help her from the couch. She stretched and took it.

"Okay, let's go over our bear-hug move first."

They practiced that a few times and Andrea was pleasantly surprised at what she remembered. What her body automatically remembered. Brandon praised her for it, too.

They spent the next hour going over how to twist out of wrist holds, and the most vulnerable points of an attacker she could hit.

The physical activity, focusing on something besides what was going on between her and Brandon, felt good. She found she had a knack for it, because it was somewhat like dancing, ironically. She just had to think of what step came next. And eventually her body knew what step came next without her having to think about it.

"Okay, one more thing I want to teach today. If someone has you on the ground in a choke hold."

He had Andrea lie on her back and he straddled her hips. He gripped her throat with one hand.

"Most of what I've shown you hasn't been dependent on strength or speed, just on basic human mechanics. Joints only turn certain ways. This is more labor intensive on your part. Someone bigger, heavier, is going to be harder to get off you."

Andrea wasn't sure she could do this. Having Brandon this close in this position? If he slid his hand over they'd be in an embrace rather than in combat. But she tried to focus.

Like all the other techniques he'd shown her, he went over the moves slowly at first: trapping his leg with her foot, grabbing his wrist and elbow, hiking up her hips and flipping him over.

She could do it when he worked with her, but once they started going at a faster speed Andrea had trouble.

"What's the problem?" he asked. "You're going to have to move more quickly and fluidly than that for it to work."

Andrea gritted her teeth. She didn't think she could do this—he was too big. And she might hurt him. *And* she really did not want to thrust her hips up against his.

"Look, I'm a little tired. Maybe we should just take a break."

Brandon's eyes narrowed as he looked down at her from where he straddled her hips. "Make me."

"I'm serious, Brandon."

The hand that held her throat squeezed a little tighter. Not enough to hurt or cut off her breath. Just enough to make the threat a little real.

She did what he had taught her but her movements were jerky and halfhearted.

"That's not going to be enough. With this move it's not enough to just go through the correct motions. You've got to have some strength behind it. Some fire."

She tried again but the results were the same.

"That's not enough, sweetheart. You've got to do this move like you've got nothing left to lose."

She tried again, chest heaving in frustration when she couldn't budge him.

"Don't call me 'sweetheart,'" she spit out.

"Why?"

"Because you don't think I'm sweet. You think I'm dirty."

"That's right, sweetheart. I'm the jackass who judged you for doing your job the last two nights. I'm the jerk who turned away from you when you needed me to help anchor you. I'm the idiot—"

Andrea let out a cry and did it. Broke his hold, flipped

her body around so she was on top of him. As he hit the ground his air rushed out with a whoosh.

She threw her head back and laughed. "I did it!" She was amazed at the sense of accomplishment.

She felt Brandon's hands resting on her knees. "Yeah, you did. Good job."

She wasn't ready for him to sit up quickly and wrap his arms around her hips, crushing his chest against hers. He buried his face in her neck.

"How I've acted the last two days, what I thought...I was so wrong, sweetheart."

"Brandon—"

"And you're wrong. I don't think you're dirty. I think you're amazing, beautiful, sweet. Seeing you in the club was hard, I'll admit. But it was *my* problem, not yours. You were doing a job. And did it damn well."

She grabbed his face so she could pull him back. He needed to understand. "When I worked before, I wore just as skimpy an outfit. Less, if I was the one onstage. And when I waited tables, I'll admit I flirted to get tips. Encouraged glances and even some touches. I didn't like it but I did it."

He brought his lips reverently to hers. "You did what you had to in order to survive. Being smart enough to work the system to your advantage is not something to be ashamed of. And I promise, I will never make the mistake of judging you for it again."

"But some of what you felt was probably correct."

"Sweetheart, nothing of what I felt was correct. And you've got to stop letting your own head think it was correct, also."

She sighed. "That's easier said than done."

"I spoke to Drackett and he said to give you his personal and professional congratulations for a job well done."

"You spoke to Steve?"

"Last night. And for the record, I agree with him."

"I thought you'd never want to touch me again. That you found me distasteful."

She felt his arms wrap more strongly around her waist before he used his powerful leg muscles to stand up in one fluid motion while still holding her.

"Trust me when I say, I find you more and more tasteful each day I know you." Keeping her legs wrapped around his hips, he carried her back into the bedroom and proceeded to show her.

Chapter Nineteen

If Brandon could've spent all day in bed with Andrea, he would've. He did his best to apologize with both words and actions, trying to say with his body what he wasn't sure she could hear with his words.

He didn't let himself think too much about why it was so important for him to repair what he'd damaged with her. That would lead to too many questions about the future. About how things could never go back to being the same between them at Omega after this case.

The warrior had the woman he craved by his side. That was enough for now.

But they couldn't stay in bed all day, because they still had a killer to catch.

And they were both pretty hungry despite their breakfast.

Andrea was making sandwiches when Brandon came out of the shower. He could tell by the way she moved across the kitchen that she was feeling lighter, happier. The shadows were gone from her eyes.

He should be surprised that she was more attractive with no makeup and messy hair, dancing around in shorts and a loose T-shirt, but he wasn't. Andrea's natural beauty would always outshine what she could do with makeup and a brush.

She felt his presence and turned to smile at him. "Lunch," she said, handing him a plate.

The silence during their meal this time was easy and light. Unlike before. They were washing dishes together when Andrea caught him off guard with her question.

"Hey, do you know who a guy named Damian Freihof is?"

Brandon stilled. She instantly picked up on his nonverbals, stilling and tensing herself.

"What?" she asked.

"Why do you ask who he is?"

"That box my aunt gave me with my stuff. It contained like fifty letters from a Damian Freihof. I have no idea who that is. I think he's got me confused with someone else and has for a long time. I only opened one letter, but they all had the same name and return address on the envelope."

"Can I see them?"

"Do you know him?"

Brandon wouldn't lie to her. He hadn't thought keeping her in the dark about Freihof was a good idea, although he'd agreed because he'd thought there hadn't been any link between Andrea and Freihof since he went away to prison.

But evidently there were fifty links between them.

Steve had been wrong when he thought Freihof had forgotten about Andrea. He sure as hell hadn't forgotten her if he'd written her that many times.

"Yes, I do know who he is. And you do, too. You just don't know that you do."

Andrea's eyes narrowed and he could see her trying to remember. "Was he part of a case I worked? I can't place the name."

"Damian Freihof was one of the three bank robbers/ hostage takers you helped stop on the day you met Steve Drackett."

He hated how stress began to fill her body again. "The third guy. The evil one."

"He was the one mostly kept out of the original press reports because of the ties he had with some other bombers and terrorist organizations. We were going to try to use him to catch some bad guys even higher on the food chain, but he decided he'd rather serve a double life sentence."

"Well, evidently he decided to make me his pen pal from prison. That's kind of creepy."

"What did the letter you read say?"

She shrugged. "Nothing threatening. Just that he wished he could've gotten to know me better and looks forward to the time we'll eventually spend together." She shuddered. "That's really frightening now that I know who he is."

"I need to send the letters to Omega, if that's okay. Get someone to check them out."

Andrea shrugged. "Sure. I don't want to read them. Why would Omega want them? Freihof is already serving two life sentences. They're probably not going to find much in the letters that will keep him in jail longer than that."

Brandon put his hands on both her arms. "Freihof escaped from federal custody last week during a prison transfer. Nobody knows where he is."

ANDREA COULD FEEL all the blood leave her face. "He escaped?"

"Yes." Brandon pulled her in for a hug and she leaned into him for a moment, needing his strength.

Damian Freihof. That was the name of the face that haunted her dreams over the past four years. She had never forgotten his eyes and the evil that had radiated from him in that bank.

She'd asked Steve about him after she'd gone to work for Omega since she'd never heard anything about him in the news. Drackett had assured her that the third man had been arrested, had just been kept out of the press for national-security reasons.

She pulled back from Brandon. "Steve knows Freihof escaped."

"Yes, and we've been keeping our eyes and ears to the ground for info about him. But Steve didn't think Freihof would come after you."

"Why would Steve even think that was a possibility? Before the letters, I wouldn't have thought it was."

Brandon's lips pursed. "During and after his trial, Freihof mentioned coming after you."

"What?"

Brandon shrugged. "Drackett didn't really take it too seriously. Freihof was in custody and he was mad that he was going to jail for the next eighty years. Steve figured the guy was just running his mouth. He also mentioned wanting to kill some other people."

"Why didn't Steve tell me?"

"Freihof was in jail. You were safe."

Andrea took a step back. "But then he got out of jail. Steve should've told me then."

Brandon held out a hand, entreating. "I agree, and even told him so. But this was right as you were coming back here. Steve felt like you had enough on your plate already."

"Well, the last letters are postmarked as late as two weeks ago."

"That's why we need to get them to Omega and see what we can find from them."

"Does anybody know where he is now?"

"He was briefly spotted in Texas. Probably heading to Mexico."

Andrea thought about all the times she'd felt someone watching her over the past few days.

"What about the lightning-storm guy? That could've been Freihof."

Brandon nodded and pulled her back into his arms. "Yes, it could've been. But he would've been taking a huge chance by coming here after you right now. Steve agrees. He's probably heading south."

"So I don't need to worry about him?" That was definitely not going to happen.

"I won't lie to you. Freihof definitely needs to be worried about. Your safety is something Steve and I will be having a heart-to-heart about when we're back at Omega. I'm not going to let anything happen to you, even if it means moving you in with me." She could feel his kisses in her hair. "I just don't think we have to worry about him right at this moment."

Andrea could feel warmth pooling through her. After the brittle cold that had settled on her insides the past couple of days, this felt wonderful. Having someone really care about her felt wonderful. And Brandon had mentioned Omega for the first time, as if what was happening between them would continue.

The thought was both thrilling and terrifying.

She pulled back to look at him, this man who had brought out so many emotions in her over the past week.

"What?" he asked.

"Nothing. Just thinking about life after this case for a second. Realizing that you know just about every single thing there is to know about me, but I don't know much about you."

"You know that I can be a conceited ass who refuses to see the truth that's right in front of him."

She smiled. "Yeah, but I mean the less obvious stuff."

He reached down and bit at her ear in retaliation, then leaned back against the kitchen counter, pulling her with him. "Okay, what do you want to know?"

"How'd you end up at Omega?"

"I was pretty fortunate when I was growing up. My parents realized early that I needed more intellectual challenge than most kids my age or I started acting out physically. That got me on the right path—graduated high school a little early, then found that studying human behavior interested me most."

"So you got a few degrees in it."

He shrugged casually. "Well, schooling came pretty easily to me when I was interested in the subject matter."

"How'd you jump from the academic world to Omega?"

"My best friend since high school, David Vickars. He and I were pretty different in a lot of ways. He was more of an action man. I always tended to think things through and find the most logical solution. He never even went to college. Got all the education he needed from the army, he told me. Anyway, he started working for Omega eight years ago. Pulled me in not long afterward."

Andrea couldn't see his face, the way he was holding her from behind, but could feel the tension, the sadness.

"You guys were partners."

"Yep. A great team, right up until he died a year ago."

"I'm so sorry, Brandon." She turned in his arms so she could face him.

"Me, too. Dave was a good man. Knew when to bend the rules and when to break them. Knew how to keep me in check."

"Do you need to be kept in check a lot?"

Andrea could see the different flecks of emotion cross over his face: sadness, resignation, fear, anger.

"The difference between you and I, sweetheart, is that you have a crooked past but a sweet, pure soul. I'm the opposite—a perfect past with a crooked soul."

Andrea's eyes flew up to his. "What? No, that's not true."

He tucked her hair gently behind both her ears. "Despite all your talents, I'm not sure you can see it because I keep it buried pretty deep. But I think David knew. He always did. That's why he dragged me with him to Omega."

"Knew what?"

"That I've got a darkness in me somewhere. Everything I learned about human behavior and criminal justice in school? I might have used that to be on the opposite side of serial killing if David hadn't gotten me involved with the right side of the law."

Andrea could tell that what Brandon said was true. Or at least he believed it to be so. "You're excellent at your job."

"I'm fascinated by getting inside the head of a killer and figuring out why they do what they do. What mistakes they might make and catching them."

Andrea had no doubt that the beautiful, brilliant man standing with his arms around her could kill someone and get away with it.

He wouldn't make any mistakes.

"With Dave around it was easy to ignore the darkness, to stay out of my own head and stay in the heads of others. Solve crimes. Fight the bad guys. But this last year it's been more difficult." His voice faded to a hushed stillness.

She realized his current demons haunted him as much as her past demons haunted her. He'd kept them a secret from everyone, just as she had.

"I won't let the darkness overtake you," she whispered.

He stiffened, and she was afraid he was going to pull away, maybe even scoff.

Instead, his arms wrapped tightly around her waist and he pulled her to him in a crushing hug, burying his face in her hair. She could feel his breath against her neck, his heart beating against hers.

They held each other for a long while, their embrace keeping all the demons away.

Chapter Twenty

A call came that afternoon from Lance Kendrick at the county sheriff's department. They had found the full phone number from the note Keira had provided.

Jillian Spires had been in contact with Jarrod McConnachie.

Brandon cursed, bringing the receiver down and putting it on speaker so Andrea could hear, too. "Yeah, we talked to him the day after we arrived in town. He was at a local bar, The Boar's Nest, with some of his buddies."

"We were talking to him because he was friends with Noelle Brumby. So that ties him to two of the victims right away," Andrea said.

"He's also attended at least some of DJ Shocker's club tour. We found him in some footage," Kendrick informed them. "So there's another tie-in."

"Damn it," Brandon muttered, rubbing a hand over his face. "To think we'd been so close to him from the very beginning."

"Andrea, is it possible the man you saw in the lightning could've been McConnachie?" Kendrick asked.

She shrugged. "Yes. Jarrod would be the correct build and weight. It was dark. I was a little freaked out. I didn't get as much detail as I should have."

Brandon slipped an arm around her shoulders. "What's the next step, Kendrick?"

"We've got an APB out on McConnachie. As soon as he's spotted, he'll be arrested. We've also got a warrant to search his place of residence, which ends up is his mother's house. This guy is quite the loser, seems like."

Brandon didn't disagree. "Can we meet your men there?"

"Sure. I'm coming, too." He gave them the address, an isolated area just outside of town.

"We'll see you there in a few."

Brandon disconnected the call.

"Jarrod McConnachie?" Andrea shook her head. "I have to admit, I didn't see that. If it's him, he completely fooled me at the bar on Tuesday."

Brandon nodded. "Me, too. He seemed too sloppy and disorganized. Let's go see what we find at his house."

McConnachie's house, or actually *Mrs. McConnachie's* house, was a small ranch outside of Buckeye. It was in surprisingly good shape based on what they knew about Jarrod, who didn't have a job and spent a lot of his time at bars.

Neither Mrs. McConnachie nor Jarrod were home, but a ranch worker who didn't speak much English and looked very nervous when the police showed up let them into the house.

They searched Jarrod's room first. Brandon and Andrea stood to the side observing as Kendrick and his men methodically looked through the room. It was what you would expect a room of someone who was in his midtwenties, yet didn't have a job and still lived with his mother would look like: unmade bed, collection of high school sports trophies sitting on the shelves, clothes strewn all around.

The officers were methodical and neat in their search. There was no need to destroy any property. They searched under the mattress, in all the drawers and thoroughly in the closet. Brandon was impressed by their thoroughness: he didn't see anywhere they would've missed.

They moved into the living room next, then the kitchen with the same methodical search methods but found nothing of substance. They searched through the mother's room and the other bedroom that had been turned into an office.

Nothing that suggested any crimes or linked Jarrod McConnachie to the women.

The ranch hand who had let them in watched nervously as they moved from room to room. Each room was clean and orderly except for Jarrod's, making the search easier. Brandon stepped outside to look around. They weren't going to find anything in the house, at least nothing concrete.

He could hear Kendrick speaking in Spanish with the nervous worker, explaining something about a work visa. The worker was worried about being deported, not being connected to a crime.

Brandon felt Andrea join him outside the door as he looked at the small barn. "I don't think there's anything in the house. We should check the barn." He called back to Kendrick. "Does the warrant cover the entire property or just the house?"

"All of it," Kendrick broke from his Spanish to respond. They all made their way over to the small structure that was beginning to become run-down.

They almost missed the hatch altogether.

Brandon saw it as they were beginning to turn away after searching the barn: a small hatch leading down into a tiny cellar. It was meant as an emergency hideout during a tornado, and unless you knew it was there, it was easy to miss. It was only big enough to fit two or three people and the hatch door was mostly covered by bags of feed.

He opened the door and turned on the flashlight function of his phone, sliding it down into the dark space.

Every law-enforcement officer there, including Brandon, pulled out their weapons as Brandon slowly took the half dozen steps down.

"This is federal agent Brandon Han," he called from the stairs. "I am armed and coming inside. If anyone is in there, make your presence known now."

He waited but no one spoke, so he slowly stepped down. Kendrick stood directly over his shoulder, ready to take a shot. Andrea, since she didn't have a weapon, had done the smart thing and gotten herself out of the way.

Brandon gave himself a few more moments for his eyes to adjust, then rapidly descended the stairs.

No one was in the cellar, but there certainly had been someone there recently.

Pictures of the dead women were all over the boxes that had been placed in the cellar. Pictures of them before they died and right after. There were candles lined all along the walls, as well as a roll of the same white mesh that had been used to cover the women when the police had found them.

This was the killer's preparation room. Might even have been where the killing took place, although getting the bodies up and down those stairs would've been difficult.

Brandon didn't touch anything, just backed out slowly. "Kendrick, call Gerardo Jennison. We need the best crime-scene investigators they've got."

"What is it?" Kendrick asked.

"The killer's preparation room. Jarrod is definitely the guy."

The older man whistled through his teeth before getting on the phone to call for the needed people to work the scene.

Brandon called an officer over to him. "Under no circumstances is anyone to go down there until the CSI people have done their thing. That room is about as pristine as it gets, and we don't want to mess it up."

"Yes, sir," the young officer said.

Brandon looked over at Andrea, shaking his head. "I guess Jarrod fooled both of us."

She nodded. "None of his emotions or nonverbal cues gave him away. I just didn't think he had it in him."

"Me, neither. We didn't give him enough credit."

Kendrick walked over to them. "Crime-scene crew is on their way. And we've got some even better news."

"What's that?" Brandon asked.

"We just picked up Jarrod McConnachie. Idiot went to The Boar's Nest, just like he goes all the time. Guy had no idea we were onto him. They're holding him in a cell back at the sheriff's office."

"Mind if I question him?" Brandon asked.

Kendrick slapped him on the back. "I was hoping you would."

As much as Andrea was saddened by the thought of Jarrod—someone she had known in high school and who had seemed friendly—as the killer, she was thankful that his arrest meant she didn't have to go work at Club Paradise that night.

Missing the DJ Shocker circus wasn't upsetting at all. Andrea was ready to retire her bustier and short skirts forever. Those days were well and truly in her past.

She wished she could talk Keira into doing the same, but knew no one talked Keira into anything. She would do it when she was ready.

Andrea was on her way to see her friend now. Brandon had ridden with the local police back to the sheriff's office to question Jarrod. Andrea would meet him there soon. But she wanted to talk to Keira first. Let Keira know that things were better between her and Brandon. She would show her Jarrod's picture while she was there, see if that jogged her memory any.

Hopefully Brandon could get a confession out of Jarrod. That would tie up the most loose ends. And then they'd be heading back to Omega.

Honestly, Andrea wasn't sure what that would mean for the two of them. But she knew, either way, it was time for her to make some changes in her life. Keeping herself distant from everyone at Omega wasn't the way she wanted to live any longer.

She pulled up to Keira's apartment, a small one not far from where Andrea had lived during her time in Buckeye, and knocked on the door. Keira hugged her as she pulled her inside.

"Hey, sweetie, what's going on?" Her hair was up in giant rollers and she had the TV remote in her hand. "I'm just catching up on my television viewing."

Andrea looked, expecting to see some drama or sitcom, but found some sort of wildlife documentary on the TV. Interesting choice.

"Just came to ask if you'd ever seen this guy hanging around Jillian. We think he might be the killer."

Keira took the picture. "Yes. Absolutely yes. More than once. But I don't know his name or how to get ahold of him or anything."

"That's okay. He's already been arrested. His name is Jarrod McConnachie. He and I actually went to high school together before I dropped out."

"Jarrod McConnachie. Bastard." She studied the picture a minute more before handing it back to Andrea. "I'm glad you guys got him."

"Yeah, me too." Andrea looked over at the TV again as Keira put it on Pause. "And I also wanted to let you know that things are much better with Brandon and me."

Keira reached up and patted Andrea on the cheek. "I'm

glad. And I'm not surprised. That man is crazy about you, girl."

Andrea laughed ruefully. "I'm not so sure about that. But we're at least doing better. He apologized for getting upset about me at Club Paradise."

"I'd like to hear more about how exactly he apologized—" Keira waggled her eyebrows "—but I'm sure you wouldn't give me the juicy deets anyway."

Andrea felt her face heat.

Keira laughed. "I thought so. He seems like a good man, Andrea."

"He is."

"And more than that, you're a good woman. Past is past. Future is future."

Andrea nodded and grabbed the shorter woman in for a hug. "I'm learning that. In no small part, thanks to you."

"Good. You're a beautiful, compassionate, intelligent, classy lady. Don't you ever forget that."

Andrea could feel tears brimming in her eyes. "Thank you, Keira."

"All right, enough with all the girl talk. You're welcome to stay here and watch my shows with me until I head into work."

"No, I'm going to the station. Help Brandon question the suspect if I can."

"Then I'll catch you later." Keira winked. "Hopefully not as long as it's been since the last time I saw you."

"I promise."

Andrea said her goodbyes and made her way out to her car. There was no message from Brandon, so evidently nothing new with Jarrod.

Andrea pulled the car out of the apartment complex and began driving north up Highway 85 toward the sheriff's office. She passed Jaguar's, slowing as she did so.

She wasn't going to let that place have a hold over her

life anymore. As Keira had said, past was past. Future was future. Jaguar's belonged in her past. She sped up, leaving it behind her.

She saw a car pulled over on the side of the road a few miles outside of town in the direction of the sheriff's office, smoke billowing from the hood. Andrea slowed, not wanting to put herself in a dangerous situation, but not wanting to leave someone stranded in the desert as it began to get dark.

A plump older lady was leaning over her engine, wringing her hands. No one else seemed to be nearby.

Andrea pulled her car over. The least she could do was offer a ride or to call someone.

"Ma'am? Are you okay?"

The woman—a little heavy and probably in her late fifties—looked over at Andrea gratefully. "Oh, honey, thank you so much for stopping! I was afraid no one was going to come along this road. Something is happening with my engine."

Andrea came to stand over next to the woman. "I don't really know anything about cars. But I'd be glad to call someone for you or give you a ride."

The woman looked vaguely familiar to Andrea, probably someone she had known when she lived here, or maybe even one of Aunt Margaret's friends. But honestly, Andrea didn't want to know. Didn't want to answer questions if the woman did know her from when she was younger.

The woman's primary emotion seemed to be anger, and maybe some firm resolution, but neither of those were unusual, given the circumstances. She could be angry at her husband for not servicing the car properly, or maybe just angry that she'd broken down in the middle of nowhere.

"That's so nice of you, dear." The woman began to walk around to the back of her car. "Can you just come back here and help me carry these cables to the front? I think

I might be able to do what my husband did to it last time this happened."

Andrea followed her, but really didn't want to stick around while the woman tried to fix her car. Andrea would help carry whatever cables, then would offer again to give her a ride or call someone. She couldn't spend hours on the side of the road.

She wanted to get back to Brandon.

She walked back and opened up the trunk for the woman. It was completely empty.

"Um, ma'am, there are no cables back he—" Andrea felt a sharp sting in her neck. She reached up to swat away whatever insect had gotten her.

Almost immediately she began to feel dizzy as the world swam around her.

"What?" She tried to focus on the woman, who pushed Andrea down into the trunk.

"Shame on you." The bitterness in the woman's eyes was clear now, although Andrea couldn't seem to focus on them. "You're just as bad as those other hussies. Leading men astray. You're even worse, since you pretend to be the police, too. But I will make sure you're purified."

The last thing Andrea processed was the trunk closing over her before the darkness pulled her under.

Chapter Twenty-One

Even before going in to question Jarrod, Brandon tried to verify the man's whereabouts during the murders. Jarrod had been at all the strip clubs for the DJ Shocker tour where the dead dancers worked. And sure enough, he *hadn't* been at the tour stop for the night the truck-stop waitress was killed.

Probably because he was too busy killing her.

Jarrod's friends, not knowing Jarrod was in custody or suspected of multiple murders, had given Brandon all the information they had. They'd been glad to talk about the DJ Shocker tour; it had been a hoot for them. They'd all independently backed up each other's stories, with just enough details—but not the same details—for Brandon to highly suspect they were being authentic in their responses.

He wished he had Andrea here to get her opinion on whether the men were telling the truth, but she'd gone to talk to Keira. She'd be here soon and he could at least get her opinion on Jarrod's nonverbal behavior.

Because, despite Jarrod's friends' confirmation of his location at the clubs and even despite what they had found in the cellar at his house, Brandon still had doubts that Jarrod was the killer.

He watched Jarrod through the two-way mirror where he sat in the interrogation room. Everything about the man was unkempt. He had on a wrinkled shirt and dirty jeans. His greasy hair needed washing and he looked as if he'd forgotten to shave for the past four days at least. Not to mention the man had been picked up at the bar he frequented. He hadn't even tried to avoid law enforcement.

Brandon found it difficult to reconcile these aspects of the man's personality with the cold, calculating nature of the purity killer. But maybe it was a disguise. Maybe Jarrod had fooled both him and Andrea, and Brandon's pride just didn't want him to admit it.

God knew he'd been wrong an awful lot this week.

Brandon knew where he would start the questioning: victim number two, Ashley Judson, the waitress who dabbled with prostitution on the side. She was the one who didn't fit in the Angels and Devils tour theory. She didn't dance, wasn't a stripper. If Jarrod had picked all his other victims at strip clubs, what had led him to pick her, also?

Brandon glanced at his watch. Andrea should be here any minute. He would go ahead and get started.

"Hi, Jarrod. Remember me?" Brandon walked in the door and took the seat across from Jarrod.

Jarrod nodded slowly. "Yeah. You're that cop that was with Andrea at The Boar's Nest last week. Why am I here, man? I told you everything I knew about Noelle then."

Brandon wanted answers, but more than that he wanted to make sure Jarrod went to jail for the crimes he'd committed. He certainly didn't want him to get off on any technicalities. He would make sure his questioning fell well within the letter of the law. Having a law degree helped make that easier.

Brandon read Jarrod his Miranda rights.

"Yeah, yeah. They already read me my rights when they picked me up at the bar."

"I just want to make sure you know them. That you can call a lawyer if you want to."

Brandon hoped he didn't want to. A lawyer would stall

every question he had for Jarrod. He prayed Jarrod would think he was too smart to need a lawyer.

"Naw, I don't need one." Jarrod sat back in his chair. "I don't got anything to hide."

Brandon smiled. If Jarrod was a wiser man he would've been wary.

Jarrod wasn't.

Brandon took out a picture of Ashley Judson, victim number two—a candid shot, a copy of one Brandon had seen hanging in the cellar at Jarrod's house. He slid it over so Jarrod could see it.

"Do you know this girl?"

"Um…I'm not sure."

There was no doubt in Brandon's mind that Jarrod recognized her. Even if they hadn't just found that picture *at Jarrod's house*, his nonverbal behavior—looking over to the side and down—was giving him away.

"I think you do know her, Jarrod."

Jarrod shrugged. "Maybe. I know a lot of girls."

"How about these? Do you know any of them?"

Brandon took out pictures of the women—all copies of the ones they had found on Jarrod's property—and placed them on the table one after another.

Jarrod's face seemed to lose more color with each picture he studied.

"What's going on here?" he finally asked.

"Why don't you tell me?" Brandon sat back and crossed his arms over his chest.

"What exactly do you want to know? I know Noelle is dead. And I know I told you I didn't really know her very well, but fine, I slept with her, okay? It was a fling. She was getting off of work and I was bored. But I didn't kill her."

"And what about her?" He pointed to the waitress.

"What? Okay, fine. I slept with her, too." He spread his arms out wide across the pictures. "Great, yes. I slept with all these women. Is that a crime? It's pretty damn freaky that the cops are taking a picture of all the girls I've banged over the last month."

Brandon's eyes narrowed. Either Jarrod was the best actor he'd ever seen, or he didn't have any idea all these women were dead.

"How'd you like these girls, Jarrod? Going to see any of them again? Not Noelle of course, but the others?"

Jarrod shrugged one shoulder. "I don't know. Maybe Jillian. She's pretty hot. A dancer." He pointed at Jillian's picture, the woman who had worked at Jaguar's.

"All of them are dancers, right?"

"Not this one." He gestured to Ashley Judson. "She's a waitress."

Brandon smiled, tilting his head to the side. He doubted Jarrod would notice his smile didn't come anywhere near his eyes. "Yeah, I heard that's not all she does. I heard she has a little business on the side with truckers or whoever's willing to pay." Brandon winked.

"Is that what this is about? You think I paid for sex? I didn't pay Ashley, man. It was completely mutual between the two of us. You can ask her."

It was time to move in for the kill. To see if he could force Jarrod into admitting something. All he needed to do was slip up that he knew any of the girls besides Noelle was dead and Brandon would have him trapped in a lie. Then it would just be a matter of wearing him down.

"No, I don't care about money. But doesn't it bother you that Ashley was a hooker on the side? All these girls you've been with aren't exactly upstanding members of society."

Jarrod grimaced. "I don't care about that sort of stuff, man. The girls were fun. I like fun girls."

"You sure about that, Jarrod? Sure you didn't realize that these girls needed cleaning up? That they were tramps? That this town would be better off without them?"

"What?" Jarrod's face wrinkled.

"You know, maybe they needed to be purified in some way. Help them get on the right track? Find God or peace or whatever?"

Jarrod let out a breath, shaking his head. "Dude. You are starting to sound just like my mom. I'm not into that sort of purity stuff. I like girls who like to have a good time. I'm not looking for someone to settle down with. I keep trying to explain that to her."

Brandon sat up a little straighter in his chair. "Your mom talks about purity a lot?"

"All. The. Time." Jarrod rolled his eyes. "I think I'm going to have to move out of her house. The lectures I get after staying out late… Unbelievable. And if she knew I was going to strip clubs? *Sleeping* with girls from strip clubs? She'd blow a gasket. Not enough prayers that could be said for my soul."

Brandon stood up. They had the wrong man. In fact, there wasn't a *man* at all. Jarrod's mother was the serial killer.

He walked over and buzzed the door to let him out. Surely Andrea was here by now. Brandon realized that having her to talk things through with had become important to him over the past few days. After David, he never thought he'd have that again. Never thought he'd want to.

Andrea wasn't in the observation room, but Kendrick was.

"You get that?" Brandon asked him.

"We're already putting an APB out on her. She's not at their house. We've still got people there."

"Have you seen Andrea?"

"No. She hasn't been here at all."

Something clenched in Brandon's stomach. He reached for his phone and dialed her number, knowing texts weren't great for her. It rang then went to voice mail. He left a message, then called Keira next.

"Glad to hear you aren't a complete ass after all," Keira said by way of greeting.

Any other time he would've joked with Keira, even apologized and thanked her. But not now. "Andrea with you, Keira?"

"No, left about forty-five minutes ago. Said you had the killer in custody. Showed me a picture of him. I recognized him as someone Jillian hung out with."

"He's not the right person. Stay in your house until you hear from me. Get a call out to all the girls at Jaguar's if you can. The killer is still out there."

Keira was silent for just a moment. "Okay. Find our girl, Brandon. And have her call me when you do."

"I will."

Brandon put a call in to Big Mike at Club Paradise to make sure Andrea hadn't gone there to tell him the good news. Mike hadn't seen her.

Brandon tried her phone again. Nothing.

Kendrick reentered the observation room. His face was grim.

"Your rental a white Toyota?" He read off a license-plate number.

Brandon nodded.

"It was found abandoned off Highway 85. The phone you're trying to call was inside."

Chapter Twenty-Two

Andrea fought to claw her way out of the darkness. Her brain didn't want to focus; her eyes didn't want to open. Reality felt distant, fuzzy. Her hands were tied behind her back and she was lying on her side; that much she knew.

She forced herself to be still, to think, to try to figure out what was going on.

She'd been drugged by that lady she'd stopped to help on the side of the road. She forced back nausea as she thought of the woman's face, how it had seemed vaguely familiar.

"I know you're waking up," Andrea heard the woman say from a few yards away. "I didn't give you enough tranquilizer for you to be out for too long."

Andrea remembered being pushed into a trunk, but they weren't in a car any longer. She opened her eyes in the smallest of slits, trying to keep the nausea at bay. They weren't outside. Somewhere inside, but mostly empty. Maybe a small abandoned warehouse? She opened her eyes a little more and saw where the older woman was sitting.

On a pew. An abandoned church building. It looked as if most of it had been burned in a fire.

Given the nature of the crimes, it made perfect sense that this was where the killer would bring the victims.

"I know your aunt, you know," the woman said from where she sat. "Met her at an AA meeting. Not that I'm an alcoholic, but my son is. I thought learning about AA might help me help him. He needs help. Needs to be shown the right path. He's so weak."

It came to Andrea then. They'd had the right house, but the wrong killer.

"You're Jarrod's mother."

"Yes."

Andrea tried to shake off the mental cobwebs clouding her mind. To think. To find some way to relate to this woman. "He and I went to high school together."

"Before you dropped out. Margaret told me."

"Jarrod is my friend. I know he wouldn't want you to hurt me."

"Jarrod doesn't know what he wants. And all you women keep trying to corrupt him. Lead him astray. It's been my job as a mother to clean up after him. To remove temptation from his sight."

"So you killed the women Jarrod was interested in."

"I removed the harlots who led him astray. All of them tempted him beyond what he could bear. All of them either removed their clothes or had sex for money." Mrs. McConnachie stood up. "All I did was what any other mother would do."

"But you killed them."

She took a step closer. "No. I stopped them from committing any further sins. From tempting any other men like Jarrod and corrupting them."

There was no reasoning with this woman about what she had done. Andrea could feel the sincerity radiating from her. In Mrs. McConnachie's mind, her actions were both logical and just. Andrea needed to use another tactic.

"I didn't corrupt Jarrod. He and I have never been romantically involved."

That stopped Mrs. McConnachie for just a moment. She frowned and looked down at her hands. Andrea realized she was holding a rope. No doubt the same one she'd used to strangle the other women.

Andrea began to slide backward on the floor, away from her.

That was a mistake.

Her eyes narrowed and she stepped toward Andrea.

"No. You work at one of those disgusting clubs. I saw you."

"Mrs. McConnachie, I was working undercover." *Trying to catch you*, but Andrea knew not to say that. "I was trying to stop the same thing you were trying to stop, women from corrupting men."

Mrs. McConnachie stopped again, but then shook her head. "No. Margaret said you two had talked, but you wouldn't forgive her, that you were still angry at her even though she had taken you in to raise when you were younger. You're just as bad as those women who tried to corrupt Jarrod."

Andrea realized the older woman wasn't interested in reason or logic. She planned to kill Andrea. The action was already justified in her mind.

Where was Brandon? Had he realized yet Jarrod wasn't the killer? Andrea had no doubt he would; she just didn't think it would be in time to save her. She had no idea where she was. How could Brandon possibly know?

Andrea scooted away on the floor as Jarrod's mother walked toward her. She tried to think of any of the self-defense techniques Brandon had taught her, but with her arms restrained and body feeling so sluggish because of the drugs, it was difficult to move, much less fight.

Tears filled Andrea's eyes. She was going to die here. Killed, ironically, by the very embodiment of a demon from her past, just as Andrea was starting to truly put the past behind her.

She'd never know what could've been between her and Brandon.

Mrs. McConnachie pulled her up into a kneeling position and quickly wrapped her strand of rope around Andrea's neck, coming to stand behind her. Andrea struggled not to fall over, knowing that would just quicken the strangulation.

"Don't worry. This won't hurt very long. Soon you'll be at peace."

Andrea felt the bite of the rope against her throat, instantly cutting off her air. She couldn't help but struggle although it didn't do any good. Her arms bit against the restraints, she could feel blood, but couldn't get loose.

She tried to suck in a breath but the sound just came out as a hoarse sigh.

"There, there," Mrs. McConnachie crooned. "Don't fight it. Find your peace. That's all you need to do now."

Andrea fought one last time, trying to throw her weight to the side, to not panic as Brandon had taught her to do. But it was no use.

Blessed blackness was overtaking Andrea when the pressure suddenly lessened. She collapsed to her side as Mrs. McConnachie fell to the ground next to her. Andrea sucked life-giving oxygen as she tried to figure out what had happened. Had Brandon found them?

Jarrod's mother's eyes stared blankly ahead as a pool of blood began to surround her on the ground. The woman was dead. Andrea couldn't get her body to the angle she needed to prop herself up. All she could do was barely hold on to consciousness as she struggled to get air through her bruised throat.

"Have you ever heard anything so tedious in your entire life as that woman carrying on?" A foot kicked Mrs. McConnachie's body to the side, then squatted down next to Andrea so she could see his face.

She immediately recognized the evil-laden eyes of Damian Freihof.

This time she didn't even try to fight the blackness as it pulled her under.

THE WARRIOR INSIDE Brandon roared to life. Andrea—*his woman*—was in danger, the most desperate kind of danger. Brandon had to do something about that.

He was turning to go back and demand answers from Jarrod—he didn't plan to be anywhere near so gentle this time—when Kendrick put his hand on Brandon's arm to stop him. He took a slight step back when Brandon turned his ferocious gaze on him.

"What?" Brandon snapped out. Kendrick, whatever good he meant, was standing in his way from getting to Andrea.

No one, not even law enforcement, was going to stop him from finding her. By whatever means necessary.

"Whoa, Han." The man held up both hands in a gesture of surrender. "Before you go in there, I just wanted you to know that a vehicle in distress was called in by a civilian near where Andrea's car was found about thirty minutes ago."

Brandon listened. This could be useful intel. "Okay."

"Lady didn't want to stop because she had two babies in the car, but didn't want to leave what looked to be like an older woman stranded. She doesn't remember the exact model of the vehicle, but it was a black four-door sedan. 'Like something from the '80s,' the woman said."

"I'm going to question Jarrod," Brandon told him. "This may not be pretty. I'd appreciate it if there were no interruptions."

Kendrick shrugged. "Actually, I'm going back out to the McConnachies' ranch, make sure there's no unknown buildings where the mom might have Andrea. I'm going to send our other men out to look around town. I'll call Phoenix police department and see if we can get some help, too."

"Good. Keep me posted."

Kendrick handed Brandon the keys to a squad car, then shrugged, turning away. "And damn if the system that records our interrogation-room interviews isn't on the fritz again."

Brandon nodded curtly. He would thank Kendrick later. After he had Andrea back safely.

He unlocked the interview-room door from the outside so he would be able to get back out, then slipped inside. Jarrod was still sitting there, looking bored, biting unkempt fingernails.

"Does your mother drive a black sedan? Late '80s-ish model?"

Jarrod rolled his eyes. "Oh my gosh, yes. She's had that thing since before I was born. I'm embarrassed whenever I have to borrow it."

Brandon refrained from mentioning that Jarrod was in his midtwenties and should have his own damn car.

"Where does your mother like to hang out, Jarrod?"

"Why?" Jarrod snickered. "You looking for a date? I'm sure she wouldn't be much fun, you know."

Brandon rammed his fist down on the table. Jarrod flew back in his chair, eyes wide.

"What the hell, man?"

"I'll tell you what the hell." Brandon reached down and got the autopsy photographs of each of the dead women. He put them on top of the photographs of when they were alive. "Do you know why you're here, Jarrod? Because every single one of the women you had a fling with over the last few weeks is dead."

Jarrod looked as if he was going to vomit. Color leaked

from his face. "I didn't do this, man. I swear to God, I didn't kill them. I have an alibi, remember?"

Under other circumstances Brandon would have handled a situation like this more delicately, broken the news to him more gently. Jarrod's mom might be a killer, but the woman was still his mother.

Brandon didn't have that kind of time.

"I know you didn't kill them. Your mother did."

Brandon's eyes bugged right out of his head. "What?"

"She must have been following you. She saw the women you hooked up with and killed them the next day or soon after."

"But...but why?"

"You said she talks about purification all the time? These women's bodies were left with purification rituals. Like your mother was cleansing them to send them to the next world or whatever."

The final bit of color left Jarrod's complexion. "She talks about that sort of junk all the time." He blanched as he tore his eyes up from the pictures to look at Brandon where he leaned on both arms against the table. "About needing to clean up the 'riffraff' in this town, to get rid of all those who would lead men down a corrupted path. I think my dad might have cheated on her or something before he died. But I never knew she meant to kill anyone. I just thought she meant starting a petition to close down the local strip clubs or something, you know?"

"Jarrod, I know this is hard. But I need your help *right now*. Another woman's life is at stake. Andrea's."

Jarrod was staring down at the pictures again.

"Where would your mom do this, Jarrod? Kill these women. We've already checked your house and barn. Is there anywhere else on your property?"

Jarrod shook his head numbly. "We don't really own

anything besides the house and barn. Most of the land got sold off when Dad died."

"Okay, then somewhere else? Where does your mom like to go? Where does she hang out?"

Jarrod said nothing, just stared at the pictures. Brandon knew he was losing the other man, shock settling in. That was unacceptable until he got the info he needed.

He reached down and grabbed Jarrod by the collar of the cheap jacket he wore and yanked him out of his chair. Under any other circumstances this sort of manhandling of a witness would be completely unacceptable. This wasn't some action movie where cops could do whatever they wanted with no repercussions.

Brandon didn't give a damn about repercussions.

"Think, Jarrod. Where would your mother go to do these things?" He shook the other man.

"I don't know. She goes to church a lot and some other meetings. I don't really know what." His voice was squeaky.

"No. It couldn't be a place other people are around. Where else? Where would she go if she wanted to be alone?"

Jarrod began to cry. Brandon pulled the younger man's face closer to his.

"Focus, Jarrod. Your mother would need to be somewhere where no one is around. Isolated, to at least some degree. Where. Would. She. Go?" He punctuated each word with a shake.

"I don't know, man, maybe the old church off Highway 85? She always slows down when we drive past. It's where my dad's memorial service was held."

"No, a church is too crowded, even if no service is going on."

Jarrod shook his head. "No, this one burned a few years ago. Congregation decided to build a new church in a more convenient location rather than pay to have that one re-built. The outer walls are still standing but the inside is pretty torn up."

That was it. It had to be.

"Where, exactly?"

Jarrod quickly explained, and Brandon was flying out the door and to the squad car in seconds, praying he wasn't too late.

Chapter Twenty-Three

Brandon parked the squad car and got out of it silently, not wanting to take the chance that Mrs. McConnachie might hear him and panic, hurting Andrea.

But he sprinted because the woman had already had Andrea in her clutches for way too long. Brandon pushed the warrior, who wanted to burst in and *fight*, aside. Logic had to reign right now. Caution. The mental state of Mrs. McConnachie was unknown. He'd radioed for help, but wasn't going to wait for backup to arrive.

Brandon eased his way through a side door that couldn't be completely closed because of burn damage. He couldn't see most of the larger section of the charred church, only the front portion near what must have once been the altar area. Brandon was shocked at what met his eyes.

Mrs. McConnachie's dead body lying on the ground.

Brandon no longer worried about silence or caution. Had Andrea been wounded in fighting the older woman? Did she need medical attention? He was glad it was Mrs. McConnachie on the ground and not Andrea, but where was she?

He burst into the room, looking around, but didn't see her. Had she made her way outside? He began looking between pews, to make sure she hadn't fallen behind one.

He sensed her behind him before he saw or heard her. Brandon turned to find Andrea standing in the aisle between the two rows of pews, as if she was a bride about to walk to her groom.

But in the shadows behind Andrea, Brandon could immediately make out another presence. He knew right away who it was.

"Let her go, Freihof."

"Ah, Agent Han, I see my reputation has preceded me."

"Yeah, your reputation as a sicko. Let her go."

"Come now, Agent Han, I'm sure *sicko* isn't the clinical term. You have too many degrees to be using such common terminology."

Brandon's eyes narrowed, but he played along. "How about 'psychopath with homicidal tendencies and sociopathic and delusional proclivity.'"

"Yes, yes. So much better!" Freihof turned to Andrea, shrugging. "Basically a sicko."

Freihof took a few steps closer, forcing Andrea with him as a shield, coming out of the shadows and into the dim light of the church. Brandon could see the knife Freihof held at her throat, which was covered with angry red marks. Andrea had been strangled.

"Miss Gordon unfortunately fell into the clutches of the crazy old lady there." Freihof gestured toward Mrs. McConnachie's body. "I had to take care of that. Wasn't going to let anyone kill our Andrea."

He kissed Andrea's cheek and she flinched. "Anyone but me, that is. Please take your gun out and throw it to the side, Agent Han."

Andrea tried to move away, but Freihof pulled her back against him, his blade still at her throat. Brandon took his Glock out of its holster and slid it on the ground over to the side. He refused to take a chance on Freihof cutting Andrea's throat. Freihof nodded approvingly.

"I've had almost four years to study you all," Freihof continued. "It's amazing how much one can find out about

Omega Sector if he tries, both by electronic and flesh-and-blood sources. Not to mention, your organization has put a lot of people behind bars. A lot of *angry* people."

"What do you want, Freihof?" Brandon asked. He needed to get Andrea away from Freihof's blade.

"C'mon, Agent Han, play along. I'm just trying to impress you with my knowledge. I know Steve Drackett is your boss and was there the night I was arrested. I know a great deal about some of your colleagues, a Liam Goetz and Joe Matarazzo. More than that."

Brandon tried to figure out the other man's endgame, in order to get ahead of him, but couldn't see it. "Great, Freihof. I am thoroughly impressed at your mental database of Omega Sector."

Freihof smiled and shook his head back and forth like a giddy child, taking a few steps closer with Andrea. "I know. I'm showing off. It's annoying, I'm sure."

He had figured the man was a psychopath, but Brandon hadn't realized just how intelligent he was. Freihof's size and strength were also impressive. He'd obviously spent some of his time in prison working out and bulking up.

Freihof was dangerous in every possible way.

"Okay." Brandon took a step closer, arms outstretched. "Honestly, I am pretty impressed. Your escape. Finding us. Knowing so much about Omega. You're definitely more advanced than most of the criminals I face."

"Thank you, Dr. Han. It means a lot that you would say that."

"Now tell me what you want, and let Andrea go."

Brandon purposefully did not let himself look at her. He didn't want to give away how much she meant to him, plus couldn't trust himself to be able to focus if he saw she was about to fall apart.

Andrea was strong. She could handle it. He had to believe that. He did believe it.

Freihof's knife stayed at her neck. "What I want? Do you mean long-term or short-term?"

"Either."

"What I want, what I plan to do long-term, is take Omega Sector apart piece by piece. Destroy you guys from within until the whole organization falls apart. And keep Andrea here by my side as a plaything while I do it."

Over Brandon's dead body. "Some grandiose plans you got there. How about short-term?"

"Short-term, I plan to sit Miss Gordon down right here at this pew—oh, please don't get me started about the church symbolism—and give her a little gift."

Freihof did as he'd spoken and sat Andrea down, awkwardly because her hands were restrained behind her back, on the pew next to him. Brandon watched in horror as he took out a small explosive device with a twine loop and wrapped it like a necklace around Andrea's slender neck. He took her hands and secured them to the arm of one of the pews with a zip tie.

Brandon could see the three-minute countdown blinking out at him brightly.

"I know we're running out of time and the rest of this rinky-dink town's police force will be here soon, so I'm going to start this timer," Freihof continued in a conversational tone. "That will give you three minutes to finish me off and get back to your love here, Dr. Han."

"Don't turn that thing on," Brandon said through clenched teeth. "How's she supposed to be your long-term plaything if you blow her up?"

"I've found you have to be flexible in your plans, Agent Han. Besides, I don't foresee any problem with me being able to take you in three minutes—it will give us both motivation to do our best work, right? Neither of us wants Andrea in little pieces."

Freihof pressed a button that started the countdown.

2:59, 2:58, 2:57…

"I have a feeling you're going to wish you'd spent less time in the library and more time in the gym, Dr. Han." Freihof's eyes were complete evil.

Brandon allowed himself to look at Andrea just for a moment. A single tear fell from her green eyes. Then he looked down at the explosives attached to her neck.

2:51, 2:50…

Freihof was wrong. Brandon wasn't going to wish he'd spent more time at the gym. He stood up straighter, immediately knowing what he had to do. For the first time in his entire life, Brandon didn't even try to keep the darkness inside him at bay. He let the cold, intellectual side of himself be pushed to the side.

As the warrior inside broke free.

He could feel his mind emptying, a complete and utter focus overtaking him. Intellect would not win this battle; the warrior would.

The warrior fighting for his woman.

He saw Freihof's eyes narrow briefly—the man realized his mistake too late—before Brandon flew at him at a speed he wasn't expecting. Freihof still had the knife, and Brandon felt its sharp sting, but it seemed to be at a distance.

Freihof was bigger, stronger and had a weapon. But Brandon fought like a man with nothing to lose.

Because he realized what the warrior inside him had known all along: if he lost Andrea, he lost everything.

The blows between him and Freihof were brutal and coarse. The countdown around Andrea's neck left no room for strategy, no room to dance around each other.

Brandon felt perverse pleasure as Freihof's nose broke under one of his punches, but then felt the burn as the man's knife found his side. Again.

The moves he'd practiced so recently with Andrea

helped him face the bigger man. He heard the snap of Freihof's arm and the man's grunt of pain when Brandon used a move he had just been showing her yesterday.

The only thing the warrior would allow his intellectual side to do was keep track of the time. Without even having to look, Brandon knew the exact second of the counter.

1:02, 1:01, 1:00...

As Freihof fell to the ground, Brandon threw punch after punch at the man's head and torso. Brandon knew at that point he would win the fight.

But he also knew he would pay a heavy price. He could feel himself becoming light-headed from blood loss, although he'd since kicked Freihof's knife away.

0:19, 0:18, 0:17...

He had Freihof in the hold he wanted. One that would subdue him into unconsciousness in a matter of seconds.

"You're running out of time, Han." Freihof wheezed. "Are you going to choose her or me?"

He was right. Brandon didn't even hesitate. He let Freihof go and ran over to Andrea.

0:10...

He had no idea how to disarm the bomb; all he could do was get it off her and away from them, praying it would not have enough power to bring the entire building down on them.

0:06, 0:05...

He slipped it off her neck and threw it as far as he could toward the back corner of the church. He snatched the knife lying beside Freihof's unconscious form and cut through the zip tie and most of the thin twine that bound Andrea's wrists. That was all he could do.

He grabbed her and slid them both under a pew, wrapping himself around her to protect her as best he could, tucking her head into his chest.

A moment later the explosion shook the entire building and nothing could be seen but darkness.

EVERYTHING IN ANDREA's body hurt. Her shoulders, her throat, her ears. But she was still alive.

The building hadn't collapsed, but given the state it had already been in before the explosion, Andrea wasn't sure how long it would stay standing.

"Brandon, are you okay? I think we need to get out of here."

She nudged him with her shoulder. He had pulled her close to protect her, but now his arms were lying limply by his side. The bonds that held her wrists were looser and Andrea tugged at them for release. Seeing Brandon lying so still gave her a burst of strength.

She bit her lip in agony as her shoulders moved back into a more natural position.

"Brandon?" More panicked now, she brought her cheek up to his mouth to see if she could feel his breath. Yes, breathing. But when she looked down at his body all she saw was blood.

Too much blood.

She tried to stop the bleeding with her hands, but his shirt was so soaked she couldn't even figure out where the wounds were.

"This is the Maricopa County Sheriff's Department," Andrea heard someone call out. "Is anyone in here?"

"Yes," she yelled as loud as her hoarse voice would allow. "Back here."

She waved her hand, but then immediately brought it back down to his wounds.

Too much blood.

"Here," she called out again. Flashlights pointed in her direction as she called out. "I need help." Her voice completely gave out with that last word.

Out of the corner of her eye, something caught her attention. Freihof. She turned and he gave her a tiny wave and evil smile before running silently out the side door.

Andrea wanted to communicate with the police officers who were making their way through the rubble to get to them. To tell them about Freihof, but she literally could not get the words out.

Besides, she didn't care about Freihof when Brandon's blood was seeping out of his body under her. He still wasn't conscious.

She bent back down to say in his ear as loudly as her voice would allow, "Come on, Brandon. I need you. I've had two serial killers almost get me today and we're not going to let them win. You fought for me. You beat him for me. Fight for *you* now. *For us.*"

She kissed him. His lips, his forehead, his cheeks.

A paramedic as well as two police officers came and took over life-saving duties. Andrea didn't want to let Brandon go but knew more qualified people needed to take over. She watched it all as if she was in a daze.

But when they rushed Brandon into the ambulance, Andrea found her spirit and fought to stay with him. She wasn't letting Brandon out of her sight. A paramedic stopped her at the ambulance door.

"I'm sorry—you can't ride here."

"I have to," Andrea croaked out, but the words came out soundless. She could feel herself begin to panic. She couldn't leave Brandon alone.

She felt someone take her arm. "I'll drive you," Kendrick said. "Consider it the beginning of restitution for all the times we let you down when you were younger."

Andrea nodded. She knew she should say something, couldn't anyway, so she just got in the car with Kendrick. Her eyes never left the ambulance the entire time.

Chapter Twenty-Four

Fifteen hours later—the longest fifteen hours of her life—
Brandon was safely out of surgery. Andrea was still watching over him. Keira had brought her a change of clothes,
much needed since hers had been covered in Brandon's
blood. Andrea had talked with her friend for a while, still
a difficult task due to the damage to her throat. Keira had
contacted Steve Drackett for Andrea so he could be updated.

The doctors had done a full scan of Andrea after
Kendrick brought her in right behind Brandon. She'd been
very fortunate, they'd told her, that although she had ex-
tensive bruising and swelling, none of her neck muscles
had been ruptured, nor did there seem to be any permanent damage to her larynx.

Ironically, if Freihof hadn't stopped Mrs. McConnachie
when he had, the damage would've grown exponentially
greater every second.

Kendrick assured her that every law-enforcement officer in Arizona was looking for Freihof even as they spoke.
Somehow that didn't reassure her. But she wouldn't let it
worry her right now. Right now she was focused on Brandon.

He had *fought* for her.

Andrea had realized, of course, when he had been
teaching her the self-defense moves, that Brandon knew

how to handle himself. He was a trained agent, so he would know hand-to-hand combat moves.

This had been more than that.

When Freihof put that explosive necklace around her neck, Andrea had not believed there was any way Brandon would be able to fight and beat someone with the size and cunning of Freihof—who had a *knife*—in three minutes. Some things were just not possible.

She'd watched as Brandon had turned into something else before her eyes. In one second a myriad of conflicting emotions had radiated from him: concern, anger, worry, pain. He'd been thinking of multiple different angles and scenarios to tip the situation in his favor, his powerful mind working in overdrive.

In the second Freihof had turned on the explosives countdown, Brandon's powerful mind had been completely shut down. Every emotion he'd been projecting had stopped. Focus and determination had taken its place.

The intellectual genius had been replaced by a dark warrior. And the dark warrior had achieved the impossible: defeating Freihof before the time had run out.

He had *fought* for her. No one in her life had ever fought for her.

Andrea held Brandon's hand as he slept. Soon his family would be here and she'd be relegated to the waiting room. But for now he was hers to protect.

BRANDON'S BRAIN WOKE UP before he could force his eyes open. That happened a lot. He was processing before he was fully awake.

But for some reason he seemed to be processing more slowly than usual. Frustrating. He forced himself to relax, not opening his eyes. To listen, to remember, to piece it all together.

His first awareness was of the pain. It seemed to radiate from everywhere in his body. Everything hurt so much he couldn't seem to figure out where his central injuries had occurred.

He heard the beeping of machines, distant talking farther away. He was in a hospital. The fight with Freihof, the knife, the explosion… It all came back to him.

"College just wasn't for me," a deep voice was saying. "I had better things to do with my time. Things that provided a much more rounded education, if you know what I mean."

Joe Matarazzo. Brandon knew his friend and fellow agent's voice.

Brandon tried to open his eyes but it was more difficult than he'd thought. The pain wanted to pull him back under.

"You're bad." It was Andrea's sweet voice, but different. More throaty. Hoarse, but damn if it didn't still sound sexy to him. He could feel his hand resting in hers.

"My friends say I'm audacious." Brandon could hear the smile in Joe's voice. "I had to look that up to see what it meant, because of the lack of college education and all. Ends up that 'coming from a billionaire family and sleeping with every available woman in a three-state area' is actually the very definition of *audacious*."

Andrea laughed. "Yeah, well, I'm a high school dropout ex-stripper. I think that might one-up you."

Had Andrea just made a joke about her past?

Joe's bark of laughter was friendly and kind. "Well, then you and I probably ought to run off and get married right now."

Now Brandon opened his eyes.

"Nope, she's taken." He raised their linked hands.

Joe smiled. "Hey, bro. You gave us a scare for a minute."

Joe said some other things, but Brandon only had eyes for Andrea. She was here. She was safe. She was at his side.

Joe cleared his throat. "I can see that you and your lady need some time, so I'll be back in a while."

Joe made his way out the door. Brandon appreciated the other man's tact.

"Hey," Andrea whispered, leaning over him so she was a little closer.

It cost him considerable effort, but Brandon reached up to bring her lips down to his. He couldn't go another second without feeling her sweetness against him.

"Are you okay?" he asked against her mouth.

"Yes. You were the one who was hurt, fighting Freihof."

"Your voice sounds different."

"That was actually Mrs. McConnachie's doing. Freihof saved me from her so he could kill me himself." He felt her shudder. "But the doctors think my voice should fully recover. And there is no permanent damage. You, on the other hand... Multiple stab wounds, concussion, dislocated shoulder. You're very lucky, all things considered. One of the stab wounds missed your kidney by a couple of centimeters."

"But you're okay." That was all Brandon could remember about his fight with Freihof. The knowledge that if he failed, Andrea would suffer. He couldn't allow that to happen.

She kissed him again. "I'm perfectly fine."

Thank God. He hadn't allowed it to happen.

"But Freihof got away. Kendrick assures me they have a statewide manhunt going for him."

Brandon's teeth ground. As long as Freihof was free Andrea wouldn't be safe. "Does Steve know?"

"Yes. I think that's why Joe is here. He said he was just passing through on another case, but I think Steve sent him to keep an eye on us in case Freihof came back."

Brandon nodded. "We'll get him, sweetheart. I promise."

Andrea smiled. "I know."

"I heard you make a joke about being a stripper with Joe. That took a lot of guts."

Andrea gave him a shy smile. "Given his past, mine didn't seem so bad. Plus, Joe's easy to talk to. He makes everything seem okay somehow."

"That's why he is so good at his job as a hostage negotiator. Everybody loves to be around him."

"Well, I just love to be around you," she whispered.

"Good, because I don't plan on letting you out of my sight."

Her past didn't make any difference to him except in how it had formed her into the beautiful, intelligent, gutsy woman she was. All Brandon cared about was their future.

A nurse entered the room. "Mr. Han, your family is here."

"Okay, you can let them in."

Andrea stood up. "I'll go wait in the waiting room or find Joe."

Brandon didn't let go of her hand even for a second. "No. Like the nurse said, my family is here." He pulled her down for a kiss. "That includes you, sweetheart. From now on."

Her soft smile balanced out the darkness inside him and appeased the warrior inside.

She was his.

* * * * *

Look for more books in Janie Crouch's
OMEGA SECTOR: CRITICAL RESPONSE
series later this year.

MILLS & BOON®

INTRIGUE
Romantic Suspense

A SEDUCTIVE COMBINATION OF DANGER AND DESIRE

A sneak peek at next month's titles...

In stores from 14th July 2016:

- **Six-Gun Showdown** – Delores Fossen *and*
  Hard Core Law – Angi Morgan
- **Stockyard Snatching** – Barb Han *and*
  Single Father Sheriff – Carol Ericson
- **Deep Cover Detective** – Lena Diaz *and*
  Be on the Lookout: Bodyguard – Tyler Anne Snell

Romantic Suspense

- **The Pregnant Colton Bride** – Marie Ferrarella
- **Beauty and the Bodyguard** – Lisa Childs

Available at WHSmith, Tesco, Asda, Eason, Amazon and Apple

Just can't wait?
Buy our books online a month before they hit the shops!
visit www.millsandboon.co.uk

These books are also available in eBook format!

MILLS & BOON®

Why not subscribe?
Never miss a title and save money too!

Here is what's available to you if you join the exclusive **Mills & Boon® Book Club** today:

* *Titles up to a month ahead of the shops*
* *Amazing discounts*
* *Free P&P*
* *Earn Bonus Book points that can be redeemed against other titles and gifts*
* *Choose from monthly or pre-paid plans*

Still want more?
Well, if you join today we'll even give you
50% OFF your first parcel!

So visit **www.millsandboon.co.uk/subscriptions**
or call **Customer Relations on 0844 844 1351***
to be a part of this exclusive Book Club!

*This call will cost you 7 pence per minute plus your
phone company's price per minute access charge.

SUBS_2016

Lynne Graham has sold 35 million books!

**To settle a debt, she'll have
to become his mistress…**

Nikolai Drakos is determined to have his revenge against
the man who destroyed his sister. So stealing his enemy's
intended fiancé seems like the perfect solution! Until
Nikolai discovers that woman is Ella Davies…

Visit **www.millsandboon.co.uk/lynnegraham**
to order yours!

MILLS & BOON®